My Kind of Trouble

BECKY McGRAW

CHAPTER ONE

The wrench in Cassie Bellamy's hand slipped off the nut she was trying to loosen, and she rapped her knuckles, then cursed a blue streak. Thanks to the crusty cowhands shooting the breeze in the barn at the Double B, she knew plenty of curse words to throw into that streak too. She didn't bring them out often though, Imelda's Ivory soap had taught her well that ladies didn't curse.

In Cassie's estimation though, the hot Texas sun burning the back of her legs and her broken down pickup were just cause right now. Shifting her boots on the bumper, she leaned farther under the hood to get better traction on the heater hose clamp nut.

With no one around for miles, her cell phone dead, and the odds of someone traveling down the dusty road that led to her daddy's ranch slim, Cassie knew fixing the damned truck was all on her. Even after she got the hose off, she had a seven mile hike back up the road to Bowie, so she could get a replacement hose.

Usually organized, Cassie was angry at herself for not charging her cell phone before she left the hotel in Amarillo this morning. Not that she thought they'd have service out here in the middle of the boondocks anyway, but at least there would have had been a chance.

The uneventful drive she'd had from Phoenix to Bowie had lulled her into a false sense of security. Once she'd hit the old Farm Market Road though, Bessie, the old pickup she'd had since she was sixteen, gave up the ghost and left her stranded on the side of the road.

She should have driven her new Beamer convertible, but she told herself she didn't want to rack up the miles on it. Deep inside though, she knew she'd driven Bessie for sentimental reasons.

Her old truck had taken her out of Bowie ten years ago to her new life in Phoenix, and now it seemed appropriate that the old girl bring her back to her daddy's ranch, which she hadn't visited since she left. But she sure wasn't visiting Bowie for nostalgic reasons.

If her daddy didn't need her, she wouldn't be here now.

Any warm and fuzzy feelings she had for her hometown were thoroughly snuffed out from her last memories of the place. Her boyfriend who said he loved her, the one she'd given her virginity to, tangled up with a half-naked girl by the lake on her graduation night, had replayed in her mind like a bad movie for the first year after she left Bowie.

Luke Matthews and Becca Harvey had done her a favor though. If not for them, she wouldn't have her freedom, and wouldn't have had the gumption to leave Bowie to find a better life. Maybe she should look them up and thank them.

Her life in Phoenix didn't include a passel of kids or a husband like most of the girls who'd stuck around Bowie. No, hers included a successful career and a business, which gave her independence, a nice little house, and as many toys as she wanted, like her Beamer. These days, Cassie depended only on herself, and she liked it that way.

Well, there was James, but she tried not to depend on her fiancé too much either, even though he was her business partner too. Depending on other people meant letting down your guard to heartache and disappointment. Cassie hadn't been disappointed in ten years...not since she left.

But she wasn't here to dig up old bones. Carl Bellamy needed her help at the Double B, and so did the woman Cassie called Mama Melda, the closest thing to a mother Cassie had known since her own mama died when she was ten. And until she got this hose off and got back to town, she wasn't going to be able to help them.

Moving her hand a little deeper into the engine compartment, she adjusted the wrench again and twisted with a grunt. It budged a little and gave her hope that maybe she could get the darned thing off.

The fact that Imelda had waited a month to call her, pissed Cassie off. It was probably her stubborn old dad's fault, she knew. He most likely forbid Imelda from calling when it happened. Until three days ago, when Imelda finally called, Cassie hadn't known her dad had been thrown from a horse and had broken his leg in two places.

The last time she'd seen him had been at Christmas when he flew to Phoenix to see her. Although he'd looked older, maybe a little more bent, the crotchety old fart was still full of piss and vinegar. *How the hell had he let himself get thrown off a horse?* The man had been riding since he could walk.

He's getting old, and shouldn't be riding anymore, that's how. Cassie gave the wrench another vicious twist. *Stubborn old cuss.*

He should just sell the damned ranch and move to Phoenix with her. Cassie had tried to convince him of that last Christmas when he'd come to see her. That hadn't gone over well...at all. Carl Bellamy had told her firmly that his place was, and always would be, on his ranch outside of Bowie, Texas. Told her she could bury him there.

That was not something Cassie wanted to think about. He, Imelda, and Bud his ranch foreman were the only family Cassie had left. Even though she hadn't been able to make herself come back to Bowie for ten years, they knew she loved them. She made sure of it with calls, letters, cards and gifts. Maybe it wasn't the same as being here, but it was the best she'd been able to do. And she'd made sure her daddy came to see her in Phoenix, at least twice a year.

Cassie knew one thing, and that was she did not want to become a rancher. She'd grown up with that life, and saw what her daddy had sacrificed to raise her by himself, the hard work he'd done to keep them going. She intended to pay him back for those sacrifices now, by coming back to help him while he was down. But there was no way she was going to stay in Bowie.

Her life was in Phoenix now, and that's where she'd return. Once it got to the point of him not being able to run the ranch anymore, he'd have to move there as well. As much as it pained her to think of how it would hurt her daddy if she sold the Double B, Cassie was not going to take over permanently. She'd made that perfectly clear to him.

Things happened for a reason had always been Cassie's motto, and so far her life had proven that. Her mother's death, her finding Luke with Becca, her move to Phoenix, and now her dad's injury, all had meaning, and purpose to teach her something.

Her mother's death had made her a stronger, more independent woman. Luke's cheating had taught her not to put her happiness or heart in the hands of a man. Her flight to Phoenix had put her where she needed to be to find a more successful life than being a small-town housewife with a bunch of kids. And now, her dad's injury might help him find some rest and enjoyment in his golden years, instead of working himself to death on that damned ranch.

Cassie shook her head to clear out the cobwebs she was spinning in her mind then put her weight behind the wrench to give it one more forceful twist. The rusty nut popped off and steam rushed up from the loosened hose to hit her in the face with a hot blast. Surprised and blinded, she reared up and banged her head on the hood, and cursed. Her boot heels slipped on the bumper and then she felt herself falling backward into empty air.

**

Luke Matthews passed a rusty old grayish-green pickup truck broken down on the side of the road, as he headed toward the Bellamy farm to check up on old Carl. He'd seen Imelda in town this morning and she'd told him that

4

Carl had been thrown from a horse a few weeks ago, and had broken his leg pretty badly.

Imelda had told him that they'd operated on Carl and put pins in his leg, but he'd be laid up for a long time. The man should be in a rehab hospital, not trying to run a cattle farm from a wheelchair. Luke planned on telling him that, and offering to help if he needed it.

He knew the man's only kid, Cassie, was in Phoenix and she didn't seem to care about anything in Bowie...not even her father it seemed. She hadn't been back to the ranch in ten years to see the old man. Anger surged up inside of Luke, but he tamped it back down. What Cassie Bellamy did was no business of his, he reminded himself.

Slowing his cruiser to a crawl, he looked inside the cab of the old truck. It was empty, so sped up a little and passed on by, but then looked up in the rearview. Lust slammed into his gut when he saw the finest ass he'd ever seen in a pair of cutoff jean shorts sticking out from under the hood. The owner of that fine behind and illegally long legs was standing on the bumper in cowboy boots leaning under the hood struggling with something under there.

Without his consent, Luke's hands twisted the steering wheel and he made a u-turn, then pulled up in front of the truck, and shut off his engine. He opened the door to get out, just as he saw steam billow out from under the hood, and saw the woman jerk upward and hit her head on the hood. Her boots turned loose of the bumper and she started falling backwards.

Quickly skirting around the front of his car, Luke saw her go horizontal toward the ground and ran to catch her in his arms before she hit the ground.

"Whoa, there," he chuckled and pulled her against his chest, then set her down in front of him.

Her face was hidden by a beat up straw hat that had slipped down over it, but he saw a mass of wilted sunshine yellow curls around her shoulders. Beautiful hair, he thought, his interest peaked, then his eyes traveled down to take in her full breasts showing clearly under her sweaty grease-streaked tank top. Luke's mouth watered, even sweaty and dirty this cowgirl had his full attention. That is until she pushed back her hat and he saw sky-blue eyes rimmed by smudged mascara set in a face he knew he'd never forget.

"Cassie Bellamy..." he said in shock and his arms dropped to his sides then he took a step back.

Her gaze flew to his and she looked as shocked as he was, but she recovered more quickly than he did. With a smug quirk at the corner of her full lips, she ran her eyes down his body and back up, leaving a scorching path. Luke shifted his stance as his uniform pants got a little tighter. It seemed this particular woman would always have that effect on him, and it irritated the hell out of him.

With a haughty tip of her chin, Cassie snorted dismissively, then turned on her heel and climbed back up on the bumper to work on the truck. Luke just stood there staring at the spectacular view she was giving him.

After a minute, she emerged from under the hood and hopped down from the bumper holding a heater hose and wrench with a look of victory on her beautiful grease-smudged face. She should have looked ridiculous so sweaty, dirty and grease-streaked, but she didn't. She looked sexy as hell. Good enough to eat. And damn if he didn't realize, even though it galled him, that he was still hungry for this gorgeous, but heartless woman.

Luke let his eyes take a journey down her slim sweat-slick throat, across her full breasts in the lacy bra he could see through the wet tank top, then down to her small waist and curvy hips, to her toned thighs and calves all the way to where they stopped at her cowboy boots.

Dragging his gaze back up to her blue eyes, he swallowed hard then said, "You haven't changed a bit." And he wasn't just talking about her physical appearance. Her attitude was the same too.

A message he couldn't decipher sparkled in her blue

eyes when she told him, "That's where you're wrong, Sheriff," then spun on her heel to sashay over to the cab of the truck. Reaching inside, she jerked out a large purse, and slung it over her shoulder. Without another glance in his direction, Cassie headed up the road toward Bowie, her ass swinging, taunting him, with each long loose stride.

Cassie pushed her hot stringy hair over her shoulder and huffed in a lungful of the dusty dry Texas air. She pulled her tank top away from her breasts where it had suctioned, then frowned at the grease on her shirt, her broken nails, dusty shorts and boots.

This was sure not how she wanted to look when she saw Luke Matthews again. She imagined he must still be laughing his ass off at the sight she made. *Oh well, what the hell did she care what he thought?* But an inner voice taunted that she did care...because she wanted him to eat his heart out.

A Sheriff? Bad boy Luke Matthews was a deputy now? She almost stopped in her tracks to howl laughing. The same boy who had gotten thrown in the pokey for underage drinking? For kicking Jimmy Jones' ass for slapping hers? For breaking curfew to try and sneak into her window? That last one had almost got his ass filled with buckshot by her daddy, but instead he'd settled for calling the cops, *thank god.*

Cassie shook her head again...a deputy.

Time had been good to him, she admitted grudgingly. He was still as handsome as sin with his dark hair, square beard-stubbled jaw and whiskey brown eyes. Tall with the hard-packed muscles of manhood now, instead of lean and rangy like he'd been as a younger man, he looked even better than he had back then. All that manliness wrapped up in that uniform made him even more delectable. But Cassie wouldn't be partaking of Luke's all-night buffet, that was for sure.

She was over Luke Matthews...had been for years now. Her sole purpose in Bowie was to help her dad get back on his feet, and maybe to convince him to retire. Besides, she was an engaged woman, engaged to a man who really loved and respected her. She twisted the two carat diamond on her left hand around in circles.

James Barton was her friend, business partner and lover. Although he could be a little shallow and a lot clingy at times, he was steady and dependable too. They understood each other.

She'd met him three years ago at a Realtor convention, and they'd hit it off, then went into business together in Phoenix. One lonely night they'd progressed to a friends with benefits relationship, then six months ago he'd told her he loved her and asked her to marry him. And she'd said yes.

He might not be her idea of a dream lover, as good looking as he was, but he wasn't all that bad. When he wasn't being selfish he got the job done...sometimes. So what if he didn't set off wildfire inside her gut, he was a good man and he treated her well.

Cassie figured she loved James as much as she would ever allow herself to love any man again. Her heart had been out of the dating and relationship equation, since she'd left Bowie. It still was. But she was ready to start a family, and not a single-parent one like hers had been after her mother had died.

When a horn blew behind her she jumped then spun around. Luke eased up beside her on the road and rolled down the window. Cold air wafted through the opening and she saw the hair on his forehead lift in the cool breeze from the vent. She swallowed thirstily, and used her forearm to wipe away a bead of sweat that trickled down her temple.

"Hot out there?" His asked, his brown eyes twinkling with amusement. He gave her a smug smile that caused the dimple that always drove her crazy to dent his cheek then told her, "Hop in, I'll give you a ride to town."

"I'd rather roast, but thank you." She turned and

marched down the road again. Cassie had gone about ten steps when he pulled up by her again, idling along as she walked.

"C'mon, cupcake. I won't bite...just nibble a little," he drawled in that lazy honeyed voice of his she remembered so well.

Her heart kicked a little at his use of the nickname and corny line that had made her agree to go out with him the first time he asked. It kind of touched her that he remembered, but then she reminded herself it was probably a well-worn line. One she'd fallen for just because she was a naive teenager who had a crush on him.

She growled her frustration, then narrowed her eyes and hissed, "I don't think so...and don't call me that again!"

Cassie started walking again and then a dust tornado swirled in front of her kicking dust and pebbles into her mouth and eyes. Raising her hand, she tried to protect her face from the onslaught and then coughed when she inhaled the gritty air. She glanced back over her shoulder and saw that Luke was still tailing her at an idle.

Being stubborn wasn't going to get her to Bowie any quicker, she decided. It was hot as cornbread in a cast iron skillet out here, and she was exhausted. Her skin was coated in a fine layer of dust that was turning to mud with every bead of sweat that trickled down her face. Her fair skin would be burnt to a crisp by the time she got to Bowie.

She could ride with him, and remain unaffected, she told herself. Luke Matthews meant less than nothing to her now. He was simply a public servant, and for right now, she was one of the public he served.

Lifting her chin, Cassie looked over toward the car where he sat smiling, waiting for her to either accept his ride or start walking again. Cassie huffed out a breath then crossed the road and walked around the car to jerk open the passenger door. When she slid inside, cold air brushed across her skin and evaporated the sweat beads there.

Breathing a sign of relief, she laid her head back against the seat.

"Feel better?" He asked then leaned forward to kick the air up a notch and point another vent toward her.

"Yes, thank you. Could you please take me to Bowie?"

"Sure thing, cup--" he started, then stopped when she opened one eye and gave him a warning look. "Cassie," he corrected then looked at the road and pressed the accelerator.

After a minute, Cassie sat up and looked out the window at the all-too-familiar landscape of her former home, dotted with patches of grass, cactus and scrub brush, broken up by copses of trees here and there. When she felt his eyes on her, Cassie looked at him to find him staring at her chest.

Looking down, she saw that the cold air had made her nipples tighten under the wet tank top. She gave him a nasty look and folded her arms across her chest, crossed her legs and shifted her body toward the door. *There, how's that for body language?* Off limits buddy--that ship sailed about ten years ago, she thought.

Silence filled the inside of the car, except for the sound of the air blowing from the vents they didn't speak. Finally, curiosity got the better of her. "So, how long have you been a deputy?"

He looked away from the road and said, "I was a deputy for three years, and I've been Sheriff for nearly four."

A grin she couldn't control eased her lips up and she chuckled. "Sheriff?"

"Surprising, huh?"

"I'd say...I kind of expected you to be on the other side of the bars," Cassie told him with a snort.

She would think that of him, Luke thought. But Cassie didn't know Luke Matthews wasn't the same boy she'd ran out on ten years ago. Luke was a man now, and respectable. His drunken father wasn't how people knew him these days, neither were his youthful indiscretions...most of which were caused by her.

Her smile faded and she asked, "How's your dad?"

"Dead. His liver finally gave out three years ago." He still couldn't force any feeling into saying that, even after three years, all he could feel was relief that his old man was dead.

She gasped. "Oh, Luke...I'm sorry."

He glanced over at her and saw her eyes filled with sympathy. It grated on his nerves. "Don't be. I'm not." He pinched his lips together and gripped the steering wheel tighter.

Luke didn't care if he came off sounding like an unfeeling bastard, that was just how he felt about it. His father got what he deserved, after years of physically abusing and mentally torturing him when he was into the bottle.

"You here to see about Carl?" he asked her to deflect the subject.

"Yeah...Imelda called me. I'll be around a few weeks to help him get back on his feet, unless I can talk him into coming to Phoenix with me."

Luke snorted. "That ain't happening, honey. You know it."

Carl Bellamy's roots were planted on that ranch and the only way she'd get him to leave was boots up. She unfolded her arms and put her hand on her thigh. Luke glanced down and saw a diamond ring on her finger big enough to choke a horse. The sun shining through the windshield hit it and it about blinded him.

A sharp pain pierced his chest and he reached up to rub it. Her eyes met his and he saw something that looked almost like guilt there. "Your Daddy never mentioned you got married."

"Engaged." She corrected him flatly and covered her left hand with her right in her lap, as if hiding the huge stone would make it go away. Like she was embarrassed over it.

He nodded. What did he expect? She had a life in Phoenix now, Cassie was a beautiful woman, how could he expect her not to be married by now? But the hard proof on her finger that another man had the right to touch her...to love her...that she loved someone else, made his heart wrench a little as what ifs flitted through his mind. *Would she still be his if she'd stuck around?*

Luke gritted his teeth then swallowed hard and said, "Congratulations."

Her blue eyes slid to his and she studied him a moment, then said, "Thank you."

She glanced down and picked up her purse from beside her leg and unzipped it. Removing a pack of wet wipes, she flipped down the visor and wiped her face, neck and then her chest.

Watching that cloth slide over her throat and chest had him hot and bothered again, so he forced his eyes back to the road to keep from torturing himself. As they rode in silence, Luke reminded himself that her flippant attitude toward him proved she was still the selfish bitch who'd left him ten years ago without explanation. No way was he going to let the pretty packaging blind him to that fact.

Luke was relieved when they finally pulled into a parking spot in front of Toby's garage. She picked up her purse from the floor then said, "Thanks for the ride," before she reached for the door handle.

"I can wait and bring you back to your truck if you want?" Luke offered without knowing why. Must be latent masochistic tendencies. All he needed was to be trapped inside the car with her any longer. Her familiar smell and half-naked body was already driving him to the brink of insanity.

"Nah, I'm sure I can get a ride," she said distractedly. "Hey--is that Cody Lawson over there?" She waved at the large blond man in the grease-stained overalls who stood at the bay door wiping his big beefy hands on a red rag.

Luke knew she'd dated the big bozo, who had been full-back for the Bowie Beavers, in tenth grade, before he and Cassie had started dating the next year. Jealousy punched him in the gut and he tamped it down. So what if she still had the hots for the big grease monkey, he thought.

"Yeah, he's worked here since right after high school. He owns the garage now. Toby retired a few years ago."

"Really? I thought Cody got a full-ride to A&M for football?"

"He did--they took it back when he got hurt that last game." The knee injury wasn't the only thing that would have prevented Cody from finishing college. The guy was dumb as a box of rocks. The only reason he finished high-school was because the teachers wouldn't dare fail their star athlete. The coaches made sure of it. This was Texas, and A&M football was much more important than education to them.

"That's too bad...he was really good," she said with sympathy filling her blue eyes.

"Yeah, he was," Luke agreed tightening his grip on the steering wheel. "He probably wouldn't have made the grades to stay on the team anyway," he told Cassie then realized what a jealous fool he sounded like. But, it was true. Cody didn't have the drive or the brains to have gone the distance.

Unlike Luke, who had worked two jobs so he could go to school and make sure he could do better than his drunken father.

Luke watched as recognition hit Cody and a big smile split his face, before he walked to the car and jerked open the door. He pulled Cassie out of the car and into a big bear hug that lifted her off her feet. "Oh, my god honey, are you a sight for sore eyes!"

She giggled...*fucking giggled*...and then put her arms around his neck then put a big smacker of a kiss on his grease-smeared cheek. Luke wanted to punch something.

That certainly wasn't the reception he'd gotten. And that guy hadn't almost been her fiancé before she'd up and left him high and dry with no explanation. Luke held that honor.

Luke had actually been on the verge of asking Cassie to marry him the night she'd left, had the ring he'd saved up for six months in his pocket. If Becca Harvey hadn't fallen into the damned lake and almost drowned, making him late meeting her at their spot, he would have. Maybe Becca saved him the embarrassment of Cassie laughing in his face, and telling him she was leaving.

He'd never been good enough for her anyway, everyone said so, and she'd probably figured it out, or had always known it too. Which probably explained why she'd had no problem at all leaving him. What Luke had thought to be sincere words of love from her had actually been a little rich girl getting her jollies by stringing him along with hot kisses, before she cut out for greener grass.

Her daddy owned a big cattle ranch...she was part of the 'haves' and he was definitely a 'have not'. Just the size of the rock on her finger told him she was still out of his league, regardless of the fact that he had made something of himself in the ten years she'd been gone. Luke was not, and would never be a rich man, someone who could keep Cassie in the style to which she was accustomed.

But he was happy with his life now without her. Things had turned out like they were supposed to. He wasn't letting a case of 'what ifs' make him forget how far he'd come. He dated plenty, got laid when he had the urge, without complications. He didn't need the tall leggy former rodeo queen complicating his life. Nope, Luke learned from his mistakes...and Cassie Bellamy was one of the biggest he'd ever made.

He wasn't sticking around for the rest of her reunion with Cody Lawson either. Leaning across the passenger seat, he grabbed the door handle. "Looks like you have things covered. See you around," he told her gruffly and slammed the door then jammed the car into reverse and pulled away. A glance in the rearview found her standing beside the big beefcake staring after him with her hands on her hips.

Luke dragged his eyes away from her in the mirror and hit the accelerator. If he hurried, he could make the trip to the ranch to see Carl and be gone before she got her truck fixed and made it there. He'd make sure of it.

CHAPTER TWO

It was dusk by the time Cassie dragged her suitcase from the bed of the truck and lugged it up to the front of the big farm house that had been her home for the first eighteen years of her life. She stopped for a moment at the steps to take all in.

The big old house looked the same, even down to the brightly colored potted flowers hanging on the hooks her mother had put along the porch eaves twenty years ago. Imelda must still be making sure flowers were hung there and they were tended. Cassie inhaled deeply and took in the familiar smell of cattle, hay, dust, rich earth...home.

The sense of homecoming that squeezed her heart, was unfathomable. Ten years faded away, as she placed her boot on the first step and then the second, before stepping on the wide boards of the front porch which led to the tall red front door with high windows. She lifted her hand to knock, but dropped it to the knob instead, and walked inside.

Stepping inside the entryway was like walking through at time warp. The antler chandelier in the high-ceilinged entry welcomed her, and the rich brown hardwood floors gleamed in the fading sunlight. She took a few steps and looked left into her mother's sitting room.

Dainty lace doilies her mother had crocheted still covered every piece of sturdy oak furniture, and the same overstuffed floral sofa sat against the wall between two sage green high-backed Queen Anne chairs.

She peeked into the small telephone alcove that was right by the front door and was surprised to see the red rotary dial phone had been replaced by a modern black push button model.

After a few more steps, she looked into the formal dining room. Her mother's fine china was still proudly displayed in the big oak hutch her daddy had bought for her. There was a white lace table cloth covering the huge table that would seat twenty people, and often had for holidays.

When she got to the end of the entry hall, instead of turning right to go into the kitchen, she took a deep breath of the rarified air smelling of lavender, lemon oil and leather then yelled "Daddy! I'm home!"

"Cassie Bee? Is that you?" she heard Carl Bellamy's deep familiar voice call weakly from the family room.

Cassie dropped her suitcase in the foyer and ran through the big doorway into the family room, and found her daddy sitting in a wheelchair near a window beside the huge brick fireplace with a crocheted afghan over his lap. Skidding to a stop on the braided rug in front of the fireplace, she stared at the frail old man in the wheelchair who looked a hundred years old. She swallowed a lump of emotion that clogged her throat. He bore no resemblance to the man she'd seen at Christmas.

Her hand flew to her mouth and she whispered, "Oh, daddy..." then ran to him and hugged him tightly.

"Dammit, I told Imelda not to call you," he said grumpily against her shoulder.

"And I'd have kicked your ass if she didn't. I'm really pissed she didn't call when it happened!"

"I'm fine girl...just leave me be," he told her then looked away to stare back out the window.

"You're not fine, and you know it. You're just a being a crotchety old fart who won't admit to needing help."

"Watch your mouth, young lady."

"I'm not a young lady anymore, daddy...and you're not a young man," Cassie told him and huffed out a frustrated breath.

He grunted and jerked the afghan off of his legs and tossed it aside. When he put his hands on the arms of the wheelchair, and moved his leg off the leg rest as if to stand, she pushed his shoulders back down. "You stay right there--what do you need?"

"I need for you to quit treating me like an invalid. I

have a ranch to run."

"I'm running the ranch until you're better. You are going to get some physical therapy to get back on your feet," Cassie told him firmly.

"I'm not going to one of those old folks homes...you can put that right out of your head."

"I'd never do that to you! You know that!" She couldn't believe he thought she'd do that to him. "We'll get someone to come out here."

"They won't do it...it's too far out in the sticks." His big hand squeezed the handle of the chair and he swallowed thickly. Her dad had been so strong for so many years, it hurt her heart to see him so weak and fragile. And to see how much he was trying to hide his frailness from the world. He was only sixty-two, but right now he looked ancient.

Cassie clenched her jaw, looked him in the eyes and said, "They'll do what I damned well tell them to do."

A grin kicked up the side of his mouth, creasing his wrinkled his weathered cheek. He reached over and squeezed her hand. "That's my girl."

He was right, the Double B was pretty rural, but somehow, she'd pull off getting someone to agree to come out. She had to...because she knew he'd never agree to leave the ranch. Cassie had come by her stubbornness honestly. Getting him to retire and move to Phoenix with her was a pie in the sky dream, she knew. But she wasn't giving up on trying. Tenacity was another thing she'd inherited from Carl Bellamy.

Forcing a bright smile, Cassie asked, "So what do you want for supper?" She grabbed the handles on the back of his wheelchair. "You know my cooking skills are limited, so take it easy on me."

"You still haven't learned to cook? How're you gonna catch a man if you can't cook girl?"

She'd heard that one before. Her mother hadn't been around to teach her, and Imelda had tried with no success.

She could make simple stuff, but she wasn't going to win a blue ribbon at the county fair for her pie that was for sure.

Without her mother's guidance in the girly department, Cassie had turned into something of a tomboy after her death, preferring to ride and rope and fish than priss and primp. It had won her the title of rodeo queen, and 4-H barrel racing champ, but hadn't done much to improve her domestic skills.

"I'm going to hire a cook like Imelda." It was good that James was nearly a gourmet chef. He was the one who cooked in their household. "Or marry a man who can cook."

He looked over his shoulder at her. "Not that prissy pants, James fella I met at Christmas, huh?"

"Yeah, Dad. James and I are engaged now."

He grunted. "When he shook my hand his wrist was as limp as my dic--"

"Dad! That's enough!" she said in exasperation.

"What you need is a man like that Luke Matthews." He shook his head then laughed and added, "Even though I almost had to pepper his ass with buckshot that time I caught him trying to climb in your window, he's a good man." He laughed again and then slapped his thigh. "You would've laughed your ass off if you'd have seen that boy's face staring down the barrel of old Annie."

Not likely, because she had invited Luke to climb that rose trellis. She had been terrified her daddy was going to kill Luke that night. But she smiled a wide smile anyway, because it was good to see her father laughing about anything right now.

"Is he still single?" She had wondered when she'd seen him earlier today, but wasn't about to ask him. Cassie hadn't noticed a wedding ring, but that didn't mean anything...nor did the fact that he was flirting with her. Once a cheater, always a cheater.

"Yeah, he's single, but there's always girls hot on his tail, I hear. He was out here a little bit ago checking up on me."

"He was?" That was odd, he must've come out right after he dropped her off at the garage. To her knowledge Luke and her father weren't close, and from what she remembered of him, Luke wasn't one to care about anyone but himself. But maybe he'd changed on that front a little. After all he'd had helped her earlier.

"He wanted to see if I needed anything. Offered his help, and suggested I go to a hospital over in Amarillo to get back on my feet. But that ain't happening." Her dad's gray eyes narrowed thoughtfully, "You know...he's worked on a cattle farm before, may---"

"No!" She shouted in frustration, stopping the wheelchair right in the doorway to the kitchen. "Why are you so hot for me to hook up with Luke now? I thought you didn't like him?"

"I changed my mind when they elected him Sheriff. He's made something of himself, and you could do worse for a husband...like that James."

"Dad, please. James is a good man and he's my business partner. I care about him, please don't talk like that."

Her daddy harrumphed. "He's just not the right one for you, baby girl. You know I speak my mind."

"If there's one thing I know, it's that." She leaned down and kissed his leathery cheek. "Okay my stomach thinks I cut my throat, let's go eat."

"You lucked out, Imelda left some lasagna in the fridge. Think you can manage to heat it up without burning it?"

She laughed and slugged him in the shoulder lightly. "Yes, daddy, I think I can manage that."

The rubber wheels of the chair squeaked across the shiny floor as she pushed him through the kitchen and parked him at the small oak breakfast table. "So how many cowpokes you have working for you these days?"

"Four, not including Bud." She set the brake on the chair before walking around the breakfast bar to the big double door refrigerator beside the huge stainless steel stove.

Bud was the foreman and lived out in the bunkhouse behind the barn. He'd been her daddy's foreman and best friend for thirty years. There wasn't anyone her father trusted like Buddy Parsons. "He's still putting up with you? Amazing."

She dug around inside the refrigerator and found the foil-wrapped casserole pan with the lasagna. James would love this kitchen, she thought when she stood back up looking around. The copper pots hanging on the rack above the center prep island, and the eight burner stove, would put him in heaven.

Reading up in the cabinet, Cassie pulled down two stoneware plates and set them on the countertop by the microwave. Maybe she'd invite James down for the weekend in a couple weeks. Her daddy might like him better, if he got to know him.

Carl grunted and said "I'm still putting up with him you mean."

"I know how the wind blows at the Double B, daddy," she said with a chuckle then dug in the drawer until she found a serving spoon. Cassie scooped out a big serving of lasagna on one plate, then the other. Brushing her finger over the spoon, she sampled the cold sauce and moaned. Delicious as always.

"It blew you right out of here didn't it? Thought Buddy would be right behind you."

Cassie picked up the plates and walked toward the microwave. "He loves you more than me, you know that," she told him then winked.

"Not a snowball's chance in hell, darlin', that man thinks you hung the moon and the stars. You practically ripped his heart out of his chest when you left."

Buddy treated her like the daughter he never had, and sometimes she thought their closeness made her daddy a little jealous. Buddy was about eight years older than her daddy...that put him near seventy now. He was getting old too. The Double B would never be the same when he finally retired. And her daddy wouldn't be able to handle things out here alone.

Sadness crept over her like a dark cloud of impending doom thinking of that day. This ranch meant everything to her daddy. He'd be heartbroken if she sold it when he couldn't run it anymore, but ranching was not the life she wanted, he knew that. She had a life...in Phoenix, a business to run, one she enjoyed thoroughly.

But for now, she'd be a rancher. It had been a long time, but she knew the ropes...mostly. And what she didn't know, her dad or Bud could fill in for her.

Cassie set the microwave timer then leaned back against he counter and crossed her arms over her chest. "How many head of cattle do you have right now?" she asked dreading the answer. It was calving season now, and soon there'd be twice as many in their herd, until they were weaned.

"Five hundred or so. About half are pregnant."

She swallowed hard. That many? How could he think to run that many at his age? "Daddy, that's a lot of cattle. Can we sell some off?"

"Not now. We'll have a sale after the calves are dropped."

"But that will be seven hundred fifty head then. And trying to watch over the cows birthing all those calves with only five hands will be nearly impossible. We could probably sell them as twofers now before the births."

"Lose too much money, Cassie Bee. Just hire a few more hands to help with the calving. Talk to Bud about it tomorrow. We need to talk about the cotton we have planted on the back acreage too. It'll need to be harvested in August, if I'm not back on my feet by then."

Oh hell. Not only did she have the cattle to contend with, she had crops. At least that didn't require too much supervision...and she had two months before she'd have to worry about it, if at all. Maybe she'd be gone by then. The timer dinged and she groaned and opened the door to pull out the plate. "How many acres?"

"Hundred."

Cassie stood up and walked over to put her dad's plate in front of him with a fork, then put her hands on her hips. "Wow dad--you sure know how to bite off more than you can chew."

"I've been chewing that for thirty years, little girl." He picked up the fork and shoved a sizable bite into his mouth.

"But you're thirty years older now too, dad. It's time for you to scale down."

"I know how old I am, Cassie. And I know how much I can handle. If that damned snake hadn't scared that new filly I was riding, we wouldn't be having this discussion."

Holy shit, he'd almost been snakebit too? She shivered. If there was one thing Cassie hated, it was snakes. Poisonous or not they all slithered and made her skin crawl. "Dad, really...a snake?"

"Yeah, big ole rattler. Scared the bejeesus outta that filly and she took off and left me behind. Good thing she's barn sour and ran right back here, or I'd probably still be out there."

"You're lucky you didn't get bit. And what the hell were you doing riding alone?" she chastised.

"I had my rifle out aiming to shoot the damned thing when she bolted. Got off the shot and killed it before I got thrown."

"Thank God for small favors." Cassie mumbled huffing out a relieved sigh as she walked back around the counter to put her plate in the microwave. "Where's the filly? Which one were you riding?"

"Fiona. Clementine's foal."

Clementine had been his favorite mare, but her dad had told her at Christmas that she was too old to work anymore, so they'd bred her a few times and put her out to pasture a while back.

Cassie grabbed two glasses, filled them with ice then poured a large iced tea for both of them then walked over to hand him one. "How old is she?"

"Four. Under saddle for less than a year. She's just green." He dismissed the filly's poor behavior.

"I think we should run her through the auction next month. We don't need unmanageable horses here. Someone else could get hurt," Cassie told him.

"No." He said and popped another bite of pasta into his mouth.

"What?" Cassie spun back around to look at him. "A spooky, barn sour horse that leaves you hurt out in the field and you don't want to sell her?"

"No--she stays. We'll just get one of the hands to work with her more."

God, the man could be stubborn. "Dad we only have five hands and they are all going to be busy working with the five hundred head of cattle and two hundred fifty calves."

"Talk to Bud--tell him to find someone. She stays."

Cassie added working with that damned filly to her ever-growing mental to-do list. She had no idea how this was going to work. There was just too much to do.

The buzzer on the microwave sounded, but she found she'd lost her appetite as she pulled her plate out. Sleep was going to be what she needed. She had a feeling that would be in short supply for the next month.

A few hours later, after she'd tidied up the kitchen, and helped her dad to get tucked into bed, Cassie grabbed her sleep shorts, fresh underwear and a t-shirt and headed to the bathroom. Her muscles ached from first sitting in the truck for so long, then her war with the heater hose in the truck. She smelled to high heaven she knew, and would probably leave a ring in the tub from the grime that had accumulated on her skin from her unplanned pitstop on the road.

Cassie ran hot water into the large claw-foot tub, poured in some bubble bath then stripped naked. She slid beneath the frothy bubbles and sighed, closing her eyes.

Tomorrow would tell the tale on whether she'd survive the next month or so. Once she talked to Bud, she hoped he'd have the answers she needed on how they were going to get through this farming fiasco.

If Bud didn't have a good solid plan, whether her Daddy liked it or not, they were going to have a mass cattle sale and he was going to take the time off he needed to heal. Maybe they could both go back to Phoenix for that. That was the ultimate solution to this problem. If she could get Bud to agree that was the answer, they could gang up on her dad and talk some sense into him.

***

The smothered chicken, mashed potatoes and gravy Luke ordered at the Bluebird Cafe tasted like sandpaper in his mouth. This was his favorite dish, so why wasn't he enjoying it tonight? To distract himself from thoughts about Cassie Bellamy, he'd called up Katie Smith, the woman he'd been dating lately and invited her to supper at the Bluebird.

The twenty-five year old redhead worked on auto-pilot with her non-stop chatter, and required little input from him to keep a conversation going. He thought that would be the answer for him tonight, but somehow it wasn't. Not even the sight of her full breasts spilling over the V in the tight bubble-gum pink tank top she wore could distract him.

Everything about the woman sitting across from him was in technicolor, big breasts, bigger hair and she was bold as a brass penny. Katie certainly provided enough visual stimulation to keep most men from thinking of little else but her. Not him, not tonight. Her endless talk about the latest gossip she'd heard down at the Cut Up Corral while she got her roots done, was giving him a headache. Her high-pitched voice, which he usually found cute, bored inside his skull like a drill.

The events of his fucked-up day kept spinning in his mind like a tilt-a-whirl. With every rotation, he got madder and madder.

Today, Cassie Bellamy had treated him like an unwelcome acquaintance, instead of the man she'd dated for a year and half then left without a word. She'd offered no apology, no explanation, as to why she'd left Bowie like her tail was on fire. She acted like she didn't owe him one either, like he didn't matter, had never mattered to her.

That pretty much cemented the opinion he'd formed of her after she left. She was a spoiled rich girl who'd chosen him as her play toy because of his reputation, to put a little excitement into her life, until she got bored and went looking for greener pastures.

He couldn't believe he'd been so blind to her true nature while they were dating. Evidently, she'd grabbed his brain along with his dick ten years ago. Well, Luke wasn't thinking with that part of his anatomy anymore. He was a different man than the one she'd fooled so many years ago, he had a different agenda.

A little revenge might go a long way to making him feel better though. Maybe he'd seduce her then leave her dangling on the limb, like she'd done him back then. Or maybe he'd fuck her enough times to get her out of his system. The thought improved his mood a little.

"Luke? What's up with you tonight, hon? You're as distracted as a bird dog in a chicken coop."

Luke dropped his fork onto his plate and looked up into the bright green eyes studying him intently. "Nothing, sugar...just work," he lied. The last thing he needed was to discuss Cassie Bellamy with his current quasi-girlfriend.

"You have a bad day, doll?" She smacked the gum she always seemed to be chewing, and blew a bubble. "Want to talk about it?"

"Nah, can't do that."

She pursed her cupid's bow mouth, the same mouth that had fascinated him since she first used it on him, then she blew out a breath. "You never want to talk to me about your work."

"I can't talk about it, sugar. I told you that." Luke picked up his iced tea and took a swallow then absently rubbed his fingers on the condensation ring where it had been sitting on the red-checked table cloth.

Katie's lips moved into a pout, and she twisted a strand of her fiery red hair. She looked about sixteen with the freckles on her nose.

"Come to think about it, there's not much you do talk to me about...other than sex," she whined.

They had nothing in common that's why. She was as shallow as a birdbath and as chirpy as the birds that swam there. Perhaps it was time for him to move on from the big-haired, big-breasted woman he was having dinner with. Three weeks was long enough to know a fourth wasn't going to improve anything.

Inside the bedroom their compatibility might be a ten, but outside? Barely a blip on the scale. Luke cleared his throat and tried to make it easy. "Listen sugar...I think it's time for us to move on. I'm holding you back from finding someone who could really make you happy."

She gasped and raised her multi-ringed hand to her impressive heaving cleavage. "Why, Luke Matthews, I think you're dumping me."

Give the lady a prize, she got it on the first try. "I think it would be the best for both of us to date other people, sugar. I work so much I hardly have time for you. You deserve someone who can give you more attention."

"Well, maybe you're right. I do deserve better, Luke." She stood and pulled down the micro-mini blue jean skirt that barely covered her round ass then picked up her water glass and leaned closer to him. His eyes automatically traveled to her cleavage.

"Go fuck yourself, Luke. Because you certainly aren't going to be fuc--" she pinched her lips on the curse and then tossed the water into his face and slammed the glass on the table, before spinning on her heel and stomping to the door.

Okay, that just capped his shitty day. Water dripped down his hair into his eyes and splotched his shirt. He reached across the table and pulled several napkins out of the holder then mopped his face with them. Eerie silence had descended inside the diner, and he looked around and noticed all eyes were focused on him.

"Just a misunderstanding folks...please, eat your dinner." Luke told them feeling a flush creep up his neck and across his cheeks. He stood, tossed a few bills on the table then picked up his Stetson and jammed it on his head as he walked to the door.

This would be all over town tomorrow, he knew. Luke hated to be the fodder for the town gossip mill. He'd had years of that with his father. It irritated the shit out of him to be there again. Not to mention, it made him look like a fool, because he was the Sheriff.

He lived a clean life, kept to himself, and tried to stay on the straight and narrow. As Sheriff he needed to keep a low profile. The scene that just played out was not helping that cause. Maybe he needed to date women from Henrietta, instead of Bowie. Taking his business out of town might be the answer to keeping it from spilling out in such a public way.

Dammit, this was all Cassie Bellamy's fault too. Why the hell had she come back to Bowie now after ten years? He thought he was way past being angry over her desertion so long ago. Way past feeling *anything* for her. Evidently, that wasn't the case, since all he could think about all afternoon, and now, was her.

He'd never admit it, but he was thirty-one years old and unattached for a reason. The gaping hole she had left inside of him when she left him ten years ago was still there, as was the lesson she'd taught him. Women couldn't be trusted. They were fickle, and flighty. Which explained why he only dated bimbos these days, so he wasn't tempted to get attached.

Well, no more. Fate had presented him with a golden opportunity to get his head on straight again, and he was going to seize it so he could finally move on from Cassie Bellamy, and find something more lasting in his life. The old scars she had left would be erased, and the unfinished business between them completed, before the leggy blonde left Bowie again.

Luke wasn't into playing games, so he didn't know how he was going to pull it off, she didn't seem overly interested in seeing him again when he was with her earlier today. No, she'd been too busy reacquainting herself with Cody Lawson at the garage to even say goodbye to him.

Cassie Bellamy better get ready, because Luke was going to be on her like white on rice until she got in the right frame of mind, and then he would accomplish his goal. Luke looked both ways at the corner then crossed the street with determination and walked to where his truck was parked.

CHAPTER THREE

At 8 a.m. sharp, Luke walked into the station and stopped at Julie Beth's desk to pick up the pink messages on his spike there.

The dispatcher wasn't around, so he went to his office and grabbed his coffee cup then headed to the kitchen for his second cup of the morning. As he neared the kitchen, he heard a low murmur of female voices inside, one being Julie Beth's.

His footsteps faltered, and then he stopped right outside the door to listen for a second. Julie Beth was in her fifties and was probably the head engineer on the Bowie gossip train.

"Yeah..." Julie Beth said a little above a whisper. She craned her neck to make sure nobody was listening and then said, "She told him to go fuck himself, and then threw water in his face!" The other woman, an administrative assistant from the mayor's office the next floor up, gasped then covered her mouth with her hand and chuckled.

With a groan, Luke slapped his hand to his forehead. It took less time than he'd anticipated for the events of last night to travel. Hell, it had probably been spread to half the town by midnight last night. This town didn't need a newspaper with all the mouthy residents who carried the news like pigeons.

"Oh and did you hear that Cassie Bellamy is back in town?" Julie Beth asked and the other woman shook her head negatively, which was Julie Beth's 'go sign'.

"Well yeah, you know her Daddy fell off a horse and broke his leg. She's back to take care of him and help with the ranch til he's back on his feet. The old man must be off his rocker, because he has over five hundred head of cattle out there and a hundred acres of cotton."

Julie Beth shook her head and took a deep breath and continued, "I don't know how the heck he thinks that city-slicker girl of his is going to hold it together for him. Bud's been asking around town for extra hands to help out, but so far he's only found one."

Luke knew Bud was Carl's ranch manager. He also knew the man would be hard-pressed to hire extra help right now. It was calving season, and most of the cow hands around town had already signed on with other ranches. Julie Beth was right about one thing, there was no way that Cassie was going to be able to handle it on her own.

One of the jobs he'd had in college was being a cowhand at a local ranch. The other had been at a horse farm, shoveling shit, cleaning stalls and feeding and exercising horses on the weekend. Neither of the jobs was pleasant, but he did them so he could go to school at night and get his degree in criminal justice.

Once he got his degree and had gone to the police academy, he left all that behind though, and swore he'd never go back. This time he'd make an exception for two reasons. Cassie needed his help, and he was going to finish their unfinished business. Once and for all.

The three weeks vacation time he had coming couldn't be put to better use, Luke thought and spun around without going into the kitchen to head back to his office.

This place could run on auto-pilot without him for a few weeks. Bowie wasn't crime central of the country, for sure. Hell, most of his calls were either for bar fights or cattle on the loose. Cole Jackson, his best friend and second in command, could certainly handle it by himself for that long.

Walking behind his desk, he picked up his phone and buzzed his friend. "Hey, you got a sec?"

"Yeah, something up?" Cole asked gruffly.

Cole was not a morning person, and it took at least half a pot of coffee for him to function. He was probably only on cup two or three right now. "I need to talk to you...grab your coffee and get in here."

"Yes, sir." Cole agreed sarcastically and then slammed the phone down.

Luke chuckled and sat back in his chair, tenting his fingers over his chest to wait. Within a second or two, his slightly rumpled best friend and deputy walked in frowning.

"What's on fire?"

"No fire--just some smoldering ashes."

"Cryptic this morning aren't you?" Cole walked to the chair in front of his desk and plopped down. "Spill it...coffee hasn't kicked in yet, so go slow."

Luke just stared at Cole for a moment, trying to frame what he was going to say. Cole wasn't going to like what he had in mind, he knew that for sure. After all, he was the one who had to put up with his sorry ass after Cassie had left the last time. His was the shoulder Luke had leaned on after he tried to drown his sorrows the same way his father had for so many years.

Cole had just barely kept Luke out of jail for the subsequent bar brawl and public intoxication. Thank God his daddy, Wiley Jackson, had been Sheriff at the time, or Luke might well not be sitting behind this desk or wearing the badge he was now.

Cole's father hadn't thrown him in jail, instead he sat him down for a conversation Luke needed to hear. "You need to get your shit together boy or you're gonna wind up just like your daddy," he said. "You can choose the side of the law you want to be on right now. If you keep this up, you won't have that choice." He went on to suggest that Luke go to school, and maybe consider law enforcement as a career like Cole planned to do.

"You gonna sit there eyeballing me or you gonna tell me what's on your mind, Slick? Cole said and took a large swallow of his coffee then asked, "This about what happened at the Bluebird last night?"

Heat crept up Luke's neck and he cleared his throat. "No, it's not about that."

"What then?" Cole asked and sipped at his coffee again.

"You hear Cassie's back in Bowie?"

Cole groaned and sat up straighter in his chair. "Yeah, but I was hoping you hadn't."

Luke picked up his coffee cup and went to take a sip, then remembered he hadn't gone into the kitchen to fill it and set it back down. "I ran into her yesterday on the road to the Double B. Her truck broke down."

"And?" Cole pinned him with curious green eyes. "Did you give her a Texas howdy when you passed by?"

No, he didn't give her the finger. "I stopped to help her. Didn't know it was her at first."

"So what happened? How's she look?" Cole asked curiously and then grinned. "That wart on the end of her nose grow a hair?"

Luke chuckled then ran a hand through his hair and admitted, "No wart. She looks the same fucking way she did ten years ago, just better." God he hated admitting that. It would have been so much easier if she'd come back toothless and two-hundred pounds heavier, and actually did have the wart that Cole joked about.

But she hadn't...Cassie Bellamy still looked like a beauty queen, and had the sassy mouth he loved to kiss. And she still lit that fire inside of him that no other woman since had been able to ignite.

"Not good man. How'd she act? She spill on why she left?" Cole leaned forward and propped his forearms on his thighs.

"Didn't say a fucking word and treated me like I had a communicable disease."

Cole shook his head and twirled his cup around in his hand. "Not good at all...you ok?"

"Not really." Luke forced out a laugh. "We have unfinished business, you know?"

"What'cha gonna do?" Cole drawled.

"Finish it." Luke told him with finality. "Once and for

all."

"Luke, you know that's not a good idea. She's not worth your time, man. You always get into trouble when she's around."

"Trouble or not, she needs help out at the ranch, while her Daddy's down. I'm taking my vacation time to help her," Luke told him firmly then asked, "Can you cover for three weeks?"

"You know that's not a problem. The problem is I'm not particularly thrilled about what you plan to do with your vacation time. Why don't you go on that Alaska fishing trip you wanted to take? Just get out of town for a while. She'll be gone by the time you get back."

"I'm going on a different kind of fishing trip, buddy." Cole smiled at his friend, ignoring the concern that pinched between his brows. "There'll be plenty of time later for that Alaska trip. This is a once-in-a-lifetime kind of opportunity to get my head right for the future, and put the past to bed."

There were a lot of things he'd like to put to bed, and the past was just one of them. Now all he had to do was convince her it was a good idea.

"Your head will never be right as long as that woman is around. It's like she scrambles your brains or something, man. Best thing you can do is stay away from her."

"Not happening, Cole. I'm doing this...I have to do this."

***

Cassie tucked her hair behind her ears and slipped on her old straw hat, before heading out the back door of the house. Her boot heels kicked up dust with every stride she made toward the bunkhouse.

After wearing a suit and heels every day for the past six years, being in boots and blue jeans felt like heaven, so there was a bounce in her step as she headed out to the barn to talk to Bud. It was early, but Bud was usually an early riser, so she'd probably catch him eating his breakfast.

The six or so horses in the barn nickered a greeting from their stalls when she stepped up on the porch to the bunkhouse. Although she was tempted to stop in there and scratch every head, she didn't.

Her mission this morning was too important. She wondered if Bud had fed the horses yet though. If not, she'd do that for him. It was going to take them a few days to get a routine down pat, one that was necessary to run the ranch right. Changing partners for the delicate dance her daddy and Bud had been doing by rote for thirty years was going to take some time, but she could do it. Her daddy had big shoes to fill, but her feet weren't small, and she was determined.

Cassie knocked on the whitewashed door of the bunkhouse then twisted the knob and walked inside. Nobody was in the kitchen, and she took a deep breath and inhaled the familiar smell of hay, leather and dust. Someone had evidently been cooking bacon in there recently, she thought, when the smoky rich scent teased her nostrils. She took a look over at the old cast iron cook stove and saw the skillet still sitting on the eye.

Walking around the long rough board picnic like table skirted with flat wood benches and across the narrow kitchen, she looked down the long T hallway to the sleeping rooms and called out for him. "Hey Buddy--get your old bones out here! I need a hug!" Her voice echoed down the hall and bounced back unanswered.

She walked down the long hallway to his room at the end and knocked loudly. "Buddy, sun's up lazy bones. Open up!" Still no answer. This was really odd, she thought. Her dad had still been sleeping when she left the house, and Imelda wasn't there yet to cook breakfast.

Maybe her dad knew where Buddy could be. But she wasn't going to wake him up. Sleep healed, and he needed a lot of healing. No, she'd feed the horses, then go see if he was up yet.

Excitement filled her at doing something physical for a change. She felt empowered as she walked back outside then into the barn and grabbed the thick hose from the spindle on the wall, and a feed bucket.

Dragging the hose to the first stall, she dropped the feed bucket then opened the latch and stepped inside. Politely, the pretty roan mare with a white blaze on her muzzle took a step backward and then shook her head.

"Morning girl," Cassie said and scratched the mare between her ears then shoved the hose nozzle into the water bucket and turned it on. When it was filled, she turned off the water and stepped back out and locked the stall. "I'll be back with your breakfast in a few minutes." The horse whinnied as if she understood and Cassie chuckled.

She made her way to all seven occupied stalls and refilled water buckets then went to the feed closet and filled up a feed bucket and grabbed a scoop. This job she'd done a thousand times in her life, it had been one of her chores as a teenager, and she loved it. Bonding with the horses in the morning and at night gave her a sense of peace and accomplishment.

After she'd given all the horses their feed and supplements, she went to the hayloft and got a couple of bales and cut the string loose. A tabby barn cat rubbed at her ankles while she peeled off several flakes from the bales. She stopped and gave the fuzzy little kitten a scratch on his back. He licked her hand then rolled on his back and she scratched his belly, which made him purr loudly.

When she lived here, she'd always spoiled the barn cats with milk, and extra food. She was glad to see there was still some around. Cassie couldn't count the times she'd come up here when she was upset and cuddled with them until she felt better. They were good listeners.

Cassie pushed to her feet and grabbed the hay up in her

arms. The smell of the rich alfalfa filled her nostrils and tickled her nose. She made another round through the stalls and gave each horse a share.

Cleaning the stalls was something she'd deal with this afternoon. They looked relatively clean, like they always did. Clean stalls was something that Buddy demanded. Hoof rot was not something he would tolerate. He loved his animals, like they were his children.

Slightly sweaty, her muscles aching a little from the unusual physical exertion, she made her way back outside and saw that the sun was up fully now, and the sky was cloudless, and a blue so vibrant it hurt her eyes. She pulled her hat down a little then headed for the back porch. Leaning on the doorframe she scraped her boots on the brush beside the door then went inside.

The wonderful smell of bacon and eggs frying and warm biscuits baking drew her to the kitchen like a zombie in a trance. Her stomach grumbled and she put a hand over it, then walked in the kitchen. Imelda was tending a pan at the stove, her ample waist cinched with a flowered apron, her gray-peppered black hair up in the same bun it was in every day. "Mama Melda!" Cassie squealed and ran over to her.

The short round woman jumped and then spun around. "Cassie Bee!" She grabbed Cassie tightly around the waist. Cassie squeezed her just as hard. "God, I've missed you girl."

"I've missed you too, mama." When her own mama had died when Cassie was ten, Cassie had been distraught and beside herself asking Imelda what she was going to do without her mama. Imelda, with five children of her own, jerked her to her breasts and hugged her tight, telling Cassie that she'd never be without a mama as long as she was around.

Cassie had started calling her Mama Melda after that day, and Imelda had been the closest thing to a mother she'd known since. It didn't make her miss her own mama any less or regret that instead of being able to go to her mother when she started her period, or when she'd had her heart broken the first time, she went to Imelda instead. But it had given a lonely, sad little girl the comfort she needed to survive.

"My goodness Cassie Bee, you're skinny as a rail. Sit down and let me feed you."

Cassie smiled. She wasn't skinny, but no matter what, Imelda worried about her, and her solution to everything was a good meal. Her own round hips told that story. "That sounds wonderful, mama. You need any help?"

"No, you just sit there and tell me what you've been doing with yourself for the last ten years. Your daddy tells me things, but I want from the horse's mouth."

Cassie walked toward the breakfast bar and sat down, then they talked for a few minutes, before Imelda put a heaping plate of scrambled eggs, grits and bacon in front of her then handed her a fluffy perfectly golden-brown biscuit. "Wow...this looks scrumptious."

Cassie picked up her fork and dove in, and had made quite a dent in her meal when the doorbell sounded. She looked up at Imelda standing at the sink washing dishes and raised a brow. "You expecting anyone?"

"Nope. Buddy told me yesterday he'd be out this morning. He was going to town to try to find some hands. He wouldn't be ringing the bell though."

Cassie set down her fork and slid off the barstool then walked through the family room to the front door, just as someone knocked. She reached for the knob and swung the door open and there stood Luke Matthews dressed in tight-fitting Wranglers, cowboy boots and a tight black t-shirt with a well-worn saddle slung over his shoulder. Her mouth went dry as all the moisture in her body fled south below her belt buckle.

"Morning, darlin'," he drawled and walked past her into the entryway.

Her mouth flapped several times as her eyes moved

down to his tight ass so well-displayed in the faded jeans, then back up to his eyes as he turned around to face her again.

"What the hell are you doing here Luke?"

"I'm here to help you, darlin'," he told her matter-of-factly.

"Oh, hell no, you're not." She walked around him and pushed on his broad shoulders trying to get him back out the door.

His boot heels dug into the wood floor and he leaned back. "Yes, I am. I talked to Buddy this morning."

Cassie huffed out her frustration. "But you can't! You're the Sheriff...not a cow hand."

Luke turned around to face her. "I'm a cow hand for the next three weeks," he told her and smiled widely showing that stupid dimple that drove her crazy.

"Why would you want to do that? We don't need you, we'll be fine."

"You do need me...and I'm not leaving," he said and reached behind him to shut the front door, his eyes never leaving hers.

Cassie stuffed her hands on her hips. "Okay then--bunkhouse is out back you can store your gear there--*and stay out there.*"

He smiled even wider then took off the sexy black Stetson hat that had been shading his brown eyes. "Bud told me to come up to the house to get some breakfast from Imelda. He's out back in the bunkhouse."

"Fine," she huffed and stormed back to the kitchen leaving him standing there. "Throw your saddle on the back porch," she said snottily over her shoulder.

Luke chuckled and walked through the house then out the back door to deposit his saddle where she'd indicated, before he went back inside and found the kitchen. He'd been inside the big rambling farm house once or twice when he and Cassie had been dating, and then yesterday when he'd come out to visit Carl.

The place hadn't changed much over the years, but could use a coat of paint on the outside, he'd noticed. Taking care of a place this size--just the house--would have to be a big burden on Carl, even with the few hands he employed on the ranch. Maybe, after Cassie left, he'd come back out and help him do a few repairs.

Walking into the kitchen, Luke went over and put a kiss on Imelda's cheek. He was friends with a couple of her boys in school, and had been to her house occasionally growing up. "Hi, Imelda."

Her wrinkled brown hand moved up and she patted him on the cheek. "Hey honey--you been keeping outta trouble?"

"Nah, you know it always manages to find me," he chuckled then looked over at Cassie sitting sullenly at the breakfast bar. Her eyes met his briefly, then she looked down at her plate. She wasn't happy about him being here, but that was just too damned bad. "How's Brandon doing these days?"

"He's living over in Amarillo. Got married a couple years ago and gave me my first grandbaby last fall." Imelda wiped her hands on her apron and then reached up for a plate, before she walked to the stove and filled it up without even asking if he was hungry.

"Oh, that's great. Boy or girl?"

"Girl, they named her Ella. She's cute as a button," She shoved a plate and fork at him and he walked around the breakfast bar and took the stool next to Cassie.

"Bet you're spoiling her rotten," he said and forked up a mouthful of eggs. They were spectacular, and melted in his mouth.

Imelda set a big glass of milk next to his plate then said, "They don't make it down here often, so I don't see her as much as I'd like. Bran is working at a factory there and his wife Sue owns a hair salon in town, so they don't have much time off. I'm thinking I'll head there soon to see them."

He nodded, and scooped up some buttery grits then moaned as the creamy warm cereal pleasured his taste buds. This was the best breakfast he'd had in forever. He was a decent cook, but he didn't have time in the morning usually. On weekends, he'd often eat breakfast at the Bluebird, but their offerings didn't hold a candle to this.

Cassie looked over at him and she licked her lips her eyes filled with more than a little heat. He wanted to moan again, and was tempted to lean over and lick her lips too. Instead, he restrained himself and dragged his attention back to his breakfast.

The stool beside him scraped on the floor when she pushed herself off then walked around to put her plate in the sink. "Is daddy up yet?"

"No, and he needs to stay in bed. I brought him his breakfast there."

"I agree. I'll be out in the barn if you need me."

"Okay, Cassie Bee. I'll have lunch ready around noon. I'll ring the bell."

"Thanks," she said and kissed Imelda's cheek again "I'm not sure I'll be in for lunch though," she said then walked to the back door without looking his way again.

Cassie found Bud sitting at the long farm table inside the bunkhouse drinking coffee and munching on one of Imelda's biscuits. He glanced over to her when she came through the door and smiled. Or at least she thought he did, his thick gray beard covered most of his lower face. "Well, look what the cat dragged in," he said and set down his cup and biscuit before sliding a leg over the bench to stand then open his arms to her.

She ran into them and squeezed him tight. Bud whooped then lifted her up in a big bear hug. "Darlin', I've missed you somethin fierce."

"I've missed you too...so much." she managed to mumble against this broad flannel-covered chest feeling the sting of tears behind her eyes. The only regrets she had since she'd left town was not seeing Bud or Imelda, and not being able to explain why she'd left them ten years ago without saying goodbye. She knew it must've hurt them.

"Well, you're back now when your daddy needs you. That's what matters," he told her in his gravelly voice.

When he finally put her back on her feet, Cassie sniffled and rubbed an arm across her eyes. "Yeah, he does need me. I'm here to help, tell me what I can do."

"Well, you've already got off to a good start. Thanks for feeding the horses."

"You know you don't need to thank me Bud, it was...fun."

He snorted. "Fun? Jesus, girl you've been off the ranch too long for sure if you think that's fun."

"It was fun. I've missed all this," she admitted honestly.

"Why the hell did you leave it then?"

"I had to Bud...but I can't talk about it. Phoenix has been good to me. I have a business there and a fiancé now." She shoved her finger toward him and showed him the large engagement ring James had given her.

"Lordy, girl that thing could choke a mule..." he said then squinted his eyes to take a better look. "You should put it up someplace safe if you're gonna be working out here."

She hadn't thought about that. He was right, she'd probably either lose it or damage it wearing it out here. At the very least get it full of horseshit or dirt. "I'll put it up when I go in for lunch. I'll just put it in my pocket for now." She slid off the large diamond ring and stuffed it in her pocket.

Cassie looked around the room and then asked him. "So, where are the other hands?"

"I told them I'd be gone this morning so I told them to come in late. I'm gonna have them out mending the fence in the south pasture."

"What can I do to help. I don't know your routine

with daddy, and it's been a long time..."

He smiled. "Yep, it's time for you to get back in the saddle for sure."

Cassie groaned, it had been ten years since she'd ridden. Riding today meant she'd be sore as shit tomorrow from using the core muscles that she only pretended to keep in shape from her twice weekly workouts at the gym at home.

"Really? I thought I'd clean the horse stalls."

"Nah, we can do that this evening. I need to ride out and cut a few of the high-risk cows from the herd. Don't want 'em losing their calves, and last time I was out they looked sickly." We'll put them in the catch pen behind the barn, so the vet can check them." He patted her shoulder. "You're a natural, honey--it'll come back to ya. Just sit in the saddle and let the horse do the work."

Her face fell and Bud chortled, then picked up his plate and walked over to put it in the sink. "Luke is gonna help us. It won't be that bad."

"That's something I need to talk to you about. I don't want him here. Can't we find someone else to help out?"

"I've been trying to find more hands for a week. I found one, and he wouldn't have been my first pick, that's for sure, rough kind of sort. It's calving season, and all the good hands are signed on elsewhere. We're damned lucky Luke agreed to help, Cassie Bee."

Cassie sighed in frustration and dropped her chin to her chest. It looked like she was stuck with the man, at least until they could find another hand to replace him.

"Okay, but will you keep looking? We can cut him loose when we find someone else."

"Sure will," he said and patted her shoulder, "Sunshine's a wastin, let's get going." Cassie followed Bud out of the bunkhouse and around to the barn. Now wasn't the time to bring up the cattle sale she wanted to have, he was busy, and she really did need to take a look at the stock before she made that decision.

CHAPTER FOUR

When they walked into the barn, Luke was there with a big black gelding in crossties, while he saddled him. His head was bent and his nimble fingers moved over the buckles and cinches underneath the gelding with knowledge.

In high school, when they dated, he'd ridden a motorcycle not a horse. Cassie swallowed hard against the mental image of the twenty-one year old bad boy he'd been, and how he'd hot he'd looked on that bike.

She'd never seen him around a horse, other than hers when he watched her barrel race at rodeos. He stood up then walked to the horse's head and expertly pinched his upper lip and slid the bit gently between his teeth, pulling the straps up over his cheeks and ears.

He glanced over at them when he was done. "Hey, Bud...Cassie."

He tipped his hat at her then pulled a hoof pick out of his back pocket and lifted the gelding's front leg to inspect his hoof. After he finished inspecting all four feet, he patted the big horse's side and unclipped the crossties and grabbed the reins. "I'll be out back when ya'll are ready."

Why his ability to groom and tack a horse would turn her on, she had no idea. But it did. Heat moved up her throat to her face and she swallowed hard and nodded.

"We'll be ready directly, Luke," Bud told him.

She watched as he turned the horse toward the back door of the barn, the sight of his broad shoulders and fine ass in those blue jeans ramping up the funny little flutters that were dancing around in her chest. Forcefully, she tamped down the fluttering and sucked in a breath.

Luke Matthews was off limits to her...she was an engaged woman, she reminded herself. And even if she wasn't, Cassie wasn't about to put herself out there again with him to let the cheating bastard hurt her again. Even for what she knew would be the best sex she'd had in ten years.

"Your saddle and spurs are still in the tack room, Cassie Bee. You can ride Honey today. She's got some spunk, but she won't give you any trouble." He led her over to a stall where a beautiful golden palomino mare stood lazily munching on the hay she'd put in there earlier. "Damn good cutter, too," Bud told her.

Cassie clicked her tongue and the horse looked up then sauntered over to put her head over the gate. She scratched her behind the ear, then rubbed her muzzle. "Hiya, pretty girl." The beautiful horse nudged her hand with her nose. "Yeah, we'll get along fine, won't we?" Honey neighed and snorted and Cassie laughed.

This is what she'd been missing for ten years...her bond with animals. Maybe when she got back to Phoenix, she'd find a barn where she could lease a horse to ride when she got the urge.

Pushing away from the stall, Cassie went to the tack room and found her saddle lovingly covered with a soft cotton cover, her spurs on the shelf above. Reaching up she pulled down the spurs and clipped them on her boots, then she removed the cover on the saddle and ran her hand reverently over the gorgeous well-oiled leather. Someone had been taking care of it for her, it had to be Bud.

She'd won the saddle barrel racing, her title and the date was commemorated for all time by the deep engraving on the fender. Feeling sentimental, she leaned over the saddle horse and hugged the saddle to her, then stood up and lifted it over her shoulder, the stirrups banging against her waist and rear.

The short, blunt rowels of her spurs sang a familiar tune as she walked back into the barn to find that Bud had cross-tied Honey and brushed her out already.

"Thanks, Bud," she said and walked over to pat the horse and run her hand along her spine, before she placed her hot pink saddle blanket over the horse's back.

She walked around front and petted Honey's nose. "We're gonna look mighty fine today, Honey. You get to wear my prize saddle." Cassie told her then gently set it on her back and tightened the cinches. When she was done saddling Honey, she grabbed a coiled rope from a peg on the wall and secured it on a clip on the saddle.

"You got your rifle with you, Bud? Daddy said the reason he got thrown was a rattlesnake."

"Always, honey," he said then patted his saddle where it was sheathed. "The snakes are pretty bad this year, but what happened to your daddy was a fluke."

"I sure hope so...you know how I hate snakes."

"I remember," he said and a chuckle rumbled deep in his chest. "That garter snake you ran up on in the garden that time really made an impression on you. I don't think your feet hit the ground more than twice, before you made it to the bunkhouse to get me."

"It certainly gave me a healthy respect for them."

"No worries, sugar. I'll shoot 'em for ya." He grabbed his reins and led his horse toward the back exit and she followed a safe distance behind.

Once they were outside, they met up with Luke who was already mounted and waiting for them. She tossed her reins over Honey's head then grabbed the pommel and put her left foot in the stirrup. With a bounce, she swung her leg over Honey's back and settled herself in the saddle.

So far, so good, Cassie thought as she clicked her tongue and Honey started moving forward toward the gate to the pasture. Bud was right behind her on the big roan mare that had been so friendly to her this morning, followed by an unusually quiet Luke on the big black gelding.

When she got through the gate, she squeezed her legs and urged Honey to a trot, then a canter. Cassie stopped her then circled her around testing the horse's response to her reining commands. Honey was soft in the mouth and responded beautifully in both directions. She pulled back on the reins gently and the horse immediately responded by backing quickly until Cassie released the pressure on her mouth. Bud pulled up beside her and she looked at him and grinned from ear to ear. "Yeah, she's real good, Bud."

"She certainly is." Luke said and she looked over at him. The intensity in his smoky brown eyes told her he wasn't talking about Honey. "I've missed seeing you ride, cupcake...I forgot how good you were."

Tingles from his deep rich voice worked their from her scalp, down her throat to settle around her nipples, which had instantly had responded to his sexual innuendo.

Lifting her chin, Cassie spun Honey toward the open pasture then accidentally kicked her sides harder than necessary. The horse took off into a gallop across the field, and Cassie leaned low over her neck. She had no idea where she was going, but wherever she wound up she'd be away from the irritating temptation of Luke Matthews.

"She's somethin ain't she?" Bud said with reverence watching Cassie riding hell bent for leather across the field, her blonde hair flying out behind her.

"Definitely," Luke agreed swallowing down the lust that mule-kicked him in the chest. He shifted in his saddle, his current position, no longer comfortable. "Let's catch up with her before she breaks her neck," Luke said then urged his horse to a trot, then a gallop.

When they rounded the copse of trees at the end of the pasture, he saw she had slowed her horse to a walk. He pulled up beside her with Bud right behind him. "You think you can wait on us?"

Cassie shrugged. "I felt like a run. It's been a long time."

"Don't forget it sweet thing. You might have been a rodeo queen, but it's been ten years since you've been in the saddle. You need to be more careful."

"You don't have to worry about me, *honey bunch*. I've been riding since I could walk."

"So has your daddy, and he got thrown." Luke was

seriously worried that she'd take for granted she was rusty and hurt herself because of it.

She pushed her hat back on her head and pinned him with angry blue eyes. "My daddy only got thrown, because of an inexperienced horse and a snake," she told him then looked away, her shoulders stiff.

Luke heard Bud chuckle behind him and shot him a look over his shoulder. The man could at least support him and give her a warning himself, but it looked like the old cowboy was just hanging back enjoying their sparring.

"Suit yourself, sunshine," he said to the stubborn woman then kicked his horse into a gallop. Two could play her game. He glanced back over his shoulder and saw that she had Honey at a gallop again and she was low over her neck, pushing her hard to catch up to him. He grinned and urged his mount faster toward the fence in the distance. When he got there he lifted the horse up and hugged close to his neck as the long-legged gelding jumped the fence with ease.

Once he got over, he pulled him to a stop and spun around to grin at her as she neared the fence herself. It was poetry in motion to watch her communicate with her horse with her body language to urge the beautiful palomino over the fence as well. She didn't stop though, she gave him a cocky smile when she passed him and then kept hauling butt across the pasture toward the herd grazing in the distance.

Instead of following her, Luke waited for Bud to catch up and got down to open the gate to let him through. The big grizzly man was grinning from ear to ear. Bud was enjoying the shit out of the sparks flying between him and Cassie. Secretly, Luke was enjoying it too. It had been a long time since he'd had this much fun.

"Thanks. Better go catch up with that girl before she has the whole herd hog-tied." Bud chuckled and kicked his horse to a canter, after Luke was remounted. They reached the herd a few minutes later, and Cassie was already off her horse, moving through the black cows inspecting the pregnant ones more thoroughly.

"I got a list of the ones we need to cut Cassie Bee, but if you wanna look them over too, that's not a problem."

She looked up at Bud distractedly then said, "I'm just thinking since we're short on hands, we might wanna think about having a twofer sale before they drop the calves."

"Your daddy would have a stroke. That's a lot of money to give away, darlin'."

"I know, but if we sold at least some of them, it would make the herd more manageable," she told him and then pushed her hat back on her head to look at him earnestly.

"Carl ain't gonna go along with that, Cassie. We'll have enough hands to handle it with the new hand I hired, and you and Luke."

"I'm sure Luke has better things to do, and if we sold of part of the herd now, we wouldn't need him." Cassie glanced at Luke then back to Bud.

So that was her angle, Luke thought. Getting rid of him. Well, she could put that thought out to pasture, because he wasn't going anywhere. "I agree with Bud and Carl. We have enough hands now, and if you sold the pregnant cows you'd be losing a fortune."

Her eyes narrowed and she shot daggers at him, her full lips pinched before she said, "And your opinion would matter why? What the hell do you know about cattle?"

"A hell of a lot more than you think, darlin'. Didn't Bud tell you I worked on a cattle ranch while I was in college?" He looked over at Bud who was still just smiling from ear to ear, but not backing him up at all.

Cassie's eyes flew to Bud as well. "No, there's a lot he failed to mention, evidently." She stomped over to her horse and remounted, then shoved her hat back on her head. "Which ones do we need to cut, Bud?"

He pulled a small notebook from his pocket and flipped back the cover. As Bud called out numbers, she and Luke moved through the herd to search the ear tags on the pregnant cows to find the one he called. Together, they worked as a team to cull them from the herd then moved them over to the corner of the pasture where Bud stayed behind to keep them cornered there.

They'd separated six cows from the herd so far, and Bud said there were ten more on his list. Her thigh muscles were aching and her ass felt like it had when she'd been paddled by the principal in sixth grade for putting a frog in Becca Harvey's book sack.

It had been worth it to see the horror on Becca's face and hear her girly scream when she reached inside to pull out her book and the slimy toad jumped out and landed on her chest. There was a riot in class when everyone jumped up trying to catch the jumpy amphibian. Mrs. Simpson was not as impressed as the kids in her class were and sent her to the principal's office.

The number Bud had last called appeared on the ear tag of the cow right in front of her and she signaled Honey and managed to work the clumsy cow over by a tree. She waved at Luke and he started toward her, then she heard a sound like crunching leaves to her left and looked down to find a dusty brown snake with a diamond pattern on his back coiled up and not looking happy.

Cassie screamed and automatically squeezed her thighs around Honey like a green horn. The mare took off from under her and a limb caught her across the chest. She somersaulted off the back of the horse then landed face first in the dirt knocking the breath out of her. Numbness claimed her whole body as shock set in and she began shaking.

She heard a rifle shot nearby and then Luke was beside her his long-fingered hands moving over her body from head to toe. "Cassie, sugar...talk to me. Are you hurt, darlin?" His voice was choked and scared, as he begged close to her ear, "C'mon cupcake. Talk to me."

His fingers certainly got her blood moving again as he gently moved them through her hair, down her neck and then her shoulders, arms and ribs.

"I'm okay," she finally told him then rolled over and tossed her arm across her eyes. "Tell me you killed that snake."

"He's dead," he told her gruffly then asked with concern, "Are you hurt?"

"Just stunned..." She moved her arm and looked around for Honey. "Is Honey okay?"

"She's fine, she's over by Bud," he told her then stood. He grabbed his rifle and slid it into the scabbard on his saddle, before kneeling back down beside her and sliding one arm under neck then the other under beneath her knees before lifting her into his arms.

He hugged her to him tightly for a second, and kissed her cheek, which shocked the stuffing out of her and caused her tongue to stick to the roof of her mouth. She thought she felt a tremor move through his big body, but she was shaking so badly she couldn't be sure if it was him or her.

When she finally got her tongue unglued, she told him "Put me down, Luke, I'm fine."

He ignored her and walked to his horse and lifted her into the saddle. She scooted forward to give him enough room to mount behind her and grabbed the saddle horn. He walked back to the tree and picked up her hat from the ground beside the dead snake and dusted it off on the leg of his jeans. When he came back, he put his foot in the stirrup and vaulted onto the horse's back behind her. He handed her the hat then grabbed the reins with one hand and put the other around her waist to pull her back against him.

As shaken up as she was, Cassie still noticed how good his body felt against hers, his strong thighs pressed against hers on the fender of the saddle. His warmth pressed against her back warmed the coldness that had settled in her chest. And he smelled so damned good. Like soap, sunshine and sexy warm male. A little moan escaped her when she took a deep breath wanting to inhale his essence.

His arm tightened against her waist. "Something hurting you?" His voice was a gruff whisper against her ear.

Just her inability to resist the big sexy man behind her. "No, really--I'm just shook up." She shivered, and not entirely from her ordeal. His hot breath on her ear was causing all kinds of havoc to her system. "I hate snakes," she said and wiggled her behind in the saddle trying to get comfortable.

Luke groaned behind her and she felt a large very hard ridge press against her bottom. Cassie wanted to groan herself now, but sat perfectly still instead and said, "Sorry."

"Just sit still," he begged his voice low and tortured as he rested his chin on her shoulder, and rubbed his jaw against her hair. "God, how the hell can you still do this to me?" He sounded amazed and then she felt his tongue lick at the side of her neck before he sucked her earlobe between his firm lips.

"Luke, stop," she told him heatedly then slid forward in the saddle. "That can't happen."

"Why not? We're grownups, darlin' and surely you remember how good it was between us."

He licked her again and she leaned away from his exploring mouth, which felt way too good. "Because I'm engaged."

"And?"

"And I'm not interested," she said with finality, although that little devil that rode her shoulder occasionally called her a liar.

His hand moved up from her waist to cup her breast and his thumb brushed over her pebbled nipple causing her to shiver again. "Liar."

She slapped his hand away. "Just get me back to my freaking horse please."

He chuckled then nudged the horse to a trot. "Yes ma'am."

When they reached Bud, he was beside himself, and quickly slid off his horse and ran over to them. "You alright Cassie Bee?" he asked putting a hand on her calf.

"I'm good, Bud. Just shook up. Damned snake scared me and I squeezed Honey like I've never ridden before and a limb got me. Poor darlin' is probably scared to death."

"Ain't too worried about the horse, girl." His voice was gruff and concerned. "Are you sure you're not hurt? We need to take you to the doc to have you checked out?"

"No--I'm fine," she almost shouted. She was tired of saying it. Why wouldn't these two believe her? She elbowed Luke in the ribs and he grunted. "Get down." Once he was standing on the ground, she tossed her leg over the saddle, but before she could slide to the ground, she felt Luke's hands at her waist lifting her down.

Her legs weren't all that steady when she landed, so she was glad he did. She pulled away from him then staggered over to where Honey was ground tied, her reins dragging in the dirt. Cassie grabbed them up and the mare looked at her with scared brown eyes.

She scratched the side of Honey's neck and cooed into her ear, "It's okay, baby girl, it was my fault, not yours." She whispered encouragement in the mare's ear a few more minutes, then eased the reins over her head and mounted her.

"What's the next number, Bud?" She asked him with fierce determination then patted her hat down on her head. They had a job to finish, and it wasn't going to be because of her they didn't finish.

"No way, Cassie Bee. We're going back now," Bud told her seriously and mounted his horse. "We'll finish up tomorrow."

"We'll finish up today." She told him through gritted teeth. "What's the next number?"

Bud studied her intently for a second. "You're as stubborn as your daddy, you know that?"

"And proud of it." Cassie gave him a bodacious grin and demanded once more, "Now what's the next number?"

The sun was setting by the time they corralled all the cows they'd cut into the catch pen, and had unsaddled their horses. Cassie was dirty, sore and tired, but happy too. They'd finished the job and had all sixteen cows back to the barn.

"I'm gonna sleep good tonight," she said as Luke took her saddle from her shoulder and walked with her to the tack room. Her stomach rumbled. "We missed lunch, so I hope Imelda has something good for supper."

"Everything Imelda makes is good."

"Yeah, she's a damned good cook," Cassie said then tilted her head and asked, "You staying for supper?"

"You inviting me to stay?" he drawled, his whiskey brown eyes hopeful.

Cassie hesitated and nibbled her lower lip. It probably wasn't a great idea, but he had worked hard today and was probably just as hungry as she was. As aggravating as he'd been today, she couldn't deny him. "Yeah, I'm inviting."

Surprise flitted across his tired face, then he grinned at her. "Thanks," Luke said then looked down at his dirty clothes and dirtier hands. "I need to take a shower though."

"You can take one up at the house in the spare room. I'm sure Daddy has something you can change into."

"I have some spare clothes in the truck. Always carry them because I never know what I'm gonna encounter when I'm on shift," he told her thinking of the last time he'd had to use them. A very unfriendly skunk had wandered into the mini-mart right outside of town. It took him a week and a case of tomato juice to get that smell off of him and out of his car. Cole had gotten a lot of mileage teasing him over that unfortunate event.

He pulled off his dusty, sweaty hat and slapped it on his thigh, then ran his hand through his wet hair. "I'll grab them and be right in...and thanks again."

She nodded and he watched as she walked off toward the house, her stride not quite as long as it usually was. Tomorrow she'd feel like she'd been run over by a truck. You didn't ride as hard as she had today after not riding for ten years and not pay the price. It had been seven years since he'd ridden, so her pain must be at least twice what his was.

Luke shook his head, amazed again at how focused and determined she'd been to finish their job after being thrown from Honey. Most women, wouldn't have even been out there in the first place. But she'd been out there and she hadn't let a little thing like getting thrown slow her down.

It seemed like he was the only one scared down to his toes from the frightening experience. When he saw her fly off the horse and hit the dirt, his heart had actually stopped until he found out she was still breathing and in one piece. People died from lesser falls.

After he'd gotten his senses back, his respect for her edged up a few notches. Her spurs weren't just for show like he'd originally thought. Working the cattle with her today had been like a well-orchestrated dance. One he wouldn't mind repeating...in bed.

He had to get control of himself several times during the day when he kept imagining her riding him as well as she was riding that horse. And then when they'd ridden double, Luke thought he was going to lose it right there like a teenage boy if she wiggled against him in the saddle again. Her salty-sweet taste, when he couldn't resist sampling her neck, had almost sent him over the edge.

Opening the door of his truck, Luke reached behind the seat and pulled out his duffle then slammed it. He walked to the porch and pulled off his boots then stomped a few times to knock the dust off his jeans, before he opened the door and walked inside.

He heard someone talking on the phone in the little

alcove down the hall to the right and a light feminine laugh had him standing still for a second to listen.

"Yeah, I'm fine, James. Just hurt my pride." Cassie's lilting voice said to the person on the other end of the line. "I'm sorry I didn't call when I got here. My cell doesn't get reception out here in the boondocks."

After a few moments of silence, she said, "I miss you too. Thanks for handling things so I could come out here." She laughed a low intimate laugh and then, "Maybe you can come out for the weekend soon."

Luke's fists clenched imagining what the man on the other end of the line was saying to her. They talked a minute or two more about some business deal in Phoenix, then she told the guy she loved him too and hung up the phone.

Luke gritted his teeth, and forced his feet to start walking. He bumped into her when she barreled out of the alcove without warning. He grabbed her shoulders to keep her from stumbling.

"Oh, hey." Her hands fluttered and she said unnecessarily, "I was just on the phone."

Luke captured her wide blue eyes with his own and tightened his grip on her shoulders. She shrugged her shoulders trying to break free, but Luke just moved closer and pushed her back into the tiny alcove. He dropped the duffle on the floor and pressed her back against the wall.

Cassie put her hands on his chest and pushed then tried to bring her knee up between his legs, but couldn't manage it. "Luke--let me go," her voice was a breathy whisper between them.

"No, I made that mistake once," he ground out then claimed her mouth with his and poured out all the anger and frustration bottled inside him, as well as a good measure of the lust he'd been smothering down all day.

What started as an angry kiss transitioned into something else when her arms snaked up around his neck and she leaned into him, her hips moving against his.

Luke groaned then deepened the kiss, his tongue seeking out hers in the warm cavern of her mouth. All the blood rushed from his head and moved south. He moved his hands down to her butt and squeezed before pulling her closer into him.

Cassie moaned, but it sounded more like a purr around the buzzing in his own ears. She lifted her thigh against the side of his leg and wrapped her calf around him, giving him access to where he wanted to be.

He pushed his erection into the V at the top of her thighs and pressed into her, moaning when he felt her heat against him. He kissed her desperately for a moment then jerked his mouth from hers to rain little kisses across her smooth cheek then down her neck, before he stopped and licked a spot right behind her ear that he knew drove her wild.

She whimpered and pressed her breasts to his chest, her hardened nipples scratching against him with every breath she tried to drag into her lungs. He moved his hand up to cup her breast and rubbed his thumb over her nipple then asked, "I bet he doesn't get you this hot, does he?"

Her body went completely still in his arms, she reached down and moved his hand off her breast then squeezed out from between him and the wall.

Luke dropped his hands from her body and turned to face her just in time to catch her hand across the side of his face. Luke gritted his teeth against the sting. For a girl, she packed a wallop and it stung like crazy, but he wasn't going to rub it.

"How dare you!" Her fists were clenched at her sides and color rode high on her cheeks. Her blue eyes were fierce and angry.

"How dare I what, cupcake? Turn you on? Or bring it to your attention that your boyfriend must fall short in that department?"

She growled, her body shaking now, practically

vibrating, as she pointed toward the door and ground out, "Get out."

He grabbed her hand and inspected it. "Where's that honking ring the bastard gave you?"

Cassie sucked in a breath and glanced at her naked finger, then pulled her hand from his. "In my pocket. I took it off at the barn, before we went out." She shoved her hand into her pocket and searched around for it. Digging in as deep as she could, she felt along the seam at the bottom and didn't find it, so she searched her other pocket.

A horror-stricken look came over her beautiful face and then tears filled her eyes. "Oh, my god..." she gasped and then turned her pockets inside out. "I lost it." He saw her swallow hard and then the tears started falling.

If there was one thing he couldn't stand it was a crying woman. Especially this woman, one he'd never seen cry before, and it made him damned uncomfortable to see it now. With a growl, he pulled her into his arms and held her. "Shh...we'll find it."

Finding that damned ring was the last thing he wanted to do. He'd be happy if she never found it. It was just a constant reminder that another man was going to have what was supposed to be his. But he was going to help her. He didn't like the heartbroken look in her eyes, or the sadness that was evidently in her heart.

Cassie sobbed into his shirt and clutched it with her fists, then hiccupped a couple of breaths, before looking up into his eyes. "I--I--have to find it, Luke."

"I'll help you first thing tomorrow," he told her then kissed her forehead and hugged her again. She sniffled, and he rubbed her back. "Let's go get cleaned up and eat. I'm starving." For more than food, he thought and squeezed her again, before pushing her away and wiping at her tears with his thumb.

***

Three days later, they still hadn't found the ring and Cassie was in desperation mode. They'd searched all over the barn, house and bunkhouse and even out by the tree in the field where she'd been thrown. It was like looking for a needle in a haystack.

Luke, true to his word, had helped her search in earnest, although he didn't look any too happy about it. He had been sullen and withdrawn since he'd kissed her at the house the other night. Grumpy. That was a good word to describe him, but still sexy as hell when he was brooding.

No matter what he was doing, he was sex on a very tall stick, and she couldn't help her body's response to him when he got near her. So she tried to avoid him as much as she could.

Thank goodness, he didn't seem intent on pursing her now, or she'd be in real trouble, regardless of what he'd done to her ten years ago. That was old news, but what she was feeling for him was the same, yet so much more intense than back then. He was a man now, filled out and definitely ready for action. And guilt for noticing that fact was riding her like a swayback mare.

James had called yesterday before she'd gotten back to the house, and she hadn't called him back. She couldn't. Between what was stewing with Luke, and the fact she'd lost the very expensive ring he'd given her, she didn't think she could talk to him without breaking down. She'd call him once she found the ring.

Cassie was in the barn this morning tearing up the tack room searching for the ring on her hands and knees. "Any luck?" Luke's deep voice sounded behind her and startled her. She lifted up and bumped her head on a saddle rack.

"Ouch." she said and lifted her hand to her head. "No, I still haven't found it."

"Get Honey saddled," he ordered gruffly.

"Why? I have to keep looking."

"We're going out to look by the tree again. That has to be where you lost it. Either there or by the fence we jumped," he said his brown eyes moving over her face then across her chest and back up.

Her blood heated and she licked her lips. "Okay, I'll be ready in ten minutes."

Luke nodded then turned away from her and walked out the door. She sat there for a moment staring after him, daydreaming about what ifs. Ten years ago, Cassie had thought Luke was the real deal. A good man that cared about her. Before he broke her heart. Before she'd gone running away like a little girl.

If the same thing happened today, she'd handle it a lot differently. She'd confront him, make him face his treachery, demand answers, and then she'd kick him in the balls. Cassie was ten years older now and knew how to face down hard truths and chip them into diamonds. The hard truth she faced right now was that she was not over Luke Matthews.

Was there a hidden diamond there? She hadn't thought so when she came here. But the facets that Luke was showing her now made her wonder.

Even though he probably hated her, he stopped to help her fix her truck. She'd tried to push him away, but he stubbornly stayed to help her manage the ranch, because her daddy was down.

Although she'd been a hard ass to him, he was tender and loving when she'd gotten thrown out in the field, and now he was helping her find another man's ring, even though she knew he wanted her badly from the way he'd kissed her at the house the other night.

It all didn't add up to the heartless bastard she'd written him off as ten years ago.

Maybe her dad was right and he had changed. Or maybe he hadn't changed at all, and she'd just misjudged him? Cassie blew out a breath and went to stand when a shadow fell over her from the doorway and she looked up to see a stranger standing there with his thumbs dangling through his belt loops.

CHAPTER FIVE

"Well, ain't you a pretty little filly," the greasy-looking man drawled, his eyes moving over her body, before a shifty grin appearing on his cracked lips. He was probably thirty-five or so but looked a lot older. He also looked like he hadn't shaved or bathed in a few days. His worn jeans were stained at the knees and his hands and nails were dirty.

"What can I do for you?" She asked firmly then widened her stance so she could run if she had to.

"Oh, there's a lot you can do for me little lady," he said and stepped inside and moved toward her.

"Who the hell are you?" Cassie took a step back from the unkempt man, but his smell still insulted her nostrils. Horse shit and sweat weren't smells she cherished.

"Name's Randy...and who are you sweet cheeks?"

Cassie bowed up at him and put her hands on her hips. "Well, Randy, I think you need to tell me what the hell you're doing on my ranch before I scream the place down and you have fifteen ranch hands on your ass."

"Ain't nobody here for you to yell for, missy. So we're gonna have us a little fun." He moved closer to her and backed her into the saddle rack. She almost gagged from his stench up close.

Pushing against his round chest, Cassie struggled against his hands which were now on her hips pulling her toward him. She brought up her knee between his legs as hard as she could, but he turned to the side and she caught his thigh. He grunted and then his fingers dug into her shoulders painfully. "Settle down now and I won't hurt you," he growled near her ear.

She sucked in a deep breath then let loose a scream that would have peeled the paint off the walls inside the house, at the same time she boxed his ears with her closed fists. He leaned back at the last minute, so her blow landed on his jaw instead, then he grabbed her shoulders and shook her until her teeth rattled.

Cassie screamed again and jerked hard enough that she got loose, but he pulled her back against him before she could take a step, and put his hand over her mouth then threw her on the ground and fell on top of her.

Breath whooshed out of her when they landed and she was momentarily stunned. His heavy weight made it nearly impossible for her to drag in a breath. Suddenly, his weight left her and she heard the sound of a fist hitting bone then a grunt, and another crunch.

She gathered her wits and rolled over to see Luke sitting on top of the man with his fist raised about to deliver another smashing blow to the man's already bloody nose.

"You fucking bastard. I'm going to kill you," Luke said in a strangled voice then cocked his elbow even higher, before he swung it downward.

"Luke, no!" she gasped and surged to her feet to catch his arm. His fist glanced off the man's ear instead of landing on his nose. She slid her hands down his forearm to his wrist and looked at his mangled fist, then placed a kiss near his wrist. "Don't honey, he's not worth it."

Luke's chest was heaving and anger poured off him in waves. He swallowed thickly, then looked at her. There was a red haze in his eyes, that was slow to clear. Anger smoldered there and something else. Hatred blacker than any she'd ever seen, especially in this man's eyes. Even when he'd kicked Jimmy Jones' ass when they were teenagers, he hadn't looked like this. Murder had definitely not been out of the question here.

When Luke's breathing calmed down a little he wiped his knuckles on the unconscious man's shirt and shook her hand off his shoulder to stand up, then he stepped over the man. He turned his back to her and leaned down with his hands on his knees. "Get me a rope. I don't have my cuffs with me."

She scurried out through the door and grabbed a rope

down from the peg. Going back inside, she handed it to him and watched as he rolled the man over and expertly hog-tied his hands to his feet like a professional roper in a rodeo. She expected to him to stand and throw his hands up for a time when he finished, but he didn't.

Instead, he walked over to her and pulled her into his arms hugging her fiercely. "You sure know how to attract trouble don't you, darlin'?"

She sighed deeply then gave him a watery chuckle. "Looks that way, darlin'," she said and snuggled her cheek against the soft cotton of his t-shirt. Her arms went around his waist and she hugged him back. "Thanks for the rescue...again," she mumbled against his chest.

"I'll always be here for you, cupcake," he said in a low growl then kissed the top of her head. Then he pushed her away and looked her over carefully. "Did he hurt you?"

"Nah, but I'd have hurt him if I'd have landed that knee to his balls. That's twice now that move has failed me. I need to practice, I'm a little rusty." She lifted an eyebrow then asked with humor in her eyes, "Care to volunteer?" Her eyes followed his hand down when he moved it to cover his crotch and she laughed.

"No way, sugar. I just barely avoided that move the other night."

She glanced over at the unconscious man lying on his side with his hands and feet trussed up behind him. "What're we gonna do with him?"

"We're going up to the house to call Cole, so he can come and haul this piece of trash out of here," he ground out between clenched teeth then leaned over and picked up his hat and dusted it off.

Luke saw interest spark in her blue eyes then she said, "You and Cole still hanging out together?"

"He's my Chief Deputy...and still my best friend. He's covering for me while I'm out here."

"Then I'll have to thank him," she told him with a grin.

"Maybe I'll ask him to come by for supper."

"He'd probably appreciate that." Although his friend was loyal to a fault, he didn't really want him around Cassie. Cole had been on the verge of asking her out himself way back when, right before Luke had.

Jealousy seemed to be a constant knife twisting in his gut where she was concerned, and Luke couldn't seem to stop it. Even his best friend wasn't immune from him. Luke didn't want any man touching her...except him. And he didn't have the right to do that anymore...not that it was going to stop him.

They walked up to the house side by side and ran into Bud on the way. Luke told him what happened and they found out the man was the newest hand that Bud had hired. They had to almost physically restrain Bud, when he grabbed his rifle from the saddle and was headed out to the barn to take care of the scumbag, as he'd called him. Instead, they managed to wrangle Bud up to the house with them and Luke called Cole.

A little while later, Cole pulled up the long dusty driveway of the ranch in his department-issued SUV and pulled to a stop in front of the house. They all walked outside and met him at the porch steps.

He got out of the truck and walked over to them. "Jesus, Luke you take a vacation, but make sure you keep me busy." He laughed and smiled widely then tipped his hat to Cassie. "Hi, darlin'."

Cassie thought she heard a growl come from Luke standing behind her to the left. She smiled her rodeo queen smile at Cole then rushed down the steps to launch herself into his arms, knocking his hat off in the process. Cole went back on his heels and hugged her to him spinning her in a circle.

"Now that's what I'm talking about," he said then set her down and kissed her on the cheek. "How's your daddy, sugar?"

"He's getting along, but being in the bed is making him

itchy. I think Imelda might put a pillow over his head and put us all out of his misery."

"That's not something you should be telling a deputy, darlin'." He chuckled and pinched her cheek.

Cassie snorted. "She'd probably tell you herself."

"So, what's going on out here?"

"Damned cowhand almost raped Cassie," Luke barked.

"Is that right, sugar?" Cole grabbed her by the shoulders and looked deeply concerned.

"Yeah, I was in the tack room and he cornered me after Luke left."

"Holy shit, where is the asshole?" He released her and she saw his hand move to the butt of the mean looking handgun on his belt. His eyes narrowed and his lips pinched into a flat line.

"Unconscious in the tack room. Luke beat the shit out of him," Cassie said and snickered.

Cole's eyebrows raised and then he said sarcastically, "Nah, Luke wouldn't do something like that. I'm sure he just used enough force to restrain the ass--suspect. Isn't that right, Luke?"

Luke grumbled then nodded. "Of course. He resisted, so I didn't have a choice. Now lock the asshole up and call Judge."

Cole saluted him and then turned to walk toward the barn and they all followed. Once inside the tack room, Cole stopped and looked back over his shoulder at Luke. "Hog-tied, Luke? Really?"

Laughter seemed to rumbled up from his toes and then Cole bent over consumed him. "Nice law enforcement maneuver, Sheriff. They teach you that at the academy?" He howled again and before long they were all laughing. Everyone except Luke. His eyes were angry and his fists clenched at his side.

"Cut the shit Cole and get him out of here before I decide to finish the job," he told his deputy gruffly and turned to walk out the door.

Cassie grabbed his arm and stopped him. "What's wrong Luke?"

"Nothing," he said and shook off her hand. "I'm going home."

She followed him almost having to jog to keep up with his fast movement toward his truck. "Wait, Luke..."

He didn't stop, but she finally caught up with him when he opened the door to his truck and climbed inside. She stepped up on the running board to stand between him and the door then leaned inside and got right up in his pinched face. "What the hell is wrong with you?"

She saw a muscle working in his jaw, but he didn't say anything. His knuckles were white where he was gripping the steering wheel, staring out over the top of it. Cassie didn't know what had put a burr under his saddle, but she knew she wasn't letting him leave until she got it out.

She leaned close to his ear and whispered. "C'mon, baby, tell mama what's wrong," then moved her hand to rub his thigh. She kissed his cheek then the corner of his mouth, her hand moving a little higher on his thigh.

Moving to his ear, she flicked out her tongue and circled the lobe, then sucked it and released it. She thought she heard him groan, and noticed that his breathing was faster than it had been. A flush stained high up on his chiseled cheekbones.

"You're playing with fire, honey. Move so I can leave."

"What if I don't want to?" She nuzzled his neck and put a butterfly kiss over the pulse pounding there. Her head spun when he jerked her inside of the cab between his muscled chest and the steering wheel right before his mouth slammed down over hers in a kiss that sent her pulse from zero to sixty in 2.6 seconds.

Luke slid his hand under her tank top and rubbed it along her ribcage up to cup her breast. When his thumb found her nipple, desire ripped through her like a summer wildfire and she linked her arms around his neck and deepened the kiss, letting out all the pent up frustration that had been building in her since she laid eyes on him again.

Cassie moved her hip to stroke his steel-like erection which was nudging against her, then opened her mouth to tangle her tongue with his. Moving her hand down to the hem of his t-shirt she tugged it out of his jeans, then slid her hand over his hard abs up and up to his pecs. His heart beat like a sledgehammer against his ribs, just like her own. Cassie flicked his nipple with her fingernail and he groaned, then put his hand over hers.

"We need to stop, Cassie," he told her breathing heavily then pulled her all the way inside the cab and sat her on the passenger seat.

Hot and bothered with her brain muddled with passion, Cassie looked over at him dumbfounded. Breathlessly she said, "What the hell?"

"We have an audience."

She looked outside the truck and saw Cole and Bud holding the battered and bruised almost rapist between them, with wide grins on their faces. Cassie dropped her head back against the seat and groaned. "Aw, shit...not good."

Luke looked over at her curiously and said in a slightly hurt tone, "Felt pretty damned good to me."

It was beyond good, Cassie thought. Kissing Luke was spectacular...being with him again would be heavenly. Something she wanted more than her next breath right now. But that was the problem. She shouldn't be feeling what she was feeling with Luke...shouldn't be doing what she was doing.

"I'm engaged Luke and when my daddy finds out about this he's gonna give me hell."

"Why's that?"

She hesitated. How the hell could she tell him her daddy had been trying to hook them up since the day she got here? "Um...you'll just have to trust me on that one."

He looked over at her and his brown eyes were dark

and intense, full of passion. "Cassie, there's something going on here between us. The way you ran off left us with some unfinished business. We need to get it out of our system, so we can move on."

The temptation to agree with him was enormous, but she resisted. "Luke, we can't go back...we'd both just wind up hurt again. And James would wind up hurt too."

Luke leaned over and grabbed her shoulders. "Fuck, James. How the hell can you marry him when you want me?"

Cassie felt the sting of tears behind her eyes and took a deep breath then forced sincerity into her voice, "I love him," she lied hoping it would end this discussion.

Luke growled and let go of her shoulders to put his hands back on the steering wheel. Without looking at her he hissed, "Get out, Cassie."

She slid away from him toward her door and opened it, but stopped to look back at him. His jaw was clenched and his lower lip was trembling with the effort.

"Luke, I'm sorry."

"Just get out, Cassie, and think about what I said. If you change your mind let me know, but in the meantime keep your damned hands off of me," he told her his voice deep and raspy.

"Okay," she said sadly then shut the door and stepped away from the truck. Luke turned the key in the ignition violently then hit threw the truck in gear and peeled out of the driveway leaving a dust cloud behind him.

Bud had evidently headed back to the bunkhouse, but Cassie saw Cole stuffing his prisoner inside the SUV. She needed to bawl like a baby, but she wasn't doing it in front of Cole. Cassie lifted her arm and swiped at the tears that had slipped from her eyes, then turned and ran toward the house.

"Cassie Wait!" Cole slammed the back door of the SUV locking his prisoner inside and caught up with her right when she stepped up on the porch. "What happened, honey?" He yanked her back against his chest, but she kept her face down and didn't turn around to face him.

"Let me go, Cole. I need to be alone."

Cole leaned close to ear and whispered as his hands squeezed her shoulders. "He still loves you, you know? If he's acting crazy, that's why."

"He doesn't love me," Cassie heard her voice waver and flinched.

"He does...he always has...since the first moment he met you. I thought he was going to rip my head off when I said I might ask you out." Cole chuckled and put his arms around her waist and led her over to the swing at the end of the porch. He sat down and dragged her down beside him. "It's always been you for him, darlin' and probably always will be judging by the way he's acting since you've been back."

"That's not true, Cole. He might want me, but he doesn't love me. The night I left, he proved it to me."

Cole kicked the swing and started it swaying back and forth then slid his arm around her shoulders. "Why do you think that?"

"It's not important now. It's been ten years, and it's water under the bridge now. I'm engaged and I owe it to my fiancé to nip this in the bud. I'm here to help my daddy, not rekindle old fires with Luke."

Today's exhibition had been all her fault...any flames fanned today were ignited by her. She'd pursued him, kissed him, touched him, because she'd been through so much since setting foot back in Texas, and because he'd been there to catch her every time she hit a slick spot. Cassie was determined to avoid any more slick spots while she was here, so she wouldn't need saving or helping.

"You owe it to Luke to talk to him, Cassie. You weren't here to see the state he was in after you left. He was a mess...still is. I told him to stay away from you, but he didn't listen."

Cassie's eyes flew to his and she swiped at new

unwelcome tears. "Luke had his chance Cole, and he blew it. So, if he's a mess, it's not my fault. He'll have to work it out himself. I'm gonna get my daddy back on his feet then I'm going back to Phoenix."

Cole looked at her intently, then stopped the swing and stood up to face her. "You're making a mistake, sugar. But it's yours to make. If you need to talk, give me a call." He reached into his pocket and pulled out a business card handing it to her. "My cell's on the back."

She watched Cole until his SUV was reduced to a cloud of dust in the distance, then got up from the swing and went into the house to go find her dad. She needed to talk to him before he got any crazy ideas from what happened between her and Luke just now.

***

It was Friday, Cassie was cleaning out the horse stalls, and Luke hadn't shown back up at the ranch in a week. Not since the scene in his pickup. And Cassie missed him a lot. She'd get over it though, she kept telling herself.

Just like last time ten years ago, each day would get better, and she'd miss him less. The hole in her heart, which felt like a double-barrel shotgun wound right now, would eventually heal to pellet size. How the hell had she let herself care about him again?

She didn't know how it happened, but Luke had managed to get a toehold inside her heart again, and she had been teetering on the cliff again, had almost fallen over the edge. The same one that had landed her flat on her face and heartbroken last time. She needed to be thankful he was staying away, not sad.

His absence was making it harder to manage the daily chores on the ranch, but much easier for her to untangle the briar bush of emotions clogging her head and making her forget how much she loved her life in Phoenix...and James. But even though Luke hadn't been around to remind her, when Cassie lay down at night, his parting words tossed around in her head like a broken record. *"How can you marry him when you want me?"*

With a sigh, she lifted the heavy shovel of manure and tossed it into the wheelbarrow by the door, before going back to repeat the process. When it was full, she pushed it out of the barn and headed toward the pile at the edge of the pasture. She was halfway across the pasture when she saw a familiar silver BMW convertible ease down the rutted driveway toward the house.

Cassie let out a whoop, dropped the wheelbarrow and took off running. She took a shortcut and hopped the fence near the house, running to meet the car as it pulled to a stop. Cassie was sweaty, dirty and probably smelled like horse poop, but she didn't care. James was here and he would make her feel better. Help her remember that she loved him.

Out of habit, her thumb went to stroke the diamond engagement ring on her finger, and encountered nothing but smooth skin and a faint ridge. She sucked in a breath and tucked her hand in her pocket.

Because of the attack by the ranch hand, and then their argument in the truck with Luke, she hadn't ever made it back out to the tree or fence to look for her ring again. She swallowed hoping James wouldn't notice it was missing, before she found it.

He opened the door and eased his long lean frame out of the car, then pocketed her keys and stretched. "Hi, sweetheart. Surprise!" he said his eyes moving over her from her dusty boots to her misshapen straw hat. He leaned forward and gingerly kissed her cheek without touching her anywhere else. "Wow, you sure look like a country girl. Gives me all kind of hayloft fantasies." He winked at her then stuffed his hands in the pocket of his sharply-creased khakis.

Okay, she hadn't seen him in almost two weeks, had talked to him maybe two times on the phone, and this was the best greeting he had in him? "I'm a little dirty. Come on in the house, while I shower and change," she walked away from him toward the house.

She was sure he didn't want her to muss up the expensive green polo the same color as his eyes, or his chinos, but still...the man played golf, he'd seen sweat and dirt before, surely.

"I'd like to take you out to dinner tonight. Is there anywhere good around here?" he said and she realized he hadn't moved to follow her.

She looked back over her shoulder and found him bent over dusting his loafers, so she stopped and faced him again. "There's a decent steak house in Bowie, but nothing to write home about, and a Mexican place." When he stood up and pocketed his shoe shammy, she turned and walked with him up to the porch and opened the door for them.

Cool air rushed over her skin as she stepped inside the entry then took a few steps toward the kitchen. "Have you had lunch?"

"Yeah I had a salad when I stopped in Amarillo." James informed her sounding stationary. She turned around to find him eyeballing the furniture and then the antler chandelier in the entry with a curl to his lip. "Wouldn't want to tangle with that thing in the dark." he chuckled and Cassie bristled at his snobbishness.

"That'd be hard to do since it's hanging from the ceiling," she told him with sarcasm lacing her tone.

His smile slipped a notch, and he looked at her curiously. "Everything okay, sweetheart?"

She huffed out a breath and reeled in her irritation. "Everything is fine, James. I'm just tired, and hot. I'll feel better after my shower." She forced herself to smile at him and then grabbed his hand to lead him into the family room where she found her dad sitting in his wheelchair reading a cattleman's magazine.

"Daddy, look who came to see us..."

Her dad looked up, his reading glasses resting on the end of his nose making him look kind of like an owl with his wild gray hair and busy eyebrows. He grunted then said, with an obvious lack of enthusiasm, "Howdy...John is it?"

Cassie wanted to strangle her dad. She knew he remembered James' name. He'd spent a week with them at Christmas, and he wasn't senile. He was just being an ass, because he didn't like him.

James, bless his heart, walked around her and extended his hand speaking loudly as if her dad was hard of hearing, "James Barton, Mr. Bellamy. It's good to see you again. How's the leg?"

"Damned leg is fine, and my name is Carl," he said grouchily.

James eyebrows shot up, and then came back down over narrowed green eyes. "Well, that's good news then, sir. That means Cassie can come home soon."

"She is home, boy," her dad told James and then dropping his eyes back to his magazine he rustled through a few pages, totally ignoring them.

"Did Cassie tell you we're getting married soon?" James asked evidently to irritate her dad further. This wasn't going well at all, and she stepped between them and put her hands on James chest and shook her head.

He let out a deep frustrated sigh, and then turned his back to walk back toward the entry. "I've got a few calls to make, but my cell doesn't have reception. Mind if I use the phone I saw on the way in?"

"That's fine, James. I'm going upstairs to get cleaned up. You're welcome to come up there when you get done," Cassie invited hoping that would keep him away from her daddy. At the foot of the stairs, she told him, "It's the third door from the landing on the right."

"He ain't going in your room, little girl. Ain't proper," Carl grumbled.

Cassie growled her frustration. "Dad, I'm twenty-eight

years old, and he's my fiancé. Stop being a stubborn old coot."

Her dad harrumphed, slapped his magazine down on his lap, then unlocked the brake on his wheelchair. He turned the chair away from them and wheeled it toward the room he was using on the ground floor.

Cassie's shoulders slumped. This was not what she needed now. She'd have a private talk with her dad in the morning, and make sure he didn't give James a hard time again. If he did, she'd just pack up her suitcase and head out, and she was going to tell him so. She looked over at James just standing at the doorway to the alcove frowning, his shoulders stiff.

She smiled at him, and said, "He's just in pain. He's been that way since I got here." Then she shrugged and turned to run up the stairs fast.

The water coursing over her skin felt like heaven. The steam billowed up around her and cleaned out the smell of horse manure from her nostrils. She picked up the floral-scented body wash and loofah she'd brought with her and scrubbed herself thoroughly, before washing her hair.

By the time she exited the shower and wrapped herself in a towel, she felt like a new woman. Bending over, Cassie towel-dried her hair then wrapped it up turban-style, so she could lotion up and work away the calluses on her hands that had developed over the last two weeks.

She took extra time on her makeup and hair, since she knew she wouldn't have to think much over what she was going to wear. The one black dress and heels she brought would have to do. Out here, Cassie didn't figure she'd have much need for her closet full of dress clothes back home. At least she'd thrown a dress in at the last minute, or she'd be going out to dinner with James in jeans and a tank top. He wouldn't like that much, she didn't think.

When she walked back to her room, she opened the door, and found James laying on the bed on his back scrolling through his cell phone messages. He looked up at her after a second and his eyes traveled over her exposed skin, lingering at the top of her breasts. "Mmm...maybe we'll skip dinner?"

Her stomach rumbled indelicately and she put a hand over it. "I'm starving," she admitted and smiled sheepishly. She'd eaten more in the last two weeks than she did in a month back in Phoenix. But she'd worked more too--hard work--so she wasn't worried about gaining weight.

She walked toward the closet and opened the door. James got up off the bed and walked over to pull her back into his arms. "Now, we can say a proper hello," he said near her ear and kissed her neck. She shivered, but not because she was turned on. His touch was repulsing her, but she forced herself to stand still while he kissed his way up her neck to her ear, then took her shoulders and turned her around to face him.

"I've missed you," he told her then leaned down to put his lips on hers, pulling her to his chest. Cassie closed her eyes and tried to capture any spark of passion his kiss ignited in her. Nothing...absolutely nothing happened.

He lifted her hand to his mouth and kissed it, then confusion crossed his face and he ran his thumb over her ring finger. "Where's your ring?"

Cassie felt the flush start at her chest, move up her neck and spread across her face. "I took it off, because I didn't want to damage it, or l-l-ose it working," she said stumbling over the last words. Thank god it was the truth, she felt relieved at not having to lie to him.

Relief passed over his finely chiseled features and he smiled. "Good, thinking." He kissed her hand again and then let it go and stepped back. "You can wear it to dinner then."

Guilt flooded her and she swallowed hard and lied, "Um...it's locked in the safe in daddy's room and I don't want to disturb him."

James' smile slipped a notch, but he nodded. "No, let's

leave him alone to rest...maybe it will improve his mood. I'll just go downstairs and wait for you in the family room." He leaned in for another kiss and she turned her cheek to him. He looked at her curiously, then walked to the door.

Cassie let out the breath she'd been holding when he shut the door softly behind him. Luke's taunting, but truthful words took a circuit through her brain. *"How can you marry him when you want me?"*

The tremors started in her hands then moved up her arms and down her body to her toes. She was shaking violently and stumbled over to the bed to sit down before she fell. The truth hit her in the face taking her breath away. She couldn't marry James. But how was she going to tell him. They were business partners, lovers and they lived together. That was a whole lot of mess to untangle.

***

Luke tossed back the last sip of his third beer, and tapped it on the bar letting Slim, the bartender know he wanted another. He hadn't been drunk in a long time, but he was working on it right now. Maybe he'd be able to sleep tonight.

The bartender looked up at him then slid the beer toward him, giving him a thumbs up. Luke nodded his thanks and took a long swallow. Someone bumped his shoulder and it spilled down his shirt, then they sat down on the stool beside him.

"Drowning your sorrows, buddy?"

"Shit," Luke said looking down at his expensive western shirt. He grabbed the bar towel and mopped at his shirt, before he wiped his forearm over his mouth.

"Give a guy some warning, would ya?" he said grouchily.

"You had supper yet?" Cole asked with concern in his tone.

"No, daddy, I haven't had supper," Luke slurred then tossed back another swig of his beer.

"This won't help you know...you should have learned that last time," his friend told him and waved to the bartender for a beer.

"Jesus, can't a guy just get shit-faced for no reason these days?"

"If you were the same guy I pulled out of this same bar ten years ago, I'd say yeah. Now, the answer is a little more complicated...Sheriff."

Luke's head dropped and his shoulders slumped. Cole was right, but he'd be damned if he'd admit it, so he didn't. He just picked up his beer and finished it one long slug before slamming it down on the bar. "Do you ever mind your own business, Cole?"

"You're my friend, that makes you my business." Cole slapped him on the back then took a sip of the beer the bartender had just put in front of him. "How bout we finish off one more then go eat at the steakhouse? There's a cute waitress over there I'm sweet on."

"Don't want food. It'll ruin my buzz. I need to get laid," Luke said then spun around on his barstool and leaned his elbows back on the bar to survey the possibilities.

Cole laughed and took another drink of his beer then turned around too, hooking his boot heel on the stool and leaning closer to Luke. "Okay...then pick one out and we'll all go over to the steakhouse." He pointed to a curvy brunette in a tight red dress standing by the jukebox swinging her ass while she picked out songs. "How bout her, she's a hot number."

Luke's vision was a little blurry, so he squinted his eyes to take a closer look at the woman, then caught himself on the bar when his stool wobbled a little. He stood up and shoved his Stetson down on his head then walked a little unsteadily toward the jukebox and his date for tonight.

He sidled up beside her and put his arm around her

waist, and whispered in her ear. "Hello, darlin'."

She pursed her red lips and looked him over from head to toe and back up. "Hi, sugar," she said and then dropped a few quarters in the machine and picked a slow belly-rubbing song by a bluesy country singer. "Wanna dance?" she asked running a fingernail along his cheek.

He put his hand over hers and then took it in his to lead her to the small dance floor where he pulled her into his arms, and put his hands on her ass to get closer. They swayed together and she pressed her full breasts into his chest and looped her arms behind his neck.

Luke bent down and kissed her neck then across her cheek before he claimed her luscious mouth with his. The beautiful woman in his arms should have sent his libido into overdrive, but she felt all wrong...she wasn't tall, she wasn't blonde, and evidently, she wasn't smart if she was letting a drunk lovesick cowboy kiss all over her.

Cassie Bellamy had done this to him...again. And he wasn't supposed to let her do that.

With determination, Luke moved one hand up to the woman's breast and gave her nipple a little brush. It hardened instantly and she moaned into his mouth. They were still kissing when the song ended and another faster one started.

A tap on his shoulder made Luke come up for air and look over his shoulder to see Cole standing behind him. "Let's go eat. Your friend want to join us?"

Luke looked down at the pretty woman and smiled. "You wanna steak, honey?"

"Some beef sounds good," she said saucily and winked at him, her pretty green eyes sparkling, before she linked her arm through his.

Cole grinned and shook his head, before turning and leading the way to the front door. "I paid the tab, buddy. You owe me."

"Seems like I always owe you, buddy." Luke chuckled and put his arm around the brunette pulling her closer into his side. He looked down at her. "What's your name, sugar? It has to be something beautiful. A gorgeous girl like you wouldn't get stuck with something like Edith." Luke laughed and staggered a little feeling her arm slide around his back to help steady him.

"Candy," she said her lips twisting wryly.

"Perfect," he said giving her a face-splitting grin and a squeeze.

She certainly looked good enough to lick all over, he thought. Maybe tonight would be the night he'd get over his obsession with Cassie Bellamy--for good.

CHAPTER SIX

The steakhouse was only a block or so from the bar, and it was a great night, so they decided to walk there. Close to the restaurant, he saw a fancy silver BMW easing along the sidewalk, looking for a place to park. The driver of the car shoehorned it into one of the only spots open. It looked like all of Bowie was at the steakhouse tonight.

Luke laughed when a tall skinny guy got out of the car bumping his head on the doorframe in the process. Slick city dude needs a pickup truck, Luke thought. Wouldn't be bumping his head then. He watched the guy go around the car to open the passenger door, then stopped right under the canopy of the restaurant when Cole's cell phone rang, and he stepped aside to answer it.

He pulled Candy up against him and leaned down to kiss her again, then stood back up and smiled at her. "You sure are pretty, darlin'." He moved a thumb to her face and wiped away a smudge of lipstick. "Thanks for coming out to eat with us."

"Thanks for inviting me..." she said then purred suggestively, "But I'm wanting to skip to dessert." Then she leaned up to gave him a quick kiss under his jaw. He growled and captured her mouth with his, his hands going to her ass to lift her up against him.

Someone's shoulder bumped his hard and he let go of Candy and grabbed onto a post to keep from toppling over on top of her. He shot a look to his left to see who the rude asshole was and groaned.

"Excuse us. Can't you find a room or something?" Cassie said snottily, her eyes shooting blue fire at him. She notched up her chin then the tall blonde guy with her slid an arm around her waist and opened the door to lead her inside.

Luke stood there frozen in place. Cassie had on a tight black dress with a ruffle skirt that flirted around the top of her thighs and five-inch 'come fuck me' heels that put her almost at eye level with him. He swallowed thickly. She'd curled her beautiful blonde hair and it floated over her shoulders and back like a cloud.

He stiffened and looked over at Cole who wore an expression that must mimic his own. Stunned. Dumbfounded. Totally blown away.

Cole lifted an eyebrow then asked, "You want to go somewhere else?"

"Who was she?" Candy asked and nudged Luke.

"Nobody you need to worry about darlin'...let's go eat," he said and leaned around her to open the door. Luke was not going to let Cassie Bellamy and her fancy pants fiancé run him off. And besides that, he was curious about the man she was engaged to....the infamous James. The man she supposedly loved.

This could be fun, he thought, his buzz giving him just the right amount of courage he needed to walk inside the restaurant behind Candy.

Cole was hot on their heels and grabbed Luke's arm when he walked up to the hostess stand and asked for a table for three, preferably near the couple that had just been seated.

"Luke," he said a warning in his voice. "This isn't a good idea man. Let's just go to the Bluebird."

"Nope, I feel like a big ole steak. Don't you darlin'?" Luke smiled down at the woman on his arm and she nodded, her big dark curls dancing around her shoulders, brushing the arm he had across her back.

Glancing back at the hostess making her way across the restaurant back to them, Luke saw her speak to the woman at the stand, then she grabbed menus and led them across the red-carpeted restaurant to their table.

Several people spoke to them as the hostess led them to their table. Luke did his best to act sober and avoid conversation. He was off duty, but he didn't need to stir up gossip that he drank a lot. He didn't. This was probably a once a year thing for him...unless Cassie

Bellamy came to town.

Candy glanced up at him adoringly when he pulled out her chair and waited for her to sit down. "Thanks, sugar," she said with a wink.

"You're welcome, darlin'," he said then scooted his chair closer to hers and sat down. Cole sat down across from them with a thundercloud in his eyes. It looked like Luke's luck was running tonight, because the hostess had seated them at a table directly behind Cassie and her fiancé. The man's back was to them, but Luke had a clear view of Cassie, and she had a clear view of him...and Candy.

Luke gave Candy a thousand-watt smile then ordered a tequila sunrise for her and another beer for himself. Leaning down he swept her hair aside and whispered in her ear exactly what he'd like to do to her at sunrise. She blushed and then giggled when he licked her ear.

Out of the corner of his eye, he saw Cassie drag her eyes from preppy boy's so she could look over at him and pin him with a lethal stare. He lifted an eyebrow at her then turned back to look down into Candy's eyes before he leaned in to give her a heated kiss, which she participated in enthusiastically. He heard Cole growl across the table from them, and smiled against her lips.

When he came up for air, he looked at Cole. "Hey, Cole I think Candy might be into a threesome tonight. You up for it?" Luke asked louder than necessary, but not loud enough for anyone other than the table next to them to hear.

Cole's mouth flopped open and closed a couple of times then he saw Cassie's eyes widen then narrow, before she picked up her water glass and took a big gulp, her hand shaking.

It looked like Candy might protest, so he covered her mouth with his again, and moved his hand under the table to stroke her thigh. He swallowed her protest with another kiss, then leaned near her ear and said not quietly,

"I can't seem to keep my hands off of you, sugar. You don't mind do you?"

She shook her head looking slightly uncomfortable, and he felt bad for using her, but he was having fun torturing Cassie. "That's good, sugar, because I'm going to spend all night long showing you how hot you make me."

Cole slapped his hand against his forehead then rested it in his palm on the table mumbling under his breath. Luke grinned. It looked like he was getting a twofer. He was torturing Cole too. He chuckled under his breath and kissed the top of Candy's head.

The waitress came back with their drinks and put them down to take their dinner order. "I'd like the biggest steak you have, medium rare, with all the fixings. I think I'm going to need my strength for later." He said suggestively and winked at Candy. "What'll you have, sugar?"

"Petite Sirloin and a salad," she said then pushed back from the table. "I'll be right back, sugar. I need to go to the powder room."

Candy leaned down and gave him a brief kiss then walked toward the bathroom, her heart-shaped ass drawing the attention of every man in the room...and Cassie. He watched Candy until she disappeared in the ladies room, then he looked back at Cassie to find her studying him with glacial eyes.

"Puttin it on a little thick aren't you, Luke?" Cole asked through gritted teeth in a voice a little above a whisper.

"Nah, needs a few more coats for sure," he said and lifted his beer to take a long draw. He licked a drop from his top lip, and he saw that Cassie's eyes followed the motion, then she took a deep shuddering breath.

"You could at least wipe the lipstick off, dude." Cole laughed dryly, then took a drink of his beer, gesturing with the bottle. "It's not your shade at all. Clashes with the green-eyed monster sitting on your shoulder."

Luke saw the preppy boy get up from the table then walk over and drop a kiss on Cassie's cheek before he headed toward the bathroom. Luke pushed back his chair and stood starting around the table, but he wasn't sure if he wanted to have a bathroom conversation with the asshole with his fists, or if he wanted to go pull Cassie up and kiss her senseless, so he just stood there and wobbled around a little.

As it turned out he didn't do either, because Cole stood up quickly and got right up in his face. "Ut uh--no way, buddy. You're not going anywhere," he grated then pushed him back to his seat, before going back around to his own chair.

"You're no fucking fun, man. When did you get so fucking boring?" Luke asked and plopped back down in his chair.

"About the time I dragged your sorry ass out of jail ten years ago."

"What are you my fucking guardian angel?"

"Not nearly. Your keeper maybe...but it's getting real old, real fast." Cole drummed his fingers on the table, then said seriously. "Luke you're gonna fuck up your career. You worked too damned hard to let that happen."

Luke took a deep shuddering breath then looked into his friends eyes. "Thanks for being here for me, man. You know this isn't me," he said and worked at peeling the label off of the half-empty bottle.

"I know. That's the only reason I'm putting up with your sorry ass."

A few minutes later the waitress delivered their food, and Luke dug in even though he wasn't hungry at all. He needed something to dilute the beer he'd drank and get him sobered up. After he'd devoured half of his meal, he looked over at Cole and asked, "Hey you think Candy gave us the old bathroom ditch?"

"Looks like it. Unless she's passed out in there, she's gone."

Luke was glad she'd left. It saved him the embarrassment and hassle of having to cut her loose when they left the restaurant. There was no way he would have been able to go through with having sex with her. He wasn't in the mood. And she didn't do a damned thing for him.

His eyes moved over to the beautiful blonde talking chattily with preppy boy, and the steak he was chewing turned to dust. Pushing back his plate, he pulled out his wallet and tossed down a few bills on the table. "Let's get out of here," he told Cole and got up.

Cole quickly wiped his mouth and threw the napkin on his plate. "Good idea. You feelin' better?"

"Yeah, but I'll need a ride home." He'd pick up his truck from the station tomorrow. He'd parked there earlier to walk to the bar. Forcing himself to ignore Cassie and her fiancé, he put his arm on Cole's shoulder and headed for the front door. "Thanks for not letting me do something stupid, man."

"That's what friends are for and I'm sure you'll be returning the favor one day."

***

Cassie wanted to vomit. Watching Luke kissing and petting that floozy had made her physically ill. Seeing that had brought back memories of the night he'd crushed her ten years ago. And he'd done it on purpose tonight. He looked to be drunk and he was trying to hurt her. If he'd wanted a pound of flesh from his performance, he'd gotten ten from her.

"James, I'm not feeling well, can we go?" Tears burned at the back of her eyes and her stomach was a burning cauldron of acid.

He looked up from his cell phone and replied distractedly, "Sure, sweetheart." He didn't even notice how upset she was.

He'd done nothing but check for text messages all night, and fiddle with that damned phone. It was like he was making up for the lack of reception at the ranch, by cramming in as much texting as he could while they were in town. She wondered what was so damned interesting that he' practically ignored her all night. "Work trouble?"

He looked up at her again, "Yeah, working on a big deal over in Mesa."

"At nine thirty at night?" She couldn't help the edge that crept into her voice.

"Yeah, it's really big. I'll tell you all about it when you get home."

Cassie twisted her lips to stop from saying what she felt like saying. "If I come home." Now that she'd decided that she was going to break things off with James, there wasn't really anything to keep her in Phoenix.

She could sell him, or someone else, her part of the business and move. She'd enjoyed the physical work on the ranch, since she'd been here--realized how much she missed working with the animals. Once, her horses had been her life. Maybe she could expand the farm to breed quarter horses and scale back the cattle operation.

James sighed then stood up and reached in his pocket to pull out his wallet. He opened it then frowned. "Aw, nuts. I forgot to stop at the bank machine earlier. Can you get the tab, honey?"

Cassie ground her teeth in frustration and reached inside her purse for her wallet. James always did this to her, and it really pissed her off. She grabbed the black folder off the table and shoved her credit card inside then waved it at the waitress.

"We're kind of in a hurry...sorry." The girl nodded and was back quickly with their ticket. Angrily, Cassie signed it, put her credit card back in her wallet and tossed the folder down on the table. "You ready?"

"You're not mad are you, sweetie?" he asked in a patronizing sing-song voice.

She replied in the same tone, "Why in the world would I be mad, *sweetie*?" Cassie's laugh was brittle and insincere, but James didn't notice.

She brushed past him and walked ahead so he didn't put his arm around her. The thought of him touching her made her skin crawl. The way he'd acted at dinner made her realize she was right, it was time to put a fork in this relationship. She was going to break up with him tonight. While she had a full head of steam going.

He'd driven *her* fucking car to Bowie, so she'd have to buy him a one way ticket to Phoenix tomorrow morning and drop him off at the airport in Dallas.

"So who was that guy you were staring at all night?" James asked glancing over at her after they'd driven a few minutes and had just turned on the Old Farm Market Road.

She couldn't believe he'd noticed anything other than what was on the screen of his cell phone. "Old friend," she said shortly and looked out the window.

"How friendly and how old?" He asked suspiciously glancing at her again.

Cassie sucked in an exasperated breath then blew it out and said, "Why do you care James? Really? I'm surprised you even noticed you were so caught up in your text conversation."

"That was business."

Business hell. She didn't believe that anymore than he believed Luke was just an old friend. Cassie would find out later when she got her hands on that damned phone.

"Sure it was," she said breezily. "Let's just drop both subjects, okay? I don't want to fight with you."

"Fine." He stomped on the accelerator and her car fishtailed on the soft gravel shoulder before he corrected to right it.

"Don't drive my car like that." She crossed her arms over her breasts and glanced at him then looked out the window again.

"It's going to be our car soon, Cassie. And I wasn't driving recklessly."

Like hell it would. This car was her baby, bought with money she'd earned. Just like everything else he'd laid claim to these days. Fuck the plane ticket, she was doing this right here, right now.

"Pull over," she demanded.

He looked at her curiously, then did as she asked.

She reached over and grabbed the keys from the ignition, then said forcefully, "Get out."

"What the hell, Cassie?" James barked incredulously.

She clenched her jaw and restated slowly as if he was a little short on gray matter. "I said, Get out! Now!"

When he didn't move, she leaned across him and opened the door then pushed on his shoulder. He finally got the message she was serious and slid out of the seat to stand beside the car.

Cassie yanked her dress up to her waist and awkwardly climbed over the gearshift to settle herself in the driver's seat. "I hope a fucking coyote eats your sorry ass, James. We're done. I'll be in touch about the business. And don't bother going by the house, the locks will be changed by the time you get home. I'll have a moving company box your shit and set it at the curb next week."

He spread his hands and almost whined. "Cassie, honey, don't do this. I love you."

"You love yourself and my money...and whoever you're so interested in on your damned cell phone."

His face pinched and his lips curved nastily. "I want my fucking ring back."

"Tough luck, Pedro. I lost the fucking ring when I fell off my horse and almost broke my neck. Not that you give a shit. And besides, I paid for most of it. You charged it on my credit card, remember? Goodbye, James," she said then slammed the door in his face.

Hitting the lock button, she jammed the keys into the ignition. Cassie felt liberated--and laughter bubbled up inside of her as she fired the engine to life and shoved the car in first before roaring down the road, leaving James staring after her on the dark country road.

She grabbed her purse from the floorboard and fished around inside for her cell, and then pulled a business card from the side pocket. Turning on the phone, she saw she still had a little reception, one bar, but it would fizzle out soon, she knew.

Quickly, she flipped the card over and punched in the cell number with her thumb. Cole picked up after one ring. "Cole, it's Cassie."

"Cassie? What's up?" She heard someone grumble in the background.

"I think you should send someone out to the Old Farm Market Road. I just dumped James out there and he'll probably get eaten by a coyote or wind up with cactus needles in his ass."

"And I'd care about that why?" he asked a little gruffly.

"I'm doing the right thing here and letting you know. I couldn't give a shit what happens to him either. Just thought I'd let you know. Goodbye."

Cassie disconnected the call and tossed the phone on the floorboard where it immediately started to ring. She turned on the radio to a country station and cranked it up then sang along at the top of her lungs.

***

"What the hell did she want?" Luke asked then belched loudly.

"I think she's lost her ever loving mind..." Cole disconnected the callback he'd made to Cassie and tossed his phone into the center slot on his console. He picked up the microphone from the dash and keyed it, then told dispatch to send a squad car to go pick up James and take him to a hotel.

Luke sat up straighter and grinned over at Cole. "She dumped him?"

"Out on Farm Market Road. She was just letting me

know so we could pick him up before a coyote ate him or he wound up in a cactus patch."

Their soft chuckles in the cab of the truck escalated to gales of laughter then uproarious hoots and thigh slaps. Cole was laughing so hard he pulled over to the shoulder and leaned over the wheel holding his stomach.

Luke was gasping for breath when he finally got control of himself again. "Oh god, that is too good. I didn't need to get drunk. I just needed to let him piss her off."

"She sounded pretty damned mad. He's lucky she didn't fill his ass with buckshot," Cole said and glanced over at him which was a mistake, because they both started laughing again.

When they finally composed themselves, Cole pulled back on the road and Luke told him, "Damn, that felt good."

"Yeah I haven't laughed like that in forever."

A few minutes later, Luke saw Cole glancing over at him like he wanted to ask something. "What's on your mind? Spit it out."

"Why do you think Cassie left back then?" His friend's voice was kind of somber.

"Who the hell knows...she sure didn't say anything to me when she left, not even goodbye. Why?" Luke threw an arm over his eyes and closed them. He didn't want to go there right now, but was curious why Cole brought it up.

"When you stormed away from the ranch the other day, I stuck around and talked to her for a few minutes. She just said something strange that got me to thinking there might be something you hadn't told me."

Luke opened one eye and stared at Cole's profile, the green light from the dash casting an eerie glow over him. "I told you everything I knew about it. What did she say?"

"I told her that you loved her...always had. She said 'No he doesn't, he proved it to me that night.'"

Luke sat up and turned toward him. "What the fuck?"

"Kinda what I thought, but she seemed so convinced...or convincing."

Luke sat back again swirling her words around in his mind, while he dissected each one for hidden meaning by tying them back to the events of the night Cassie had left him.

It was the night of the Bowie High School graduation and Luke had made plans to meet up with Cassie that night at their favorite spot to star gaze and make out. It was damned hot out that day and he was early, so he decided to go for a swim first.

He'd just gotten his shirt and shoes off when he heard a girl screaming and looked out into the lake to see what was going on. He saw hands flailing and a head go down under the water, so he ran down the dock and dove in.

Luke had been a lifeguard at the Henrietta Rec Center pool during the summer when he was in high school, so he knew what to do. He swam out to where he'd last seen the girl and dove under the water swimming in a grid to try and find her.

His hand finally rubbed against her skin and he found a piece of clothing to grab on to. Unfortunately, it was her bikini top and it had come off in his hand, so he tossed it aside and managed to wrap his hand in her hair and swim with her to the surface. When he got her back to shore, he lifted her in his arms and carried her, while doing rescue breathing on her at the same time. He didn't even notice it was Becca Harvey, the girl that had been after him all summer just to piss off Cassie, until he laid her down on the dock. He kept up breathing for her until she coughed and turned to the side to spit up half the lake.

By the time she came around and help arrived, he knew he was way past late meeting Cassie. He picked up his clothes and looked around for the ring he'd bought to ask her to marry him, but couldn't find it.

He hadn't had time to take it out of his pocket before he dove in the water, and figured the pretty little ring he'd scrimped and saved to buy for her was at the bottom of the lake. He didn't stick around to look more, because he knew he had to find Cassie and explain what happened. Why he'd missed their date. After he went and checked their spot on the rocks, and she wasn't there, he rode his motorcycle hell-bent-for-leather to the Double B, where her Daddy told him she'd taken off.

Cole was about to turn into Luke's driveway when Luke vaulted up and shouted, "Holy Shit!" and slapped the dash. Cole slammed on the brakes and Luke slid forward, but caught himself by bracing against the dashboard.

"What the hell is wrong with you man?" Cole screeched.

Excitement, relief and then finally anger flooded Luke's chest and he rubbed a spot between his pecs. "I think I might know what happened."

"What happened when?" Cole asked in confusion staring at him like he was nuts.

"The night Cassie left." If he was right, Luke would be sick that ten years had passed with her thinking what she did about him. It all made sense now. Ten years too late.

***

Cassie got back to the Double B and waltzed up the steps and through the front door. "Daddy, I'm home!" She yelled running through the house and down the hall to his bedroom.

When she burst through his door and flipped on the light, he sat up in bed and rubbed his eyes. "Baby girl, are you drunk?"

"Drunk on life, daddy!" she told him and giggled. Since she'd only had one glass of wine with dinner, she was nowhere near intoxicated.

"What's got you so fired up then?"

"I dumped James' sorry ass out on Old Farm Market Road tonight. I'm hoping maybe a coyote will eat him."

Her daddy's eyes widened and his jaw dropped open. "Well slap my ass and call me Sally," he hooted. "Come here and give me a hug."

Cassie laughed then walked over and sat down beside him, pulling him into a big hug. "I love you daddy," she said close to his ear and then kissed his cheek with tears burning behind her eyes.

"I love you too, baby girl." He laid back on the bed and gave her a grizzly smile. "So, what made you feed him to the coyotes?"

"I just finally realized what an ass he is, and that he was using me." And probably cheating too, based on his sudden obsession with his text messages. "I guess it took being away from him for me to finally see it." Cassie knew now it had been there all along, his selfishness and snobbery, she had just been blind and stupid.

"Don't guess Luke had anything to do with your decision?" Carl Bellamy's eyes sparkled with hope.

Cassie shook her head. "Nope...nothing at all. He pretty much ripped his britches with me tonight. I'm through with men for a good long while, daddy. I'm going to stay here with you and raise horses."

"Do what?" Carl sat up straighter and grabbed her shoulders.

"I think we should scale back the cattle to something you can manage, and I'm going to raise and train quarter horses."

Tears filled his eyes and Cassie swallowed. "That would be just fine, Cassie Bee."

"Tomorrow I'm getting a full-time nurse out here to get your physical therapy program going. You've sat around here moping long enough. I need your help."

***

Up bright and early the next morning with a new sense of purpose, Cassie raised her face to the sun when she stepped off the porch and strode to the barn with a spring in her step. Bud and his hands were standing by the bunkhouse hashing out their chores for the day, and she walked right up and shouldered her way into the circle of men.

All eyes moved to her and Bud gave her a warm smile. "Morning, Cassie Bee."

"Morning, Bud," she said and then looked at each man in the circle and gave them a head nod. "Morning, guys."

Bud took a step to the center of their group and took off his hat. "Fellas, you haven't had a chance to meet Carl's daughter, Cassie. She's gonna be working with us to get through the calving, while Carl's laid up." They all appeared to be dumbstruck, and none too happy about her helping them.

They maintained respect though, and each introduced themselves to her with a tip of their dusty hat. The hands probably thought she wouldn't be much help, and they'd wind up babysitting the boss's daughter, instead. When they broke up and headed off to saddle up, Cassie pulled Bud aside to talk to him privately.

"Bud, I'm staying in Bowie...coming home for good."

His face split with a big grin, he told her, "It's about damned time, Cassie Bee. Your daddy's missed you."

Although he didn't come out and say it, Cassie knew he'd missed her too, because he sniffled a minute then pulled his red bandana from his pocket to wipe his eyes and then stuff it back in his pocket.

"I'm going to get a stud and a few good mares and start raising and training quarter horses."

"Damned good idea, darlin'. I'll keep my eye out for some good stock. You might check with Tommy Tucker at the Rockin' D up near Amarillo, I hear him and his daddy's herd have thrown some mighty fine foals the last few years."

"Thanks, Bud. I'll do that. But first, we have some babies to get born and cattle to get sold," she told him with a smile then turned back toward the house. "I have a few things to do this morning to settle up things in Phoenix and get daddy's therapy set up, so I'll be back out here in a couple hours. Just tell me what you need me to do."

"Go on, darlin'. Let me know when you get done."

CHAPTER SEVEN

Back at the house, Cassie made a list of the calls she needed to make, and then sat down in the alcove. There were a lot of things she could handle by phone, but she'd have to go to Phoenix in a few weeks to tie up loose ends on some of her outstanding real estate deals, and to get her stuff sold, or packed up to move here.

First, she called a locksmith and got the locks on her house changed. Then she called her friend Betsy, a fellow Realtor about her age that she should have gone into business with instead of James. Betsy was very professional, and was named Arizona Realtor of the Year last year. Cassie had been nominated, but Betsy had edged her out for the award.

She thought Betsy would probably jump on the chance to buy her interest in the firm she co-owned with James and had worked her ass off to make a success. Although, she wasn't positive Betsy would be interested. Over the last couple of years James' reputation had suffered from his lack of attention to detail and laziness. Maybe Betsy could whip him into shape.

When Cassie called, Betsy wasn't in though, so she left her a message that she wanted her to list her home and that she had a business proposition for her.

Next, Cassie called a mover she knew and set up an appointment for them to pack up James' belongings and move them. She'd arranged for the locksmith to give her assistant a key, then she called Diane and told her what was going on with James and she agreed to meet the movers for the appointment.

Finally, Cassie called a nursing service, and put them on the hunt for just the right nurse with a lot of patience and physical therapy experience to help her dad recover. They assured her they'd find a good fit in the next few days. She'd been trying to get physical therapy set up for him since she'd gotten to Bowie with no luck, so she'd believe it when it happened.

When she hung up the phone, Cassie felt a sense of relief. Like a fifty pound sack of potatoes had been lifted from her shoulders. She went to the kitchen and ate breakfast with Imelda, and told her the good news, before she headed back out to the barn.

Imelda had burst into tears and then hugged the breath out of her. The people on this ranch were the ones who truly cared about her, loved her for who and what she was. She wasn't leaving them again. This was her home.

Cassie walked with purpose to the barn and stepped into the dimmer light, then walked toward Bud's office. It took her eyes a moment to adjust, but when she got to the door of the office, she didn't need her eyes to recognize the voice she heard inside, talking to Bud, who was bragging about her plans. Luke was here.

The smile that had been pasted on her face all morning fled, and she put her back against the wall, hoping they didn't see her. No such luck.

"Cassie Bee?" Bud called out to her.

With little choice, because he had indeed seen her, Cassie pushed away from the wall and went into the small room. Her eyes flickered over Luke sitting in the chair by Bud's desk, who was leaning back casually with his hat tipped up and his elbows propped on the arm rests, his long legs crossed at the ankles in front of him.

The sleeves of his black t-shirt accentuated the roundness of his well-defined biceps and the color made his eyes look almost as black, while he studied her with some strange emotion reflected there.

Her still raw heart felt like someone poured salt over the open wound in her chest. Time and distance from him was what she needed for it to get better, but it didn't seem like he was going to give her that.

She dragged her eyes away from Luke and looked at Bud, then tried to work up some saliva in her suddenly dry mouth. "Yeah?"

"I've been talking to Luke and he's got a proposition for us. I think you might wanna hear him out."

She looked back to Luke with a raised brow and said, "Oh, yeah?"

Luke uncrossed his legs and sat up in the chair then said, "Yeah, I want to buy the herd and lease some acreage."

"You want to be a cattle rancher?" Cassie asked incredulously with a snort.

His eyes glittered angrily as he drawled, "Looks that way doesn't it?"

"Five hundred head? That's a lot to chew for a newbie, Luke." She wondered if he'd suddenly hit the lottery, or where the hell he was getting the money it would take him to pull off his plan.

"Cole and I are going to be partners. He's got the money from the sale of his daddy's land, and I've got the experience, as well as some cash."

"But you have a full-time job. How the hell do you think you're going to have enough time?"

"My term as Sheriff is up in a year, I can swing it until then. Bud knows a good manager I can hire."

It looked like Luke had put a lot of thought into the idea, but she still didn't think he realized the enormity of what he was undertaking. "I don't know, Luke."

"I'm going up to the house to talk to your daddy," he told her and pushed up from the chair.

Luke was evidently determined to do this, no matter what she had to say about it. If her daddy agreed, there wasn't a damned thing she could do about it either, and he knew it. She'd have to see him every day...the last thing she wanted for her new lease on life.

"You'll have to build a new barn and bunkhouse, because I have plans for this one," she said firmly. If he did that maybe she could minimize having to see him.

"Not a problem." His firm lips quirked up at the corner. "Anything else?"

"Yeah, I don't want you in my way over here. I'm going to be busy."

"So, I've heard," he said and his eyes moved over her hotly. "Good luck, darlin'. Glad you're coming back." His fists clenching and unclenching at his sides didn't escape Cassie's notice.

Something strange was going on with Luke, but she didn't have a damned clue as to what. He looked determined, but there seemed to be anger simmering right below the surface of his determination. *What the hell did he have to be angry about?*

Well, Cassie didn't have time to worry about it. She had plans to make now that it looked like her horse farm was going to become a reality quicker than she anticipated.

"Thank you, but I don't need luck. I know what I'm doing, so I'll wish *you* good luck," she said nastily then spun on her heel and walked out.

Watching Cassie's stiff back as she stomped out of the office, Luke dragged in a deep breath trying to calm himself. His epiphany last night might have given him an understanding of why she'd treated him like shit since she'd come back to Bowie, but her attitude was beginning to wear out his patience, because he didn't deserve her apathy.

Well maybe he deserved some of it...after what he'd done last night at the restaurant. He'd been a total ass and made a fool of himself to boot. And he should probably apologize, but her attitude didn't put him in a real remorseful mood.

But his stupidity from last night shouldn't be compounded by the imagined sins she'd laid at his doorstep ten years ago, that he had cheated on her. Luke planned to confront her about it, but he was going to do it on his time. He wanted to settle things with Carl first, and get over his anger at her lack of faith in him.

Luke turned to Bud who was now standing behind the scarred old wood desk with his hands on his hips. "I don't know what's gotten into that girl."

Luke knew what was wrong with her, or thought he did, but he wasn't going into it with Bud. "Don't worry about it. I'm going up to the house to talk to Carl. I'll let you know what he says."

***

Honey's coat glistened after all the brushing Cassie had given her. The beautiful mare had just stood there munching on the treat Cassie had given her, while Cassie brushed out all of her anger and frustration at Luke along with the bits of mud and grass caught in her coat.

She patted the mare's neck lovingly then threw the body brush in her grooming kit to pull out the tail and mane brush. She should be doing other things, but this relaxed her, and she deserved a break. Since her feet had hit Bowie, Texas dirt two weeks ago, she'd been busting her ass and battling problems.

It was a gorgeous clear day, hell she might even go to the lake later this afternoon and swim. At the last minute before she'd left Phoenix, Cassie had tossed her bikini in the suitcase right before she'd zipped it up. She was glad now that she had and would enjoy the cold fresh water after how hot it was today.

Maybe tonight, she'd call up an old girlfriend or two and see if she could find someone who wanted to go out for a beer. It would take her a while, but Cassie was determined to reclaim her life in Bowie.

Cassie was hot and sweaty after she finished cleaning the horse stalls again. It was nearly three o'clock when she made it back to the house and went upstairs to change. A swim in the lake was going to feel fantastic, she thought as she stripped then donned her bikini.

She put on a pair of old cut off shorts and slid her feet into rubber flip flops wiggling her toes to let the air cool off her hot feet. Boots were good for working, but they sure didn't allow any airflow.

She grabbed an old romance novel off the bookshelf in her room and then got a towel from the bath and shoved both into a canvas tote she'd found in the closet. Smiling, she pulled down a big floppy straw hat with a huge hot pink flower on the front from the top shelf of the closet and plopped it down on her head. The flower matched her bikini.

Imelda had packed her a lunch and snacks with some bottled water, and she put that bag inside the tote as well. Once she was well-equipped for her excursion, she headed downstairs and across the yard to her truck.

Glancing over at the barn, then the bunkhouse, Cassie saw the door open and Luke came striding out smiling. When she saw him notice her, she looked away and hurried her steps to the truck then opened the door and threw her bag across the seat before she hopped in. The last thing she wanted to do was talk to him.

Cassie grabbed her sunglasses from the dash and shoved them on her nose, then cranked the truck and threw it in reverse then forward and hit the gas. The trail of dust behind her was so thick when she glanced in the rearview she couldn't even see him.

Good, she didn't want to see him. Let him go find that tramp he was with last night--or Becca Harvey, for all she cared--if he wanted female company. She was sure either of them would accommodate him.

A strange, but familiar, pain darted through her chest then went away. You've been through this before Cassie, it'll get better, she reassured herself. Today, she was one day closer to getting over him...again.

At the lake, Cassie parked her truck by the road along the trees and grabbed her bag then headed down the well-worn path she'd traveled many times before. She inhaled the rich-earthy smell of the woods once she stepped inside the dim canopy of trees. A cool breeze ruffled the hair at her shoulders. Carefully, she picked her way along the trail and slowed when she reached the steep decline that led to the spot she sought. A spot that held too many memories for her, but one she couldn't resist revisiting to prove that she truly was moving on.

The first clue she was almost there was the sound of waves lapping against the shore, then the air got thicker with moisture right before she walked out onto the wide rocky ledge into the bright sunshine.

Even with her sunglasses on, the brightness blinded her for a moment and she shaded her eyes staring at the wide blue expanse of water. She saw a sailboat or two in the distance, then a motor boat pulling a skier. The traffic on the lake wasn't busy today, since it was a weekday. This weekend would be a different story. She dropped her bag to the ground and slid to her knees pulling out her towel and sunscreen.

Laying the towel in a flat spot, she sat down and then smoothed sunscreen over her body and face, before pulling out her book and laying back. Later, she'd take a hike down to the dock and go for a dip, but she wanted to relax a little first. She opened the book and quickly forgot everything around her as she became engrossed in the love story. After a while, she became sleepy and laid the book beside her and closed her eyes.

A whiff of warm air fanned over her skin and she opened her eyes lazily then stretched and yawned. Cassie glanced to her left and saw a towel was spread down beside hers, and standing on it she saw a pair very large male feet.

Her eyes traveled up long muscular legs covered in soft dark hair, over navy swim trunks that led to a slim waist, then followed a tantalizing happy trail upward over a ripped abdomen and firm chest to a square jaw bristled with a five o'clock shadow that framed a blinding white smile. Her eyes met sexy brown eyes filled with desire.

"I thought I'd find you here," Luke told her in a low intimate rumble.

The vision of his perfect body and that voice, smooth as dark chocolate, wrapped around her libido and all the moisture left in her body flooded southward. She pushed up to her elbows to glare at him.

"What are you doing here, Luke?"

"Sunbathing, relaxing...looking for you," he said then sat down on the towel he'd spread beside her.

"Why?" She scooted over a few inches to put some space between them. The temptation to reach over and rub her hands over his smooth skin was too great. "Is everything okay at the ranch?"

"Yeah, it's fine," he said lazily then picked up her sunscreen and poured a glob in his hand then smoothed it over his chest. "Lay back down and relax, darlin'."

How the hell was she supposed to relax watching him rub lotion all over his delectable body? This was torture of the highest form, and she didn't think she could take much more without losing it. It was bad enough trying to resist him when he was fully clothed.

Cassie licked her lips and tried to drag her eyes away from him, but couldn't. As if pulled by a magnetic beam, her eyes followed his hands down his chest to his chiseled abs then to the waistband of his shorts. When he pulled the hem of his shorts up to rub lotion on his firm thighs, she groaned then stood and jerked her towel up from the ground.

Grabbing the handle of her tote, she said angrily. "I'm leaving."

Luke looked up at her and she saw his throat work a couple times before he said, "Well at least you're telling me this time."

"And just like before, you'll have the floozy you slept with last night to console you," Cassie spat then turned her back to him and headed up the path into the woods.

She heard a fierce growl behind her, then rustling and before she knew it she was on the ground and Luke was on top of her, pinning her there. He rolled off of her then took her shoulders and turned her over to face him. Cassie was so stunned she couldn't do anything but stare at him like he'd lost his mind. He most likely had, she thought. Luke had never been rough with her. Not that his tackle had been rough, even when he was subduing her she felt the care he'd taken not to hurt her.

Fierce emotion filled his icy brown eyes and a muscle worked at his jaw. He grabbed her shoulders and leaned down into her face to say in a grating hiss, "Listen to me well, Cassandra Bellamy. I. Did. Not. Cheat. On. You! And it pisses me the fuck off that you even think I did. And I didn't sleep with that floozy last night." Luke shoved her shoulders and then stood.

He put his hands on his hips and bent at the waist. "Maybe you did me a fucking favor running off ten years ago, because I would have asked a woman who thought I was a piece of trash to marry me, and she would probably have laughed in my face. Or if she'd said yes, I'd have found out what she thought of me too late. So, thank you for saving me that humiliation....goodbye, Cassie."

Luke stood up straight, his shoulders and face hard and unyielding, then turned and walked back to pick up his shirt, shoes and towel. Without another word, he gave her a disgusted stare then around her and up the trail at a fast clip.

His words and the solemnity of his tone finally ripped through the confused stupor that had claimed her. The fact that his goodbye rang with such finality settled in her heart and she was afraid she'd never see him again.

Cassie vaulted to her feet and ran after him. "Luke, wait!" she yelled, but he was too far ahead to hear evidently, or he was ignoring her. "Luke, don't just say that shit and run off. Please stop!"

She picked up her pace to a jog, but he still he outdistanced her. His fists were clenched at his sides and he took long ground gobbling steps up the steep incline.

"Goddammit Luke, stop! I love you!"

His step faltered and he slowed down a second, then he clenched and unclenched his fists, but he started moving again at the faster pace and yelled back to her. "That doesn't mean a damned thing to me now. Those are words, your actions say something entirely different. I'm done, Cassie."

"No, Luke don't say that! Just stop and let me talk to you," she begged and then tripped on a tree root, her ankle rolling painfully.

She felt something snap, before she fell on the soft packed dirt on her face, hitting her head on another root in the process. The pain shooting up her leg was excruciating and she rolled onto her back and grabbed her ankle, rocking back and forth and moaning.

She heard Luke yell, "Fuck!" from down the trail, and then he was at her side running his hands over her body then down her legs to her already swelling ankle. It was obvious he was beyond angry and didn't really want to help her, but he'd come back and she was thankful. "I think it's broken," she told him and moaned again.

"Oh, this is fucking perfect," he said shortly then reached into his shorts and pulled out his cell phone and dialed a number. "Cole, get your ass down to the lake. Cassie needs you to take her to the hospital for an x-ray."

Cassie felt nauseous and rolled onto her side away from Luke, just in case she had to throw up. He really wasn't going to help her, she thought dejectedly. He was pawning her off on Cole. Her heart shattered into a million pieces and silent tears rolled down her cheeks onto the ground. She curled up into a tight ball of misery and sobbed quietly. Luke finally finished his explanations to Cole, then grabbed her shoulder to turn her over.

"Just leave me alone," she said in a whisper. "Go, ahead Luke. Cole will help me."

"Cassie stop being dramatic and turn over, so I can look at your pupils. Did you hit your head when you fell? Do you feel nauseated?"

"Yes and yes...but it's no big deal," she told him weakly. "Cole will take me to the hospital...just go away." Cassie closed her eyes against her pain and let the black dots that had been filling her vision turn into a dark curtain of peace.

When Cassie woke up she was being wheeled on a gurney from an ambulance through glass double doors with big red letters spelling EMERGENCY. The scent of antiseptic hit her in the face when the two men beside the gurney pushed her inside.

She gagged and said, "I think I'm going to be sick," before putting her hand over her mouth praying she wouldn't be. An IV tube pulled in her arm and she dropped it back beside her.

One of the men walked away and spoke briefly with a nurse. He came back and handed her a small rectangular pan. "Here you go, honey. Use it if you need it. I told the nurse to see if the doctor would order something for your nausea."

Cassie licked her dry lips then thanked him. "Where's Cole?"

"Is that the Sheriff's deputy who was with you when we got there?" She nodded and wished she hadn't, because pain sliced through her head causing another wave of sickness to surge to her throat.

"He was following us and will be here in a few minutes."

"Thank you." Cassie gripped the pan the medic had given her and turned her head to the side closing her eyes to focus on not getting sick.

They wheeled her into a room, transferred her to a bed carefully, then zipped a curtain around her. The other medic that had helped her picked up a call button from the rail on the bed and put it in her hand.

"Ring this if you feel sick again, or need anything. A nurse will come to help you."

She nodded and gripped the small white cylinder, her

finger hovering over the button. Cassie hated feeling helpless. She couldn't stand hospitals or being sick. If anyone thought her daddy was a terrible patient, they hadn't seen her sick.

The curtain around her parted and an older brunette woman in scrubs walked in with a long syringe filled with liquid. She was followed closely by Cole, his face pale and his lips pinched into a tight line. He stood over to the side to give the woman room.

The needle was so big, Cassie cringed and said, "If you think you're sticking that in my ass...you better think again," she told her flatly with misery lacing her tone.

The nurse chuckled and walked around the bed to the IV pole and slid the needle into the tube. "This is for nausea, and it goes in your IV, not your, um..."

"Ass..." Cassie filled in the blank and then said, "Good. When is the doctor going to get in here? If he can patch up my ankle, I'm good to go."

Just mentioning her ankle made it throb. Her toes were cold and numb, and the pain was as intense as an earache. Her head hurt just as bad.

"I'm afraid it's going to involve more than that, sweetie. You probably have concussion, and your ankle looks to be pretty badly broken. We'll have to wait for the doctor to find out when you'll be released."

Cassie gritted her teeth and pushed on her forearms to sit up. Pain sliced through her ankle and head at the same time, bile surged up into her throat and her vision blurred around the edges. She moaned and then laid back against the hard bed and closed her eyes.

Cole was at her side in a flash, and leaned over her. "Stop being a horse's ass, Cassie and let them take care of you."

She swallowed hard and nodded gingerly then opened one eye to look at the tall blonde man she considered a friend. "Where's Luke?"

Pushing against the bed, Cole stood upright then

shoved a frustrated hand through his hair, anger pulsing from him like heat from a woodstove. "Not here," he ground out.

She looked into his angry eyes and said in a hurt whisper, "He really meant it then..."

Her throat went dry and she felt a hot tear slip down her cheek. Luke didn't love her anymore...he didn't even care enough to make sure she was okay. It was a hard pill to swallow, and something she couldn't face right now. Turning her face away from Cole, Cassie pulled the sheet up to her chin and closed her eyes.

She felt a thumb gently rub her cheek and then smelled the distinctive woodsy aftershave that Cole wore when he leaned next to her ear and said fiercely. "He loves you, Cassie. He's just hurt--he'll come around. Trust me, darlin'."

Well if he did, he sure had a fine way of showing it. No, she had a bad feeling in her stomach that Cole didn't know his best friend as well as he thought he did. Luke was sending her a message by not being here. And she'd received it loud and clear.

***

Luke paced back and forth in front of the fireplace in his living room. His hair was standing on end from the many times he'd run his hands through it waiting on Cole to call and give him an update on Cassie's condition. He wasn't related to her so the hospital wouldn't tell him anything.

It had been the hardest thing he'd ever done in his life to leave her in his best friend's care and not go to the hospital with her. But he'd had to do it. For his own sanity, he could not keep going on this emotional merry-go-round with her.

After he and Cole had a long talk about the situation with Cassie when they got back here last night, his friend had convinced him to give her another chance. To go after what he wanted, because obviously their ten year separation had all been a result of a misunderstanding.

By the time they finished talking, his anger and resentment toward Cassie had subsided, and he was on board with trying to work things out with her. They'd even formulated a plan to help him do that. He and Cole were going into the cattle business together....buying Carl Bellamy's herd.

Cole's intention was to invest his inheritance wisely, and Luke's goal was to set himself up where he made enough money to provide for Cassie properly...to feel like they were equals financially.

Then, Luke planned to sit her down and explain what happened that night, and see if she apologized for misjudging him. If she did, he hoped they'd be able to heal the past and see if there was a future for them. He'd thought maybe he'd finally be able to ask her to marry him, ten years too late.

Carl Bellamy agreeing to sell him the herd when he asked earlier today, meant he was able to check off his first goal. The man had been more than willing to sell him the herd and lease him the grazing land he'd need to work them. Truth be told, the old man looked relieved.

Luke knew that buying the cattle would help Cassie out and take some of the burden off her shoulders. That had been part of what drove him to the decision. Her daddy was getting on in years, and wouldn't be able to run the cattle part of the operation for much longer anyway. He also knew from his conversation with Bud and Carl that it was Cassie's dream to raise horses...not cattle.

His deal with Carl would help her do that much sooner than if they waited for the calving and sales. Carl and Bud had both told him that if Cassie was able to start the horse farm, she was planning on staying in Bowie. That news thrilled him, and made him determined to make sure she could do that sooner, rather than later.

It was like the sun, moon and stars were all aligning perfectly to help him.

Now, however, Luke realized it had all been a pipe dream. Instead of being open and receptive to him when he'd gone to the lake to find her and have that talk privately, she'd been the same way she'd been to him since her return to Bowie, hostile and unwelcoming. He finally faced the sad fact that she was never going to respect him.

To her, he'd always be that poor kid whose daddy was a drunk to her...the guy she'd simply given a few minutes of her time to make him feel like he was something special.

Luke meant what he'd said to her at the lake today. He was well and truly done chasing her. Being able to say that to her was supposed to bring him closure. Instead, she'd messed up his mind with her love words, then broke her ankle and probably cracked her skull. Now, all he felt was guilt.

Worry wrapped itself around his heart and squeezed painfully. "Call me, dammit," he said to the empty room.

Exhausted and wrung out, Luke sat down on the couch to wait after a while, and evidently dozed off, because the sound of the doorbell echoing loudly off the log walls of his cabin startled him awake.

His heart pounding inside his chest, Luke looked around disoriented for a moment, before he launched himself up and ran for the door. He flung it open and a very somber Cole stood on his porch with his hands fisted at his side, his jaw clenched.

Before he could invite him in, Cole marched past him, his shoulder slamming against Luke's as he did. Luke shut the door and followed him across the room. Glancing at the clock above the mantle Luke realized it was almost midnight. His friend should have been off-duty about six hours ago, but was still in his rumpled uniform.

"Did something else happen? Why the fuck didn't you call me? How's Cassie?" Luke asked in rapid succession as he walked to sit in a chair across from the sofa.

Cole didn't say anything, just stared at Luke with anger glittering in his green eyes, his lips pinched shut.

Panic raced through Luke and he shoved out of the chair and ran over to the couch to grab Cole by the shirt front. In a strangled voice he demanded, "What the fuck's wrong? Is Cassie okay?!"

Cole brushed his hands off then leaned forward to shout in his face, "If you were so fucking worried about Cassie's condition you should have been at the hospital. They kept her overnight for observation. I stayed until she was settled in a room." Cole pushed against his chest and Luke stepped back a few paces.

Cole knew why he couldn't go to the hospital, Luke had told him what had happened by the lake, and that as far as he was concerned he and Cassie were done-- permanently. That his friend didn't have more sympathy and understanding for him in this situation pissed him off.

"What did they say was wrong?" Luke asked his fists clenching at his side in frustration.

"Broken ankle and moderate concussion. They're watching her overnight to make sure her brain doesn't start swelling," Cole finally answered.

Panic edged back up inside Luke, but he tamped it down. "Did they say she'd be okay?"

"Yeah, they think she'll fully recover in a couple of weeks. But she needs rest, and that damned farm isn't the place for her to get that." Cole ran a hand across his face then sighed. "She's so fucking stubborn, she'll probably be out wrangling cattle in the cast they put on her leg."

"You're probably right." Luke knew he was right. Cassie was not one to sit on her laurels when there was work to be done. She was just as stubborn as her old man.

Resignation then determination filled Luke and he said before he could change his mind, "I'll take her up to your dad's fishing camp at the lake for a week."

Surprise and then wariness flickered across Cole's face. "I thought you didn't want to see her?"

He didn't...but there wasn't anyone else to take care of her. Imelda and Bud were pushovers where she was concerned, she'd run right over them. Her dad was laid up himself, so he couldn't do it.

"I don't, but I'm not a total asshole. I'll make sure she gets the rest she needs, then in a week I'll dump her ass back on the front porch of that ranch and walk away. Can you take care of helping Carl and Bud with the cattle for the week? Until we can get the paperwork done?"

"Since you're still on vacation for a week, that's gonna be kind of tough. I'll contact that manager Bud suggested though, and get him on board now instead of waiting. Then I'll go by there in the evenings and help out."

"Thanks, man. Do you know what time they're cutting her loose tomorrow?"

"They said the doctor makes rounds at eleven, and if she's okay, they'll probably release her around noon."

"I'll be there."

CHAPTER EIGHT

Cassie was tired of being poked and prodded. She wanted out of this godforsaken place now. The nurse had removed her IV earlier, and she was thankful. But she could probably use another painkiller because her head and ankle were starting to ache again.

The doctor who'd been in earlier to release her had given her a prescription for pain and another for nausea, but those pieces of paper sure wouldn't help until she could get them filled. She hoped Cole would get here soon to take her home.

The doctor had had also given her instructions on caring for her ankle and told her to rest as much as possible. But rest was not something that was going to happen. Even though she was banged up, she had a ranch to run, and her daddy to take care of. And she damned well wished Cole would get here soon so she could get to it.

Her eyes moved down over the green scrubs she'd put on to go home and she grimaced. Last night, they'd brought her here barefoot and in her bikini, so she didn't have any clothes or shoes to change into.

Thank god, the nurse had mercy on her and had brought the scrubs and a pair of surgical booties to wear, or she'd have had to ride home in that split-back hospital gown with her backside mooning the world. The nurse had slit the leg on the scrubs to accommodate the bulky florescent green walking cast they'd put on her leg. Her bikini was in a bag next to the chair where she was sitting.

Cassie glanced over at the utilitarian black and white clock hanging on the wall by the TV and saw it was almost noon. Surely, he'd be here to get her soon. She owed Cole a lot for helping her out last night. He had been there for her every step of the way, holding her hand, encouraging her to be cooperative when she'd gotten fussy, and comforting when thoughts of Luke made her weepy. His kiss on her cheek before he'd left her last night let her know that he cared about her.

More than she could say for Luke, who'd run out on her like his tail was on fire.

She looked up when a nurse came in smiling while she pushed a wheelchair over to Cassie. "Your ride's here, sugar."

Cassie grabbed the crutches they'd given her beside the chair and used them to push up to stand, then pivoted to sit in the wheelchair.

"Thank goodness. I'm ready to blow this popsicle stand!" she said then chuckled weakly.

Once she was seated, the nurse leaned over the wheel to release the brake. Or at least she thought it was the nurse, until she looked down and saw a muscular male arm beside her doing the job. Cassie looked over her shoulder expecting Cole, but saw Luke's unsmiling handsome face instead. She gasped, "Where's Cole?"

Luke didn't answer her question, he just stood back up then spun her around and pushed the chair toward the door at a swift clip. When they went past the nurse's station, the pretty nurse who'd brought in her chair smiled at him. "Be seeing you, sugar," she said to Luke and winked. "Hope you get to feeling better Miss Bellamy."

Cassie growled. Every woman on the planet must be susceptible to the man. Well, she wasn't going to be anymore. Let some other woman deal with him and his stubbornness. Luke said he was done...we'll she was about two clicks past that. "I asked you where Cole was. He was supposed to pick me up."

"He had other things to do," he told her flatly when he stopped at the steel door of the elevator and leaned over her to push the button.

Luke made it sound like she was totally inconveniencing him and everyone else, because she'd gotten hurt. "Push me back to the nurse's station, I'm calling a cab to take me home."

The double doors swung open and he pushed her inside instead, then jabbed his finger on the button for the main floor. Anger coiled up inside of her then unfurled in her chest.

"Ah, hell no..." Cassie pushed herself up from the chair and put a crutch under either arm. Pain shot through her ankle, but other than a grimacing, she ignored it. He was not going to bully her around anymore. And she was not going to be trapped in the truck with this angry hard man from Henrietta to Bowie. No way.

"What the hell are you doing, Cassie?" His hands gripped her shoulders tightly. "Sit your ass back down before hurt yourself."

"If you haven't noticed, I'm already hurt. Not that you'd give a shit," she said heatedly. "I'm going to call a cab to take me home. Any obligation you felt to help me is unnecessary. I'll call Cole and thank him for his help last night and pay him for his trouble."

A muscle worked at his jaw as he ground his teeth then spat, "Cole doesn't need your fucking money, and neither do I."

"Fine then." she said and hobbled past him when the door opened. "Goodbye, Luke."

Cassie had gotten about half way to the information desk and a phone, when her feet were suddenly taken out from under her as Luke swept her up into his arms. Her crutches fell to the floor with a loud clatter and a woman in a pink striped uniform ran over to them.

Luke smiled at her then asked sweetly, "Can you bring those for me, sugar?" The girl nodded then he headed toward the exit with his arms tightly around Cassie.

"Put me down, now!" she grated next to his ear.

Luke ignored her taking long easy strides toward the door, then went outside to his truck which was parked in the circular drive designated for patient pick-up.

The young woman who'd walked beside them opened

the door for him, and he put her on the hot leather seat, then leaned over and jerked the seatbelt across her and clicked it. He slammed the door, took her crutches from the candy-striper and threw them in the back of the truck before stomping around the truck to get behind the wheel.

"You do know that kidnapping is illegal, right Sheriff?" Cassie turned toward him to ask.

"Yeah, it's a good thing you're not a kid, Cassie. So stop acting like one."

She harrumphed and then sat back against the seat and crossed her arms over her chest. All the jarring she'd been through while he carried her, then the jarring when he dropped her on the seat, and now the pot-holed road leading from the hospital, made her leg ache.

Cassie reached a hand down and rubbed her knee, because the cast prevented her from rubbing where it really hurt. It also felt like her ankle was starting to swell inside the cast. It had gotten tighter than it had been when she woke up this morning, and her toes were numb again.

He glanced over at her and asked, "Hurting?"

"Yeah, I should probably have it propped up." She groaned as he hit another hole and the truck lurched.

He glanced at her and then back to the road a few times, before telling her gruffly, "Lay down on the seat and put your leg in my lap."

"No, thank you." She'd endure the pain before she got that close to his lap, or any other part of his body, ever again.

With his knuckles turning white on the steering wheel, he glanced over at her again and shouted, "Quit being stubborn, Cassie! Just do it!"

She scooted her butt to the edge of the seat and pivoted so she could lay down then lifted her left leg up. The cast was too heavy and when she groaned, he slid a hand under her knee and pulled it up for her, then moved his hand to the top of her thigh to hold it steady. Her other leg, bent beside the seat, rubbed on his calf. Cassie swallowed hard as his heat burned through the thin scrub pants to brand her skin.

Once she was settled, he looked down at her with concern in his whiskey-brown eyes. "Better?"

Cassie huffed out a breath and tried to relax. "Yeah, thanks." He gently patted her thigh then rubbed it, his long fingers sliding along the inside seam of the thin scrubs. She swallowed down the needy moan that wanted to escape from her lips as electric sparks of desire traveled up her leg to her center. What she wouldn't give for him to move his hand up, just a little, and put her out of her misery.

She covered her eyes with her arm, so he wouldn't see the desire she knew must be revealed there, and so she didn't have to look at his handsome profile for the next eighty miles.

When the bouncing finally stopped, and she heard the humming of the truck tires on asphalt, she guessed they'd finally reached the main road. The monotonous drone and cool air blowing from the vent on her face, worked together to lull her to sleep.

Cassie eased into a hot dream where she imagined Luke's hand had traveled up higher on her leg, and he was whispering words of love and longing while he brought her to a spectacular climax.

When the truck started bouncing again, and Luke's hand tightened on her thigh Cassie was jarred awake. "We home?" she asked him, her heart pounding, as she let go of her erotic dream reluctantly, then sleepily rubbed her eyes.

"Just be still..." he said quietly without looking at her, and absently stroked her thigh again.

She laid perfectly still, but dug her nails into her palm, as the lustful urges that had been increased tenfold by her dream ramped up even more. She sucked in a breath and let it out along with a little mewl.

His gaze swung to hers and he raised one dark brow in question.

Breathlessly, she told him, "Either move your hand off my thigh or finish the job."

Both eyebrows shot toward his hairline over eyes that were filled with molten heat, then a grin kicked up the corners of his mouth and his dimple popped out, causing her mouth to go dry.

"I'd be happy to darlin'," he murmured in a sexy drawl then skimmed his fingers up the seam of the scrubs until he reached the spot that was aching for his touch at the V there. His fingers hovered over her lightly and she could feel the heat of them just millimeters from where she wanted them. Cassie gasped and licked her lips then lifted her hips toward his hand trying to increase the contact.

Instead of touching her though, his grin widened then he lifted his hand and placed it on the steering wheel and turned his focus to the road.

What a bastard, she thought! and jerked to a sitting position. He yelped and grabbed himself when the heel of her cast caught him in the crotch when she pulled her leg off of him.

Cassie smiled evilly then scooted to her side of the truck and jerked the seatbelt back in place across her chest. Served the bastard right if she'd flattened his nuts to pancakes. He deserved it for teasing her like that.

"Guess I'll have to see if Cole's up for finishing the job then. He seems to be the one who cleans up all your messes," she taunted then crossed her arms under her breasts.

Cassie heard a rumbling in his chest, then he slapped his hand against the steering wheel, and steered the truck to the shoulder of the road. Cars whizzed past them as he turned and gave her a hard look. She pushed back as far as she could against the door, and looked at him.

His eyes were like a black hole dragging her inside to drown her in his misery and anger. She couldn't ever remember seeing Luke this angry. His face was mottled red and his lips were peeled back over his teeth as he snarled, "You stay the fuck away from Cole, do you hear me? He doesn't need you messing with his head like you're doing with mine. The only messes he's cleaned up are the ones you created."

God, why was she always antagonizing him? Even when he was trying to help her, she needled him just to get a rise. Probably because if she kept him angry, she didn't have to deal with her feelings about the softer side of Luke. The one that made her want to curl up against his chest and kiss him like she used to and tell him that she loved him.

And his walking away yesterday, the finality of it, had opened her eyes wide to the fact that she did still love him. As much as his actions made her hate him sometimes.

If she wanted him to open up and tell her what he'd meant by his shocking words at the lake yesterday, she needed to rein in her mouth and do more listening.

Her lower lip trembled when she told him, "I'm sorry...I didn't mean it. You know Cole and I are just friends."

Luke took a deep breath then blew it out slowly, seeming as if he were trying to control his anger. He dropped his eyes from hers to look at his hand where it was fisted on his thigh. "Cassie, I can't do this with you anymore...."

She undid her seatbelt and scooted over toward him on the seat until she sat right beside him. She put her hand over his on the fist on his thigh. "Do what, Luke?"

His chin wasn't too steady when he looked into her eyes. His throat muscles worked a couple of times and then he said, "Can't love you anymore. It's driving me crazy....you're driving me crazy. One minute you're hot, the next you freeze me out. I just can't take it anymore. That's why I didn't come to the hospital last night."

He shook his head, pulled his hand from under hers then turned back to face the steering wheel. "Shove over, I'm taking you home."

She gasped, and jerked the keys from the ignition, before tossing them on the dash.

"No--you're gonna listen to me for a second first," she told him forcefully.

Luke's fists clenched on the wheel, and he didn't look at her, or say a word. His face was hard and his jaw worked as he gritted his teeth.

Cassie knew she had to frame her words right or he was going to shut her down and take her home. She hesitated a second contemplating, then said, "I told you yesterday that I still love you. I meant it, Luke." She leaned up and put her hands on the side of his face to make him look at her.

The emptiness in his eyes made her stutter, "T-t-here's a lot we need to work out between us, I know. A lot that needs to be said. It would have probably been said by now if I hadn't been so stubborn and ornery. I haven't given you much of a chance to say anything, I've been so busy fighting with you."

His lips were a flat line and he still didn't say a word. She rubbed her thumb along the muscle ticking in his jaw. "I'm sorry for that...truly sorry. I'll give you that chance Luke, if you still want to talk," she told him and then leaned forward and pressed her lips against his tenderly. "I don't want to fight with you anymore," she whispered against his unsmiling mouth.

She eased back down on the seat and moved her hand down over his chest to cover his heart. It was beating like a ticking bomb, which told her wasn't as unaffected by her touch or what she'd said as he was trying to appear.

A little ray of hope parted the dark cloud of hopelessness inside her. "Say something, Luke."

She saw his Adam's apple bob a couple of times, then he said, "Okay, Cassie, I'll give it one more chance, but that's it." He didn't sound like agreeing to that made him very happy, or that he held much hope it'd work out.

Well, she had enough hope for the both of them.

"I only need one more darlin'," she told him and leaned up to give him one more quick kiss before she scooted back on her side of the truck.

After one more intense look, he reached up on the dash and grabbed the keys. Luke seemed to be deep in thought the rest of the ride to Bowie, and she didn't break the thoughtful silence with needless words.

She'd said her piece, and thank god he'd listened...and agreed to try to untangle their issues. Her heart was lighter than it had been in several days.

When Luke passed the turnoff to the ranch, and kept going down the main road, she glanced over at him. "You just missed the turn."

"We're not going to the ranch."

"So where are you taking me then?" she asked and chuckled. "You really kidnapping me?"

He glanced over at her with a teasing glint in his eyes. "Hey, you accused me of it, and put the thought in my head. It's always been my fantasy to kidnap a hot blonde and tie her to my bed. Guess it's about time I give it a go."

She felt blood rush to her face and moisture to other body parts. His low sexy voice vibrated in her ears and then sparks of desire traveled along her nerve endings straight to her core.

Visions of the big handsome lawman handcuffing her to his bed and doing wild and wonderful things to her danced through her head. Her heart kicked, her breathing picked up and she pinched her thighs together to stop the throbbing there. It had been a long time since sex had been anywhere near wild and wonderful for her. About ten years now.

As delicious as that sounded though, she couldn't forget her responsibilities at the ranch. "Luke, I really need to go to the ranch. Dad--"

"Cole is handling the cows. And a nurse showed up for your daddy yesterday after you left for the lake. Bud and the other guys hauled in the equipment she brought with her, and Imelda helped her set it up. You don't need to worry...just relax for a change."

She heaved a relieved sigh and settled back against the seat. "I owe you and Cole so much, Luke. Thank ya'll for all you've have done since I've been back. I've been too stubborn to tell you that."

"You're welcome," he sounded surprised.

A few minutes later, she realized they were near the lake. She flipped off the air conditioner and rolled down her window to inhale the rich fishy smell that always hung in the air. She pulled the rubber band from her hair and ran her fingers through it as the wind whipped her hair into a frenzy. She laughed then asked, "So this fantasy of yours...it includes the lake?"

"Lake house," he corrected. "We're going to the place Cole's daddy left him on the other side of the lake."

She squealed, then wished she hadn't when pain pierced her brain and a wave of nausea rolled over her. "Oh god, I thought that was gone," she said and leaned over her knees.

"What the lake house?" he asked in confusion looking over at her.

"No--the headache that makes me want to throw up," she told him and groaned when another pain throbbed inside her skull. "Jesus, Luke..."

"What can I do to help? Need me to pull over?"

"No, I just need to get the prescriptions the doctor gave me filled. They're in the bag I have with me, but the pharmacy is way back in town. I forgot." She didn't forget, she just hadn't planned on getting them filled or taking them. Cassie didn't like the out-of-control loopy feeling pain medication gave her. She never took it.

"That's not a problem. Let me get you to the cabin and settled, then I'll go back to town for it. I need to buy some groceries anyway."

She smiled her thanks as she sat back up and leaned her head against the seat, letting the brisk wind from the window cool her skin. "I'm sorry I'm such a pain in the butt."

"I like your butt," he said and chuckled. "Just relax, cupcake. If you remember how to do that."

It had been a long time since she'd relaxed, but she thought she could remember how. If she could just get her head to stop pounding, and her stomach to stop heaving, maybe she'd be able to do it.

They pulled up in front of a cozy little wood cottage painted bright yellow with green shutters. The front door was by stark contrast, painted bright red.

Cassie hadn't been here before, so she let her gaze wander around the yard. Two canoes were leaned up against the side of the house, and she saw a floating dock on the water down a hill behind the house. A small aluminum motorboat sat tied to the dock. There was a huge deck on the backside of the house, but she could only see a portion of it.

Luke hopped out of the truck and shut his door. As she picked up her bag and reached for the handle on her door, it was flung open and then he was standing there reaching inside for her. Before she could say anything, Luke pulled her into his arms then kicked the door shut.

"There are probably holes in the ground around here, and I don't want you hurting yourself again," he said by way of explanation as he walked with her up to the porch. He shifted her weight, then used one hand to open the door then carried her inside.

He didn't put her down once they were inside the cabin though, he just walked swiftly across the large room and turned down a short narrow hallway to the right. "You can put me down now you know. They put a ball on the bottom of the cast, so I can walk on it."

"Ain't happening, darlin'," he said and stopped at a last door on the left at the end of the short hall. Once he managed to open it, he walked across the room and gently laid her on a huge king-sized bed covered in a wedding ring quilt. "There you go." Luke smiled at her.

She sat up on her elbows and said in a whiny voice, "Luke I can't stay in bed all day."

Luke put his hands on his hips and smiled sexily. "I'll bet I could give you reasons to like it...when you're feeling better, of course."

Blood rushed to her face and her mouth went dry. She would love nothing better than to have him demonstrate that incentive, but she knew he wouldn't, because she was hurt. "Can't I go out on the back porch instead?"

"Not today, honey, you need to rest. Now lay back," he ordered and pushed her shoulders into the mattress. When he leaned across her to grab two of the other pillows on the bed his chest brushed against her breasts. Cassie sucked in a breath and held it while her nipples hardened to sharp points and darts of desire coursed through her.

He raised back up with the pillows in his hand, and she let the air trapped in her lungs escape slowly, but the tingles remained as did the sexual tension between them. She met his eyes and they glittered with desire telling her he was just as aware of her as she was of him.

With hands that trembled slightly, he bent to lift her cast and put two pillows beneath her leg. "That ought to help with the swelling," he told her and moved to squeeze her numb toes. "Your toes are icy and blue darlin', you need to keep that leg propped up, or we're going to have to go get it checked out again. I think you've got some swelling going on."

"Thank you...doctor," she said saucily and gave him a heated stare. "That's one of my fantasies, you know...playing doctor with you. So let's throw that in the mix with the kidnapping."

Luke growled and sat down on the bed then leaned toward her. "We'll throw in anything you like honey, and a lot more. We have a lot of catchin' up to do."

Capturing her mouth with his in a heated kiss, Luke

coaxed her lips to open, then sealed his lips to hers and devoured her mouth. Heat poured through her and she put her arms around his neck, and kissed him with everything that had been pent up in her for weeks. It felt like she was finally home.

After a few moments, he pulled back from her and sat up breathing hard. Her eyes traveled down his chest to his fly and she noticed his breathing wasn't the only thing that was hard. She moved her hand to his thigh and then slid it upward. When she reached her destination, he placed his hand on top of hers, held it there and groaned.

"Not yet, cupcake." His voice was low and gravelly.

She squeezed his steely length and tried to move her hand against him, but he pulled it away from him and up to his mouth where kissed her palm.

"We'll get there soon, but you need to rest now...and I've got to go to town." He stood and gave her a quick kiss, moving away before she could grab him for more. "I won't be gone long."

He took his cell phone out of his pocket and left it on the night stand for her. "Cole is number one on speed dial. Call him or 911 if you need something."

She smiled at his thoughtfulness. Her cell phone was in the tote bag she'd had with her yesterday, probably still down by the lake where they'd been.

"I need to go get my tote bag from our spot at the lake. My phone is in there," she told him, hoping he'd go get it for her.

"Cole picked it up and has it in his SUV for you. I'll get it back from him."

"Thanks," she said and watched his muscular jean-clad butt as he turned and left her. She sighed dreamily.

***

Luke dug Cassie's prescriptions out of the plastic bag she'd left the hospital with and dropped them off at the

Bowie Pharmacy, telling Clyde the pharmacist he'd be back by in a little while to pick them up.

When Clyde looked at the name on the prescriptions, he asked if they were for Carl's daughter, and when Luke said yes, that led to a lengthy conversation about what had happened to her and then to how Carl was getting along. It had about taken an Act of Congress for him to get away from the chatty man.

Finally, Luke got back to the truck and glanced at the dash clock and groaned. He had already been gone an hour and a half, and still hadn't made it to the grocery store. He'd told Cassie he wasn't going to be gone long, and he didn't like leaving her out there alone. She was hurt and immobile. He'd be quick at the grocery and get back to her.

The big pink pig on the sign at the grocery store waved at him when he pulled into the parking lot. A parking spot opened up near the front door, and he gunned the truck to get there before someone else did. This store stayed pretty busy, because it was the only one in town. To get a prime parking spot usually meant you were living right.

Luke slid out of the truck and went inside. He grabbed a buggy and headed directly to the produce section. You couldn't cook without proper seasonings, and a salad and baked potato with the steaks he planned to grill for them tonight sounded great.

He was perusing the tomatoes, when someone stepped up beside him, and then an angry male voice grated, "Hello, asshole, where's Cassie?"

Luke dropped the tomato to turn and face the name caller, his hand automatically reaching for the butt of the weapon he wasn't wearing. He dropped it to his side. "I think she said all she had to say to you the other night, didn't she *asshole*?"

James, Cassie's ex-fiancé, didn't look quite as slick as he had two nights ago at the restaurant. His khakis were wrinkled and dirty and had about two inches of dirt up the legs from the hem. His formerly pristine green polo shirt had stains under the arms and it was ripped at the sleeve. The thick brown hair he'd had perfectly slicked back with gel the other night was sticking up in every direction, and he had a two-day old growth of beard on his face. Luke wanted to laugh. If Cassie could see him now, she probably would too.

"I went by the farm and her old man wouldn't tell me where she is. I saw how she stared you down at the restaurant the other night, and saw you at the lake with her," he said accusingly.

Luke stepped into the man's personal space and ground out, "Are you stalking her? How the hell would you know she was at the lake?" Luke had panicked for a minute thinking he meant he knew she was there now, but then he realized he meant when they were there the other day. The asshole must've followed her.

The man, who was a couple of inches shorter than Luke, and about fifty pounds lighter, took a step closer to him, and put a brazen finger in Luke's chest. "Just tell me where she is...our business is none of your business."

Luke pushed the man with the foul breath back from him then grated, "You don't have business with Cassie anymore. The best thing you can do is get out of town, bud."

James snorted then said, "It's a free country, I'll leave when I damned well please. Who are you anyway telling me what to do?"

"I'm the Sheriff," Luke informed him then leaned down to within inches of his face. "And I think you following Cassie to the lake constitutes stalking, and your visit to the Double B was trespassing. So if you don't want your ass thrown in jail, I suggest you get out of my face, and out of Bowie right now."

The other man's face paled, but he didn't back down. "I'm not leaving until she talks to me. She owes me an explanation...and a hell of a lot more than that...and I'm going to get it, one way or another." Luke saw a strange glitter in the man's eyes that bothered him. This guy was one pancake short of a stack.

Luke grabbed him by the shirt collar and jammed him into the potato bin. "She doesn't owe you a fucking thing. You want to know why she broke up with you? Because for one you're a smarmy city-boy asshole. And secondly, she loves me--*she's mine*--and you leave her the fuck alone. Is that clear?"

A crowd had gathered around them now, and Luke looked around at the familiar faces, he'd sworn to protect and swallowed hard. He let James go and took two steps back. James jerked his collar straight, before he said loudly, pandering to the crowd, "Why Sheriff, I think that constitutes assault, and I wish to press charges."

That's all Luke needed right now. Why did he let this asshole goad him into grabbing him? Because he was a threat to the woman Luke loved. Luke would probably lose his job over this one, the mayor and city council weren't going to be happy.

Luke flinched when he saw Cole push through the crowd then come to stand beside him giving him a lethal stare. He didn't say a word to his friend, he turned his back to him and put his wrists behind him. The cold metal cuffs snapped shut, and he felt Cole squeeze them hard to tighten them, before he pushed him up against the apple display and searched him while he read him his rights.

When Cole was done, Luke told him loudly. "Arrest him too, he poked me in the chest and threatened Cassie. He also trespassed on Carl Bellamy's property."

"They haven't pressed charges, Luke. I can't arrest him, you know that." He turned to the crowd and asked, "Did anyone see him poke Luke in the chest?" Luke saw them all shake their heads negatively and groaned. "Sorry bud, can't do it, but you can file a complaint if you want when we get to the station."

The crowd erupted in a flurry of conversation as Cole

grabbed his arm and led him away. He heard James the asshole snickering, and he wanted to beg Cole to let him go so he could at least make the assault charge with worth it.

When they walked outside, Cole led him to the SUV and gave him the full criminal treatment by putting his hand on top of his head and shoving him into the backseat roughly. Luke couldn't keep his balance and wound up laying across the seat. He deserved it and more for being so damned stupid.

Now, Cassie was at the lake house alone, and the asshole was on the loose. Panic surged through him and he sat up and leaned his forehead against the wire cage in front of him.

"Get someone out to the lake house to keep an eye on Cassie," Luke demanded. "Call her on my cell and warn her that James is still in town and may be stalking her."

Cole looked him in the eye in the rearview mirror, and said. "You're not the Sheriff right now Luke. Sit back and quit giving me orders."

Luke gritted his teeth. "He fucking threatened Cassie, Cole. He's been stalking her. Please, do it," he begged.

"She's fine, Luke. He doesn't know where she is."

Luke slammed himself back against the seat and growled his frustration.

CHAPTER NINE

Gingerly, Cassie got out of the bed and went to look for the bathroom. Luke had been gone a long time, much longer than she'd expected, and her bladder couldn't wait any longer for him to get back to help her to the bathroom. If he'd just left her crutches, she'd have been golden, but he'd forgotten to get them from the back of his truck.

Using one hand on the wall to steady herself, Cassie picked her way down the hall, then balanced with her outspread arms across the living room and teetered toward a door near the kitchen that must be the bath.

In the very quiet house she heard the faint ring of Luke's cell phone down the hall, and thought about trying to get back to pick it up, but knew it would go to voicemail before she got there. Whoever it was, she hoped it was Luke, she'd call them back when she managed to hobble back to the bedroom.

It took her fifteen minutes to take care of her business and get back to the bedroom. Being stiff and sore made every step she took torturous. Her ankle was hurting now, and she wished Luke would get back with her pain pills. Although she didn't like taking them, she was going to make an exception this time.

She sat down on the bed with an exhausted sigh and reached for the cell phone. The only missed call she saw was from Cole, so that must have been him on the phone. She noticed that there wasn't much of a charge left on the phone, and wondered if Luke had left a charger laying around here somewhere. There was no way she was going to go looking for it though, that much she knew. She'd wait until he got back and ask him.

Pushing the number one, she brought the phone to her ear and heard it ringing. It rang five or six times then she heard Cole's deep-timbered voice on the recording asking her to leave a message. She disconnected, figuring he'd call her again when he had time. Luke had been gone a long time, but she wasn't really worried about him yet, because he'd had a lot of errands to run. It was almost dusk now, and she'd start worrying if he wasn't back after dark.

As soon as her head hit the pillow, her stomach growled noisily, and she realized she was damned hungry. She hadn't eaten since the bland breakfast she'd had at the hospital this morning. Dreading it, but knowing she had no choice, Cassie got to her feet again to go to the kitchen and see if she could scrounge up something to eat.

She should have gone to the kitchen when she went to pee, but hindsight was twenty-twenty. Cassie stood and leaned back to pick up the cell phone then dropped it in the pocket of the scrub shirt. At least, she'd remembered to bring that with her this time.

As she made her way slowly down the hall, Cassie flipped on lights, because the interior of the cottage was getting very dark, and she didn't want to trip over something, and break her other leg. Cassie chuckled amazed at what a klutz she'd become lately.

She hadn't had a broken bone in her life, and now she'd fallen off a horse and almost broken her neck, and then tripped on a tree root and broken her damned ankle...all within a couple of weeks.

When she reached the kitchen, she turned on the light and made her way to the pantry then flung it open. There was one can of hot dog chili and a box of strawberry toaster pastries. Other than that, the cupboard was bare. No wonder Luke was taking so long grocery shopping. She grabbed a silver wrapped package from the box of pastries then decided to check the refrigerator.

The phone in her pocket chimed and vibrated at the same time, sending strange tingles through her chest. She giggled and pulled it out then pressed talk. "Hello."

"Cassie?" Cole's voice sounded tired and agitated.

"Yeah, it's me, Hopalong Bellamy." She heard him

snort on the other end of the line, and chuckled. "What's up?"

He groaned and then told her, "Luke's in jail, and James is still in town."

Her legs turned to rubber, she wobbled then almost fell down, and would have if she didn't drop the Pop Tart and grab hold of the counter. "You threw Luke in jail?!" she screamed incredulously into the phone.

"I had to. He did something really stupid in front of a lot of witnesses."

"What did he do?"

"James saw him at the Piggly Wiggly and gave him a hard time. Supposedly, he told Luke he'd followed you to the lake and that he'd been out to the ranch and Luke went off on him."

"Going off on him isn't a crime."

"No, but jerking him up by the throat against the potato bin is."

"Oh, crap..." Cassie groaned but hysterical laughter bubbled up inside her as a mental picture of the scene formed in her brain. Then she sobered and asked, "So James is stalking me?"

"Looks that way. You wanna press charges?"

"Damned right I do." She wasn't letting that asshole press charges against the man she loved and not return the favor.

"Good, I'll be there in twenty minutes to pick you up." Cole sounded excited and relieved for some reason. "Think your daddy might want to press charges for trespassing?"

"Yup, I know he will. He hates James."

Cole chuckled then said, "We'll stop by the Double B then on the way back to the station."

Cassie let out a whoop then told him, "That sucker isn't getting away with this. He ain't seen Texas justice yet, but he's about to get a taste of it! I'm surprised my daddy didn't fill him up with squirrel shot when he went over there."

"Me too, darlin'...glad he saved him for me. I'm going to enjoy throwing that asshole in jail."

Cassie laughed and said, "See you in a few." She hung up the phone, tossed it back in her pocket, then reached down to pick up her dinner.

***

Luke shoved a hand through his hair and made another circuit in the jail cell mumbling as he cursed himself for getting locked up, cursed James for goading him into doing what made him get arrested, and finally he cursed Cole for throwing him in here and refusing to protect Cassie.

Cole hadn't even called the judge so he could set bail, and Luke could get out. He was just being a dick because he was pissed at Luke. His ex-best friend would probably let him simmer in here all night.

Luke had no idea what time it was, but he figured it had to be close to midnight. When Cole had finally taken statements from James and several other witnesses, and booked him, it was around seven, and that was hours ago. It felt like an eternity, and evidently it could be another before he was released. He didn't care about himself, but he was worried about Cassie.

Hearing keys clank against the main door to the holding pen, Luke ran to the bars to see if it was Cole or someone who could help him get out of here. He took a shocked step back when he saw Cole leading James down the corridor in handcuffs.

James had a split lip, and bloody nose, and Luke wondered who'd finally had the honor of punching the bastard in the face. He should have done it at the grocery, instead of just grabbing him.

Cole gave him a meaningful stare and then his lips quirked up at the corner smugly, when they passed by.

Luke smiled at their backs knowing that his best friend had been the one to pick up his slack. Like always. He shouldn't have doubted him.

After he shoved a very quiet James in a cell, and locked the door, Cole strutted back up the corridor and stopped at Luke's cell. "Called Judge. He said to release you on your own recognizance for now, and he refused the charges until we see what happens. I told him the situation." He nodded his head back toward James cell.

Luke gave him a tight smile of thanks and grabbed his shoulder through the bars. Cole nodded then put the key in the door and let him out. "Cassie's waiting for you up front," he told him with a pat on the back. Luke stumbled out of the cell then walked quickly toward the gate down the corridor.

When he finally walked into the outer booking area, he saw Cassie sitting in one of the hard plastic visitor chairs, slouched over, her chin resting on her chest as she snored softly. His heart twisted in his chest and love for her poured through every part of his soul. He walked over and sat beside her and gently nudged her shoulder then rubbed his thumb over her cheek.

"Wake up, Sleeping Beauty," Luke said gently.

"I went and got her medicine from the pharmacy before they closed. She took a pain pill, so she's pretty out of it," Cole said standing beside his chair.

Luke's voice was choked when he turned to Cole and said, "I can't thank you enough, man."

"No thanks needed...I've got to go. Call me if you need me, and tell Cassie I said goodnight." Cole turned to leave then looked back once more. "Oh, and your truck is out front, I had someone drive it over here from Piggly Wiggly. I put the suitcase she packed while we were at the ranch in the back." Cole reached into his pocket and tossed him the keys.

"Jesus, Cole...you're my knight in brown khaki. I think I'm in love." Luke chuckled and winked at his friend.

"Yeah, yeah...you're in love alright, but not with me," Cole's eyes wandered to Cassie then back to Luke's. "Take care man, and stay out of trouble!" He gave Luke one more meaningful stare then turned and walked away.

Watching his friend's retreating back, Luke reached over beside him and pulled Cassie over onto his lap and held her against his chest. He noticed she'd changed from the green scrubs into cut-off shorts and a pink tank top.

She must've done that while she was at the ranch with Cole, he thought. He was glad she had a chance to pack some stuff. Those green scrubs she'd left the hospital in were the only thing she'd had with her and they weren't going to last the week they were going to stay at the cabin.

The beautiful, blue-eyed angel in his arms looked up at him with a sleepy smile. "Luuuuke," she said as if they'd been apart for years this time and not hours, then put her arms around him and snuggled into his neck, placing light kisses there. "I missed you."

It kinda sounded like she meant all those years they'd been apart. He smiled, maybe he was finally getting the welcome he'd wanted that first day he'd seen her again.

"I missed you too, sugar...a lot," he told her then gave her a squeeze. "And I'm sorry you had to get dragged out here for this mess when you should be resting." He stood up with her in his arms. "Let's get you back to bed."

"Mmm...." she purred and snuggled into him again. "Only if you're there with me this time."

"Oh, I plan to be, darlin'," he drawled. "Just as soon as I can scrub this jailhouse stench off of me."

Cassie stuck her nose up against his neck and he heard her inhale deeply. "You smell pretty good to me, darlin'," she said then he felt her small but deadly tongue lick up his neck to his ear. "Taste pretty damned good too."

He shivered and then missed a step on his way across the parking lot to his truck, his jeans feeling suddenly too tight. She giggled near his ear. Leaning his head down, he gave her a loud kiss on the lips and then whispered over them, "Stop that sugar, or I'm gonna drop you on your ass."

"No you won't," she told him then looked up into his eyes seriously, "I trust you." Her eyelids flickered then she closed them and snored softly against his chest His heart did a little dance in his chest then settled.

Luke had waited a long time to hear those words, and wished like hell they weren't given now, while she was under the influence of narcotics. If she said them to him sober, he'd believe her, and believe he was one step closer to having her respect. Their key to forever. He shook his head and opened the door of his truck to gently deposit her limp, sleeping body on the front seat and buckle her in.

They had a long road ahead of them to get to forever, but Luke was hopeful again. Spending this week alone with her should be a good start for their new beginning, as long as what she'd said to him about wanting to try to work things out was true, and as long as he didn't lose his job and his freedom over his latest screw up.

If he did, it didn't look like he was going down alone. He chuckled thinking of how sullen and bruised James Barton had looked when Cole had incarcerated him. He knew he'd been released because she and her daddy had pressed charges against James.

The state motto of his home state flitted though his mind. "Don't mess with Texas..." and then he looked over at Cassie and added mentally, "Women." Texas women would chew you up and spit you out like a plug of cheap tobacco.

On the drive back to the cabin, Luke saw an all night convenience store and pulled in. He was starving, because he and Cassie hadn't eaten lunch or dinner...that he knew of anyway.

Cole might have picked her up something while they were out, but his friend hadn't given Luke the same consideration. He'd meant for Luke to suffer, while he was in the pokey, and he had done a good job of making him miserable.

Luke didn't want to wake Cassie, so he eased out of the truck and softly shut the door then walked inside and picked up a couple of pre-made sandwiches from the cooler, a couple of bags of chips, and some items for their breakfast tomorrow. He'd make his second attempt at a grocery shopping trip tomorrow morning after they ate. Hopefully, it'd go better than his last one. Luke chuckled, paid the cashier and walked back to the truck. He saw Cassie sitting up stretching.

Opening the door he hefted the two full bags onto the seat between them, and then jumped inside. "You hungry, sleepyhead?" Luke asked her digging around in the bags for the sandwiches and chips.

She yawned and nodded taking the sandwich he offered her then she grabbed a bag of nacho chips she saw sticking out the top of the other bag. "Thanks. Are we almost back to the lake?"

"Yep. Not too far," he said and started unwrapping his sandwich.

He glanced over at her and saw she was looking out the window staring upward. "The sky is beautiful tonight. Lots of stars out..." she told him.

"Yeah, a full moon too." He'd noticed that earlier when they'd left the station. It probably explained all the crazy shit that happened to him today. It felt like there had been two solid weeks of full moons.

He felt her eyes on him and looked at her again. "What?" he asked her raising an eyebrow.

"Are you tired?"

"Tired, but too keyed up to sleep probably." No probably about it. What Luke had been through today had him wound tighter than a two dollar watch. "Your head hurting? Ankle?"

"Nah, the pain pill took the edge off, I'm good now." She smiled at him, a small secretive smile that had him wondering what she was thinking about. He didn't have to wonder long. "If we go to our spot for a picnic, you think you can carry me down to the water?"

"Hell, yeah." Luke would carry her fifteen miles if it meant they could spend time stargazing like they used to. It would also give him a chance to clear his head, so he had some hope of falling asleep tonight. It was around one o'clock in the morning, but a couple hours of relaxing would probably do them both good.

"Great idea, darlin'."

She gave him a wide smile and rewrapped her sandwich then asked, "Got a blanket?"

"Yep always carry one behind my seat for emergencies. Does this qualify?" He rewrapped his too and put it in the bag.

"Damned straight it does. Let's get going."

Luke didn't have to be told twice. He shoved the keys into the ignition and peeled out of the parking lot. When they reached the secluded spot that held so many memories for him, he parked at the road then reached behind the seat to pull out the blanket and unfolded it to put their food in there. He handed her a soft drink then put one in the blanket for him and tied it hobo-style and put his arm through the loop.

He slid out of the truck and walked around to her door and opened it. Excitement poured off of her as she scooted to the edge of the seat and put her arms around his neck. He slid his arm under her knees, lifted her into his arms then kicked the door shut.

"We're gonna have to go slow. It'll be darker in the woods, and I don't want to trip over a tree root," he said sarcastically and winked at her.

She slugged him in the shoulder and he laughed. Luke walked down the path and into the woods, darkened by the thick canopy of trees that blocked the moonlight. Night creatures sang their songs, their music sweet to his ears. It was a tune he hadn't heard at this particular place for ten years.

When they reached the decline down to the rocks, he went sideways carefully picking his way to the bottom. The scene when he exited the woods into the night was breathtaking.

The moon was a huge glowing orb bathing everything around them in soft iridescent yellow light. It shone off the water lapping gently at the shoreline below, creating one of the most romantic settings Luke had ever seen. He hadn't been back here in the moonlight in ten years, and he knew why.

This was his and Cassie's special place...the place where they'd fallen in love...and he hadn't wanted to share it with anyone else, or relive those memories. Until now.

Luke swallowed hard against the emotions churning inside of him, then walked over beside a huge flat rock that hung over the edge of the cliff and sat her down there.

"You doing okay, darlin'?"

"Perfect." she said and gazed at him dreamily with her moonlit eyes. He unwound the blanket and set the food beside her on the rock, then shook out the blanket spreading it on the ground, before placing the food in the middle.

He picked her up in his arms again and set her down on one corner of the blanket then dropped down beside her. "Your buffet is served, ma'am," he said and handed her sandwich to her.

He watched her dig in hungrily, and he did the same and was just about done with his chips too, when she took a long sip of her Coke then asked out of the blue, "Were you really going to ask me to marry you, Luke?"

The chip he'd just popped into his mouth lodged in his throat and he coughed and pounded his chest to break it loose. When it finally dislodged and traveled on down, he took a drink of his soda too then looked her directly in the eyes, "Yes, I really was...the night you left."

Her only response to his pronouncement was a jerky nod. Still holding his eyes, she lifted her drink to her mouth again and took another long sip. His eyes traveled along the smooth contour of her throat as she swallowed. The urge to kiss her neck was strong inside of him. He wanted to feel that soft skin on his lips and the quick little pulse that he noticed jumping there.

Luke licked the salt from the chips off his lips and asked a question of his own, "Did you see me at the dock with Becca Harvey that night?"

He watched as the moonlight caught on tears that welled up in her eyes. "Yeah..."

Luke wanted to clear the air between them more than anything, but not now. The night was too beautiful, and so was she, and he didn't want to waste it on what he felt would probably turn into an argument. He needed to unwind, not ramp up the tension inside of him. There was peace between them now, and he wanted to pretend the heavy baggage hanging over there heads didn't exist, just for tonight.

"Let's not talk about all that right now, sugar. Let's just enjoy ourselves," he told her and scooted closer, then laid on his back and extended his arm. "Come here."

Cassie shoved their trash off of the blanket then crawled over to him and laid down on his shoulder facing skyward, before reaching up to lace her fingers through his where he'd curled his arm around her shoulder. Luke sighed in contentment and squeezed her hand.

"Hey, you see our star?" he asked.

Glancing over at her, he saw her eyes squint as she concentrated on the sky. He leaned his head closer to hers then pointed. "Right there."

It was a game they'd played when they were dating. He'd told her that even if they couldn't manage to be together that night, they'd both look at the same star at midnight and know that they were thinking about the other right then.

Warm moist lips pressed a kiss to his cheek and lingered, and he turned his head to search them out, then brought his arm over Cassie's waist to pull her closer. When his lips met hers, he kissed her gently, testing, tasting her sweetness with his mouth then shifted his hand to the hem of her tank top and slid it underneath to feel the soft skin of her stomach. He felt her shiver and slowly licked over the seam of her mouth until she opened for him.

"My god, you taste good, darlin'...I just want to eat you up," Luke whispered over her lips right before he claimed them in a long deep kiss that made the tendrils of desire coursing through him knot into a tight ball in his chest.

He was as hard a spike, and wanted take her right then, but he was going to take things slowly. Luke wanted her on the same runaway train he felt like he was riding. Turning on his side next to her, he moved his hand up her side to cup the roundness of her breast and kissed her deeper.

Her soft moan was captured in his mouth when he found her tongue with his and teased it into an erotic dance. Moving his thumb, over the peak of her breast, he slowly circled her nipple until she whimpered softly and lifted toward him. Luke reached down to pull at the hem of her shirt and lifted it over her head. "I've got to taste you, cupcake," he told in a fierce whisper by her ear.

The sight of her perfect breasts bathed in the moonlight pulled a groan out from the depths of his chest and he leaned down to kiss each beautiful mound where they spilled over her ice blue bra.

Cassie's hands moved to the side of his head and she held him to her as he moved his lips down to her nipple to wet it with his tongue through the material, before he caught it in his teeth.

Her body launched against his and she moaned loudly. The sound of her pleasure filtered into his brain and sent sensational waves of desire crashing over his body. His cock hardened painfully against his zipper and he blew a hot breath against her nipple then whispered, "I've missed you so damned much."

"Oh, god Luke," she lifted her hand between them and moved it up to his fly to stroke him. "I need to feel you...," she begged sliding her hand up and down his length.

She squeezed him under his jeans and pressed harder with her strokes. The friction sent pulsing sensations through him that made him want to howl. He sucked in a tortured breath and closed his eyes.

If she didn't stop, this was gonna be over before it even started. He put his hand over hers to still it. "Slow down, darlin'. We've got ten years of loving to catch up on..." he told her then placed a kiss behind her ear, before moving down her throat. He licked the underside of her jaw, then kissed his way across her chin to recapture her lips in a heated kiss.

Luke slid his thigh over hers and she began wiggling her hips against him, her breathing coming in heavy pants, punctuated by needy little sounds of pleasure. Luke lifted his lips from hers and stared deeply into her passion glazed eyes. "We're just getting started, cupcake...I'm going to make you come at least twice before I get inside of you. Then I'll make you come again...for me." He felt a tremor move through her.

His fingers found her nipple again and he rolled it between his fingers, then he palmed her breast and squeezed it, before moving downward to the clasp at the front of her bra. Scooting down, he kissed a path down the valley between her breasts and his fingers found the front clasp of her bra and flicked it open.

When it spread apart like a rose opening in full bloom, the sight of her took his breath away. "So damned beautiful..." he growled and then bent his head to take one firm peak into his mouth.

Cassie moaned and ran her hands over his back and down to the bottom of his shirt tugging it up inch by inch.

"Take your shirt off, Luke," she ordered him in a frantic whisper.

He lifted up and pulled it over his head then tossed it over by the rock. She put her hands on his abs and her heated fingers traveled up to trace each indentation, before she stopped at his pecs and flicked a thumb over a nipple.

"God, you make me want to lick you from stem to stern," she told him with a groan.

Lust surged through him and he felt the electric sizzle of her words and touch all the way to his toes. Luke laid partially on top of her and pressed his chest against her breasts. It was heaven to feel her against him again...pure heaven.

"Oh god, darlin', I forgot how good you feel," he moaned and closed his eyes imprinting the feel of her on his dazed brain. It just made him want more. Rising up to his knees, he moved his hands over her thighs and spread them, gently positioning her casted leg, so he wouldn't hurt her. He moved inside the V he'd created and gently crawled upwards until their bodies were pressed together intimately.

They fit together perfectly, touched in all the right places now to drive him insane, it had always been that way with them. His mouth went dry when she gyrated her hips against him and he growled then matched her rhythm as he bent to kiss the side of her neck, down her throat to lick along the ridge of her jaw line again and up to her ear.

"You're mine cupcake, *only* mine," he said in a possessive whisper then skimmed his hands up the sides of her arms to link his fingers with hers and raise them above her head.

He looked deeply into her eyes and demanded, "Say it," then ground himself against her hips, placing himself so he hit her at the perfect spot.

She whimpered then he felt her shiver, before she repeated, "Yes, Luke I'm yours...only yours." Her hot breath danced over his lips with her words, and she leaned up and sucked his lower lip into her mouth.

Luke thought he was going to explode right then and

there, but he held on and claimed her lips in a fiery kiss, pouring all his emotions out to her, showing her the depth of his passion with the kiss.

Cassie worked her long fingers over the muscles in his back then moved down to his ass and slid her fingers inside the waistband of his jeans. Kneading him, she pressed him closer to her, as her hips moving needily against his.

"You need to take these off too. I want to feel you, Luke...all of you," she told him unsteadily in between short gulping breaths.

Ignoring her plea, he lifted himself up on his arms to hover above her then licked his way across her chest, down the valley between her breasts, stopping to give each nipple a suck, then moved across her flat stomach to circle her navel with his tongue. Her skin quivered against his mouth, and he felt a tremor move through her.

Luke looked up into her eyes intently, then he lowered his head and grabbed one edge of the closure on her shorts with his teeth. He bit down then yanked the loop over the metal stud, before catching the zipper tab with his teeth. Slowly, inch by inch, he worked it down, stopping to place little kisses and licks on her skin as he exposed it.

Cassie's hips gyrated against his mouth, and he saw her chest heaving as she drew in desperate breaths. He looked down again to continue his task and smiled against her skin right above the top edge of the matching ice blue panties he'd just revealed.

"Wow, sugar, you sure do know how to wrap the merchandise," he told her, his own breaths not coming easily.

With a kiss on her hip, Luke pushed up on his knees between her thighs then lifted her hips to slide the cut-offs down her legs. He eased them carefully over her cast then threw them on top of his shirt over by the rock.

She arched against him and bent her uninjured leg around his waist trying to pull him closer. "I can't wait ten more years Luke. I need you now, please."

He reached behind him and gently put her leg back on the blanket, then moved back between her thighs. "Not yet, darlin'...I still have some ground to cover first."

He dropped on his elbows and inspected every inch of her body, up her thighs to the wet spot at the center of her panties, over her mons, across the smooth expanse of her abdomen and over the hills of her breasts, until he found her sparkling eyes.

"Be patient, baby. This is my favorite part," he said and gave her a wide grin.

"Well my favorite part is when you finally stop messing around and put out this fire you've started inside of me," she told him in an agitated tone and he saw her fists clench where they rested at her sides.

Luke slid his hands up the inside of her thighs, then slid them underneath her thighs to gently lift her hips up to him, and anchored her with his hands on her hipbones. The first open mouth kiss he placed on the inside of her thigh had her gasping and reaching for his hair. The second one had her clamping her thighs against his shoulders and whimpering.

God, he loved how responsive she was to his touch. It increased his own pleasure tenfold. She'd always been like that with him. He certainly didn't have to wonder if he was doing things right, he thought, as he shifted his attention upward to trace the lower edge of her panties with his tongue. Her sweetness traveled over his taste buds, and he inhaled sharply taking in the heady smell of her arousal into his senses and savoring it.

He ran his tongue over her through her panties and then pulled them aside and spread her then flicked his tongue over the bud that he knew would send her soaring.

"Oh my god, Luke...I'm coming...oh, god don't stop...don't stop," she begged him as her muscles contracted and she let out a keening wail. He kept licking the spot giving her pleasure and then he rolled the bud between his lips. Her body shook, practically vibrated, against his mouth and she wailed again, the sound ratcheting up the tension inside of him to unbearable levels.

When her body stilled except for an occasional tremor, he let her panties fall back in place then licked his lips and asked her, "How's that fire darlin'?"

The sexy deep timber of his playful voice rumbled through Cassie starting new fires. She took a deep satisfied breath then sighed as the last remnants of her incredible orgasm waned.

"Smoldering, but not out," she told him and sat up. "That was...amazing." It was more than that--incredible, stupendous--the best orgasm she'd had in ten years, but she needed more.

He pushed up to his knees again and pressed her back against the blanket. Shaking his head he told her, "Ut uh, darlin' you just lay there and enjoy. I'm not letting you hurt yourself."

"Luke I need you inside of me...please." She grabbed his shoulders but he pulled away.

Skimming his hands down her body, he grabbed the thin bands at the side of her hips and drew her panties off, tossing them over by the rock. Even though it was dark, the heat of his eyes felt like the fiery sun on her nether regions. His glittering eyes met hers and he grated, "I said I was going to make you come twice, but I'll have to take a rain check on round two. I need you now."

Cassie's mouth watered as he stood up and unbuttoned then unzipped his jeans, the muscles of his arms and chest flexing as he worked. He pushed his jeans down to his ankles, and she swallowed hard when she saw his steely erection pushing against his tight white boxer briefs.

She licked her lips thinking of how much she'd like to taste him there. Her hands itched to touch him like he'd touched her. But the damned cast on her ankle prevented her from being mobile, so she could indulge.

When he pushed his briefs down and sprang free, Cassie gasped and her inner muscles clenched. He was just as she remembered, her fantasies hadn't been lying to her. She'd thought of Luke every time she was with another man while they'd been apart, because they'd all fallen short of his glory. But she wasn't about to tell him that. His ego was big enough.

She saw him dig in the pocket of his jeans and pull out a small foil packet before he tossed them over by their other clothes. He quickly fell to his knees beside her and tore the packet open. She couldn't help herself, she had to touch him.

Sitting up again, Cassie took the latex ring from his fingers and placed it on the swollen head of his member then rolled it down in place. She closed her fingers around him and stroked him, her other hand going to gently cup his sac. "I want to taste you so badly, but I know it'll have to wait."

Luke's hips moved with the rhythm of her hand and he grasped her shoulders for balance. His breathing was tortured and he groaned then placed his hand over hers to still her movement. "Darlin', stop, I'm almost there and I want to be inside of you when I come."

She swallowed hard and nodded then lay back on the blanket and opened herself to him. With arms spread, she welcomed him inside. He eased down into her arms and slid his hands under her shoulders. Her head lolled to the side as he placed tiny kisses on her throat, sending tingles of pleasure dancing along her enflamed nerves. Her hands found his narrow waist then moved to his firm butt to pull him closer to her. She needed to feel him inside of her now.

Luke moaned then shifted his hips and picked up her uninjured leg and held it over his forearm. He positioned himself at her opening and looked into her eyes with a fierce expression on his face. "Mine..." he grated before thrusting halfway inside of her.

Cassie gasped his name, trying to relax to accommodate his fullness. Her inner muscles were stretched tautly, and the feeling although wonderful was one she hadn't experienced in a long time. Moving her hips, she tried to get him to enter her all the way, but he remained still, his face a mask of tension.

"It's okay, Luke, I'm fine. You feel so good," she whispered in desperation and lifted her hips against him.

Something inside him broke and he roared before shoving inside her to the hilt. He was breathing heavily, his muscles twitching from holding back.

"You're so fucking tight....so wet." His Adam's apple bobbed several times and he closed his eyes as if savoring the sensation of being inside of her, feeling the sense of homecoming that she was feeling too.

"Luke...make love to me," she whispered to him, looking deeply into his eyes, her love for him filling her up to overflowing. She felt the earth shifting beneath her as he started moving inside her in a rhythm as old as time.

The friction he created sent her spiraling swiftly toward another release, and she regulated her breath trying to delay it so she could go over the edge with him. He wasn't having any of it though and lifted her hips, shifting his position slightly, and shortening his stroke, so he hit a hidden spot inside of her on every reentry.

The feeling he created was so intense she almost thought she'd black out, or hyperventilate from the short gasping breaths she was forced to take. She moved her hips in small circles with him to increase her pleasure and his.

"Oh shit...Luke, I'm..." He moved his fingers and manipulated the bud at the apex of her thighs and she went sailing over the edge into another mind bending release, her inner muscles contracting around his thick length inside of her. The sensation was expanded and intensified when he lengthened his stroke again and increased his pace, slamming against her now, his chest heaving. He stroked a final time and then howled his release, his fingers digging into her hips.

He stayed there buried deep inside of her for a long moment, until his breathing finally slowed, then he slid out of her, gently easing her hips back to the ground.

Cassie was speechless and closed her eyes and let her head drop to the side, every muscle in her body sated and relaxed. She felt Luke kiss her cheek then move to her side, before he drew her into his arms. He took one corner of the blanket and pulled it over them, then snuggled his face into her hair and hugged her fiercely to him.

Neither of them spoke, she didn't know about him, but she didn't have energy left to say a word. She turned on her side and threw her arm over his abdomen and cuddled into his neck. She heard his soft breathing and felt his tense muscles relax and knew he'd fallen asleep. Being in his arms made her feel safe and warm...loved. Cassie reveled in the comfortable familiar feeling and closed her eyes welcoming a short nap herself.

A loud mocking voice woke her up from a fabulous erotic dream. "Got a report from a boater that there were some nudists sunning themselves out here. Would that be you two?"

Cassie vaulted up and her hand flew to her chest to cover her wildly beating heart. Her unfocused eyes searched for the owner of the somewhat familiar voice. Luke stirred beside her then opened his eyes. They widened as he looked up and his sleepy brown gaze landed on Cole standing above them with his hands on his hips, his legs spread. His eyes were shaded from the early morning sun by a pair of dark aviator sunglasses.

A slight breeze kicked up and wafted across her skin, and she glanced down and realized she was naked. Jerking the blanket to cover herself, she uncovered Luke in the process. He didn't seem to be bothered, because he just laid there staring up at his friend, a sardonic expression on his handsome face.

"Well?" Cole prodded in his stern cop voice. "What have you got to say for yourself?"

"Get the fuck out of here and leave us alone?"

"Seems you're determined to give me plenty of reasons to arrest you lately, or to make the mayor fire you." Cole said then continued gruffly, "Ten years of clean living and all of a sudden you, the Sheriff of this town, are my worst nightmare...kind of ironic don't you think?" He glanced over at Cassie his lips pinched.

Irritation bubbled up inside of her and she harrumphed. "I am not the reason he's getting into trouble."

"You're his kryptonite, babe, his weakness...you crook your little finger, and he's following behind you like a dog on point, and ready to chew off the face of anyone who crosses you."

"Shut the fuck up, Cole..." Luke snarled then added, "And don't call her babe!"

Luke pushed up to his feet and stomped over to the rock to grab his jeans. He stuffed his legs into them without putting on his underwear. Self-conscious Cassie pulled the blanket around her and tied it sarong style across her shoulder then stood too.

With a smug smile Cole spread his hands in front of him. "See, sugar? Pure kryptonite," he said to Cassie with a brittle laugh.

"Quit needling him, Cole. We're leaving...you can go now." Cassie said and then started to hobble over to the clothes pile, her movement unsteady on the loose rocks littering the ground.

Luke ran over to her and picked her up on his arms to carry her over to the rock and sit her there. "Don't do that!" He yelled, frustration radiating from his every pore, agitation tingeing his voice.

She dropped her chin down to her chest and twisted her hands in her lap. The fact that Cole, Luke's best friend, thought she made him weak and caused him trouble, gnawed at her. Now, Luke was yelling at her like she was an idiot, making her feel worse.

When she'd left Phoenix, Cassie had been a strong independent woman with a good head on her shoulders, a successful business and a good life. Now, she felt weak and dependent, her future uncertain. If anything, Luke was *her* kryptonite.

Maybe staying in Bowie wasn't a good idea after all, she thought. She and Luke just weren't good together...they didn't strengthen each other as much as they set each other on fire. If being together didn't make them stronger, their lives better, they shouldn't be together.

"Luke, can you take me back to the ranch?" she asked quietly as she bent over to pick up her clothes from the ground. She worked under the blanket to put on her panties and bra, then slid on her shorts and tank top. She only had one tennis shoe, and Luke was going to carry her to the truck, so she didn't bother with it.

Cassie didn't regret last night. Regardless of Luke's arrest, it had been the best night of her life, hands down. Being with Luke again had restored her belief in him, and in love. He was a good man, and he deserved better than the trouble she brought him. She didn't want him to lose the job he loved because of her, or his best friend.

It was time for Cassie to head back to Phoenix and get her head on straight, and let him get his life under control again. She'd think things over while she was there and decide if she wanted to move to Bowie permanently or not. Her dad had a nurse to take care of him now, Luke was buying the cattle herd...so, he didn't need her here anymore.

CHAPTER TEN

Luke argued with her out at the lake for about thirty minutes, before he finally agreed to bring her back to the ranch, instead of taking her to the cabin. She'd stared at his angry profile and tense shoulders all the way home.

When he pulled to a stop in front of the house and got out and slammed the truck door, Cassie opened her own door and slid to the ground without waiting for him. She'd had enough of his surliness. She grabbed her hospital bag from the floorboard and had the door shut before he made it around to her side.

He growled, then bent and swept her up into his arms and stomped across the yard to the porch. "Stubborn woman," he grated as he marched up the stairs to the door and opened it, walking inside without knocking. He strode through the house to the kitchen and then deposited her in a chair, before pulling out another one and propping her casted leg up on it. "Stay," he ordered and spun to stomp back through the house.

Imelda rushed around the breakfast bar wiping her hands on a dish towel, her round face curious. "Whatcha doing back here, sugar? I thought you were going to be at the lake house for the week."

"Changed my mind, mama," Cassie told her flatly.

"Your ankle doing okay?"

"Yeah, it's doing fine. Not even hurting yet today."

"You and Luke have a fight?" she asked with concern and put her hand on Cassie's shoulder.

"Not exactly...." Cassie knew she was being difficult, but she wasn't going to discuss her late night activity or early morning eye-opener with Mama Melda...or anyone else.

Imelda walked back over to the breakfast bar and picked up the tray of steaming food from the counter. "If you need to talk, sugar...I'm here," she said and then walked out of the kitchen.

Luke passed Imelda in the doorway of the kitchen and stopped to kiss her cheek. They exchanged a few words that Cassie couldn't quite hear, then he strode over to her with crutches in one hand and her suitcase in the other. He leaned the crutches against the table, and plopped the suitcase down beside her chair.

"Think that's all," he said shortly his whiskey-brown eyes glittering with intense emotion she couldn't identify.

"Thanks...for everything," she told him letting her eyes drink him in, storing the images in her memory to tide her over when she got to missing him too bad.

He huffed out a frustrated sigh, then leaned over to gently kiss her lips. Tears burned behind her eyes, and it was all she could do to hold back the storm she felt brewing inside her. When he stood back up, she put her hand over her lips and whispered, "I love you, Luke." Even she heard the finality in her tone and flinched.

He just stood there with his hands on his hips, his eyes glittering dangerously. Then, as if dragged from the depths of his soul, he finally spoke in a harsh choked voice, "I love you too. Don't ever forget that." He shoved a hand through his hair then said, "Take care of yourself. I'll try and stop by tomorrow," then he turned and strode out of the kitchen and her life.

He didn't know it, but she wouldn't be here tomorrow when he came calling. It was best for both of them. Cassie put a hand on the table and pushed up out of the chair to reach for her crutches. With even strokes she used them to push herself across the floor at a steady pace toward her dad's room.

He was sitting up in a wingback chair with his white ankle to thigh cast propped up on an ottoman, his breakfast tray on his lap, when she made it inside.

"Morning, daddy," she said forcing brightness into her tone.

He looked up, his gray eyes shining happily under his equally gray wiry eyebrows, a smile splitting his face.

"Morning, sugar. You look plum tuckered out. A lot of excitement yesterday, huh?"

"There's been a lot of excitement around here for two weeks..." she told him as she walked past to sit on the edge of the bed to face him. "How's that nurse working out for you?"

"Crotchety old filly is like a drill sergeant. Bosses me around something terrible," he grumbled and forked a piece of scrambled egg into his mouth. "Kinda like those sponge baths though," he said around the egg and chuckled.

He would, she thought with a chuckle. "She sounds like just what you need, old man. Otherwise, you'd be running all over her."

"You're one to talk little girl. That wimpy ex-fiancé of yours still in jail?"

"As far as I know. Between your trespassing charge and mine for stalking, he'll either have to drop the charges against Luke or spend more time than him in jail. I'm going to get a restraining order against him once I get back to Phoen--" she let her sentence trail off and her dad's eyes narrowed.

There was dead silence between them for a minute or two then he asked in a low even voice, "So you're going back?"

"Yeah, for now. I've got a lot of loose ends to tie up with the business, and I need to really think about where I want to live and what I want to do. I made a snap decision to stay in Bowie because I was excited about the horse breeding thing..."

"You can still do that, I have plenty of money darlin', more than I could ever spend."

"I know daddy, but if I do it, I want to do it on my own. It will mean more that way. But I'm not sure yet if that's what I want or not." She saw his eyes mist up and she reassured him. "I still might do it daddy, there's just a lot I need to deal with before I can make a decision...a lot I need to work out."

"You tell Luke?" he asked studying her intently.

"No, I didn't...and I'm not. He wouldn't let me go. The time I've spent with him these past few weeks has been great...I love him, daddy...but I don't see things working out between us. We don't make each other stronger."

He threw his fork down on the tray and spat, "That's horseshit, girl. You two were made for each other, and it's a crying ass shame you can't see it. That boy loves you...he'll take care of you."

"See that's the thing daddy--I don't want him to take care of me. All that's done so far is get him into trouble. His life was solid until I came back. Even Cole said so. I think the best thing I can do for both of us is go back to Phoenix. For now, anyway."

"You've got some strange notions about love, honey." He shook his head and picked his fork back up. Staring down at his plate, he continued, "Your mama was the love of my life, and we argued every day. It didn't mean we didn't love each other. Love's hard work...not for the faint of heart."

He stuck his fork into a piece of cantaloupe and waved it at her. "You're one of the strongest women I know, Cassie Bee...and you could work it out with Luke, if you'd just stick around and try." His eyes pleaded with her to change her mind.

He just didn't understand...they weren't good together. "Since I've been back in Bowie, I've gotten thrown from a horse, almost raped, broken my ankle and cracked my skull, then was stalked by my crazy ex--and Luke has tried to save me from it all.

For his trouble, he's been antagonized by me, risked everything he has to buy a herd of cattle he has no use for, has had to beat the shit out of the cowhand who tried to rape me, been thrown in jail once, almost twice now, and he's arguing with his best friend over me. How can you say that we're good for each other?"

That got a chuckle out of her dad, but he sobered quickly. "None of that has anything to do with the price of tea in China--or love--girl. If Luke was there for you through all that, and you were there for him, that's what love is. Life ain't easy, you have to take the fleas with the dog."

"Well, I'm taking my flea circus and heading back to Phoenix for a while, daddy."

He looked up at her and asked quietly. "Why did you run away after graduation, Cassie Bee?"

She looked down at her hands and twisted her fingers in her lap. She figured she finally owed him the explanation she'd never given him.

"Luke was supposed to meet me at the lake that night, and I went to find him. I found him tangled up with Becca Harvey, and thought he was cheating on me."

"Did you talk to him before you left? Ask him about it?"

"No...I was too hurt."

"So you just got your ass over the dashboard and left him dangling on the limb to head to Phoenix."

Cassie looked up at him and swallowed hard. "Yeah, I guess I did. But he didn't come after me either."

"You're wrong there. He came over here right after you left that night looking like he could eat nails. He grabbed me by the collar and yelled at me trying to get me to tell him where you were. I thought he was gonna cry when I told him you left, but didn't say where you were heading."

Her daddy had never mentioned that to her before, and a wave a guilt surged up to strangle her. "I didn't know."

"So now you're doing it again. Leaving him dangling without talking to him and heading off to Phoenix to run away and hide."

Was she doing that? Repeating history by being a coward and running away instead of confronting Luke?

Her conscience whispered, *hell yes you are.* "Okay, daddy you've made a point. I'll call Luke and talk to him."

"There you go, Cassie Bee. I'm proud of ya, darlin'."

She got up and hobbled over to put a kiss on his weathered cheek. "Thanks for setting me straight, daddy. I love you."

"I love you too, sugar," he said and swatted her behind. "Now, you go take care of that business and let me finish my breakfast before the battle ax gets here."

Cassie chuckled feeling sorry for his nurse. Although her daddy was a hard man to handle sometimes, he had a heart of gold...and he was pretty damned smart too.

***

Cassie sat on the front porch swing waiting for Luke to show up. She had her bad leg propped up on the swing and her other toeing the floor to set it rocking in a slow steady rhythm, as she sat back against it and watched for the dust cloud that would announce his arrival.

At first when she'd called him, Luke was kind of cold to her. He said he was too busy to come by again today. After she begged a little, he finally agreed, but he didn't sound too happy about it. He was still on vacation, how busy could he be?

His brush off made her uneasy, because the way he sounded gave her a bad feeling he'd already figured out she was planning on leaving. Either that, or he'd decided the same thing she had about their relationship, and was trying to cool it.

That thought made her heart twist in her chest. Whatever the result of this conversation, things needed to be said, to give them peace. It was time for them to have the talk that was ten years late in coming.

A lump formed in her throat when she saw the dust, then his big pickup broke through the cloud, barreling down the drive toward the house. When he pulled to a stop, she saw the firm set of his jaw, and flat line of his lips through the windshield. He didn't get out right away, just stared at her for a minute from the truck. She saw him lay his head down on the wheel for a minute, then he lifted it back up and opened the door.

Her mouth went dry watching his loose limbed strut across the yard toward the porch. Memories of last night and how he'd loved her senseless caused her heart rate to pick up, and her breathing to shallow. His boot heels beat a steady tune on the porch as he made his way over to the swing and picked up her leg, before sitting down and putting it on his thigh.

"What's up?" he asked not looking at her, just staring straight ahead, his shoulders stiff. His voice was as cold as it had been earlier on the phone.

Cassie swallowed hard, "I was thinking of going back to Phoenix."

She saw a muscle tick at the side of his clenched jaw. He finally loosened it and said, "I know. So why are you still here, and why did you call me out here?"

"I didn't want to leave without talking to you this time."

He lifted her leg up off of his lap and stood, then laid it back on the swing, before he said sarcastically, "That's mighty nice of you, Cassie, but why break with tradition?" He turned one hip toward the porch steps making to leave then said, "I didn't mean a fucking thing to you then, and I certainly don't now, so why bother?"

Cassie felt her lower lip tremble, but hung on for dear life to the tears that threatened. "You do mean something to me, Luke...you mean everything. I love you."

An angry flush suffused his face and he turned back to her and leaned very close to her face. "That's total bullshit, Cassie," he spat then turned toward the steps again. At the top step, he stopped with his back to her, his shoulders tense and his hands fisted at his sides.

"Becca Harvey almost drowned that night. I jumped in to save her. I was trying to save her life when you saw us, not kissing her," his voice was low and choked. "Goodbye, Cassie...have a nice life."

Cassie found her voice, and yelled after him, standing up to wobble on her cast. "Don't leave, Luke--I have more to say!"

"I don't want to hear it," he said curtly and continued across the yard toward his truck.

She screamed at his back anyway, "I didn't want to cause you to lose your job or your best friend!"

With a sob, she took off toward the steps after him. A loose board caught on the ball of her cast and sent her rolling across the porch until she finally came to a stop at the top of the steps dazed.

She heard Luke yell "Fuck!" and tried to get up and go after him again. She'd managed to shove to her knees, before he came stomping up the steps and jerked her up to stand then stepped back. "You're going to kill yourself! What the fuck are you doing?"

Cassie took two steps forward and put her arms around his waist. "I d-don't want to be your k-kryptonite...or the cause of you losing your job. Cole is right, I'm nothing but trouble for you," she whimpered and then the tears fell down her cheeks unchecked. She sobbed and hugged him tightly. She wasn't going to let go, until he listened to her.

Luke peeled her arms from around him, then stepped away again and grated, "Cole is a fucking idiot. I was over at the station chewing him a new one when you called me. He was way out of line," he told her brusquely then skimmed his eyes over her body seeming to assess her. "Are you hurt?" he asked her gruffly.

Just her pride...and her heart.

"No, I'm fine." Cassie stepped toward him again and put her hand on his cheek. "I don't want you two to be fighting over me, Luke. I don't want to cost you your job or your best friend trying to protect me. That's why I was *thinking* of going back to Phoenix..." Her lip trembled again and she bit it then finished, "Even though it was gonna kill me to leave you again."

Luke ran a hand through his hair. "Fuck the job. I was going to resign anyway. I want to raise cattle, and be able to give you a good life." He dragged her back over to the swing and made her sit down.

"But you can't quit your job, you're Sheriff! People depend on you...respect you. You don't even like cattle ranching," she yelled desperate talk some sense into him.

"What the hell do you know about what I like?" he asked with glittering eyes, then sat down beside her and rubbed his palm on his thigh. "You've been gone ten years! I like it well enough and it sure pays a helluva lot more than being Sheriff."

"I don't give a damn about money, Luke," she said and put her hand on his arm. "I give a damn about you. You should be able to do what makes you happy, not have to settle for something because of a paycheck. You're fucking brilliant, and have more determination than anyone I know, you could do anything you set your mind to."

He looked over at her. "That's what I always loved about you...even when I didn't believe in myself, you believed in me, made me believe in myself," he said and then turned to look out over the porch rail. "But when you left me, I thought you'd figured out I was just the town drunk's son and not worth a plug nickel. I figured you ran off because you finally realized I wasn't good enough for you."

She gasped, shocked that he would feel that way, have so little confidence in himself. Then anger filled her that he thought so little of her.

"I'm not like that, Luke and it pisses me off that you ever thought I was. If all we had was a one bedroom shack with no running water, I'd still have been happy as a clam as long as you were with me."

He looked back at her and gave her a small grin. "I felt a little better when I figured out why you really left. But then that pisses me off too."

"When was that?"

"That night I was drunk and saw you at the restaurant..." His grin turned sheepish.

She felt blood rush to her face and anger coursed through her. "The night you and *Candy* and Cole had your threesome?" she asked in a hurt tone spiked with anger. "That give you your insight?"

He groaned, then admitted. "That didn't happen honey. I only did all that to make you as crazy as you were making me. Candy went to the bathroom after she ordered dinner and didn't come back. I was pretty obnoxious."

"You were more than obnoxious, you were...an obnoxious asshole."

"I apologize...I was a *jealous* obnoxious asshole, I agree."

"Okay then, if Candy was off the menu that night, when did you have your revelation?"

"After I heard about you throwing that city boy to the coyotes."

She shook her head and laughed. "That was an eventful night for sure. But how did that help?"

"After Cole and I finished laughing our asses off on the side of the road, he asked me about something you'd said to him and it got me to thinking."

"Something I said?" she asked curiously.

"Cole told me you said I proved I didn't love you that night you left. For a second, I thought you were just trying to shove the blame off on me. Then he said you seemed pretty convinced, and I ran back over that night in my head and figured out what you must have thought you'd seen."

"Very astute of you, Sherlock. I was damned and determined you weren't hearing it from my lips."

"How the fuck could you think I'd do that to you, Cassie?" he said in a hiss. "I told you I loved you...proved it. There was nobody for me but you."

"I left because I couldn't confront you and hear you tell me you'd been seeing Becca all along, and laugh in my face. It would have killed me," her voice trembled over the words.

Luke ran a frustrated hand over his face then told her, "You need to communicate instead of running scared, darlin'. It cost us ten years that we could have been together...and here you were about to do it to me again..."

His whiskey-brown eyes were filled with emotion, then he finished with, "I can't trust you not to run out on me again the next time you get a wild hair or crazy notion."

She slid her hand over his and uncurled his fist to lace her fingers with his. "Please don't give up on me, Luke. I know I don't deserve your forgiveness...or trust...but I'll work on talking instead of turning tail. I promise."

The woman sitting beside him with so much sincerity in her eyes and pleading in her tone tied him up in knots so tight he couldn't get them out with a fork. She always had. But she was also the only woman for him...he loved her. That wasn't going to change even if she did go back to Phoenix and leave him. Ten years had proven that. And even if he cut her out of his life himself, he knew he'd never be able to cut her out of his heart.

Luke studied her a minute or two more and then said, "Promise me that no matter how mad you get, or hurt and confused, you'll yell at me instead of running off. I can handle anything but that."

"I promise, Luke. I'm done running," she vowed and squeezed his hand.

He squeezed hers back then pulled her up into his lap to give her a hug. "Don't make me regret this, darlin'," he murmured against her hair.

"You won't regret it," she told him then leaned back in his arms to look up at him. "Luke, will you come with me to Phoenix, so I can tie up things? It shouldn't take more than a few days."

He smiled down at her. "That's more like it...I'd love to," he said and hugged her closer then dropped his lips to hers.

CHAPTER ELEVEN

Luke walked into the station, breezing right past Julie Beth's desk, heading down the hall to Cole's office. When he walked inside, Cole was leaned back in his chair on the phone with his feet propped on the desk. Wariness entered Cole's eyes and Luke knew the reason for it. Their last conversation when he'd threatened to beat his ass if he didn't apologize to Cassie, and make things right.

He sat down in the chair across from Cole's desk and waited for him to finish his conversation. After a minute or two, Cole dropped his feet to the floor, and put the phone down, then leaned forward and folded his arms on the desk. "What do you want now?"

"I'm sorry...I was out of control yesterday."

"You've been out of control a lot lately," Cole told him, his green eyes glittering angrily.

Luke huffed out a breath. He knew Cole was right. "Yeah...I know."

"So, whatcha going to do about it?"

Luke knew that he meant *what are you going to do about Cassie*. "I'm going to ask her to marry me."

"Oh, that should solve things....are you fucking *crazy*?"

"We talked and things are okay now. I'm going to Phoenix with her," Luke told him and shoved a hand through his hair.

"Wow, you really are being led around by your dick.. You're throwing away your career and life to follow her to Phoenix?" Cole launched the wheeled chair back and stood to slam his hands on the desk and lean over it. "I thought you had more sense than that, man!"

Luke raised a palm and said calmly, "I'm going to help her pack up and then we're coming back. We'll only be gone a week at the most."

"You're vacation will be up in four days," Cole reminded him then sat back down in the chair.

"I know that...I quit. You should've been Sheriff

anyway...I was never cut out for it."

"The people elected *you*, Luke, not me. You are the Sheriff...but damned if you've been acting like it since Cassie came back. And I feel like shit now for encouraging you to go after her again."

"I'm glad you did. I think I'm finally getting handle on what I want out of life."

"What? An unemployment check and all the heartache you can handle?" Cole snorted derisively then drummed his fingers on the desk.

Luke was the one to vault out of his chair this time and slam his hands down on the desk putting him almost nose to nose with his best friend. He leaned into Cole's face and said forcefully, "Butt out, Cole. This is my life, and I'm going to live it, my way."

They stayed that way for a minute, then Luke told him as he stood back up, "I'm headed to the mayor's office to turn in my resignation. I just wanted to tell you first. They'll probably name you interim for the rest of my term."

He pulled his service weapon from his belt, made sure it was on safety, then put it on the desk, then unbuckled his service belt and put that down too, before he reached into his pocket and handed over his badge.

"Good luck, buddy. You'll be great, just like your dad was," Luke told Cole then stuck his hand out, but Cole didn't move to take it. It hung between them, like the bad blood he'd stirred up with his threats yesterday.

Luke dropped it to his side and put his hands on his hips. "We're still friends, Cole. Even though I'm not Sheriff anymore. Nothing is going to change that. You still in with me on the cattle herd?"

Cole hesitated a long time...long enough that Luke started grasping for alternate plans to accomplish his goal of buying the herd. "Yeah, I'm in. Just let me know when the details are worked out."

Luke nodded and then walked out of the office and

breathed a sigh of relief. It was like a heavy weight had been lifted from his shoulders, and his step was lighter than it had been in a long time as he headed for the elevator to go talk to the mayor.

***

Imelda had helped her get a shower earlier, and Cassie was sitting at the vanity in her room putting the final touches on her makeup when Luke walked through the bedroom door. She felt like a million bucks this morning. Luke had stayed with her last night, and although he'd forbidden James to share her bed under his roof, her daddy hadn't said a word about Luke staying.

Last night, they'd eaten the supper Imelda had fixed for them, and her daddy seemed to be in a great mood. He was getting better and it did Cassie's heart good to see it.

When they finished supper, her daddy had gone to bed, and she and Luke had gone back out to the swing with a bottle of wine, where they'd talked half the night. What they'd done the other half of the night was what had put a smile on her face this morning.

Catching his eyes in the mirror, Cassie smiled at the handsome cowboy she loved, then turned around to face him. An answering smile spread across his face from ear to ear. There was a lightness to his mood she hadn't seen in a very long time. It was almost like ten years had melted away in the last few hours he'd been gone. "You look happy."

"I am, cupcake...very happy." He said seriously then stopped beside her and leaned down to give her a kiss that curled her toes.

"Mmm..." she murmured and reached up to put her hands at the side of his face to deepen the kiss.

He grabbed her hands then stood holding them. "We need to get on the road, sugar."

"A few hours won't matter," she said suggestively and

waggled her eyebrows.

"Yes it will, darlin, we have a schedule to keep. You packed?"

"I never unpacked," she laughed. "That suitcase I packed for the lake house has all my stuff in it. All my other clothes are in Phoenix."

They were going to drive his truck to Phoenix, so she could load her necessities to haul back. The movers would carry the rest to Bowie.

Happiness bubbled up inside of her at the thought of actually leaving Phoenix behind for the last time. She knew now this was what she wanted for certain, her horse farm and Luke.

Tilting her head to the side, Cassie told Luke something she'd meant to tell him when he first walked in. "Cole called me a while ago and said that James has offered to drop the charges against you if we agreed to drop the ones against him. He also said that James was going to leave town and not come back. I agreed...you okay with that?"

He grinned, "Hell, yeah!" he hooted then his smile dropped. "I resigned as Sheriff. I hope you're okay with that."

She swallowed down the lump that formed in her throat as momentary panic surged through her. "I'm happy, if you're happy, Luke. Whatever you want to do with your life, I'm with you."

"I want to be a cattle rancher. Although Cole is pissed off at me, he's still going to be my partner."

She sucked in a breath. Dreading his answer, she asked, "Because of me?"

"Yeah, but my decisions in life aren't dependent on Cole liking them, darlin'. He's my friend, but my life is my own. He doesn't realize it now, but he's going to be a helluva lot better Sheriff than I've ever been."

"I don't believe that could be true, but I'll take your word for it. I just hope that I don't come between you two."

"We'll be fine...he'll get over it when he sees how happy I am," he said and brought her hand up to his lips and kissed it. "Now let's get this show on the road."

Luke loaded up the truck, and she kissed Imelda and her daddy goodbye, then he carried her to the truck even though she told him she could walk just fine in the cast.

After they'd been driving about four hours, and they'd covered about all the conversation topics at their disposal, Cassie's eyes got scratchy and started to drift shut. The sudden sound of Luke's voice made them come back open.

"Ut uh, sleepyhead, we have a stop to make soon, and you need awake for it," he said in his deep sexy drawl.

She sat up straighter in the seat and gave him a curious look. "Oh yeah, where are we stopping?"

"It's a surprise," he said with a mysterious grin.

Cassie harrumphed and crossed her arms over her chest. Patience was not a virtue the good Lord had seen fit to bless her with. "Luke Matthews, you know I don't like surprises. Tell me."

He just shook his head and pinched his lips tighter. Cassie sat on the edge of the seat trying to gauge where they were. Probably near Amarillo by now, but the signs weren't a big help. They were on a long stretch of highway with no exits nearby, only long stretches of fence, scrub brush and fields sparsely dotted with either cattle or horses.

He drove another twenty minutes or so, and she saw a green and white sign saying 'Amarillo 95 miles' just past an unmarked exit. He took the exit and then turned off on a one lane road with lots of pot holes. She sat back in the seat so she wouldn't be bounced off, and glared over at him.

Fifteen miles or so down the rutted road, he turned onto a road covered in loose pea gravel. The back end of the truck fishtailed sending her sliding across the seat to his side, before he smoothed it out. She put a hand on his thigh to steady herself and felt him harden against her wrist.

There was more than one way to get the information she wanted, Cassie thought smiling. Watching his face for a reaction, she stroked his thigh then slid her hand to his fly and pulled the zipper tab down a few inches.

The truck swerved to the left, and he yelled, "Shit, Cassie! Stop!" then flung her hand off of him. "You trying to make me wreck the truck?"

"Nah, I'm trying to get you to tell me where we're going."

"Stop messing around. We'll be there in a minute," he told her and grabbed her hand with his to keep it from wandering again. "There, now be good."

She laughed and told him playfully, "Honey, I'm always good. If you'd have let me finish, you'd know that."

"Oh, I'll let you finish..." he shot her a heated glance, his topaz eyes filled with desire. "Right after I show you my surprise."

"I really wanna see your surprise," she purred sexily then leaned up to lick his earlobe.

He growled, "Stop it!"

She laughed and leaned back on the seat and pouted. "Okay, I'll be good."

"Not likely," he glanced over at her and chuckled.

A few minutes later he turned off the gravel road onto a smooth paved driveway lined on both sides by black board horse fencing. She saw beautiful muscular quarter horses of every color happily grazing on either side, their tails swishing to swat pesky flies.

Cassie sucked in a breath and excitement filled her. "Oh, Luke," she said breathlessly and leaned closer to the windshield to get a better look. This place looked pretty close to what she imagined heaven would look like. She smiled over at him. "You sure know how to show a girl a good time, sugar."

He smiled back, happiness shining in his eyes. "You

ain't seen nothing yet, darlin'."

"Be still my heart. I swear those are the most beautiful horses I've ever seen."

"They're not as beautiful as the ones you're gonna raise."

Cassie swallowed hard. Her dreams were not nearly on this scale, she'd be happy with three or four mares and a good stallion. But she sure loved seeing her dream multiplied by a hundred spread out before her. It gave her hope that maybe she was going to be able to pull this off after all.

"You know these people?" There hadn't been ranch markings at the entrance, so she had no idea who they were.

"I've been talking to the owner for a couple of weeks," he admitted then she realized he wasn't going to tell her anything more, when he took his hand off of hers and put it on the steering wheel.

They pulled up in front of the huge Southfork-type house and he turned off the engine. The front door immediately opened and a long-legged cowboy with a white straw hat stepped out onto the porch and waved at them then hitched his thumbs in his belt loops and waited for them to get out and walk up to the porch.

Luke didn't let her walk, he flew around the truck before she could get out and eased her to the ground then put his arm around her waist and half-carried her up to the porch, going really slow to make sure she didn't stumble.

"Luke?" the man asked and stepped down two steps to stand in front of them. He shoved his hand out to Luke after smiling at Cassie.

"Yep. You must be Tommy...thanks for inviting us out," he said and grasped the man's hand in a firm shake.

The tall, leanly muscled cowboy with the kind face glanced down at her, "And you must be Cassie. Nice to meet a fellow horse nut, ma'am," he said with a wink. "Don't look like you're gonna be riding today though," he chuckled his eyes traveling down her legs to her bright green cast.

She gritted her teeth against the disappointment. "Damned ankle," she grumbled.

Luke chuckled and squeezed her side. "You'll get to do plenty of riding real soon, darlin'," he reassured her.

She stuck her lip out and leaned against him. "I know, but there're so many beautiful babies out here, and we're not gonna be back when I get this dagblamed cast off."

Tommy piped up, "Honey, you're welcome to come back and ride any time you please," he told her, then looked at Luke, "You bring her back out here when she gets the cast off."

Luke nodded and squeezed her tighter to his side. "So, where's what we talked about on the phone?" he asked cryptically shooting the other man a meaningful look.

"In the far barn. Let me go get a golf cart, I'll be right back," he told Luke with a pat on the shoulder. A few minutes later he drove around the end of the house in a bedazzled golf cart with big knobby tires and a fringed hot pink canopy.

Cassie giggled seeing the good looking, very masculine cowboy driving what looked like a Barbie Buggy. She heard Luke chuckle beside her too. When Tommy pulled up closer, Cassie saw the tortured look on his face accompanied by a wry grin, which kicked up the corner of his mouth. "My baby girl's golf cart was the only one parked behind the house. She loves this thing...rides all over the ranch with it."

Cassie's heart clenched picturing Luke instead of Tommy in the feminine transportation, saying the same words about his 'baby girl', one she imagined would have her daddy's dark hair and her blue eyes. The little girl would be the apple of his eye and have him wrapped around her little finger.

With a shake of her head, she cleared away those very appealing, but probably farfetched thoughts. She and

Luke were still renewing their old feelings for each other, getting to know each other again. It would be a long time before they were in at that place, if they ever were.

"Climb in if you're brave enough, man," Tommy offered in challenge to Luke and chuckled.

Luke grinned from ear to ear and helped her into the seat beside Tommy, then sat on the backseat. "Have to be pretty secure in your manhood to ride in this for sure," he laughed.

Cassie grabbed the pink-ribbon wound bar beside her when the cart lurched into motion and smiled. This was going to be great, she thought. She looked over at Tommy and said smugly, "I'd ride in it. Your daughter has excellent taste."

Luke chimed in from the back seat, "You would think that. I remember that time you streaked your first pony's mane and tail with pink hair paint saying you were making him a 'My Little Pony'. Cole and I bout died laughing, and felt damned sorry for that gelding."

She shot Luke a nasty look over her shoulder for making fun of her. That pony had looked spectacular when she finished.

Tommy's laughter was loud and boisterous. "You and Dixie would be two peas in a pod!" he hooted and slapped his hand on the wheel of the cart. "I'll have to introduce you before you leave."

They passed several smaller barns and a couple of sheds and he rounded a curve then she saw a huge barn that took her breath away. Off to the side was a large round pen and there was a massive outdoor arena surrounded by light poles reaching toward the sky. "Wow, this is amazing," she said breathily.

If his operation was this grand on the outside of the barn, she could only imagine how fantastic it'd be inside. She saw several other regular golf carts parked beside the far fence, and a couple of workers milling about doing odd jobs.

Tommy slid out of the cart and waited for Luke to help her out, then he waved at a couple of the men before leading them inside the brightly lit barn. When they stepped through behind him, Cassie gasped at the huge indoor arena. Her eyes traveled up to the built-in sprinkler system to wet down the dirt and keep the dust down, and the extra tubing that must be a fly control system.

There were twelve open top stalls lining each wall of the arena. Her breathing sped up and she put her hand to her chest to calm her racing heart. Tommy looked back over his shoulder and smiled at her. "You like it?"

"Like is a very weak word. I think I might be in heaven."

"Yep, you've got the fever," he chuckled then said, "Wait til you get a look at Titan. You better prepare yourself, darlin'."

"Can you saddle him up? I want to ride him for her." Luke asked him.

"Sure thing. Just a sec." He walked down the stall aisle and found a man hosing off the concrete at the end of the row of stalls. Leaning in toward him, he gave the man instructions then pointed at them. With a pat on his back, he walked back over to them.

"Jud will bring him around. Won't be long. I need to go check on a mare in the other barn, I'll be back in a few minutes. Ya'll have fun," he said with a wink at Luke then walked back out the barn.

Cassie grabbed Luke's hand and stared her fill at the gorgeous horses sticking their heads over the stalls and staring at them curiously. She'd love to take a trip around the whole barn and scratch their noses and give them treats, but with her leg in a cast that wouldn't be happening.

After a few minutes, she saw a dark-skinned man lead the most amazing buckskin stallion she'd ever seen into the riding arena. His color and markings were striking and his bearing regal. When her eyes met the stallion's, she fell in love. He took her breath away.

Without giving her gimpy leg consideration at all, she walked to the gate and let herself into the dirt-packed arena and walked over to the stallion like she was in a trance.

When she reached him, she held his eyes and ran her hand along his jaw. "Well hello handsome, aren't you a gorgeous hunk," she said reverently, and scratched behind his ear, then ran her hand along his neck and down his back feeling his tightly bunched muscles dance under her fingertips.

Luke walked up beside her and laughed, "Careful darlin', you're making me jealous."

Mesmerized, she put her hand on the horse's rump to let him know where she was then walked around behind him and ran her hands over his other side back up to his head. Her eyes traveled down to his perfect legs and she bent to run her hand down his front leg, then lifted his hoof to inspect it. Gently she let it back down and patted the side of his neck.

"Wow," she said and walked back over to Luke. "This is one fine horse," she told him with longing seizing her. "I sure wish I could ride him...I bet he moves like a dream."

"Let me show you," Luke said and led her back over to the fence where he lifted her up to sit on the top rail. He stood in front of her with his hands on her hips. "You sit right here and enjoy, darlin'."

Her position put her at the perfect height to lean over and kiss Luke's lips tenderly. "Thank you for bringing me here."

His response was a soft smile and a pat on her thigh, before he walked back over to the stallion and took the reins from the man holding them.

With athletic ease, she watched him swing up on the stallion's back. Titan stood perfectly still while Luke mounted him then his ears perked and tilted back a little so he could pay attention to Luke's commands. Exactly what he should have done. His manners were impeccable.

Luke squeezed his sides and the horse moved to the rail walking smoothly. Luke's muscular body moved with him and they looked dynamic together, perfectly in tune. After walking half the arena Luke gave him a leg and he picked up his pace transitioning seamlessly to a slow lope.

They were in perfect harmony, and Luke rolled with his movements hardly bouncing in the saddle at all. Both the horse and rider looked happy and relaxed.

Luke loosened the reins and brought him back down to a walk, and Titan didn't miss a beat. The horse was focused on Luke and reacted immediately to his every command. She was just as focused on the incredible picture they made, so she didn't notice when Tommy walked over and leaned his elbows on the rail beside her.

"What'cha think?" He asked, his voice smug and proud.

"I think I'm in love," she said wistfully then chuckled. "He's amazing, Tommy."

He grinned like a proud papa and told her matter-of-factly, "I knew you were gonna love him."

"I'm going to start an operation at my daddy's ranch. I'll have to get with you when I get it up and running. I'd love to have him cover some of my mares," she said earnestly, looking down at him.

A strange expression came over Tommy's face and then he told her, "That might not be possible, darlin'."

Disappointment flooded her and her shoulders slumped. "He'd make some beautiful babies. He booked up?"

"Something like that," he told her vaguely then pushed off the railing and told her he had to take care of something else then walked away quickly, seeming as if his tail was on fire.

She glanced back at Luke and saw him lead Titan to the middle of the arena where he circled him four times to the left then reversed direction and circled four more. Titan didn't hesitate at all. Luke put him into a canter right out of the last circle and then performed a sliding stop. It was a beautiful thing to behold, when the horse's back legs slid under him and then he stood back up perfectly still.

She heard Luke laugh and then he patted Titan's neck. The urge to be on the stallion's back was a driving need inside of her. She would definitely make Luke bring her back out here to ride him when she got her cast off. Luke led him back over to her and stopped at the rail. She scratched Titan's nose then looked up at Luke. "That was so beautiful, Luke. You were amazing with him."

"He's one helluva ride, honey. I can't wait for you to be able to give him a try."

"Yeah, we'll have to come back sometime," she said kind of sadly. Luke swung his leg over the horse's back then dropped to the ground. He walked over to her and stood real close before he looked deeply into her eyes, then handed her the reins.

"Luke, I can't ride him," she told him wistfully.

"He's yours, cupcake...this is your new stud. You can ride him whenever you damned well please."

Blood rushed to her head and Cassie wobbled on the fence, and she felt like she was going to pass out. Luke grabbed her legs to steady her then lifted her down to her feet.

"He's your wedding present," Luke fished around in his pocket then dropped to one knee in front of her. "If you'll do me the honor of marrying me, darlin'. We're a package deal," he said then flipped open a small blue box to show her a small square cut diamond, surrounded by sapphires. His eyes held hope and all the love she'd ever hoped for.

A hollow ringing started in her ears and she grabbed for the fence. "Luke, I think I'm gonna pass out, sugar," she said weakly right before her knees gave out and she felt herself falling.

Passing out was the last reaction Luke hoped to get from Cassie when he acted out the on again, off again plans he'd been making with Tommy for weeks. He'd been talking to him since Bud had first told him what Cassie wanted to do. The proposal had been a recent decision, but he had been planning to buy Titan for her to make sure she stayed in Bowie.

Luke grabbed her up in his arms and sat down on the hard-packed arena floor, holding her close. He gently patted her pale cheeks, and said, "Wake up, baby. Talk to me." His fingers went to her throat where he felt her pulse beating much too quickly. Her skin was hot and clammy, and he got a little concerned her faint wasn't just from over-excitement. He fanned her face, and then patted her cheeks a little harder, before he shook her gently. "Wake up, Cassie Bee."

Tommy walked into the barn right then and then ran over to them. "Oh my god, what happened?" He slid to his knees beside them and felt her face.

"Too much excitement, I think...she's just getting over a concussion," Luke told him and asked him to get a cold rag.

When Tommy stood up to go get it, her eyelids fluttered and then opened. She lifted her eyes to Luke's and put her hand on his cheek. "Yes," she whispered.

Luke whooped then pulled her into his chest for a tight hug. Supreme satisfaction and then love tangled up inside of him making him feel like it was his turn to pass out. He took a deep breath and released it slowly.

"I miss something?" Tommy asked grinning.

"She said yes," Luke said with a relieved sigh.

"How could she turn down Titan?" Tommy told him and they all laughed.

Once Cassie cooled off and got her wits about her, they rode around in the golf cart while Tommy proudly told them about his operation. She saw some beautiful mares she planned on talking to him about buying, once everything was settled. Everything at the Rocking D was top notch, and she got some great ideas for her own farm.

By the time they left the Rocking D, her head was

spinning and she was hot and thirsty, but so damned excited she could barely contain it. She scooted over by Luke on the truck seat and squeezed his arm, putting another kiss on his cheek, probably number fifty since he'd given her Titan and proposed.

She held out her hand and stared at the gorgeous ring he'd given her. Then a thought occurred to her, and not a comforting one. "Luke, how much did you pay for Titan?"

He glanced over at her then back to the road. "That's none of your concern, darlin'."

"But as good as he is, Tommy probably wanted a fortune for him. And you're buying the herd..."

"Cassie, I'm not a rich man, but I'm not destitute either. I've been frugal and saved my money, invested some of it and it paid off. I have enough for both. Don't worry," he told her flatly his fingers gripping the wheel a little tighter.

"I was being rude. Thank you for my present, darlin', but you didn't have to do all that to get me to marry you. I'd have said yes, if you'd just asked me. I love you, not things."

"Can't a man just go out his way to impress the woman he loves, without her worrying about how much it cost?" he asked her with irritation tingeing his tone. "I wouldn't have done it if I couldn't afford it, darlin'." He pushed out a breath.

"I wanted to give you a grand proposal...something you can tell our grandkids about," he said looking deeply into her eyes, his love blatantly displayed there.

"I think you accomplished that goal, and then some," she said with a small smile that grew quickly into a full blown grin, then she laughed. "I don't think anyone in Bowie, or hell--Texas--can top it. This story is going to become an urban legend."

He snorted. "It was pretty spectacular wasn't it?"

"My fainting didn't push that point home?"

A chuckle rumbled in his chest then he broke into full blown laughter and she joined in.

CHAPTER TWELVE

They chatted amiably as they drove the rest of the way into Amarillo, then Luke told her they were going to stop for the night. He pulled up in front of a hotel then grabbed her suitcase and his duffle bag from the back of the truck. "You okay walking, darlin'?" he asked when she made her way around the front of the truck.

"Yep, steady as a stump," she told him then laughed.

It seemed to her like all she did these days when she was with him was laugh. She sidled up beside him and took his arm then said, "You are gonna get so lucky tonight, cowboy."

"I'm already, lucky darlin'." He leaned down and kissed her upraised lips gently. "You're gonna marry me."

She put her arms around his waist and hugged him tight. "I'm the lucky one, Luke. So damned lucky."

Cassie just wondered how long her luck would hold out though. With all the crap that had landed on her and Luke's doorstep lately, how could she not? But until this thin bubble of euphoria burst, she was going to enjoy the hell out of it.

The next day when they were on the outskirts of Phoenix, she got her answer. The other shoe dropped squarely on her head with a call from her assistant. "What do you mean the account is overdrawn? We had over ten thousand in there!" she shouted into the phone incredulously.

"The escrow account too?" she groaned when her assistant told her it too was empty according to the representative from the bank who called this morning. "I'll be there shortly," she told her then disconnected the call.

"Problems?" Luke glanced over at her with a worried expression.

"I think James emptied our business accounts. Messing with escrow funds is a fiduciary breach, and criminal."

"So, call the police and file charges."

"The real estate board will file the charges, and they could charge me too, since I'm listed as the principal broker for the firm. At the very least, I'll lose my license," her voice wobbled over the words as tension from the severity of this situation settled over her.

"Calm down, honey. We'll figure things out, and make sure that sack of shit gets what he deserves," Cassie looked over at him and his jaw was clenched, his eyes sparkled dangerously.

"Hell no, Luke. This isn't your battle, you calm down and let me take care of it." She was very afraid her words were falling on deaf ears. Luke was blind when he thought she needed protecting, and she had to stop him before he got wound up and did something stupid. "Promise me, Luke."

He looked over at her and then back to the road without saying anything.

"I mean it, Luke--you're staying out of this one. I can handle it, I don't need or want you getting involved. Promise me, dammit!" she demanded.

It was minutes, not seconds, before he finally hissed out between his teeth. "I promise."

"If you can't trust me to take care of things, to be your equal partner in this relationship, it's not going to work, Luke," she warned him and saw him swallow hard. "Trust me on this one, darlin'."

He nodded, but she saw how much it cost him to agree. His muscles were so clenched under his t-shirt, she thought the soft well-worn cotton might burst at the seams.

"Thank you," she said then lifted her cell phone to make the calls she needed to make.

First she called the police, then her banker, and finally the real estate commission. She tried to get James on his cell phone and he didn't answer, of course. Luke sat silently beside her as she did this, just following her directions to take them to the office mutely.

His quietness worried her, Luke always had something to say. She wondered what he was thinking. Leaning back against the door of the truck she said, "Luke, I don't want to cut you out of this completely. I want your advice, I'll take it into consideration. I just don't want you directly involved. Talk to me..."

His eyes dropped to her feet then moved up her legs quickly over her chest then to her eyes. "Don't you think you need to change before you go to the office?"

Cassie hadn't even thought about the shorts and cherry print sleeveless shirt she'd put on at the hotel this morning, and how it would make her look to the people she had to meet with. She groaned and knew she couldn't go there looking like she did. What she needed was the armor of her power suits and heels to fight this battle, but her cast meant she'd be wearing flats instead...and she didn't have any suits with her.

"I wasn't planning on going to the office today. I only packed jeans and shorts when I came to Texas."

"You packed that hot little black dress you wore to the restaurant..." he suggested and wiggled his eyebrows making her laugh.

"Yeah, I forgot...that'll work. I packed some flat black shoes that will work with it too. Can you stop at a gas station so I can change?"

"Yeah," he said and wheeled off the interstate exit and found a station right off the exit. He hopped out and opened the tailgate then dragged her suitcase to the end and unzipped it then stepped aside so she could dig through it.

She kissed his cheek and hugged his waist. "Thanks for understanding, Luke."

"I get it, we're partners darlin'," he told her then finished gruffly, "I'm not used to operating that way, so you'll have to remind me."

"Oh, you can bet I will..." she laughed shortly and then

rifled through her suitcase to pull out the slightly wrinkled black dress and shoes. "I'll be right back," she told him then walked in her uneven gait to the bathroom in the convenience store.

Luke watched her hips sashay and his mouth went dry. Frustration ran through his body like a runaway wagon headed for a cliff. He gritted his teeth and tried to get a grip on his out of control emotions.

Being in this state of mind had gotten him nowhere but in trouble lately. Cassie expected him to take a backseat and let her deal with her asshole ex, and he was going to try, for her, because he promised, but he didn't hold out much hope for success. He had a score to settle with that prick.

He climbed up on the tailgate and folded his arms over his chest to wait for her to come back. You never knew what kind of riffraff hung out at places like this right off the interstate, he thought. There was no way he was going to let anything else happen to the woman he loved. That asshole ex of hers better believe Luke would kick his ass if he tried to hurt her, whether she liked it or not...and the guy was well on his way to deserving it.

The tall blonde woman who exited the store wearing the black dress with her wavy curls pinned up loosely on top of her head, didn't look anything like the country cowgirl who'd gone in a few minutes ago.

Gone was the one cowboy boot she'd had on her uninjured foot, replaced by a shiny black flat. Even with the cherry print shirt and shorts swinging in her hand, she looked competent and professional.

He didn't know this Cassie, he realized as she lengthened her stride with determination, her one shoe tapping an interesting tune on the concrete in concert with the bright green cast that reached halfway up her left calf. But he was sure going to enjoy getting to know her.

Smug satisfaction gripped him when the sun glinted off of his ring on her left hand. That was a sight that would always bring him pleasure, knowing it meant this bright, beautiful woman was his to love.

When she reached him she pirouetted and asked, "Better?"

"I liked you just fine before...but I wasn't sure your co-workers would appreciate the sexy cowgirl look as much as I do."

She laughed and slapped his chest playfully. "No they wouldn't have...thanks for noticing, or they'd have gotten an eyeful."

"My pleasure, darlin'," he said then took her clothes tossed them in the suitcase and zipped it. He slammed the tailgate and said, "Let's go kick ass, sweet cheeks."

He followed her directions and pulled up in front of a fancy brick building that had a sign out front pronouncing it Bellamy and Barton Realtors. The Preppy Boy's name attached to hers in anyway made hot fury pulse through his veins.

"You're gonna need to change that sign, darlin'," he told her gruffly.

"I'll probably just take the damned thing down. There won't be much left after this fiasco," she told him and her lip trembled. "But I have bigger fish to fry right now."

"Yes you do. And as your assistant on this job, I'll be heating up the grease for you, honey."

She smiled at him, "Thanks, darlin'," she said then pulled the door handle and slid out of the truck.

He saw a police car parked a few spaces down and knew when she walked through that door, she wasn't going to be smiling.

His own smile slipped as he exited the truck and followed behind her up the steps to the glass door that also had her and Preppy Boy's name in gold lettering. He bit down the growl that bubbled up from his toes, and walked into the snazzily decorated office.

Cassie walked over to the desk where a woman he assumed was her assistant sat looking wary and scared.

She patted the redhead's shoulder and then leaned down to talk softly with her.

He saw a Phoenix cop sitting in a chair across the room fiddling with his cell phone. There was another woman sitting two chairs down from him, who looked like she'd stepped out of one of those women's magazines. Her black hair was wound up tight against the back of her head, and her red suit fit her body like a glove. She glanced up from the organizer book spread in her lap and gave him a wide smile with even white teeth accentuated by full red lips.

Her black eyes moved over him with interest, then met his gaze and she licked those red lips. After a few seconds, she evidently noticed his lack of sexual interest in her, because her lips drooped then she shifted her gaze back to her book.

Sitting next to her was a skinny bird-like man in a pin-striped suit and shiny shoes. There was a briefcase leaning against the chair by his leg. It looked to Luke like the party was about to begin. He pegged the woman as the representative from the real estate commission and the man as Cassie's banker.

Cassie was still busy talking to her assistant he noticed, so he went and sat down in a chair right by the door. He felt like a pigeon in a flock of peacocks here in his faded black t-shirt, worn jeans and dusty cowboy boots. He reached up and removed his Stetson and put it in his lap, his fingers fiddling with the crease.

Cassie walked over to the three people there to see her and introduced herself with a tight smile, then took them down a hallway that evidently led to her office, or a conference room. She didn't glance at him at all before she led them away.

A few moments later, he was surprised to see her reappear in the doorway and crook her finger at him. He got up and walked over to her, feeling her assistant's gaze wandering over him, sizing him up, but he ignored it.

"Come on back, sugar," she told him.

Her invitation shocked him down to the toes of his boots. "You sure?" he looked down at himself then back to her. "I'm not exactly dressed for a meeting, darlin'."

"You look good enough to eat...as the woman from the commission noticed," she smiled wryly then grabbed his arm and pulled him into the hall. "You're just going to watch. I need some moral support."

He huffed out a breath and told her, "That I can do."

Cassie led him down the hall and into a big conference room with cushy looking maroon chairs and sat him in one against the wall. Luke shifted a little bit in the chair then finally found a comfortable position, and watched as she walked to the head of the table and sat down in between the banker and the cop.

Clearing her throat, Cassie began, "As I told you my banker informed my assistant this morning that a large amount of money was missing from my business accounts. I recently broke up with my fiancé and business partner, James Barton, and I believe he is the one who took the funds." She looked over at the banker, who had a stack of papers in front of him. "Do you have copies of the transactions?" she asked him.

"Yes, I brought copies of the cancelled counter checks. Some have your name on them, although I doubt the authenticity of your signature. There's also a large one cashed yesterday by James Barton. I only looked at the records for the last few weeks, but you may want to consider having your entire account audited from the date it was opened," the man suggested then slid the copies over to her.

Cassie looked through the stack as the banker continued, "I've requested copies of the checks written on the escrow account, but haven't received them yet. They were written from your printed checks and not cashed at the bank, so it will take a little longer. I've also frozen the accounts and bank cards."

Luke saw the cop writing in a small notebook he had open on the table, then he looked up and asked when the banker had finished, "Can I get copies of those, Miss Bellamy?"

"Sure, Officer Melton...let me get my assistant to make copies. I'll be right back."

Luke stood up and met her by the door. "I'll do that, sugar, you go ahead." She smiled her thanks and he walked down the hall to the front office.

Her assistant, a thirty-something woman with pretty auburn hair and green eyes stood up and smiled at him when he walked out of the hall. "Cassie needs copies of these," he held out the stack to her. He could tell she was extremely nervous and he wondered why. Nobody was here to question her, that he knew of. "What's your name, sugar?" he drawled.

Her fair-skinned cheeks flushed and he saw her hand shake when she grabbed the paperwork out of his hand. "Diana...who are you?" she asked him her voice not quite steady.

"Luke Matthews, Cassie's fiancé."

One finely arched brow rose over her green eyes and her lip quirked. "Fiancé?" she snorted and then said, "My, my she certainly works fast..." Her eyes brazenly roved over him, then she finished, "And has good taste too."

Luke didn't miss the strange undercurrent in her voice. Luke felt like doing a little digging of his own. "How long have you worked here, Diana?"

"Three years," she said. "Too long, considering the mess she's made of things here."

"What do you mean?"

She pinched her lips together, evidently realizing she'd revealed too much with her off-the-cuff statement. "I'm going to make these copies. I'll bring them in when I'm done."

Luke recognized that he'd been dismissed by the mouthy assistant, and turned to go back to the conference room. When he walked back in, Cassie's face looked strained and pale as she talked with the lady from the real estate board. "My license can't be suspended now. I've got a mess to clean up!"

"I'm sorry, you're the principal broker and until this situation is resolved, there's nothing I can do. I have to suspend you while the investigation is being conducted."

"How long will that take?" Cassie asked the woman, desperation filling her tone.

She shook her head. "As long as it takes, Miss Bellamy. You never know about these things. We have to locate your business partner first. I'm sure the police will help us with that," she said then gave the cop the same sexy smile she'd given Luke earlier, and he gave her a brief twist of his lips and shook his head affirmatively.

Luke had just sat back down when Diana brought in the copies and put them in front of Cassie along with the originals. Cassie flipped through the copies and then the originals and then looked up at her. "Where's the copy of the large check cashed yesterday?" she asked. "It's not in either stack."

The woman shifted her weight from one foot to the other, then her face turned beet red. "I didn't see it. Maybe it fell out of the stack of originals before I made the copies?" she offered.

Luke stood and walked over to her and took her arm. "Let's go see if it's in the copy room," he said his voice low and lethal.

Diana jerked her arm from his grasp then shot Cassie a look before throwing her chin up and walking out. He followed her down the hall and into the copy room. She walked over to the copy machine and made a show of lifting the lid to see if it was under there. It wasn't. Then she bent over and looked behind the copier on each side.

"It's not in here," she said after her cursory search.

Luke walked over to the paper shredder he saw beside a table where the fax machine and postage meter sat.

Leaning down, he saw a document hanging from the teeth of the machine that looked like a copy of a check.

"Wow, looks like it fell into the shredder..." he said sarcastically then picked the machine up and yanked the plug from the wall. "Move," he ordered her with a lift of his chin toward the doorway.

Her eyes widened then filled with tears when she met his gaze, but she didn't move. "Look, Luke was it? Why don't you just forget you saw that. That will make me very happy...and then I can make you *very* happy," she said suggestively then walked over to run her red nail down his shirt front.

What was it with women in this town, he thought. He'd been here less than an hour and had been propositioned by two of them. "Like you made James the asshole happy?" he fished for confirmation with a grin. "Why would I want his seconds?"

"You're engaged to Cassie aren't you? She's his seconds." She raised an eyebrow and her eyes glittered.

"Not likely, I had her first. Cassie has always been mine...and I'm not interested in your offer," he told her then nodded with his chin again. "Now haul your ass back to that conference room."

She turned her back to him and walked in front of him down the hall, her shoulders slumped. When he followed her into the conference room with the shredder in his arms, Cassie looked up at him with a question in her eyes. The rest of them looked at him as well.

"I think Diana has something she needs to tell ya'll," he looked at her with a warning in his eyes. "Don't you, sugar..."

"I shredded the check."

That isn't the part Luke wanted her to tell. "Tell them why you shredded the check," he prompted.

She shook her head and pinched her lips. Cassie stood up and walked over to her and got in her face. "Tell me now, Diana...or I'm going to stomp a mud hole in your ass."

Luke chuckled because even though she was dressed to impress, when push came to shove, her inner cowgirl had come out fighting. The other woman's eyebrows flew to her hairline and she took a step back into the wall with fear in her eyes.

"I'm not kidding, Diana. You tell me what you and that weasel have done to my business, or I'm gonna kick your ass and love every minute I get in jail for it." Cassie stepped closer, and pressed her body against Diana until their noses almost touched.

The cop stood up from the table and grabbed Cassie's shoulder. Luke took a step toward him and the cop's hand went for his gun. Luke stopped and took a step back raising his hands. The cop nodded, but kept an eye on him when he pushed Cassie to the side and grabbed Diana's arm.

"Turn around," he told Diana and she did. The cop kicked her feet apart and frisked her, then pulled the cuffs from his service belt and put them on her wrists. "You're under arrest for suspicion of grand theft and fraud."

"Wait!" Diana yelled and turned around to face the officer. "She's the one you should be arresting! She signed the checks!" she rushed over to the table, turned around and grabbed the papers. "Look!"

Luke watched Cassie run over and look closely at the signatures on the checks. "This isn't my signature, you lying bitch, but it sure as hell looks like yours!"

Cassie stomped out of the office and went up front, then came back a minute later with a checkbook and other papers in her hands. She slammed them down on the table. "Take a look at this and you tell me who signed those checks."

Officer Melton walked over and looked at the copies then looked at the carbon copy check register that belonged to Diana. Then he examined the incorporation papers that Cassie had signed to open the business.

"I'm no handwriting expert, but it sure doesn't look like Miss Bellamy's signature to me. She doesn't loop her y like it is on these checks, or dot her i with a circle. The slant is different too, but you do that in your signature Miss Tomley," he turned toward the redhead and gave her a lethal stare. "So, that means you're still under arrest."

He left her side and walked over to Luke. "What do you have there?" he said eyeing the shredder curiously.

Luke pointed to the check still hanging from the teeth of the shredder in his arms. "Looks like she shredded a check signed by James Barton. Guess that was the most incriminating evidence against him," Luke said then laughed, "Pretty stupid of her to do that though, considering these are only copies that can be replaced. But then she doesn't appear to be too bright to begin with by hooking up with that prick anyway."

He pushed the machine into the cop's arms. "Guess you'll be needing this for evidence."

"Yeah, thanks," the cop said shaking his head. He put it down on the table and read Diana her rights, while she sobbed and wailed hysterically, then he led her out of the room. He came back a couple of minutes later and got the paperwork and the shredder.

He shook Luke's hand, "Looks like this one is going to be open and shut as soon as we locate Barton. I think Miss Tomley will tell us anything we want to know once we get her down to the station and in a cell for a few minutes."

Luke didn't think she'd last that long. He just hoped she could help the police find James Barton. He had an itchy feeling in his gut and he didn't like it. He knew that feeling well from his years in law enforcement. It mean something ugly was about to come down the pike.

"I sure hope so," Luke told him before he left.

Cassie, who had sat back down at the table, looked over at the banker, who was busy flirting with the real estate lady, then asked, "James banks at your bank too, can you freeze his account before he can spend all that money he stole?"

"Not without a court order on personal accounts," he said then smiled at the woman in the red suit beside him.

"How can I get one?"

"Hire an attorney, he'll be able to tell you."

"But I don't have any damned money--he stole it all!" Cassie yelled and stood up to lean over the table. "If that bastard gets away with all my money, I'm going to sue your ass for taking those checks Diana signed. You have my signature card on file, and it's as obvious as your toupee that they were not signed by me."

The banker flushed red and patted the top of his head, before clearing his throat. Luke wanted to howl. Cassie really could take care of herself, he was proud of how she was handling herself.

"Now, do you think you could make an exception and freeze the damned account? Let him try and get the court order to have it unfrozen. He won't have a leg to stand on."

The man paled then and tugged at his tie. "Well, I can talk to the bank president, I suppose. He might agree to do it considering the circumstances."

"Then stop flirting and get your ass to it! Call him now--do what you have to. Time's a wasting!"

The man shot up from his chair and shoved his papers back into his briefcase, gave her an agitated look, then said goodbye to the real estate commission woman and left.

Two down, one to go, Luke thought. Cassie must've been in the same mindset, because she rounded on the real estate commission woman who had just stood to gather her things to leave.

"No, you don't...you're not leaving yet," she told her fiercely. "As you can see, I had nothing to do with the missing escrow funds, so there's no reason for you to suspend my license."

"You'll have to talk to the appeals board, file an appeal

of the decision and wait for their monthly meeting for an answer," the woman told her as if reciting from a rule book.

"Ah, hell no...I'm not waiting that long," Cassie told her then pinned her with a stare. "Tell me...do you have a boss?"

The woman swallowed then nodded as she slung her purse over her shoulder.

"I want his or her name. I think I need to file a complaint against you for unprofessional conduct."

The woman snorted and stiffened her spine. "What have I done that's unprofessional?'

"Well, first you flirted with my fiancé, then you moved on to the cop who was here, and when neither of them was interested, you moved on to the mealy-mouth banker. I'd say that's pretty unprofessional when you're supposed to be conducting an independent investigation into such a serious matter as fraud."

She harrumphed then patted her hair. "That's absurd. I didn't do that."

"I'd beg to differ, and I feel very sure I can get statements from all three that you did," Cassie told her firmly. "I'm asking you to reconsider your decision, *nicely*." Cassie let her eyes purposely travel to the woman's left hand where there was a very large wedding ring. The woman didn't miss her unspoken point.

After engaging Cassie in a stare down for a good while, she finally sighed and said, "I'll wait two weeks before I file the suspension of your license, since the accounts are frozen...unless one of your affected clients files a complaint against you with the licensing board."

"They won't. The escrow account had less than two thousand dollars in it, and I plan on putting that much back in there to settle it."

"Good, that will help. But if you have pending deals, and the account is frozen, you won't be able to close on those homes. They might still file a complaint against you."

"I'm going over my pending deals when you leave and calling the clients to explain the delay," Cassie told her shortly, hesitated a moment, then asked, "I know he's not the principal broker here, but he's an associate and a partner. You've seen the evidence of what he's done, are you going to suspend James' license?"

"Yes, definitely, right away."

"Good," Cassie told her and then walked past her and out of the room with her head held high.

Luke followed behind the real estate lady who kept walking to the front door, while he hooked a left into the office Cassie had gone to. He wanted to fucking applaud, Cassie had been spectacular. She was already sitting behind her desk, flipping through her organizer, when he walked into her office.

"Well done, sugar. You were amazing...instead of selling real estate you should have been a Philadelphia lawyer," he told her and laughed loudly, before he sat in a chair in front of her desk.

She huffed out a relieved breath. "Yeah, it worked out pretty well for now. At least I bought some time...you were the amazing one, sugar. Spill on how you figured out Diana was involved?"

"I guess my years of law enforcement didn't go to waste," he said and chuckled. "She was nervous as a long-tailed cat when I handed her those papers to copy...and stupid. She said some things that raised red flags. Then when she brought you the copies and you saw the missing check...it just clicked."

"Well it's a good thing you're so damned smart, because I was blind about her...and James." Cassie dropped her chin to her chest and fiddled with her organizer.

"It's not your fault, darlin'. Those two deserve each other and they just took you for a ride."

"I've got a lot to do here, but I really want to go check on my house. Make sure he hasn't done something there too. I had the locks changed, but that doesn't mean he couldn't get in if he really wanted to."

"You're right...want me to go check?"

"I need to go with you to see for myself, besides I don't want to be stranded here, my car is in Bowie."

"So that little silver number is your car?"

"Yeah. I just bought it a few months ago."

"Why the hell did you drive that old pickup truck back to Bowie then? he huffed out a frustrated sigh. "That damned thing is on its last legs. You're just lucky it waited to break down until you got to Bowie," he told her with worry.

She grinned at him then said, "Lots of memories tied up with old Bessie. Good and bad..." Cassie knew her words would give him a flashback of the night they'd made love in the bed of that truck. "And I thought it was appropriate since she'd carried me out of Bowie to drive her back."

Luke grumbled under his breath something about women and their notions, and then he pinned her with his eyes. "Okay, so you want to make your calls now or go check on your house?"

"I have four important calls to make, and I can do that on the road." She grabbed the organizer and her purse then stood. "There's really no reason for me to be here, I'm not doing any new business for now, so I can just do the rest from home tomorrow."

Luke stood and pulled her into his arms then kissed her on the forehead. "Lead on darlin'. Just tell me what I can do to help."

God, she loved this man. She'd asked him to let her handle things, and so far he had. He'd been supportive, and loving and helped her without trying to take over. "Luke thank you so much for helping me...you've been fantastic."

"You don't need to thank me, sugar...I'm doing it because I want to help you tie up your loose ends, so I can kidnap you back to Bowie and marry you before you change your mind."

"There you go again with that kidnapping thing," she chuckled and swatted his chest. Cassie pressed up as far as she could on her toes, which wasn't far because of the cast, and gently kissed his lips.

" I won't be changing my mind, Luke. I love you."

Luke growled and hugged her to him tightly. "Let's go before I put that desk behind you to good use."

Thirty minutes later, they pulled up in the driveway of her modest two-bedroom bungalow in a quiet suburban neighborhood.

Like most homes in Arizona, hers had a rock and cactus garden in front, instead of flowers. The sandy rocky soil didn't suit them...or grass...she hated not having grass. That was one thing she didn't like about Arizona, how dry and colorless it was in places. Her backyard was pretty nice, with a few palm trees for shade, and a couple of hardy shrubs, but it was mostly rock and dirt too.

Cassie slid out of the truck and walked toward the porch with Luke right behind her. When they reached the front door, she unzipped her purse and dug around for the key the locksmith had mailed to her at the ranch. She'd just pulled it out, when Luke pushed her to the side and studied the door. He put a finger to his lips indicating she should be quiet then mouthed for her to call 911, before he pushed the door open without even turning the knob.

She gasped and Luke shot her a look, then pointed firmly at her to stay there. With a nod, she stepped back off the porch and pulled out her cell, swallowing down the fear that someone was actually inside her house and Luke might get hurt. As far as she knew, he was unarmed.

Her fingers trembled over the keypad of her phone, but she managed to dial the numbers and whisper to the operator what the problem was. The woman wouldn't let her off the phone, and she desperately wanted to go and find Luke to make sure he wasn't hurt. She decided she'd go through the back and see what was going on. Cassie moved around the side of the house between the high wooden privacy fence and stucco wall, then carefully took small quiet steps to the back gate.

Right as she reached for the latch to open the gate, she heard loud male voices arguing and then a gunshot. Cassie screamed and the operator asked her what was going on. She told the woman to send help fast, because someone might be shot then disconnected the phone and dropped it into her purse.

Hobbling as fast as she could back toward the front door, Cassie tripped on a rock right at the edge of the house and went down on her knees hard. She looked up and saw James run from the house with a gun in his hand, and her heart fell to her stomach. Luke was right behind him running out of the house and she saw him holding his side, his hand covered in blood.

CHAPTER THIRTEEN

Cassie screamed at the top of her lungs and pushed back up to her feet, chasing after them. Although she thought he was injured, Luke didn't seem to be affected as he ran after James chasing him down the street.

When she finally reached the street and looked down the block, she saw Luke tackle James then twist one arm up behind his back, and hold the other over his head. She didn't know she could jog with a cast on her leg, but Cassie managed it somehow and reached them to see Luke slam James hand against the pavement several times until he dropped the gun and it skittered away.

She saw a few of her neighbors had seen the ruckus and were either on their porches or on the sidewalk gawking. She yelled, "Call 911 someone's been shot," and then went over to kick the gun out of James' reach. It slid along the pavement and came to a stop by the tire on a black sedan, evidently where James had been running.

Luke was breathing heavily and she saw blood dripping down the thigh of his blue jeans. She ran over to him, but he looked up at her with desolate eyes and said, "Stay back, baby."

He was holding onto James tightly, while James struggled underneath him. Luke put his knee in James' back. "Be still or I'm going to slam your head against this fucking pavement," he ground out and then flinched.

"Oh, god, Luke. Are you okay?" She felt tears pool up in her eyes and then trail down her cheeks. "I called the Police, they should be here any minute."

"Call them back darlin' and tell them to send an ambulance too," his voice was getting weaker and she was afraid he was going to pass out.

"I did, Luke...they're on their way too." She looked down the street and saw a couple of big guys she didn't know standing on the sidewalk a few houses down. She ran toward them and yelled. "Can you come help? He's been shot and needs help."

The burly men, who evidently worked out regularly, jogged toward her, and she grabbed one's arm and said "Please help hold that guy down he shot my fiancé."

The two men went over to Luke and one took over holding James down, while the other helped Luke to his feet. Luke wobbled and the guy slung Luke's arm over his shoulder and walked him over to the curb to sit down. Cassie went to him immediately and raised his shirt up to look at the wound. It was raw, ragged and bleeding profusely.

"Oh god, Luke...it's bad," she said weakly then dropped the shirt.

"Nah, it's okay, darlin'. Just a flesh wound," he said looking into her eyes, his eyes cloudy and somewhat disoriented. "Preppy Boy is an awful shot...couldn't hit the broad side of a barn."

"Don't feed me that bullshit, Luke," she grated and heard the blessed sound of sirens in the distance.

"Does anyone have a towel?" she yelled loudly to the crowd that had formed around them. She saw someone run back across the street to their house, and before long she had two or three towels in her hand. She put one on the ground and said, "Lay back, Luke."

He did and then closed his eyes. "Don't you dare die on me! Open your eyes and look at me," she demanded and lifted his shirt to place one of the other towels over his wound and press down firmly.

He didn't open his eyes, and she whimpered and pressed down harder on the towel. *God, please don't let him die.* She prayed and pressed her fingers to the weak thready pulse in his neck. "Wake up, Luke...look at me!"

He finally opened his pain-filled whiskey brown eyes and looked into hers then swallowed, then said in a low, weak voice, "I love you, Cassie Bee, I'm not going anywhere darlin' until you marry me."

She felt a hand on her shoulder push her to the side,

and two paramedics moved beside Luke then began working him. Gulping a deep breath, she took another step back to give them room to work. Luke had closed his eyes again and they cut his shirt off and started an IV in his arm.

Cassie looked around her and saw that two police officers had handcuffed James and were hauling him up to his feet. She stomped over to them and without warning, balled up her fist and punched James in the gut as hard as she could.

It must've been hard enough, because James doubled over with an oomph. One of the cops dropped James' arm and grabbed her and shook her. "Ma'am you can't do that," he said sternly.

"That piece of thieving crap shot my fiancé," she wailed. "He stole my money, and ruined my business...not to mention broke into my home." She pulled away from the officer to put her hands on her hips. "I'd say I *can* do that, and I'd like to do more!"

"What's your name?" the officer asked.

"Cassie Bellamy. You can talk to Officer Melton, I met with him earlier at my office. He was looking for James to arrest him."

The officer walked away from her and talked into the microphone on his shoulder. A few minutes later, he came back to her. "I spoke with Melton and he filled me in on what was going on. We're taking Barton down to the station for booking. We'll need you and your fiancé to come down there for a statement."

Cassie whimpered, "Sure if he's still alive, we'll be sure to do that," then turned on her heel and ran back over to where Luke was now being loaded onto a stretcher.

She grabbed one medic's arm and asked, "Please tell me he's gonna be ok...please."

"I can't do that ma'am. You'll have to talk to his doctor, but his vital signs are stable for right now. Do you want to ride with us?"

She walked alongside the stretcher, then stopped when they lifted Luke inside the ambulance. "I need to check on my house and bring the truck in case they release him."

The medic's eyes told her he didn't think that was going to happen, but he nodded and then hopped up inside. He told her what hospital they were taking him to then closed the door.

Oh, god, she needed to call her daddy...and Cole to let them know what had happened too. Panicked and numb, Cassie went back to the house and gasped in horror at the mess James had made of it. Things were strewn all around, and a lot was broken. The whole house had been ransacked.

Police personnel were scattered throughout the house. Cassie felt violated and out of control, as she picked her way through the mess to find the man in a suit who looked to be in charge of the other people.

"Excuse, me...I'm Cassie Bellamy and I own this house. How long will you be here?"

She swallowed down the sick feeling that surged through her as she saw a woman with blue gloves squatting down over a small blood stain taking photos, and another with a knife and baggie digging a bullet out of the wall near her kitchen.

"A few more hours probably..." he told her, a closed expression on his face.

Cassie nodded and asked, "Can I go change in my bedroom?"

"Sure, just don't move anything, if you can avoid it."

Ignoring the mass destruction around her, Cassie went into her bedroom and found a pair of yoga pants and a top, then quickly changed and put on one running shoe on her uninjured foot.

She hobbled over and grabbed her purse off the bed, then a thought occurred to her and her stomach sank to her toes. Luke probably had the keys to the truck in his pocket. She was stranded...and Luke was dying.

A sob tore from her gut and she ran back through the chaos in her living room then out the front door, slamming it behind her.

A vision of the black sedan parked down the street, the one that James had been trying to escape to, flitted through her mind. Maybe that idiot had left the keys inside. He would have if he wanted to make a quick getaway, she thought, and that had obviously been his goal.

Taking quick loping steps across her yard and then down the sidewalk, Cassie kept going until she reached the vehicle. The door opened when she pulled on the handle and she breathed a sign of relief, then slid into the driver's seat and felt the ignition for the keys, and they were there.

Releasing the breath she'd been holding, Cassie twisted the key in the ignition, and the car roared to life. She threw it in drive and slammed her foot on the accelerator.

A few minutes later, she slid to a stop in a parking spot near the emergency room. When she opened the door to get out, the edge of a metal box that had slid out from under the seat poked her in the ankle.

She reached down beside her leg and brought it up to the seat, then tried the latch and it opened easily. What she saw inside made her heart stop beating, and hope fill her. Money, lots and lots of banded money was stacked in neat rows inside.

Shutting the latch securely, she grabbed the box and stuffed it back under the seat then got out and locked the door. Luke was more important than any amount of money, so what she'd found was not her first priority. But it thrilled her nonetheless.

It looked like James and Diana weren't going to get away with robbing her blind after all, she thought, then made her way through the sliding glass doors and moved quickly to the admitting desk. "Luke Matthews...where is he?"

"Are you a relative?"

"I'm his fiancé....his next of kin. He doesn't have any other relatives." Her statement drove home the point to her that Luke really was alone in this world, except for her.

The nurse's eyes filled with sympathy, and she walked around from behind the desk to stand beside Cassie. Cassie whimpered and prayed, God, don't let her tell me he's dead.

"He's in room seven, I'll show you where it is."

Deep resounding relief flooded through her as the woman led her to Luke's room. When Cassie walked inside and saw the number of people working on him, that relief fled. He had a tube in his nose and wires stuck all over his body. Cassie's stomach lurched, as fear roiled there in a tight knot.

A doctor leaned over him examining the wound, while several nurses worked with him, all of them functioning as a well-oiled machine. That gave her comfort at least. He had good people caring for him. The nurse that had led her to the room, took her arm gently and said, "There's a family waiting room down the hall. I'll let them know to keep you informed of his status."

Cassie nodded at the kind woman and followed her to the waiting room. Once she was there, she sat in a plastic chair and stared at the TV mounted on the wall, not really seeing it.

After a moment, she took her cell phone out of her purse and dialed Cole's number. He picked up on the second ring, and said, "Cassie?"

"Oh, god Cole, Luke's been shot," she told him in a shaky voice then groaned.

"What?" Cole yelled across the line, and Cassie flinched.

"James shot Luke...we're in the emergency room in Phoenix."

The line was silent for a long time, and she almost thought he'd hung up when he finally said, "What's his condition...where was he shot?"

"In the side, and I don't know, they haven't told me anything yet."

"Call me back when they tell you something," he said then she heard computer keys tapping. "I'm going to try and find a flight."

"Cole, wait! Let's see what they say first. I just wanted to call and let you know."

"Thanks for calling me, Cassie. I appreciate it."

"I know you love him too," and she knew in her heart that was true. He and Cole were more like brothers than best friends. They'd been together through thick and thin since before Cassie had even met Luke. And she'd known them since she was ten.

Cole didn't say anything for a second, then he said. "Where's James?"

"In jail...Luke caught him. He broke into my house, and was there when we got there."

"I knew I shouldn't have let that bastard go. I just had this feeling in my gut he was going to do something stupid."

Cassie heard the guilt in his tone and quickly said, "It's not your fault, Cole. James is crazy, and you had no reason to keep holding him."

"Yeah, you and your daddy dropped the charges because I asked you to, so we could get Luke off the hook."

"It. Is. Not. Your. Fault." Cassie repeated trying to make Luke's bullheaded friend understand.

"If you say so," the stubborn man persisted.

"Luke would not want you blaming yourself, Cole. You are his best damned friend in the world. He loves you too."

Cole growled in her ear, "I'm not waiting. I'll be there on the next flight. I'll call you when I get there." He hung up the phone in her ear and she stabbed the end button.

Cassie called her dad and filled him in on what had happened and he was madder than a bear, and threatened to come to Phoenix and fill James' ass with buckshot. She managed to calm him down after a while, and told him she'd keep him updated on Luke's condition. '

Cassie didn't tell him that she and Luke were engaged, or about Titan. That, she wanted to tell him in person.

Just when she'd ended the call, a nurse came in and walked over to her. "Cassie Bellamy?"

She moved to sit on the edge of the chair, swallowed down her fear then said, "Yes?"

"Mr. Matthews wants to see you...*now*. He's awake now and yelling the place down for you. Please come with me."

Cassie gave her a teary chuckle. "Yep, that's Luke."

"We've moved him to a regular room on the fifth floor, and they allow you to stay with him there, so that should make him happy," she grinned at Cassie.

When Cassie walked into the room, she saw Luke's face was bright red and his fists were clenched on top of the covers. Wires were taped to his broad, firmly muscled chest, and the IV was still in his arm, but the tube in his nose had been removed. Progress, or so she hoped. She ran over to him, kissed his cheek and then laid across his chest to hug him. "Oh, Luke..."

He grabbed her shoulders and pulled her away a little flinching.

"Oh shit, did I hurt you..." she backed away from the bed her hand flying to her mouth. "Are you in pain, I'll get the nurse..." she spun toward the door.

"Come back here, darlin'," he said weakly and opened his arms to her. "Just be careful, the bullet glanced off a rib over here. He pointed at the spot and she flinched.

Sucking in a sob, she went back to him and laid over his chest gently this time and kissed him. "What did the doctor say?"

"They gave me twelve stitches and said I have a cracked rib. The bullet just grazed me darlin' like I said." His words were slightly slurred, and he gave her a wobbly smile then kissed her head. "But they're going to make me stay in this damned hospital tonight to watch me."

"I've got to call Cole, before he books that flight..." Cassie dug around in her purse and pulled out her cell, quickly dialing Cole's number. He didn't answer, and she sighed and left a message for him.

She'd barely ended her message, when her phone rang in her hand. Looking at the display, she saw it was Cole. "Hello--Cole?"

"Is Luke ok?" There was an wary edge to his voice.

"Yes...twelve stitches and a cracked rib. The bullet just grazed his side."

She heard Cole inhale deeply then exhale. "Thank, god," he said, his voice shaky with relief.

The relief in Cole's voice made guilt flood Cassie. She'd gotten Luke into trouble yet again. It was her fault for bringing him here. In a voice much higher-pitch than usual, Cassie asked him, "You want to talk to him?"

Cole said he did and she handed the phone to Luke without looking at him, then stepped out into the hall, as relief and numerous other emotions threatened to overwhelm her.

They swirled inside of her head like clothes in the spin cycle of a washing machine, guilt, anger, fear, relief and resignation. Back and forth they went, taunting her, torturing her, making her think about what could have happened to the man she loved if James had been a better shot.

And it *was* all her fault. Cole had said it was his, but he was wrong. She was the one always causing Luke problems...trouble. If she'd just come back to Phoenix alone like she'd planned, Luke wouldn't have gotten hurt. She didn't want to mess up his life with her drama. Maybe she just needed to end things now...make him go back to Bowie without her.

But the promise she made him to talk about things rather than running, or doing something hasty, because she was emotional or confused came back to taunt her.

Luke had done his best today to keep his promise to her, and she needed to make the first step toward fulfilling hers to him, by changing her standard mode of operation, talking to Luke about what was going on in her head instead of hauling tail. She pushed off the wall and walked back into his room.

Luke was off the phone and held it loosely in his hand, while he just stared at her in the door, something like fear shining from his eyes, his jaw tight. "Thanks for not running off."

"How did you--"

"Your eyes, cupcake...they always get this panicked look in them before you take off...like a scared horse. I'm starting to recognize the signs," his voice was low, gravelly and intense. "My getting hurt was not your fault...wasn't Cole's either. That blame lays only on James Barton."

"But I brought you here, if you weren't with me, you--"

"Would still be a cop and probably have a bullet in my head instead, killed doing a job I didn't even like. And I'd be miserable as hell without you."

Tears stung her eyes and Cassie swallowed hard against the emotion flooding her. "I don't want to be without you either...but I don't want my selfishness or drama to get you hurt."

"I couldn't imagine a better way to die, darlin'. I'd at least be in your arms when I did."

She gave him a watery smile and walked over to gently kiss his lips. Luke's arms wrapped around her and she sighed letting go of all her misgivings. He loved her, and wanted to be with her no matter what. The feeling was mutual.

"That's more like it," he said and kissed the top of her head. "Now, go call the police and have them come here to take my statement. I have a helluva lot to say."

"Luke, you're hurt. You need to rest," she said looking seriously into his dark eyes.

"I want to get this wrapped up quickly, so we can get

back home."

Home. Bowie. That never sounded so good to her, because Luke was going to be there with her. They'd raise horses and babies, and be happy...finally. She found his business card and dialed Officer Melton and related Luke wanted to give a statement.

"Did you convince Cole not to come?" she asked him curiously, hoping he had talked some sense into his friend.

"Nah, he's pretty damned hardheaded, he thinks he can help us. He'll be here first thing tomorrow. I won't get out of here til around noon...can you go pick him up at the airport at ten?"

"Sure, no problem...Luke, I have to tell you something." she told him gnawing her lower lip.

Worry came into his eyes, and his lips flat lined. "What now?"

She couldn't blame him for expecting the worst...more trouble. It's all he'd gotten since he'd been with her again. She laughed and his eyebrows raised.

"It's not bad..." she told him.

"What is it?" his voice was short and impatient.

"I kind of stole James' car to get here. You had the truck keys, and I needed to get here fast...so I thought about that car he was trying to get to when you tackled him, and saw the keys were in the ignition..."

"Jesus, Cassie!" he yelled and sat up grimaced then laid back down. "That car might have been stolen by him! The police probably need it for evidence. You could've been arrested!"

"Well, here's the thing..."

"What else?" he asked and groaned.

"I found a long flat metal box with a lot of money in it under the seat."

A smile crept over his face and his eyes danced. "Oh, yeah? How much money?"

"Looks like it could be all that's missing. It was all banded together--large bills."

Luke whooped and pumped his fist, which brought a nurse running into the room. Cassie stepped aside as the woman ran over to the bed and started checking machines and making sure his wires were still affixed.

"Sir, you're going to have to stay calm. You set our monitors off, not to mention you're disturbing our other patients."

"Sorry..." he said sheepishly and let her check him out. The nurse shot him one more warning look, then left them alone again.

"See, I'm always getting you in trouble," she said with a brittle little laugh.

"You're the kind of trouble I like, darlin'...the best kind," he told her with sincerity sparkling in his eyes. "The kind I'd gladly welcome for the rest of my life."

Cassie almost believed him.

She took his hand, and asked, "What do you think I should do about the money?"

"Give it to the cops, and get a receipt. Once the case is settled, they'll return it to you... probably."

"I can't do probably...I need that money, it's mine." Cassie couldn't afford not to get that money back. Settling her business affairs depended on it. Starting her horse farm depended on it.

"You know any good attorneys here?" Luke asked her.

"Yeah, I know a few, what kind?" There was no way Cassie was going to pay outrageous attorney fees to get *her* money back.

"Criminal, Civil...either one would probably work."

"I think I'll just deposit it back in my account then tell the cops," she told him petulantly.

"You could be charged with tampering with evidence, darlin'...or maybe even obstruction. Hell, they might even charge you as an accomplice."

"I'll get the attorney if and when that happens. I'd rather ask for forgiveness than permission. I need my accounts unfrozen." She needed to get her business settled so they could get out of this godforsaken state, and away from James.

"Don't even think that, honey. I need you with me, not in jail. Just do it the right way...we'll deal with the money issue when it comes up."

She dropped her chin to her chest. "How the hell could I have been so stupid to not see what James was doing?"

"This isn't your fault either, so stop blaming yourself and stiffen up your backbone. We're in this together, baby," he reassured her with a squeeze of her hand.

She sat on the beside him and leaned her head on his chest again. "I'm so glad."

A few minutes later, Officer Melton walked into the room followed by a pretty female officer in a black skirt suit. Cassie stood up, but didn't let go of Luke's hand.

"Hello Miss Bellamy, Mr. Matthews..." he nodded at them then turned to the petite dark-haired woman with him, "This is Detective Sabrina Roberts from our vice division. She's been assigned to your case, and has some questions for both of you."

Sabrina Roberts walked over and shook each of their hands and then pulled a chair up beside the bed. She pulled a small notepad from her purse and a pen, then flipped it open. Officer Melton stood over at the other side of the room observing.

The friendly, but professional, woman asked them a succession of questions about James, Cassie's business and how he was involved and what they believed he'd done, and then she took detailed notes on Luke's statement regarding the shooting.

When she was done, and was about to shut the pad, Cassie piped up. "There's one more thing you need to know..."

"What's that?" the detective asked and reopened her pad.

Cassie's eyes moved to Luke and he encouraged her

with a squeeze of her hand and his eyes. Looking back at the detective, she said, "When Luke tackled James, he was trying to get to a black car he had parked down the street at the curb. After the ambulance took off, I realized Luke had the keys to his truck, so I took that car to get here..."

"You stole a car?" The other woman's eyebrows lifted and her deep blue eyes widened.

"Not exactly...I borrowed it. I didn't have any other transportation, and didn't think James would mind considering he stole thirty thousand dollars from me."

A wry grin kicked up one side of the woman's full lips. "And?"

"Well, when I got here and went to get out, and a metal box slid from under the driver's seat. I looked inside and I think it might be the money he stole from me. There's a lot of large bills in there."

The detective shut the notebook and shoved it and the pen in her purse, then stood and smiled at her. "Let's go have a look."

Cassie led her out of the room and down to the parking lot, then went to where she'd parked the black sedan in the emergency room lot earlier. She fished around in her purse and pulled out the keys handing them to the detective, before stepping back.

The woman took the keys, but didn't open the door. She reached into her purse and pulled out a pair of blue latex gloves and put them on, before she opened the door. Cassie gulped and said, "I guess my fingerprints are in the car now, since I drove it here."

That could be a problem, if they wanted to make it one, Cassie thought, as she ran over the possible implications in her head. Thank god Luke had talked her out of depositing the money in her account. Thinking about the implications of that now, made shivers run down her spine.

It could have looked like she had stolen the money, instead of James, or that they were in cahoots to defraud their clients.

"I don't think you'd be giving back thirty thousand dollars in cash, or giving us this car instead of just wiping it down and dumping it, if you were involved, Miss Bellamy. I think you're smarter than that, even though your ex-fiancé isn't," Sabrina said then she assured her, "I'll have the techs take your fingerprints for exclusion."

Walking around the back of the car, she jotted down the license plate number. "Todd, can you call in this plate and see what you get?" She looked over at Officer Melton who'd followed them outside, but had remained silent.

"Sure, Bri..." he said with a smile, then walked behind the car.

Detective Roberts walked to the driver's door and opened it, leaning inside to look around. She pulled out her phone and took several pictures then reached under the seat and pulled out the metal box and snapped a photo of it. She pulled it out of the car and put it on the hood, where she opened it then whistled.

"Wow...you may be right, Miss Bellamy. This is a lot of money," she agreed then leaned in and took more photos of the banded money.

Officer Melton walked up beside them and whistled too, putting his hands on his hips he said, "Car's stolen."

"This gets better and better..." Cassie said with a groan.

"Well, the good thing is Miss Bellamy...I think your ex-fiancé doesn't have much wiggle room now. We'll probably get him to plead, which will get this money back to you much sooner than if we had to go to trial."

"He's a lying weasel, so he might not," Cassie informed her.

"Oh, he'll plead. All of these charges combined could mean thirty years or more in prison for him, unless he does. We also found out he has a prior record for embezzlement in New Mexico, which won't look good in court, if it's admissible."

Cassie gasped, she really hadn't known James at all.

And she felt like ten times the fool, for not checking him out better before she went into business with him. "If he pleads, how fast will I be able to get the money back, so I can straighten out my business?"

"That's up to the judge, but if you get a good attorney, probably not long."

That was Luke's advice too, so she'd do that right away. Sabrina Roberts carefully took out each band of bills, and counted them, with Cassie standing there watching. She counted a second time, and came up with the same total. After she finished, she gave Cassie a receipt for the money, and took the box over to her car and locked it in the trunk.

The detective and Officer Melton told her they were staying around until a tow truck came for the vehicle, but Cassie decided to go back to Luke. She thanked them and then went back up to his room.

When she went into the room, he was dozing peacefully and she didn't wake him. Instead, she sat down in the chair beside the bed and called her real estate attorney for a recommendation on an attorney to handle this situation.

After she talked to Mike Peterson, the attorney he referred her to, Cassie felt tons better. He heard her tale, then assured her with all the evidence against James and Diana, he felt sure he could convince the judge to release the money to her immediately. She called the woman at the real estate commission next, and told her what was going on, and that the money had been recovered.

The woman told her that if James took a plea agreement and admitted guilt, that she would close the investigation immediately, and her license wouldn't be suspended. Cassie agreed to keep her informed, then called her banker and told him that James had been arrested, and that the police had recovered the money.

After a few minutes of her needling the man, he agreed to unfreeze her accounts after he called the police and verified what she'd told him. That wouldn't really do her any good until she could redeposit the money, because all of her accounts were empty. But at least she could close her pending deals, because she would use her own money to get the escrow account fixed. As much as it galled her, she'd dip into her personal savings account to take care of that.

She saw Luke move in the bed, then his warm brown eyes popped open and he gave her a sleepy sexy smile. "God, I love waking up to see you," he said in a low voice.

Love for him poured through her, filling her heart to near bursting. She stood up and placed a soft kiss on his mouth, then whispered, "You're going to get tired of seeing me, because I'm not going anywhere, Luke. You're stuck with me for good, cowboy."

"Can't think of anywhere I'd rather be stuck," he told then put a gentle kiss on her lips, then his arm snaked around her waist to pull her closer and he tried to deepen it, but she pulled back and sat down.

"None of that right now..." she smiled then said smugly, "I need to tell you my good news."

He lifted an eyebrow and smiled. "I need some good news...shoot."

"Well, Detective Roberts took the money, and gave me a receipt..."

"That's good news?"

"She said that with all the evidence they have now against James, he'd probably accept a plea deal, so we don't have to go to court, which means I'll get the money back soon. I talked to an attorney and he agreed. He's going to contact the judge they assign to the case and work it out."

He grinned broadly, then said, "Now that is good news. Congratulations, darlin'."

"There's more..."

His other eyebrow raised and he put his hand over his heart. "Be still my heart..."

"The banker is going to unfreeze my accounts, and the real estate commission is closing the investigation, once they verify everything I told them."

Luke sat up then cringed, grabbing his side. She put a finger over her mouth to shush him from the whoop she knew he was about to let loose, then pushed him back down on the bed.

"Stop that!" she ordered in a harsh whisper.

He grabbed her by the shoulders and dragged her down to him, then claimed her lips in a kiss that curled her toes, one that got interrupted by the nurse who cleared her throat behind Cassie.

Cassie pulled away from Luke and spun to see the dour nurse standing there with an angry expression, her hands on her round hips.

"You two are something...this needs to stop. Mr. Matthews needs his rest," she said disapproval pinching her thin lips.

"What Mr. Matthews needs is to get the hell out of here," Luke said in a feral tone, and began ripping the adhesive patches off his chest, flinching as they pulled the hair on his chest.

The nurse gasped then ran over there and took them out of his hands, and shoved him back down onto the bed. "You're going to make your wound start bleeding again!"

"I don't give a damn, get this crap the hell off of me, *now*," he demanded and ripped off the last white circle from his chest and handed it to her.

"The doctor is not here, that's not possible."

Luke stuck one of his long naked legs out from under the cover and went to sit up again. God, he was an even worse patient than she was, if that was possible. He needed to get a grip on himself, before he opened up that wound again.

"Luke!" Cassie yelled and walked over beside the nurse, "Settle yourself down or I'm gonna hog-tie you."

He stopped his motion and then looked up into her eyes with a sexy grin. "Now that definitely sounds like something I'd be okay with, sugar."

The nurse looked at them like he'd lost his mind. Cassie glanced at Luke and grinned then their shared laughter bounced off the walls of the room. With a harrumph, the nurse turned off the monitor that was attached to the leads, mumbling something about wishing she was the doctor so she could get him out of her hair, before she stomped out of the room.

They laughed again and she gently pushed him back to the bed, "Now, you be good, and you'll be out of here tomorrow."

He scooted over in the bed and patted it. "I'll be good, if you come lay down here with me. It's late and I'm tired, but I'm not going to sleep without you beside me."

Chewing her lip, Cassie looked back over her shoulder where the nurse had exited, then looked back at him. What the hell? What were they going to do kick him out? He'd be happy as a hog in shit if they did.

Cassie laid down on the bed beside him, careful to avoid his injured side. His arm instantly went around her and he pulled her closer to him, snuggled his nose into her hair and sighed closing his eyes.

"Love you, darlin'," he said then she heard his soft snores in her ear.

Cassie smiled peacefully then closed her own eyes. *I love you too, sugar*, she thought, *so damned much*, right before she drifted off herself.

CHAPTER FOURTEEN

Taking a sip of the tarry black coffee she'd gotten at the hospital, before she left, Cassie changed lanes to avoid a slow dump truck up ahead of her on the interstate near the Sky Harbor airport exit. She swerved Luke's big truck back over in front of the dump truck then immediately took the airport exit, studying the signs to see where she needed to go next.

The exit to terminal three came up on her fast, and she almost missed it, and spilled a little of her coffee on the seat, but she managed to ease into the chute at the last minute. Navigating airport roads always made her nervous, she was even more nervous than usual considering she was driving Luke's big pickup with a cast on her left leg.

Cassie eased up under the terminal canopy and glanced at all the people standing on the sidewalk, looking for Cole. She slammed on the brakes when she saw him step off the curb in her path and wave. Damned man, must have a death wish, she thought, as he walked around to the driver's side and threw his duffle bag into the bed, then opened the door.

"Shove over, sugar," he drawled authoritatively.

Cassie scooted over to the passenger side, more than glad to let him drive. He smiled over at her, his eyes warm and friendly. "How's your leg?"

"It's good. Other than feeling like I'm wearing a concrete shoe, I don't even notice it anymore," she told him and laughed.

His smile faded and then he looked back at the road and asked, "How's Luke?"

"Ornery, agitated...a worse patient than I was. I thought that nurse was going to shoot him herself last night," she chuckled.

"He must be feeling okay then," Cole said and huffed out what sounded like a relieved breath.

"Yeah, he's going to be okay, Cole," she told him seriously. "Thank, god...and thank you for coming. As much as he protested, I think it'll make him feel better."

"Cassie, about what I said by the lake..." his voice was low and apologetic.

"You only said that because you care about him, Cole. I understand...and I did seem to be the cause of him getting into trouble. That's why I was thinking of leaving Bowie again. I didn't want to ruin his life or your friendship." She looked out the window and crossed her arms over her chest.

"You're the best damned thing that could have happened to him. You coming back to Bowie has made him face things he'd brushed under the carpet for ten years," Cole told her and hesitated, then admitted, "I've thought it over and him resigning as Sheriff, is probably for the best. I pushed him into running for the job in the first place, and he hasn't been happy...I saw that, but didn't want to admit it."

"Thank you for saying that," she said and felt tears burn behind her eyes, but she held them back with effort.

Silence filled the cab of the truck as he took the road to get back on the interstate, toward Phoenix. It lasted until he had been on SR 143 for about ten miles.

Suddenly, he glanced over at her with serious green eyes and said, "Don't leave him, Cassie...he was a wreck last time...this time, it would kill him."

Surprised, she turned toward him then stuck out her left hand to him. He glanced down at it then up into her eyes, his eyes held tons of questions.

"Luke asked me to marry him in Amarillo," she told him and smiled widely. "I'm not going anywhere without him, Cole."

He looked back at the road then slammed his hand on the steering wheel. "Well I'll be damned. That's great news, sugar. Congratulations," he said with an ear to ear grin, then shook his head and said, "Lucky bastard."

218

Relief poured through her that Cole wasn't upset about their engagement, that he even seemed happy for them. She'd been worried about that. With happiness filling her, Cassie related Luke's grand proposal in Amarillo, and then gushed on about Titan and how gorgeous he was.

Cole laughed and listened intently, but she could see something was bothering him. "What's bothering you?"

He shook his head, hesitated then asked, "So Luke is planning on helping you with the horses now instead of the cattle?"

"No--why would you think that?"

"Honey, there's no way he could afford to do both. He's saved up money, but not enough to buy into the cattle herd and buy the stud you've just described."

Shocked, Cassie sat back against the door and stared at him for a second. His face was an unreadable mask now.

"He said he had enough. I told him I didn't need for him to buy Titan for me. I have money."

"He was trying to make sure you stayed in Bowie. He'd been talking about it, but once he started talking about doing the cattle thing with me, I figured he'd changed his mind."

Cassie was furious with Luke. He'd lied to her, and she didn't know what was rattling around in that head of his. Maybe he planned to take out a loan for the money he needed for his stake in the herd. He should have talked to her about it. So much for him and his communication speech to her. She huffed out a breath then slammed herself against the seat back, refolding her arms over her chest.

Cole gave her a concerned look then asked, "What's going on in that pretty head of yours, Cassie? I don't want to cause trouble with you and Luke."

"Oh there's trouble all right, but none you caused. He should have talked to me..." she huffed out a frustrated sigh, "He's still in on the herd with you Cole. You don't worry, I'll fix it, but don't tell him anything...I want him to stew a while more, he deserves it."

Cole chuckled then and said, "Honey, he's definitely met his match with you. I have a feeling you'll keep him in line just fine."

When they got to the hospital, the parking lot was almost full, and Cole had to take a spot on the last row, a good trek from the front entrance. They walked across the lot, then went inside and up to Luke's room. When they walked inside, he was standing there in a pair of dark blue scrubs beside a wheelchair with his hand to his side, arguing with a nurse about needing a wheelchair.

Even though she was still mad at him, laughter bubbled up inside of her at the incredibly delicious, but ridiculous sight he made in those scrubs and his cowboy boots. He looked like a hot cowboy doctor, and her mouth watered. She walked over to him and put her hand on his arm. He turned his angry brown eyes to look at her.

"Excuse me, doctor...." she said suggestively, and winked at him knowing he'd remember their kidnapping/doctor fantasy. "What's a girl got to do to get kidnapped around this place?"

Desire sparked in his eyes and his face turned beet red, before he gave her a sexy lopsided grin that caused all kinds of tingles to dance through her. Then his gaze drifted over her shoulder and he saw Cole behind her. "Bout damned time you got here," he said grumpily.

"Bout damned time you let Cassie make an honest man of you," Cole flipped right back at him. "Congratulations, man." Cole walked over and stuck out his hand, but Luke pulled him into a man hug and slapped his back.

"Thanks for coming, although I told your hardheaded ass you didn't need to."

"I wanted to come and check out the scenery in Phoenix," he said and his eyes traveled to the pretty blue-eyed nurse who'd been arguing with Luke when they walked in. He gave her a wink and she blushed. "Looks pretty damned good so far," he said exaggerating his drawl.

Luke bristled and said gruffly, "If you'd quit being a hound dog, I want to get my ass out of this place."

The petite nurse moved to put her finger in Luke's chest, her nose barely reaching above his navel. "Then you need to sit your *ass* down in that chair," she pointed at the chair then brought her finger back to poke him again, "and I will gladly roll your *ass* out of here!"

Cole and Cassie hooted in laughter, but Luke just stared down at the woman angrily. Cole walked over to Luke and grabbed his arm then told her with an amused chuckle, "Sugar, I like your style," before he forced a grumbling Luke down into the chair.

Once they reached the front exit, Luke made them leave the wheelchair at the hospital exit, insisting on walking to the truck. He didn't want to wait in the crowd of cars under the canopy, or in the throng of people on the sidewalk waiting for their ride, he told them.

As they made the hike toward the truck, the Arizona sun was out full force, and the heat radiated off the pavement, scorching Cassie's toes where they peeped out of her cast. She noticed Luke was sweating profusely, and breathing hard by the time they got his surly ass to the truck.

Texas was hot, but Arizona was in a different league than her home state...this felt like hell. She noticed that although Luke was sweating and his cheeks were flushed, his face was paler than it had been inside the hospital. She and Cole wrangled him up in the truck, then she walked around the truck and slid in the driver's side before Cole, so she could sit between the two men. Luke put an arm around her shoulders and pulled her closer to him.

Heat poured off of him in waves, and she tried to pull away from his stickiness. "Darlin' it's too hot for cuddling right now. Let Cole get the air going first," she said and slid back over to the middle. He grunted and then leaned his head against the window.

Cole slid in the truck and cranked it up then fiddled

with the dash to crank up the air conditioner to high.

"Man, I couldn't take this heat day in and out. I'd fucking melt," Cole said.

"It feels like it sometimes for sure," Cassie agreed.

"He doing okay over there?" Cole glanced over at Luke.

Cassie saw his eyes were closed, and his shirt was drenched. "We need to get him to my house and in bed. The nurse gave me a prescription for antibiotics and pain medicine. We need to get them filled on the way home."

Cole nodded and put the truck in drive. She gave him directions to a nearby pharmacy where she went in and got Luke's medicine, fresh bandages and other supplies to redress his wound, then headed back to the truck and gave Cole directions to her house.

They pulled up in front of her cozy little stucco house with the teal blue shutters and clay tiled roof, looking so neat and pristine on the outside, but Cassie hadn't forgotten the mess James had made of it on the inside. She groaned and told Cole, "I'll clear off a spot on the couch for him, until I can get the bedroom cleaned up."

"Maid take the week off?" Cole teased.

She felt tears burning behind her eyes and told him, "No, James decided to redecorate, before he shot Luke."

"I'm sorry, Cassie," he told her with sincerity.

"Things can be replaced, Luke can't. I'll clean up the mess."

Cole opened the door and let her out. They walked around the truck to help Luke out and each of them took an arm to guide him to the porch. Cassie was concerned that his color hadn't gotten better even with the air conditioner in the truck cooling him off.

She reached up and felt his forehead, and his skin was still burning up and noticed his cheeks were still flushed. He was also too quiet, not himself for sure. That worried her more than the flush.

The nurse had told her he might spike a fever and to

give him Tylenol if that happened, but Cassie wasn't sure if he was just overheated or if he truly had a fever. She'd get him settled, give him his prescriptions and keep an eye on him.

Dropping Luke's arm, Cassie put her key in the lock then opened the door. Cole helped Luke inside and then whistled. "Jesus, Joseph and Mary..." he said his eyes traveling over the piles of her things, which now amounted to garbage strewn across her home.

"Amen," Cassie said and walked inside where she began picking up stuff to clear a path for them. Once she had a trail cleared to the couch, she swept all the stuff off the sofa and motioned for Cole to bring Luke over. She fluffed a pillow and put it in the corner by the arm and helped Cole ease him down. Luke groaned, and she felt his head again. He was still scorching hot.

"I'm going to get a cool rag for his head," Cassie said, then ran to the kitchen. Quickly, she filled a bowl with water and a few ice cubes, then searched the drawer and found a couple of clean dish towels. Walking back to the living room, she set the bowl down then dipped a towel into the bowl. After wringing it out, she put the towel on his throat, and repeated the process to put one on his forehead.

"Luke are you awake, baby? Talk to me."

He opened one glazed eye and said weakly, "Yeah, I'm awake," then closed his eye.

She grabbed the white pharmacy bag from the sofa table where Cole had put it when they came in. With a glance at Cole, she asked, "There's bottled water in the fridge, can you grab a couple? There's a beer in there too, I think, if you want one instead."

Cole went to do as she asked, and Cassie quickly read the dosage instructions for the meds then opened the caps to pull out the correct amount of pills.

When she looked up, Cole handed her one of the cold bottles that he'd already opened for her. "Sit up if you can,

Luke. You have to take your medicine."

"Can't..." he said in a voice as weak as a kitten.

She swallowed hard and looked at Cole. "Can you help him sit up?" He nodded and went over and slid his arm under Luke's shoulders to hold him up.

"Luke open your eyes, sugar," Cassie told him, then set the water down and picked up his hand to drop the pills in his palm. "Open up, Luke," she said then guided his hand to his mouth and he popped in the pills.

Quickly, she lifted the bottle of water to his lips and encouraged him to drink the whole bottle. When Luke was done, Cole slid him back down on the pillow.

"I'm worried about him..." Cassie said quietly.

"Me too--what do you think it is? He was pretty perky at the hospital, but after we got him across the parking lot to the truck, he looked pretty bad."

"The nurse said he'd probably spike a fever...maybe the antibiotic will help. I'm going get him some ibuprofen too." She was back with the pills in her hand, and Cole lifted him up again, and they managed to get them down his throat.

"Okay you keep an eye on him and I'll go get the bedroom cleaned up."

"Sure you don't want me to help?" Cole asked then his eyes traveled around the disheveled living room again.

"No, you stay with Luke, and I'll take care of it. I'll set up the spare room for you too."

"Don't go to any trouble for me, darlin'. I can clean it up when I go in there later."

Cassie nodded and took off for her bedroom before she broke down in tears in front of Cole and Luke. She was worried sick about Luke, and was an emotional mess over the state of her home, but she'd managed to keep it together, so far. She didn't think she'd be that lucky once she was alone.

She walked into the room and saw her clothing strewn all over. Some of it was ripped to shreds, mostly her lingerie. She ran into the bathroom and got a big garbage bag out of the linen closet then started stuffing things into the bag without looking at them. If she looked, she would lose it.

Bowie was a fresh start for her, and she wouldn't be needing suits and heels to ride horses, or lingerie to impress Luke. He loved her clothed or naked, and she didn't have to worry about enticing a response from him that was for sure.

When she filled one bag, she went and got another out of the closet and repeated the process, until her floor was cleared. She went into her walk-in closet and re-hung the clothes on the floor that weren't ripped, reorganized her shoes, then saw her safe at the back of the closet was open. She swallowed hard, not wanting to look inside.

Her mother's jewelry was in there. The only thing she had left of her. And her rodeo queen crown, and the little stuffed bear that Luke had won for her at the State Fair in Dallas on their second date. Her original paperwork for Bellamy & Barton was in there too, along with her investment information and a couple of large cashier's checks for commissions she'd earned, she hadn't had a chance to deposit them yet.

Feeling like she had lead in her feet, Cassie took a couple of steps to stand in front of the safe. She stooped down, then sat on the floor in front of it and opened the door fully. She felt along the top shelf, and sighed when she found her crown. It wasn't worth a lot to anyone else, but to her it meant the world. It represented her youth and her roots and was a wonderful memory that could never be replaced.

She reached to the back of the shelf and found the bear, and it was in good shape too. After a quick hug to her chest, she put it back inside and went to the second shelf to find her mother's jewelry. Her heart stopped when she found the shelf was clean, and a loud wailing sob erupted from her and tears started rolling down her cheeks.

Sticking her head farther inside, she looked around each shelf carefully, but still didn't find it. All the paperwork she had in there was gone too, as were the checks. She sat back on her haunches and tried to calm her unsteady breathing. She didn't hear Cole when he came into the closet, but she felt his hand on her shoulder.

"You alright, darlin'. What's the matter?"

"H-he took my mama's jewelry...and my papers," she said in a broken whisper.

"Do you know if he had them with him when they arrested him?"

She hiccupped then said, "N-no I don't know anything. Detective Roberts didn't mention it."

"It had to be with him, if you think about it. Luke caught him here, and he didn't make it to the car. Either that or it's somewhere in this mess."

She looked up at him with hope surging through her, and she sucked up her tears. "You're right."

Cassie pushed up to her feet, and hugged him. His arms stayed loose around her for a second, then he hugged her back. "Don't cry, darlin', we'll find it."

"You call that detective guy and I'll look around the living room," he said and then started out of the closet.

"It's a woman," Cassie said to his back.

He stopped and looked back over his shoulder at her. "What?"

"The detective is a woman," she gave him a watery chuckle. Funny that he automatically assumed it was a man.

Cole shook his head and then walked out through the bedroom door. Cassie thought about the pretty detective, and wondered if maybe she should introduce her to Cole. She seemed like his type...and they were both in law enforcement. Maybe they'd hit it off. Cole was too wrapped up in his career, he needed something else in his life...or someone. He was always worried about everyone else, he needed to worry about himself more.

But first things first, she needed to call the detective and find out if that snake James had her mother's jewelry. Cassie walked back into the living room and fished her cell phone out of her purse. She saw Cole on his hands and knees searching through the rubble. Luke was laying quietly on the couch and she saw that his color had gotten a little better, which relieved her. Grabbing the white card Sabrina Roberts had given her, she dialed her cell number.

Detective Roberts told her James had some paperwork belonging to her on him when they arrested him, but Cassie's mother's wedding rings, the pearls her father had given her mother on their fifth anniversary, and the antique brooch that had been passed down from mother to daughter in their family for a hundred years, was not among his possessions.

Fresh tears welled up in her eyes, as she thanked Sabrina Roberts then hung up the phone. She sucked in a deep breath trying to calm herself. Cole looked up at her from the floor. "They don't have it?"

"He had the paperwork, but the jewelry wasn't on him."

"Then it has to be here...maybe you should go check out in the yard," Cole suggested.

"Good idea..." Cassie said and walked out into her yard. Carefully, she worked her way around the perimeter of the yard. The sun was higher in the sky than it had been at the hospital, so she was baking as she searched inch by inch, working around the yard in passes, until she reached the center. Next, she searched the rock and cactus garden, then around the steps, and on the front porch, and found nothing.

Standing in the shade of the porch for a second, Cassie thought about the path that James had taken when he'd run from the house, and decided to follow it to where Luke had tackled him. Walking slowly, she scanned the sandy brown earth on both sides of the sidewalk.

Against the brown sandy earth, and muted bushes, a slash of rich purple velvet snagged her gaze when she neared a prickly bush by where Luke had tackled James.

It had to be the Crown Royal bag she'd always stored the pieces in, she thought. She just hoped they were still in there, and it wasn't just the bag.

Cassie walked quickly to the bush and dropped to her knees then carefully stuck her hand under the bush and untangled the gold cord from needles on several branches. When she finally got it free, Cassie pulled the drawstring cord and held her breath as she stuck her hand inside.

Her breath came out in a whoosh as she felt something in the bag, and she wanted to wail with relief. Opening it wider, she saw that all three pieces were in the bag, and it looked like they weren't harmed.

Hugging the bag to her chest, Cassie walked back to the house. Once she got inside, she shrieked, "I found them!" then went over to show Cole.

He smiled at her, whooped loudly, then picked her up and spun her around in a circle. "That's great sweetheart!" he said then kissed her cheek.

Luke sat up just then and looked at them with angry eyes over the back of the sofa. "Get your damned hands off of my woman, Cole," his pained voice was low and fierce.

Cole set her back down on the floor and dropped his arm around her shoulders. "Well, looks like you must be feeling better.," Cole told Luke and gave him a smug grin. "Too bad...I was really enjoying Cassie's company."

Luke growled and started to get up off the sofa. Cassie pulled away from Cole and ran over to push him back down. "Lay down, Luke! You're not in any shape to be up."

Picking up the second bottle of water from the table, Cassie uncapped it and shoved it in his hands. "Drink this--all of it," she told him forcefully and removed the rags from his throat and chest to refresh them in the bowl of ice water then put them back in place.

"Now you stay down there. I'm going to fix the bed for you."

"He stays here," Luke pointed at Cole who gave him an arrogant grin.

"Luke, drink your damned water." Cassie said then stomped to her bedroom. "Damned jealous fool," she cursed under her breath then yanked off the gold and blue comforter that was half off the bed anyway. She removed the sheets and pillow cases and tossed them across the room into the hamper then went to the linen closet in the bathroom and pulled down more.

Cassie was laid across the bed with her butt stuck in the air, while she fought to tuck in a corner of the new sheet when Luke staggered into the doorway and leaned against the doorframe.

"Now that's what I'm talking about," he slurred and tried to give her a sexy grin, but it came out looking more like a grimace.

Bouncing off the bed, she strode over to him and put a finger in his chest. "I told you to stay on the couch!" she yelled at him and gave him a poke.

"Didn't want to...missed you," he said slurring again, a good sign the pain medication she'd given him a while ago was working.

"You big stubborn jackass..." Cassie grabbed Luke's arm and led him over to the bed, then pushed him down to sit on the edge. Bending over, she pulled off his boots and socks then stood. After fluffing the pillow behind him, she shoved his shoulder to try and make him lay down. Instead of laying down though, Luke grabbed her around the waist and tossed her over him onto the bed pinning her with a thigh, before his mouth came down over hers in a heated kiss.

She squirmed trying to get free, but he wasn't letting her up, and after a second, she didn't want to get up. His drugging kiss had her reaching for him and deepening it, putting her tongue inside his mouth to entice his out to play. He groaned and moved his hand up to cup her breast and she rotated her hips against his thigh trying to put out the fire that had started in her core. Cole's voice at the door brought her out of the trance that Luke had put her under.

"Lord have mercy, I swear you two are like rabbits...even with him gut shot he can't keep his hands to himself."

Cassie slid out from under Luke and off the side of the bed. "Luke!"

"Don't Luke, me darlin' you wanted it as much as I did."

"That's beside the point--you're hurt you big oaf!"

He brought his hand down over his crotch, where he was very visibly aroused. "I"m hurtin' but not where I got shot..."

Cassie clenched her fists and grumbled, then strode over to the bed and threw the covers over him, then leaned in and gave him a quick kiss, before moving back outside of his reach.

"Sleep!" she demanded then backed away from the bed.

"Not unless you're in here with me," he told her and patted the other side of the bed.

"Well then you just stay in here and stare at the ceiling, because I've got things to do, and Cole is helping me."

His face became a thundercloud and he said in a low growl, "I'll help you," then flung back the covers. She ran over there again and threw the covers back over him.

Grating the words out between her teeth she threatened, "If you put one toe on that floor, I'm going to hog-tie you to that bed, Luke Matthews. I love you dammit, but you are a pain in my ass."

"Promises, promises darlin'. That ain't the first time I've heard that threat, and you've yet to carry it through," he slurred then grinned at her.

Emotion clogged her throat and her lips trembled, as

she walked over to put her hand on his cheek. "Please stay in bed. My house is torn up and I've got to fix it. I can't stand to see it looking this way," she pleaded.

His smile dropped and he pulled her to his chest and hugged her. "I'm sorry, darlin'. I'll stay put and let you get it cleaned up. Don't be upset, I can't take it..."

She lifted up and looked into his whiskey-brown eyes, then placed a tender kiss on his lips. "Thanks, darlin'."

Turning back toward the door, she saw Cole standing there shaking his head, a quirky little smile on his face. She didn't acknowledge him, but just brushed past him in the doorway and walked into the living room to start sorting piles.

Three hours later, she and Cole had made a dent in the cleanup, and Cassie was on her hands and knees with peroxide trying to get the small blood stain out of the carpet. Cole had left in the truck to go and pick them up something to eat. When the doorbell rang, she got up, and wiped her hands on a towel to go answer it.

She opened to door to find Sabrina Roberts on her doorstep, and smiled at her, then stood back to let her enter. "Come in..."

"I was in the area and decided to come by and bring you the papers we recovered when we arrested James Barton," she said and stepped inside removing her mirrored sunglasses then pushing them up on her head. Sabrina's hair was down today, and swung in shiny brown waves at her shoulders.

Cassie saw her eyes move around the room and then surprise flickered on her face. "Looks like you've been busy...the photos I saw of how it looked before were pretty bad."

"Yeah it was awful. I wish I could have made that weasel clean up the mess, but I'd rather he be in jail," Cassie told her then walked toward the kitchen. "Would you like something to drink? It's damned hot out today. Bottled water, tea?"

"Water would be great, thanks," Sabrina told her standing near the kitchen door.

Cassie turned back toward her with a bottle of water for each of them. The detective looked a little wilted from the heat, the black pants she had on weren't really perfect attire for Arizona weather. The light blue sleeveless shell she'd paired them with was stuck to her breasts.

At least the woman had taken off the black blazer that must've gone with the pants to cover the very lethal looking gun attached to a thick belt at her waist.

Handing Sabrina one of the cold dewy bottles, Cassie uncapped her own and took a long drink, then asked, "So what's the latest with James anyway? Did he agree to the plea deal yet?"

"The D.A. and my captain are still working it out. The D.A. wants to go to trial, because it's so cut and dry. He's a barracuda on white collar cases...hates to settle them if he thinks he can win and get the maximum sentence."

Cassie groaned, it would be her luck that the case would be assigned to someone like that. "Can I talk to him? I really need this over and done with so I can get moved," she said with a frustrated sigh.

"You're moving?"

"Yeah, back to Bowie, Texas...my hometown."

"So, what's in Bowie? I thought your real estate business was doing pretty well here?"

Cassie grinned at her then said, "Luke's in Bowie...and I'm going to start a horse breeding operation on my daddy's cattle ranch.'

"Oh, god that sounds like heaven," the other woman told her and sighed dreamily.

"You like horses?" Cassie was always up to talk about horses with a fellow lover.

"Love 'em. My dad had a few on our farm growing up and I rode every day. When I moved to the city after I graduated, I missed them terribly. I've been thinking about leasing one at a barn on the north side." Sabrina tilted her head to the side and then asked, "So how's Luke doing anyway? He out of the hospital yet?"

"Yeah, and he's ornery as a bear. It's all I can do to keep him in bed." Cassie's face flushed as the double meaning of her words sunk in and she chuckled. "Well, that wouldn't be a problem if he was feeling better..."

Sabrina chuckled too, "I imagine not."

"Let's go sit down and cool off," Cassie invited and walked toward the sofa. Before they got there though, the front door opened and Cole walked inside with three white bags in his hand and a liter of drink under his arm like a football.

"Oh, hey! I thought you got lost!" Cassie laughed and went over to relieve him of his bags. She walked over to the sofa table to set them down then turned back to see him still standing in the doorway with his mouth open, while he stared at Sabrina Roberts like she was Thanksgiving dinner.

Cassie smiled and then introduced them, "Cole this is Detective Roberts. She brought by the papers that James stole from my safe. Sabrina this is Luke's best friend Cole Jackson, Sheriff of Bowie, Texas."

Sabrina licked her lips, then found her voice and said, "Wow, they sure do grow them tall in Texas...it's nice to meet you Sheriff."

Cassie heard the part the detective had left out of her sentence, and good looking. Sabrina didn't need to voice it, because it was there on her face in her somewhat dazed and dreamy expression.

"Cole..." he corrected still acting like he was struck dumb by the sight of the pretty detective.

"Well, I'm going to bring Luke his lunch and check on him...I'll be back in a few minutes," Cassie told them, but neither seemed to hear her. She tamped down the giggle that bubbled up in her chest and grabbed a sack off the table, and headed for the bedroom.

Luke was snoring when she went inside. He looked so

damned adorable, she thought, all snuggled up to a pillow on his good side. The scrub shirt was pulled up on his injured side and the sight of blood on the bandage made worry run through her.

He'd been moving around too much, she knew it! She flew over to the bed and put the bag down on the night stand, then went to lift the white tape holding the gauze down.

He woke up and rolled over grabbing her wrist. "Whatcha doing, honey?"

"You're bleeding again...be still so I can take a look and make sure you haven't ripped your stitches."

He groaned a little when she tugged the tape off of his skin and she said, "Don't be a baby...you were shot and didn't whine, so don't whine now over a little tape."

She felt the vibration of his chuckle rumble under her fingers and smiled. He was playing her. Lifting the edge of the gauze she took a peek at the raw red wound which was wound tight with black thread. Nothing had broken loose that she could see, but blood was seeping out from the corner.

"You need to take it easier, Luke. You didn't tear the stitches loose, but you're bleeding. Let me go get my supplies and I'll fix you up."

"Thanks, darlin'," he said then sniffed. "Is that hamburger I smell? I'm starving."

"Yeah, Cole went and picked us up lunch. Go ahead and eat, I'll be right back."

Cassie walked back into the living room and stopped short. Cole and Sabrina were sitting on the sofa next to each other, sharing his lunch. He'd split the cheeseburger in half and had divided up the fries. They were talking quietly and seemed to be engrossed in whatever they were talking about.

As she walked behind them to go to the kitchen, they didn't seem to notice and Cassie smiled. She made Luke a glass of tea, then she walked over to the sofa table and picked up the pharmacy bag and her own lunch then went back to the bedroom, and they still didn't acknowledge her. Cole and Sabrina seemed to be in their own little world that consisted of only the two of them. All she'd had to do was introduce them, and it looked like mother nature was taking care of the rest.

Cassie walked back to the bedroom and Luke was just shoving the last bite of his hamburger into his mouth, his face a picture of bliss. "Damn, either that was fantastic, or I was starving."

"Probably both," she laughed and walked over to sit on the bed beside him. She handed him his tea, then set the pharmacy bag down and opened her lunch bag. Her stomach rumbled loudly. "I know I am."

Careful not to spill on her bed, Cassie unwrapped her chili dog and took a bite then moaned. "Mmm...this is good," she said around her bite, and looked up at Luke. His eyes were heated and he licked his lips.

"Stop that!" she said laughing, Cassie knew that look, and it always made her insides quiver.

Giving her an innocent look he said, "What?"

"You know what," she chuckled, then said, "Looks like Cole is really liking the scenery here in Phoenix."

"Oh, yeah? Not surprising, he's a hound dog," Luke grumbled putting his hand on her thigh. "As long as he ain't looking at your scenery, I don't care."

"He didn't even notice I was in the living room a minute ago...neither did his new friend Detective Roberts."

Luke hooted, "What the hell?"

"She came over to bring me the papers James stole, and he came back with lunch..."

"And?" Luke asked and stole one of her french fries to pop it in his mouth.

"From the minute his eyes latched onto her, he was like a bird dog on point."

"Interesting..." Luke smiled at her then said, "She was pretty cute."

Cassie grumbled and stuffed the rest of the hotdog into her mouth then slugged him on the shoulder.

"Just sayin, darlin'..." he laughed shrugging away from her, then said, "But she's not nearly as cute as you are."

"That's what I thought you said," she growled then nudged him again.

Luke helped her put her trash back in the bag, then pulled her to him for a hug. "Not anywhere close."

Cassie snuggled into his chest for a second, enjoying being held. "I have some things to do at the office this afternoon. I'm meeting with Betsy, a Realtor friend, to talk about selling her what's left of my business."

"Is it really that bad?"

"Well, the good thing is it hasn't hit the paper, and hopefully I can keep that from happening, by getting that money back in the bank fast. Sabrina said that James hasn't been offered the plea deal yet...the D.A. is fighting to take it to court."

He groaned, "Awww shit, I'm sorry, darlin'."

"I'm going to call and talk to him. You probably could too...."

"Get me his number, and I sure will. That bastard James isn't going to keep me from getting you back to Bowie," he growled and hugged her again.

"I'll call my lawyer too and see if he can put some pressure on the D.A."

"Great idea," he said then asked, "You want me to go with you to the office?"

"No...you are staying right here, Luke. I've got this."

"I know you do, darlin', but...."

"No, buts, Luke. If you want to help you can make that call to the D.A. I'm not gonna be gone long."

CHAPTER FIFTEEN

It took a week more in Phoenix for Cassie to get everything settled and she was more than ready to be back in Bowie. She knew Luke was ready to be back home too.

Between her attorney and Luke's calls to the D.A., they had finally convinced the stubborn man to go ahead and offer a plea deal to James, but not without a hefty jail term. He'd told them he wasn't negotiating, it was a take it or leave it deal for James.

Sabrina said James' attorney had strongly encouraged him to him to accept it, because he faced forty years in prison instead of twenty without parole if it went to court. Reluctantly, James took the deal.

The final result satisfied Cassie, but Luke still wanted to kick his ass before they left town. She assured him that James would probably get plenty of ass-kicking once he got transferred to where he was going.

Her meeting with Betsy had worked out well, although her friend was sad to see her leave, or so she said. Cassie doubted that, because she had definitely been competition to Betsy in the local market. Without hesitation, the woman had agreed to her terms, and had even agreed to assume her building lease.

As for James' portion of the business, she had her attorney filing a civil suit for damages against him, in the exact amount of his interest in her business, plus court costs. The attorney had wanted to go for more, but she thought it was useless. James didn't have funds of his own, he'd been leaning on her for years. After the suit was filed, she was going to have the attorney contact James in jail and offer to settle with him by signing over his part of the business to her.

When she met with Betsy, she'd also given her the listing on her home. To Cassie's surprise the market value turned out to have appreciated almost double since she'd bought it five years ago. That's why she'd bought in an 'up and coming' neighborhood, she had a feeling it would be a good investment. But she'd never expected it to appreciate that much in so little time. Betsy assured her it would sell quickly, and that she would be in touch soon.

The judge had released the money James had stolen, and she closed out all her business and personal accounts. She was walking away with a good amount to start her new life and new business in Bowie.

More than enough, she thought, and walked up to load the last lamp in the back of the truck. The moving people had loaded up most of her stuff in the moving van earlier. She'd only kept a few things to get started in Bowie until the bulk of her stuff was delivered, and they were hauling that in the back of Luke's truck.

When he wasn't out with Sabrina Roberts, Cole had been a huge help. He'd packed boxes with her, moved things around, and helped her keep Luke resting. Cassie was glad he'd come to Phoenix, she couldn't have done all she had without his help.

She thought Cole was glad he'd come too, or he wouldn't have met Sabrina Roberts. It seemed like Luke's friend really liked the lady detective. His sullen mood today, because they were leaving, pretty much said it was true.

"That's it, I think..." Cassie said smiling at him where he stood at the side of the truck on his cell phone. If men pouted, he was as much in that mode as he could be. Cole ended his call then grunted and stomped off to the house. She giggled watching the big handsome man storm into the house.

Yep, he had it bad...and he'd given Luke such hell about her, he deserved it.

Cassie had left one chair inside the house, so Luke could sit there while they finished loading up. Walking back inside, she saw Cole help him up then he yanked the chair from under him.

"Hey, easy there..." she said breathlessly as she went to

Luke's side and took his arm. He didn't look any happier than Cole. Oh, this was going to be a lovely ride back to Bowie, she thought, sandwiched in between two men in a snit.

She had to do something to get their mood improved, and fast. "I know a great BBQ place near the city limits...let's get going so we can stop there on the way out."

Like little boys, both broke out in grins, and her heart flip-flopped at the sight. "That's better....let's go," she said and turned Luke toward the door. Cole brought up the rear carrying the chair.

Cassie stopped at the porch and got a little choked up when she closed the door of her little house for the final time. She swallowed hard and put her key in to throw the deadbolt, then sucked in a deep breath.

"You okay, sugar?" Luke asked with his hand on her shoulder.

"Yeah, it just all hit me...I'm really doing this," she told him putting her hand up on the door and leaned on it.

He moved up behind her and put his arms around her waist, then kissed the top of her head. "It's going to be great, darlin'" he told her then leaned next to her ear and said in a fierce whisper, "I love you, Cassie Bee."

"Would you two quit with the dramatics and get your asses in the truck?" Cole spat behind them. Turning she saw him standing there with his hands on his jean clad hips, his lips pinched.

"Why don't you call Sabrina and have her meet us at the Pig-in-a-Poke on Pima Freeway?"

Cole's eyes brightened, then his shoulders slumped. "She was supposed to come by here before we left, but she got a call. She probably won't be able to."

"You won't know until you call her...so do it!"

He gave Cassie a wry grin and pulled his cell phone out of his pocket, then dialed a number and turned his back to walk toward the truck. When he let out a loud whoop after he disconnected the call, Cassie knew Bri was going to meet them there. Country boys and their whooping, she'd never get tired of it.

"She'll meet us there," he said happily.

Cassie snorted. "Thank, god...I don't think I could have looked at your hang dog face for a thousand miles."

Luke put his arm around her and they walked to the truck and got inside. Cole followed her directions to get to the interstate, then put the hammer down once they merged into traffic. He looked like he was definitely in a hurry to get to the Poke. But she knew it wasn't the BBQ he was hurrying for.

"Slow down, Cole, what's on fire, other than your breeches?" She teased him and he shot her a hot look.

She laughed enjoying needling him immensely. This was going to be fun, she thought, and Luke elbowed her. Oh, hell no, she wasn't done with him. "Think she'll bring her handcuffs?"

He shot her another look, then his lips flattened and he looked back at the road.

"Maybe you could let her check out your...gun," Cassie suggested with her tongue in her cheek, and Luke chortled beside her, but put his hand on her thigh and squeezed a warning.

Cole grated between his teeth, "You done yet?"

"Not nearly, sugar...." she told him and chuckled.

"Cut the shit, okay?" he demanded, pinning her with glittering green eyes.

She held his gaze and then her laughter overflowed and she doubled over with it. Luke joined in then grabbed his side and groaned.

She sobered immediately, "Sorry, darlin', I'll be good."

Luke snorted. "Not likely...but I like it," he told her with humor still sparkling in his eyes.

It took them about twenty minutes to get to the Poke, and they were sitting inside at a round picnic type table with delicious sweet teas in front of them, when Sabrina walked in. Backlit by the bright sun outside, her skin practically glowed when she came through the door, and a halo formed on the top of her shiny hair. The door shut behind her and she pulled off her mirrored sunglasses then squinted and searched around the restaurant for them.

When he spotted her, Cole gasped then stood up and smiled. Sabrina's face lit up when she finally saw him across the crowded restaurant, then she wove her way through the tables, without breaking eye contact with him. When she reached them, he put an arm around her waist and she leaned up on her toes and gave him a kiss on the cheek.

"Glad you could make it, darlin'," he drawled and helped her onto the bench seat beside him, then sat down again himself.

"Me too...thank goodness it was just a B&E and we got it wrapped up pretty fast," she looked over at him and her gaze lingered a moment, then she dragged it away.

"Lots of excitement here in Phoenix..." Cole said then waved at their waitress. "Most of my calls are about cattle in the road," he told her with a chuckle.

"Too much excitement sometimes," she admitted then huffed out a breath. "I'd almost welcome a cattle call," she said laughing, then she looked over at Cassie. "Get everything packed up?"

"Yeah, the movers finished up this morning," she said then took a sip of her tea. "We should be back in Bowie sometime tomorrow night."

"You have any room for a stowaway in the back of that truck?" her voice was teasing, but Cassie saw in her eyes she was only half-joking.

"You're welcome down at my daddy's ranch anytime...just call me. We've got plenty of room."

"That might be darlin' but you're going to have a lot less real soon," Luke said close to her ear and flicked the lobe with his tongue. She shivered, then looked at him.

"Oh...we haven't talked about that yet, have we?" Cassie said.

"No, but we have a thousand miles to work it out," he told her, and she knew they weren't going to be living apart once they made it back to Bowie. That was more than fine with her. Either way, if they lived with her daddy, which would be more convenient, or at Luke's cabin, they weren't going to be apart anymore.

"Even with you around, there will be plenty of room for guests though, darlin'," she told him and snuggled into his shoulder, then kissed his cheek.

Cassie looked back at Cole and Sabrina and saw them chatting quietly. The star struck look on Cole's face, as he listed intently to whatever she was saying was pretty darn cute.

"You have any vacation time coming, Bri?" Cassie asked her. Sabrina had asked her to call her the shortened version of her name the last time they talked.

The woman dragged her gaze from Cole's then said, "I have about three weeks accrued. I have to plan thirty days in advance if I want to take it. Why?"

"I could probably use some help getting things set up at the farm, once I get Titan and the mares delivered. I just wondered if you'd want to come down and help me." Cole's eyes met hers shining with gratitude and a small smile kicked up the corner of his mouth.

Sabrina sucked in a breath and her hand flew to her chest. "I'd love to...I can't believe you're asking me. I used to ride, but I'm as green as grass these days, so I don't know how much help I'd be."

"You'd be plenty help...and you can refresh your riding skills while you're there."

"When do you think you'll have all your stock there?"

"Oh, I'm planning to have them all there in a couple of weeks. I have the money now to go ahead and buy the mares," she said and smiled widely at Luke. "And my darling husband-to-be gave me the most magnificent stallion on earth as a wedding gift."

Luke swallowed thickly then gave her a smile that

didn't quite reach his eyes. "Yes, I did, darlin'. But he's not nearly as magnificent as you are," he leaned down and kissed her heatedly.

When Luke lifted his head, Cassie felt Cole's eyes on her and she glanced over at him and winked. "He and Cole are gonna buy out my daddy's beef cattle herd as soon as we get back to Bowie."

Cassie felt Luke stiffen beside her and saw a little smile kick up the corner of Cole's lips, right before he hid it behind his glass when he sipped his tea.

"Wow!" Sabrina said and looked at Cole. "Cattle ranching and Sheriffing...you sure keep busy, don't you."

"You have no idea," Cole admitted and shook his head.

"Well, I hope when I come to Bowie, you'll be able to squeeze out some time to show me the sights."

"Darlin', when you come to Bowie, my time is yours. You just tell me what you want to see or do."

She smiled at him, nudged his shoulder with hers then said in a low intimate tone, "I like the sound of that."

She looked back at Cassie then asked, "So, I should probably go ahead and schedule my vacation?"

"That'll put you there in the thick of things," Cassie told her.

"Sounds like it's gonna be the best vacation I've had in years," Sabrina said with a happy smile at Cole. She picked up the menu that was written on a paper bag and studied it, the asked. "I've never been here before, what's good Cassie?"

"Everything's good..." she moaned picking up her own menu.

They laughed and ate, then Sabrina had to leave and Cole quickly got up to walk her to her car. Luke and Cassie stayed at the table and ordered a cherry cobbler to share, which they lingered over to give them some privacy.

Finally Cole came back inside grinning widely and walked back to their table. "That woman is something," he said and plopped back down in his chair with a breathy sigh.

"Glad you got to say a proper goodbye to her after all." Cassie grinned and shoved the last spoonful of the rich cobbler into her mouth. Luke grumbled and grabbed the spoon from her to scrape the sides of the tinfoil bowl.

"Sure put you in a better mood. I might not have to shove you out of the truck before we get to Bowie, after all," Cassie told him.

With a raised brow, Cole gave her a look that said he'd welcome her trying, and then smiled again. Luke paid the check and they all walked back to the truck to get on the road to her new old home.

Two days later, Cole made the final turn of their trip up the long dirt drive to the Double B. Excitement mixed with melancholy welled up inside of her. This was the beginning of her new life and a fresh start for the Double B, but at the same time it was the end of the Double B as it had been for fifty years.

Her grandfather, and then her father had built up the successful cattle operation on the ranch through their sweat and tears. The new equine venture she planned would add a nuance to that operation they'd never had before, and she was determined to make it just as big a success.

Luke squeezed Cassie's hand and kissed her hair, then whispered intimately near her ear, "Welcome home, baby." It was hard to believe how much his life had changed in so little time. The joy he felt inside was hard to contain.

As Cole pulled them to a stop in front of the big rambling farm house, Luke felt like the sun looked brighter, the sky more vivid and the colors of the landscape more vibrant than they'd been in years. It was like someone had replaced his old TV set with a brand new hi-definition plasma...but this was real, and it was because Cassie was back in Bowie and his life for good.

The front door of the house swung open and Imelda

came out first waving at them excitedly, a big smile on her face, then he saw Carl Bellamy come out behind her using a walker to steady his steps.

Beside Luke, Cassie squealed and leaned over him to open the door. He slid out, before she could push him out, and watched as she hurried in a loping gait across the yard toward them.

When she reached them, she was swallowed up in Imelda's considerable bosom as they hugged tightly. Carl stayed up on the porch, and Cassie ran to him there and he let the walker go to grab her in a fierce hug.

Luke swallowed against the emotion that boiled up inside of him. It looked like Cassie finally being home for good made *everyone* feel like their home was complete again, not just him.

Luke shut the door, then walked across the yard to join their happy group. Imelda immediately pulled him down and kissed both cheeks and then hugged his waist, then Carl patted him on the back when he went up on the porch to throw his arm around Cassie's shoulders.

"Oh, my god, daddy -- ya'll come in the kitchen and let's get some tea. Luke and I have something to tell you," she said with excitement making her blue eyes sparkle. Her wavy blonde ponytail danced at the back of her head, because she couldn't seem to keep her feet still.

She grabbed Luke's hand and led him past her daddy and the group migrated inside to the kitchen, where they all took places at the kitchen table and Imelda and Cassie made them all glasses of iced tea. Cole came inside but he told them he had to go to the station and check on things, but he'd be back later. He said he'd called Elmer, one of his deputies, to come and pick him up.

Luke sat next to Cassie, and he hoped she was going to tell them about their engagement and Titan, but he sure hoped she didn't bring up him and Cole buying the cattle herd again. He had some things to work out on that front, but he wasn't going to tell her or Carl that and worry them.

He slid his arm around the back of her chair when put a tall glass of iced tea in front of him then sat down..

"What's the news, baby girl?" Her dad was smiling, but his eyes were a little concerned, Luke noticed.

"Luke asked me to marry him, and I accepted."

Imelda yelled, "Thank the good Lord!" at the same time her father hooted and said, "About damned time!"

She held up her hands and settled them down, "There's more...he bought me an amazing stallion as a wedding present."

Love shone brightly from her sky-blue eyes when she looked up into his, before she leaned up to give him a tender kiss. He'd give every penny he had to see that look in her eyes. Everything else would work itself out one way or another. If he had Cassie, and she was happy, that's all that mattered to him.

"Wow, that's something, darlin'," her dad said and then looked at Luke with questions in his eyes.

Luke couldn't answer those questions right this minute, and he felt guilt riding him. He'd made promises to buy that herd, and he would do it, even if he had to mortgage his house, the only thing he owned free and clear, to the hilt. But that would be kind of difficult since he didn't have a job now. He'd have to think of something else...maybe a business loan on his part of the herd.

Cassie and Cole had happily discussed the herd venture the entire trip from Amarillo, where they'd spent the night last night, to Bowie today. Every word they spoke sent a knife of guilt plunging into his gut. Mostly, he'd stayed out of the conversation, because he couldn't even work himself up to mildly interested in talking about it.

Cassie looked over at him and he must've been frowning, because she asked, "Everything alright, darlin'?"

He forced a smile on his face and leaned down to give her a kiss. "Just fine, sugar...I'm a little tired, how bout you?"

"Oh, *oh*...is your side hurting?" she asked with concern

and stood up beside his chair.

Carl Bellamy studied them intently and then suggested, "Why don't you go get Luke settled upstairs, honey, then come back down here and talk to me."

"Sure thing, daddy. C'mon darlin'," she said then grabbed Luke's arm to encourage him to stand.

"My side isn't hurting, Cassie. I'm just a little worn out from the trip," he said so she'd stop worrying about him. The stitches on his side itched and pulled now, and his rib was a little sore, but other than that, he was fine.

"Then you can take a little nap, and I'll wake you up for supper," she insisted. Luke agreed, not because he wanted a nap, but because he didn't want to talk about the herd, which he felt would be the next topic on the agenda. He'd go take that nap, and consider possible solutions to his problem. Since they didn't have cell phone towers out here, making calls in the bedroom was out of the question.

"Sounds good, honey. Lead the way." She took his arm and led him up the stairs and to her bedroom, then pulled back the covers and patted the mattress.

"There you go...need help getting your boots off?"

He chuckled and gave her a grin. "No, but if you're volunteering to help me undress, I'm as weak as a lamb, and would welcome your help," he said with a waggle of his eyebrows.

She laughed and then swatted him in the arm. "You're a mess, Luke Matthews. If I went along with it, you'd have me in bed with you all day long."

"Damn straight," he agreed and pulled her to him to kiss her long and deep. She moaned and pressed herself to him tightly, her hands roving over his back and starting spot fires wherever she touched.

His own hands had moved down to cup her butt and pull her against his growing erection. God, he'd never get enough of her. Luke tried to waltz her to the bed, but she pulled away from him and told him breathlessly, with desire sparkling in her eyes, "We'll have to pick up here later, sugar. I've got to go see what my daddy wanted."

Luke groaned and dropped his chin to his chest trying to get the sexual storm brewing inside of him under control. Cassie apologized, but left with one final kiss on his cheek. There was no way he was going to be able to sleep now, he was keyed up on two fronts now. A shower would probably help, he thought, so he went downstairs to get his duffle bag out of the truck.

When he came back inside, he heard Cassie and Carl talking at the table in the kitchen, but their voices were too low to hear what they were saying. He wasn't going to walk closer and eavesdrop, because he might not like what he heard.

Her daddy wanted to talk to her privately for a reason, and Luke feared he knew what the subject was. With a curse under his breath, Luke climbed the stairs and went to the bathroom.

"I know daddy--it was not what I wanted or expected him to do," Cassie told her father seriously. "I guess he was desperate to keep me in Bowie, and that was his solution." If she was a cartoon character, Cassie knew steam would be billowing out of her ears right now, she was so mad and put out with Luke.

Her daddy chuckled, then said, "Men do some pretty crazy things when they're in love."

Cassie harrumphed then crossed her arms over her chest. "I'm going to turn the tables on him. I want to buy the percentage of the herd for him as a wedding gift. I'm going to talk to Cole."

"I have a better idea, sugar. The herd is yours anyway...when I pass on, the Double B and everything on it is yours."

Panic surged up inside of her, and she leaned forward with tears in her eyes, "Don't you dare say that--I don't want to hear it!"

"Settle down, Cassie Bee. I'm not planning to kick the bucket anytime soon. But I'm not young anymore...and we have to talk about it sooner or later."

"Later," she spat. "Not now. I'm buying that herd for him...it's the principal of it, daddy," she said firmly her tone brooking no argument.

Carl Bellamy shook his head then said, "You are as stubborn as your mama was darlin'."

"I take that as a compliment," she told him with a amused twist of her lips.

"It was meant as one, sugar. Your mama was one fine woman, and you're just like her. So much it hurts my heart to look at you sometimes. I can sure understand why Luke did what he did."

"Whatever his reasons, I need you to get your lawyer to draw up the papers, and I'll cut you a check for the cost of Luke's stake in the herd...then I'm going to give it to him and chew his butt out good for lying to me."

"I'll call him right now," Carl said then positioned his walker and pushed to his feet.

"When are you two getting hitched anyway?"

"As soon as possible. I thought we might have a big Bar-B-Que and invite all the neighbors and town people. Maybe a month from now?"

Her daddy laughed, "You and Imelda better get to planning."

She smiled, "I've been planning since he asked me, after I woke up from my dead faint."

"You fainted?" he hooted incredulously.

"Yep, passed right out," she responded with a grin.

Her daddy howled with laughter, then grabbed the handles of his walker, "Can't wait to see what you do for an encore at the wedding."

***

Two days later, her daddy presented her with the paperwork to transfer the herd to Cole and Luke, and a 99-year lease on the ground they needed to work them.

She wrote her daddy a sizable check for Luke's portion, then stuffed the papers into her purse.

She'd arranged with Luke for them to go to dinner at the steakhouse in town tonight, so she could give him his 'gift'. She'd just told him that she felt like celebrating their engagement, since they were back home, and he'd agreed. Cole had gone to the lawyer's office to sign the papers and pay for his portion earlier, before her daddy had gotten the paperwork. It was all set now.

There was a bounce in her step as she went up the stairs to find Luke, well as much of a bounce as she could have with the cast that was still on her ankle. Luke had been working in the barn with Bud, and he was getting cleaned up for their 'date'. She walked into her bedroom and her mouth went dry, when she found him naked and drying himself off.

Desire surged through Cassie and she knew her plans had just got delayed a little, which didn't disappoint her at all looking at the incredible man she loved.

"Well, don't you look good enough to eat," she said saucily and closed the door behind her locking it. He gave her a sexy smile and dropped the towel he was holding to the floor, just as she dropped her purse and started unbuttoning her blouse.

Cassie walked over to him and had the blouse and her bra off by the time she got there. His eyes latched onto her breasts and his gaze was hot as it traveled over her. She stopped in front of him to lightly trace her fingers over his shoulders and chest, while she licked the remaining water droplets from his skin. Her attention started at his chest, then she moved across his stomach and down his abs, then lower.

"Mmmm...you taste so good...just like sugar," she said and licked a stray droplet from his hip.

A groan rumbled deep in his chest and Luke put his hands on either side of her head, trying to pull her back up to him. Cassie shook loose and dropped to her knees in front of him and took him in her hand, stroking him as she looked up into his heated whiskey-colored eyes. She licked her lips, and his gaze followed her tongue then he hardened in her hand. Smiling up at him Cassie bent to lick a droplet from the head of his cock. His body jerked then a fine tremor passed through him.

Cassie smiled up at him again and holding his eyes she swirled her tongue slowly around the head then slid her tongue down the vein running underneath and back up, before she took him into her mouth. Luke growled and tangled his fingers in her hair, and shivered as she began to work her mouth around him in rhythm with her hand.

Running her other hand up his thigh, she stroked his dewy skin then moved to gently cup his testicles. His fingers tightened in her hair and he pulled her closer to him. She took him deeper inside and sucked at the same time she gently squeezed his sack. A throaty low-pitched moan escaped him and she saw his breathing was short and shallow. She sucked harder and moved her hand faster at the base of his cock.

He tried to pull her away from him and said in a low desperate voice, "Move darlin', I'm real close..."

She shook her head, then slid her hand to his ass to hold him close, while she continued moving her mouth over him. After a second, his whole body tensed and she heard him roar his climax then felt warm spurts of his essence against the back of her throat. She held him until he finished and then slid her mouth off of him with a pop and licked her lips.

"Yep, sweet as sugar," she said in a low sensuous tone.

"Good god, darlin', you almost killed me," he growled and pulled her up to him to claim her mouth in a rough kiss.

Her breasts pressed against his still damp chest, and the soft hair there teased her nipples into erect points that sent waves of desire washing through her. Luke put his hands on her bottom and lifted her up against his still steely hardness, then took kissing her to another level, as he devoured her mouth. After a few moments, she was the one breathing frantically, desperate for him to be inside of her. She lifted her uninjured leg to wrap it around his calf and whimpered.

Luke held her to him and walked her backwards until the back of her legs touched the bed. He gently laid her down, then came down beside her never breaking from feasting on her mouth. Cassie moaned when he pressed his erection against her thigh, and wiggled her hips to ease the ache building in her core. The friction against him had her panting and gasping as she reached down to unzip her shorts with a trembling hand.

Quickly, his hand replaced hers on the zipper and he made quick work of pushing her shorts and panties down her legs. As soon as they were off, his fingers found the nub at the apex of her thighs and he massaged her there until she was wet and wild for him.

"Luke, I need you inside me now," she gasped against his mouth.

He shook his head and continued kissing her and touching her, as if she were his last meal. An orgasm of epic proportions bore down on her and she surfed along the waves of pleasure pounding through her.

"Oh, god, Luke..." she whimpered moving her hips in rhythm with his magical fingers. "Oh, yes..." Cassie shouted as waves of pleasure washed over her and her body vibrated with her release, while her brain was seized by the extreme sensations gripping her as she rode it out.

Her inner muscles were still pulsing when he moved over her and lifted her leg over his forearm then pushed inside of her to seat himself fully. Once inside, his body stiffened and he remained still, his jaw clenched.

Gasping at the incredible sensation of having his fullness stretching her, Cassie felt another orgasm building inside and started moving her hips against him. With a groan, he gripped her butt and moved with her, faster and faster as if they couldn't get enough of each other.

She felt him stiffen again and then he looked down into her eyes, "*Mine*...." he said fiercely and then shouted his release at the same time she shattered and floated over the cliff with him.

"Good, god, Luke...that was something," she panted when he lowered himself down beside her and pulled her into his arms.

"Unbelievable..." he agreed with a sigh. After a few moments of silence, Luke asked her, "You on the pill honey?"

Panic ran through her for a moment when she realized they hadn't used a condom, but it was quickly replaced by contentment...and hope.

"Nope..." she admitted and chewed her lip. "But if it happens, darlin', I'll be happy."

He pulled back to look down into her eyes. "Really?"

"Yeah, I can't think of anything I'd rather do than have your baby," she said with heady emotion causing tears to fill her eyes.

Luke hugged her to him fiercely and a tremor passed through him. "God, I love you, Cassie Bee."

Cassie and Luke went to the bathroom where she duct taped a trash bag over her cast, a routine she'd become used to, and showered while he cleaned up. Afterward, they went back to the bedroom to get ready for dinner. He dressed pretty quickly, he was a man and didn't have much to do, but she wanted to dress up for him tonight. With a kiss, Luke left her to get ready while he went downstairs to talk to her daddy.

Glad she'd packed most of her remaining clothes, the ones James hadn't destroyed, she rifled through the boxes and picked out a stretchy silver dress with a ragged uneven hem that hugged her body. Digging deeper she found flat silver sandals with sparkly jewels on the straps and took one of the pair and put it on her right foot.

She sighed in frustration over the fact that the gaudy

green cast was going to be her mandatory accessory for another week or so. She couldn't wait to get it off. It itched something fierce these days, and she couldn't scratch inside, which drove her crazy.

After putting on her makeup, she fluffed her hair and turned upside down to spray it into Texas big hair, a trick any good southern girl knew. She smiled and grabbed her purse from the floor where she'd dropped it earlier when she'd seduced Luke.

Her hand went to her flat stomach and she rubbed it in circles, hoping she was actually carrying his baby. Tingles flooded through her just thinking of the pretty dark haired girl with blue eyes...or the blonde little boy with whiskey brown eyes like is father.

Luke would be a good daddy, he felt things deeply, cared deeply and fiercely protected those he loved. He hadn't had a family to speak of growing up, and his father certainly hadn't been a good example, but Luke had turned out to be a good man, regardless. Cassie wanted to give him the family he'd never had.

Going downstairs, she found him in the kitchen at the table with her daddy, and they were laughing and joking. He looked up when she came in and his face froze, then he whistled. "Damn, Cassie you trying to get me into trouble again?"

She laughed, "Any trouble you find is your own doing, darlin'."

"You look beautiful, sugar," Luke said with a sense of awe in his tone.

"Thank you..." She walked closer and gave him a soft kiss. "We'd better get going, my stomach is growling." Then she looked at her daddy and asked, "Daddy you want us to bring you anything back?" Luke stood up and she slid her arm through his.

"Nah, I ate earlier, I'm just going read then go to bed. Ya'll have fun." he said, then pinned Luke with a playful glare. "And you have her back home before midnight boy...or I'll fill your ass with the buckshot I saved from the night you tried climbing in her window," Carl chortled then guffawed.

Cassie saw a blush stain Luke's cheeks. "Yes, sir, I sure don't want to ever stare down the business end of that shotgun again," he said and swallowed.

Her daddy chuckled again then gripped his walker and stood up. "The next time you see it will be at your wedding, if you aren't careful, boy."

Luke took a step back and got even redder if that was possible. Her daddy must've heard their caterwauling earlier, and she felt blood rush to her cheeks too. "No need for that daddy--we're getting married soon," she reminded him.

"Bout damned time too," he said grumpily then walked past them and out the kitchen door.

Laughter bubbled up inside of Cassie and she couldn't contain it. She leaned over gripping her stomach and said between gasping breaths, "Busted again, darlin'."

Luke grumbled and took her arm, pulling her up. "Let's go," he said shortly then towed her through the house, still laughing.

CHAPTER SIXTEEN

When they got to his truck, Luke opened her door and helped her inside, then shut it behind her to walk around to his side. Cassie unzipped her purse to get a tissue to wipe away the tears of mirth at the corners of her eyes.

The paperwork she'd stuffed in her purse earlier in the day taunted her. Quickly grabbing the small pack of tissues, she zipped her purse back up as Luke slid behind the wheel, then pulled out a tissue and dabbed at her eyes.

He studied her for a second, then smiled and said, "You look like a goddess out here in the moonlight, sugar. That dress shines like moon beams."

"Jesus, Luke, you're a poet..." she whispered as his words touched her. "That was beautiful." Her gruff cowboy had a tender heart, how the hell had she gotten so lucky? He had layers, and the more she unwrapped the more she loved him.

Cassie scooted across the bench seat to sit beside him, and he wrapped his arm around her shoulders. "I love you, Luke," she told him then leaned up to place a gentle kiss on his mouth. He gave her another of his own, then lifted his arm off her shoulders to start the truck.

Their trip to the steakhouse was a lot more pleasant than her last one had been with James. That night, it was all she could do to keep from strangling both James and Luke. Tonight, as she walked inside with him, pride and anticipation filled her. Pride that she was beside the best looking man in Bowie, and he loved her, and anticipation that she'd finally get the mess of the herd purchase settled by giving him his wedding gift.

Luke pulled off his sexy black dress Stetson, and held it at his side as he asked the hostess for a table. She led them through the restaurant to a table near the back. Eyes of the citizens of Bowie followed them across the room as they walked behind the hostess to their table. Cassie saw heads turning to study them intently, and she heard whispers behind their backs.

She didn't care what these people thought. Luke Matthews and Cassie Bellamy were together now, and they'd better just damned well get used to it. She smiled at familiar and not so familiar faces with her chin held high. She felt Luke's grip tighten on her elbow, and it seemed to her that he was not as unaffected as she was.

After he'd pulled out a chair for her and she sat down, he sat in a chair beside her. She looked over at him and saw his shoulders were tense, and his jaw held tightly. Cassie grabbed his forearm and squeezed, "Relax, Luke...it'll be fine."

"I guess word has gotten out that I resigned..."

"Hold your head up, darlin' and don't let 'em see you sweat. You made the decision that was right for you, and they'll understand...eventually. And if they don't fuck 'em," she told him saucily.

His lips moved up on one side to a semi-smile. "I like how you think, darlin'," he told her and notched his chin up then leaned over to kiss her in front of God and everyone in the steakhouse.

Cassie heard more whispers and slid her left hand up to his cheek as she deepened the kiss, hoping they would see her gorgeous engagement ring. They wanted fodder for their gossip mill? She was going to give them plenty of grist, and get some sweet kisses from the man she loved in the process.

The waitress cleared her throat, and they ended the kiss that had gotten a little out of control. "What can I get you to drink? Beer?" she said shortly, her pen hovering over her pad.

Luke cringed when he realized it was the same waitress that had served him, Cole and Candy the last time he'd been here...a night he wished he could erase. And here he was again, making out with a different woman, even though this woman was his fiancé.

"Um no, sweet tea please," he said sheepishly. Cassie

ordered the same then the woman walked off.

"Wow, wonder what her problem is?" Cassie said watching the waitress storm off toward the kitchen.

"She probably remembers me from last time..." he told her and then flinched.

"Same waitress?" she chuckled.

"Yeah...unfortunately," he groaned and ran a hand through his hair.

Cassie threw her head back and laughed. "Serves you right. I wanted to kill you that night too."

"I'm sorry about that, honey..." his voice was low and sincere.

"You said that already...forget it," she waved it off and took a sip of the tea the silent woman had just delivered to their table.

Cassie let her gaze wander around the room trying to identify the faces seated at the tables in the packed restaurant. After their initial curiosity about her and Luke, they'd all gone back to their discussions, thank goodness. Her eyes snagged on a familiar redhead sitting near the wall on the left side.

"Is that Becca Harvey over there?" she asked in a strained voice nodding her chin in that direction.

"Looks like her, but I haven't seen her in years," he told Cassie with disinterest. Automatically, Cassie glanced up at his face, and saw that he truly wasn't interested. She believed him when he said he hadn't cheated on her, but old habits and thoughts died hard.

She glanced back over at Becca, who was with an older man, or at least he looked older. He had a bald head and florid complexion with deep lines by his eyes and mouth. There was a red-haired boy of about nine sitting beside her, a toddler on the other side in a high chair, and she rocked an infant in a car seat with her foot by her chair.

As the old saying went, Becca Harvey looked like she'd been rode hard and put up wet. Haggard and much older than her age, which was twenty-eight, the same as Cassie.

Becca must've felt Cassie staring at her, because she looked back over her shoulder and their eyes met. Becca's went instantly refrigerator cold, and she whipped her head back around to talk to the man at the table with her, then she got up and carried the car seat around the table and sat it beside him.

Cassie watched her smooth her floral print sundress over her round hips and then she turned to walk across the restaurant toward them with a sashay more suited to someone a lot less...full figured.

"Oh, shit..." Cassie said and Luke looked up at her from his menu then followed her gaze and repeated the words. He sat the menu down and grabbed her hand under the table.

"Just be nice, darlin'," he said near her ear as the woman got closer to their table, then came to a stop standing before them with her hands on her hips.

"See all you needed to?" she asked with spite tingeing her cigarette-roughened voice. "Thought I'd come over so you could get a really good look."

"I was just surprised to see you again, Becca," Cassie said and gave her a tight smile.

"No more surprised than I am to see you back in Bowie. And with Luke Matthews on your tail again, no less." She gave Luke a once over then looked back at Cassie. "Guess you're the reason he quit his job."

"Actually, no...I'm going into cattle ranching," Luke informed evenly.

"I'd think you'd have learned your lesson from the last time she left you high and dry, Luke." Becca told him nastily, then warned, "She'll haul ass out of here again if a better opportunity comes along, just like she did last time."

Luke stood up, and Cassie went to stand too, but he pushed her back down with a hand on her shoulder. "I think you need to sashay back over to your table, and your kids, Becca."

"Or what? You're going to arrest me?" she spat and

then put a finger up to her temple, "Oh, that's right, you can't do that, you're not Sheriff anymore." An evil laugh followed her words and people were starting to stare at them again.

Cassie had heard enough of the blustering bag of wind that had been her high school nemesis. She stood and walked around the table to get really close to Becca and stare down at her. The woman was short, and Cassie wanted to intimidate her, so she took one more step closer then said in a low whisper, "You didn't have any class in high school, and it looks like that hasn't changed. If I'm wrong, walk your ass back over to your table and leave us the hell alone."

Becca took a step back and Cassie saw her chubby cheeks flush, and her hands were fisted at her hips. She hoped the shorter woman would make the mistake of taking a swing at her, because Cassie owed her a few, and by god she'd enjoy giving them to her.

Evidently, Becca thought better of it, and spun on her heel to stomp back across the restaurant, knocking things off of several of the closely spaced tables as her hips bumped them.

Cassie stifled the hysterical laughter that wanted to escape her then stiffened her spine and went back to her seat. "Damn that felt good." she said and sat down then took a drink of her tea. "I think I need a real drink, darlin'.'"

Luke threw back his head and laughed, then waved at the waitress. She came over and he ordered Cassie a tequila sunrise. "You're a force to be reckoned with, Cassie Bee."

"You better believe it," she said then grabbed both sides of his face and planted a smacking kiss on his surprised lips.

When the waitress delivered her drink, she removed the straw and drank it down from the glass, then put it down on the table and sighed. "Thanks, darlin', I needed that," she said then her smile faded as a latent thought hit her. What if she was pregnant?

"Oh god, Luke..." her hand flew to her tummy, and she said anxiously, "What if I'm pregnant..." Her lip trembled and she grabbed his hand. "I shouldn't have drank that."

A concerned frown pinched between his brows, but he assured her, "If you are, I don't think one drink this early on would be a problem. Especially as watered down as they make them here. Just don't drink anymore, darlin'."

"I won't. God, I'm terrible..." she moaned and put a fist to her forehead.

"It's okay, Cassie Bee," he told her and gently put his hand over hers on her stomach. Something fierce, elemental and protective sparkled in his eyes with the gesture.

Her smile felt wobbly on her lips as she grinned at him, and they shared a moment of intense emotional connection. He leaned over and gave her a whisper of a kiss and she sighed.

Shaking her head to break from the dreamy haze he'd woven around her, she said, "I think we need to order, so I can soak up the alcohol quickly."

"Good idea..." he said then flagged the waitress down again.

They chatted and ate the delicious steaks and potatoes, then declined dessert, because they were both stuffed. After they talked a few more minutes, while the table was cleared and the check was delivered, Cassie knew her time had run out.

Cassie picked up her purse from the chair beside her and set it in her lap. Luke evidently thought that was her cue she was ready to leave, and he started to stand up.

She stopped him with a hand on his forearm. "Wait, Luke. There's something I need to talk to you about." He sat back down and looked at her curiously.

"You gave me my wedding present and I need to give you yours." Cassie unzipped her purse and pulled out the paperwork her daddy had given her earlier that day. "This is for you darlin', and it's a package deal, just like Titan was."

He took the papers from her and unfolded them then skimmed over them, and she saw a red flush stain his cheeks as he gritted his teeth. He handed the papers back to her and said, "I can't take this Cassie."

She swallowed hard, never expecting this reaction. "Why not? I accepted Titan graciously."

"That's different," he said and looked away from her.

"How the hell do you figure it's different?"

"It just is...I don't want to talk about it. I'll buy the damned herd, but with my money."

"What money, Luke?" she asked incredulously. "I know what you did--then you lied to me about it. I should be really pissed at you, but I'm not. I accepted Titan as the heart-felt gift he was, and you should do the same with this."

"Who the hell told you?" He kept his voice just under a shout as he stood up suddenly and put his hands on the table. "It had to be Cole--I'm going to kick his ass."

"Sit back down, Luke," she grated through her teeth. "My gift isn't any more extravagant than yours was...now act like a loving fiancé and accept it."

"I do love you, Cassie, but I want to do this on my own," he told her then sat back down.

"And I wanted to start the horse operation on my own..." she countered and shoved the papers at him again. "Take it, Luke. Don't let this come between us."

"A goddamn Philadelphia lawyer...that sure as hell is what you should've been," he said and jerked the papers from her hand then folded them and put them in his pants pocket.

She smiled at him brightly, enjoying her victory. Hesitantly, his own lips curved up in a smile, and he said grudgingly, "Thank you, Cassie Bee," then he grabbed her hand and pulled her into his lap and gave her a kiss that curled her toes.

"Let's get out of here so I can thank you properly," he said in a hot whisper against her mouth then set her off his lap, before throwing some bills in the black check cover and shoving his Stetson back on his head. Grabbing her hand, Luke led her out of the restaurant and into the night air.

When they reached the truck, he pushed her back against it and pressed his body to hers then tilted his head and claimed her mouth kissing her senseless. She moaned and linked her hands together behind his neck, and deepened the kiss.

A grunt behind them, broke the sensual haze and she looked around Luke's shoulder to see Becca Harvey with a baby on her hip and one hand holding the toddler she'd seen in the high chair earlier.

"Get a room..." Becca said in a growl then stomped on by followed by the bald guy that must be her husband.

Cassie started chuckling, then it turned into a belly laugh, and she wound up bent over slapping her thigh. When she finally got a grip on herself, she stood up and said to Luke with mirth still dancing inside her, "God, that's rich...karma is surely something, isn't it darlin'?"

"That it is, sugar," he snorted and opened the truck door to help her inside.

**

Cassie had talked to Luke and he'd agreed to a wedding at the ranch, with a Bar-B-Que for the reception. She'd spent the last two weeks working with Imelda to get all the reception plans made, while at the same time hiring a contractor to build the outbuildings she needed for the horses that would be delivered on Saturday.

The contractor was working fast and had finished the indoor arena, most of it being prefabricated, and had graded up the ground for the outdoor arena. All that was left was for him to put up the lights and fencing, and she'd be in business. He said he should be done by the weekend, which fit perfectly with Titan's homecoming.

Last week, she'd finally gotten the cast off her ankle, and she felt like she was a balloon let off of its tether. Although, her ankle was still a little weak, she was so ecstatic, she felt like dancing across the field naked, just because she could. Luke would probably like that, she thought and giggled.

Her daddy was doing better too, he was on crutches now, and the nurse told them he'd probably be able to get his cast off in a couple of weeks. He told the woman in no uncertain terms, it would be off by the wedding, so he walk his daughter down the aisle, or he was taking it off himself. Cassie knew he wasn't bluffing, and she hoped the nurse did too.

Rock, the manager that Cole and Luke had hired to help them was doing such an outstanding job, there wasn't much for Luke to do, so he was bored and agitated. She sent him out to help the contractor to get him out of her hair. Cole hadn't been around much, because he was catching up on all the paperwork he'd missed while he'd been in Phoenix with them.

Luke had asked Cole to be his best man, which was not a surprise. Cassie had asked Sabrina Roberts to be her maid of honor, which was a big surprise to Cole and Luke. She didn't have any other girlfriends she'd kept in touch with in Bowie, and most of the ones who'd been her friends had moved away anyway. In Phoenix, she had business acquaintances, but no real friends. She'd been so busy building her business, she hadn't had time for it.

When Cassie had called Sabrina in Phoenix to ask her, Sabrina had been surprised as well, but excited. Cassie thought her excitement might be more about seeing Cole again, but whatever the reason, she had a maid of honor to stand up with her.

Cassie had gone to the bridal store in Henrietta and

found a wedding dress, and picked out a dress for Sabrina. They'd go back for a fitting when Sabrina got to Bowie the Saturday before the wedding. The alterations lady told her that would be plenty time for her to get the dresses ready in time for the wedding. Everything was coming together.

Now if she could keep her daddy from sawing off his cast, and Imelda from popping a blood vessel over the reception, and keep Luke from diving off the deep end because he was bored, until they said 'I do', she'd have done well.

Working on the third part of her list, Cassie climbed the wooden steps up to the hayloft with the picnic supper Imelda had packed for her. The supper had kept Imelda busy, so she worried less, so she'd killed two birds with one stone. She walked over to the open window on the far side of the loft and spread a blanket she'd found in the top of her closet of her bedroom.

It was almost dusk, and the heat in the upstairs room above the horse stalls had somewhat dissipated. A soft breeze filtered through the window, cooling her even more. It was going to be a beautiful night and this would be a great place to stargaze...among other things.

Like clockwork, she heard Luke ride his big black gelding into the barn and stop. Cassie unbuttoned a few buttons on her shirt and then walked over to the edge of the loft leaned over with her hands on her thighs to yell, "Hey Luke, is that you, honey?"

"Yeah," he yelled gruffly back up at her. She was sure he was sweaty and tired, he'd been out working on the fencing for the outdoor arena all day. Cassie had popped out there a few times today just to watch him working shirtless in the hot summer sun, his muscles flexing under his skin as he pounded the stakes into the ground, his Wranglers riding low on his hips. Heat surged through her just remembering what a scrumptious sight he made.

"Go take a shower in the horse bay then come up here. I need your help with something. I put a change of clothes in the tack room for you."

She heard him grumble, but then the sound of water hitting the concrete floor of the wash bay filtered up to the loft, and Cassie smiled. She walked back over to the blanket and pulled out the food Imelda had packed for them and spread it around the center of the blanket.

There was cheese, and fruit, fluffy biscuits and thick slices of country ham. There was also a cold bottle of sparkling non-alcoholic cider and a couple of cold beers.

Cassie heard the water shut off and then a few minutes later Luke's wet head popped over the edge of the loft, his face pinched and his lips flat. That quickly changed into a smile though when he surveyed her country buffet.

"What's all this, sugar?"

"Our supper, sugar," she said in a low intimate tone then finished unbuttoning her shirt and tossed it aside, so she sat there in her hot pink lace bra and cut off shorts. She saw his Adam's apple bob a few times and then he shot up the steps and crawled across the loft to the blanket.

"Now that looks like my kind of buffet," he said his voice gravelly with desire, his eyes fixed on her chest, not on the food spread on the blanket.

She put her hand on his chest and drawled, "That's dessert darlin', now be a good boy and come sit right here," she patted a place beside her and he moved over there, then gathered her into his arms and captured her mouth in a hot kiss.

When his hands started roving, she pushed back from him and said, "Let's eat."

Luke grumbled, but scooted a few inches away from her and dragged his eyes to the food. "This looks great," he told her. Then he evidently noticed the sparkling cider and he lifted a brow to her. "What are we celebrating, sugar?"

She leaned over to the plastic bowl in the center of the blanket, and plucked a piece of ripe cantaloupe out then brought it to his lips and rubbed it over them, "Why do we have to have a reason?"

He opened his lips and she dropped the fruit inside. Chewing around it, he said, "I don't know, I just wondered...you're acting strange darlin',"

"Okay, well let's see what I have to celebrate then, if you need a reason. I'm marrying the hottest cowboy in Texas, living my dream of starting a horse breeding operation, that stupid cast is off my foot, my daddy is getting better and should be on his feet soon..." she listed, then put a finger beside her mouth. "Oh--" she said and raised her finger in an exclamation point. "And we're having a baby."

Since they hadn't used a condom again after their first slip-up, Cassie knew it had only been a matter of time before the rabbit died. From the home pregnancy test, and then her subsequent doctor's visit today, it looked like it had happened that first night anyway, the night she'd given him his wedding present. Looks like he'd gotten more than he bargained for.

Luke let out the loudest whoop she'd ever heard, one that had all the horses in the barn shuffling and whinnying in their stalls. She imagined that Imelda who she'd told earlier could hear him in the house. Luke stood up and pulled her to her feet then into his arms and spun her around in circles hugging her to him tightly.

Cassie chuckled again and pushed against his chest, so he'd let her back down to her feet.

"Don't be spinning me in circles darlin', my stomach is pretty delicate these days."

Concern immediately filled his gaze and he grabbed her shoulders. "Oh, god, Cassie--I didn't hurt you did I?" his voice quavered as he asked. He gently pushed her down to sit on the soft hay, and fell down to his knees beside her, his hands moving over her face.

"Calm down, Luke, that's not what I meant...and no you didn't hurt me. I've just been getting sick in the morning for the last few days."

"Have you been to the doctor," he asked frantically and plopped down on his butt beside her then grabbed her hand.

"Yes, darlin' I went there this morning. I am pregnant, due in Spring of next year."

"Did the doctor say you're okay...everything's okay with the baby? Dammit, Cassie you should have told me so I could go with you!"

"I'm fine, strong as a horse...and the baby is too. Stop worrying, Luke. We're fine."

"Shouldn't you be in bed with your feet propped up or something?"

"Nope, the doctor said I could do most everything I'm used to doing...even having hot sex with my cowboy."

"He said that?" Luke hooted incredulously.

She grinned at him and squeezed his hand. "Well maybe not in those exact terms..." Her grin faded and she finished, "But I can't ride, until the baby is born. He was concerned I'd get thrown."

"Damned right you're not riding," Luke said firmly, his eyes glittering.

"Don't start bossing me around, Luke..." she said and pinned him with her eyes. She knew she had to nip this in the bud, or he'd have her cushioned in feathers and put behind glass before she had this baby.

"I'm going to do what's best for the baby, although not riding for eight months is going to kill me. Especially since Titan is going to be here next weekend, and I was looking forward to riding him for the first time."

"Since Rock is doing such a bang up job with the herd, I'll have plenty of time to help you with the horses, darlin'."

"I know, but I want you to know, I'm still going to work them on lead line and from the ground. I'll probably even give lessons."

"Yes ma'am," he said and placed a gentle kiss on her

cheek.

"But you can help by exercising them, and working on the breeding program with me."

"Can't think of anything I'd rather do, sugar," he said with a waggle of his dark brows, making a double entendre of the last part of her statement.

"Okay, then...let's celebrate," Cassie told him then crawled on her knees to grab the cider. She removed the foil and unscrewed the cap, then poured each of them a portion in the red Solo cups she'd unpacked.

Handing him his cup, she lifted hers and tapped it to his. "To our successful breeding operation," she told him then grinned and took a sip of her cider.

***

Cole came out to the farm every night for the next week after he got off work to help Luke and the contractor finish putting in the fence. Cassie worked hard in the Double B barn to get it cleaned and ready for the new arrivals Tommy Tucker was delivering day after tomorrow. Bud was back from Wyoming and had been helping her in the barn. They'd made a lot of progress. The tack room was neat as a pin and the saddles, bridles and bits all gleamed.

The only fly in her ointment was that they'd all been treating her like she was made of glass, since she'd told them she was pregnant. It frustrated her to finally have the darned cast off her leg only to be held back again, now by the people who loved her. But the reason she was being held back this time was worth it, she thought, and placed her hand over her tummy.

Bud wouldn't let her muck out the stalls, insisting that lifting that weight wasn't good for the baby, so she'd let him do it, although letting him do that at his age wasn't a good idea either. He'd managed it though, and she'd rearranged the stall assignments for the seven horses currently in the barn, then put down fresh bedding for Titan and his pretty fillies.

Cassie sighed as she neatly wound another coil of rope and hung it up on the peg in the barn. Titan would be here day after tomorrow, and she was so excited, she knew she wouldn't be able to sleep a wink tomorrow night. It was almost like she was having a baby tomorrow, a twelve-hundred pound one, a beautiful baby boy.

The wedding was next weekend, and she was nervous and excited over that too. She'd sent out the invitations on Tuesday, and ran an announcement and invitation to the town in the local paper. Her daddy was well-respected in Bowie, so they'd probably have a pretty spectacular turnout, at least for the reception. She had kegs of beer on order and enough meat for the spit to feed an army.

A caterer was coming in to handle the spit, and Bud was going to supervise. They'd hired servers to keep the buffet line filled up, and bartenders for the open bar. All of the hands still working at the Double B had offered to help set up the chairs and build a gazebo for the ceremony.

Most everything was done, except the final fitting on her dress, which was happening tomorrow as soon as Sabrina arrived. She hoped that her tummy hadn't expanded too much, or the dress wouldn't fit. It was pretty tight the last time she tried it on.

At least she could wear both of her white boots to walk down the aisle now. She'd found the perfect pair at the Western store in Bowie. They had patterned cutouts and sparkly stones embedded in the toes, and a crisscrossing pattern of stones around the top. She'd also bought a new white Stetson at the store that she'd have to bring with her to the fitting, so the shop lady could help her attach the veil.

Luke had taken Cole and her daddy into town and they all got fitted for tuxes. Her daddy had griped about having to wear one, but she could tell it was for show. He would wear a potato sack, she imagined, as long as it assured she and Luke were married next Saturday.

She almost thought he was as excited about having Luke as a son-in-law as she was about having him as her husband. Cassie was dying to see Luke in his western tux. Her mouth watered just thinking about it.

He'd set up their honeymoon, but he hadn't told her where they were going. As usual, her patience was almost non-existent, so she'd been snooping and pestering him for a week to tell her, but he hadn't given in. She still had a week to get it out of him though, and she wasn't giving up.

A barn cat rubbed up against her leg, and Cassie bent down to pick it up for a cuddle. The tabby began purring on her chest and she rolled it over in her arms to scratch its little belly, then she bent her nose down and rubbed it to the kitten's nose and he swatted her cheek with his little paw. She laughed and did it again.

"What the hell do you think you're doing, sugar?" Luke boomed as he stomped down the corridor to her.

"Wow...hello to you too, husband-to-be," she said bristling at the tone he'd taken with her.

He reached over and pulled the cat out her arms by the scruff then put it on the floor and swatted its behind gently. The playful kitten swatted his hand, but then took off down the aisle. "Hey--why'd you do that?"

"You're not supposed to be handling cats, darlin'," his voice was frustrated and terse. "I've been reading up on it, and the book I got says--"

"It's litter boxes, nimnuts. Not cats. Pregnant women all over the world have cats...and they manage to birth healthy babies just fine."

"Well yeah, but...cats all play in their litter boxes, and the bacteria is probably on their fur too," he defended.

"Bullshit, Luke...and barn cats don't even use litter boxes," she said with a incredulous laugh. A hurt expression flickered over his face and his jaw tensed. Cassie hated that she'd put that look there.

Walking over to him, she slid one arm around his waist and put her hand over his heart, before looking up at him. "If it bothers you though, sugar, I won't play with the cats anymore. I know you're just trying to protect me and the baby."

He dipped his head down and gave her a sweet kiss. "Thanks, cupacake," he said then hugged her to him.

Cassie sighed out her frustration, but she was glad she'd appeased him. Although he set her britches on fire with his over protectiveness, if he was any other way, he wouldn't be the Luke that she loved. She smiled up at him, "You done for the day?"

"Yep, we finished," he told her grinning proudly.

"Why don't you give me a grand tour, and then we'll go take a shower...together...to conserve water of course. You know how dry it's been lately," she told him with her tongue in her cheek.

"Oh yeah, very dry...." he agreed then bent to lick her earlobe, before tracing kisses down her neck. "Mmm...definitely need to conserve water," he told her kissing back up her neck then along her jaw, before he captured her mouth in a fierce kiss.

Bud cleared his throat behind them and they broke apart like guilty teenagers. Cassie felt her cheeks heat up and she saw Luke's were similarly red.

"Sorry to interrupt, but someone named Sabrina is on the phone up at the house for you, Cassie Bee."

Alarm skittered along Cassie's nerve endings, but she shut it down, telling herself it could be something as simple as matching her shoes to her dress that could have Sabrina calling her the day before she was supposed to arrive in Bowie.

"Thanks, Bud...I'll head up to the house."

CHAPTER SEVENTEEN

Cassie started to walk away, but Luke's hand on her elbow stopped her. "Wait up, I'm coming with you," he said and dropped his arm around her waist to lead her toward the back porch.

"I can't imagine what she could be calling for," Cassie told him a little out of breath.

Luke didn't respond, just held her by his side and led her up on the porch and through the door, then to the alcove where the receiver was sitting by the phone. He stepped back and let her pick up the phone.

"Hello...Sabrina?" Cassie said forcing brightness into her tone.

Sabrina didn't respond for a second, then she asked Cassie in a tense and hesitant tone, "Hi, Cassie...is Luke there with you? Are you sitting down?"

No, this definitely wasn't good, Cassie thought, and gripped the phone a little tighter, before she said, "Yeah, he's here...just tell me what's wrong Sabrina."

Glancing over at Luke she saw he was studying her with concern in his eyes.

"James escaped this morning," Sabrina informed her in a voice tinged with anger and frustration.

Cassie felt like an anvil had just dropped on her chest. She couldn't catch her breath and the phone dropped from her fingers, as she leaned back against the wall and slid to the floor.

Luke pushed inside the small alcove and picked up the phone. "Sabrina, what happened?!" he yelled into the phone, then sat down beside Cassie on the floor and grabbed her wrist checking her pulse, it was rapid and shallow. He pressed the back of her head down and shoved it down between her knees. "Breathe, honey."

"James was being escorted to the courthouse this morning for sentencing, and his guard was new and female and he talked her into taking his cuffs off so he could go to the bathroom...he slipped out a window," she told him.

"How the hell could they let that happen?" he shrieked in disbelief.

"Your guess is as good as mine, Luke. Tell Cassie, I'm not coming tomorrow...I rescheduled my flight for next Friday. I'll do my best to find him."

"Thanks, Sabrina. Keep us posted," he said then put the receiver back on the cradle, before he lifted Cassie into his arms and sat on the floor to hold her to his chest rocking her gently.

"Oh, god Luke, what if he comes here..."

"I'll put a bullet in him," Luke told her matter-of-factly. And he would. Nobody was going to hurt Cassie and their baby. Not on his watch.

She whimpered and buried her face in his chest, her fists clutching his shirt as her tears soaked the front. Luke reached up and pulled down the phone to the floor, then he dialed Cole.

"Sheriff Jackson," Cole said into the phone, sounding distracted.

"Cole, we have a problem..." Luke told his friend.

"My specialty...what's up?"

"James Barton escaped from jail in Phoenix this morning."

"*What!*" Cole shouted and Luke pulled the phone away from his ear for a second.

"Yeah, that's what I said." Luke told him angrily, "Cassie's a mess, and I think we need to get Judge to put out a restraining order, and we should probably give everyone notice to look out for him."

"I'll do that right now."

"And Cole?"

"Yeah?"

"If he shows up here, I'm gonna shoot first and ask questions later."

Cole hesitated a moment then told him with seriousness in his voice, "Make sure it's self defense, buddy."

"If he gets within a half-mile of Cassie, I won't care," he told Cole in a lethal tone. "If she had walked in that house instead of me in Phoenix, he'd have shot her. That could have been why he was there in the first place. I'm not taking any chances. Get that restraining order."

"Will do," Cole told him then disconnected.

Luke lifted Cassie higher in his arms then he pushed up the wall to stand and then carried her up the stairs to their bedroom. Gently he laid her down on the bed and kissed her forehead before he slid in behind her and pulled her into his arms.

"Shhh, don't cry, sugar. The baby will be sad too," he cooed close to her ear and kissed her again. She hiccupped and nodded then rolled over to press her face into his chest, and he tightened his arms around her. "I'm not going to let anything happen to you baby, you believe that?" She nodded again then sighed brokenly.

After a few minutes, he felt her relax in his arms and he sighed in relief letting the tension ease out of his muscles. When she miraculously fell asleep, Luke slipped his arm from under her and eased out of the bed. He was going to put everyone on the farm on notice about James Barton and tell them to arm themselves, just in case. Like he'd told Cole, he wasn't taking any chances with Cassie and his baby.

He talked to Bud first and he assured Luke that he'd take care of informing and arming the hands. Then he went and spoke with Carl, and boy he'd never heard such blue curses fly from the man. Before Luke left the office in the barn, Carl was strapping on an old Colt 45 that Luke wasn't even sure would fire. He felt slightly better when Carl walked to the corner and loaded his old double-barrel shotgun.

Luke knew from personal experience, the man knew how to use that one.

Imelda's weapon of choice was her rolling pin and as a backup her cast iron skillet. She assured Luke that she wouldn't hesitate to use either should that fancy pants show up on their doorstep.

Luke's next step was to go down to the station to talk to Cole in person, and get him to arrange for off-duty deputies to secure the perimeter of the Double B at his expense.

Next, Luke went to his house and unlocked his gun cabinet, pulling out every rifle, handgun and shotgun he owned, and he had a lot. After getting ammo for each, he loaded them into his truck and headed back to the Double B. If that sonofabitch was dumb enough to show his ass up at the Double B, Luke was going to make sure he didn't live to regret it.

Anger surged through him, and the longer it stewed, the hotter it got. By the time he got back to the Double B, it was like lava coursing through his veins about to erupt. He knew he had to get a grip on himself, and keep his cool so Cassie would too, but damned if he could manage it.

That bastard wasn't going to have a chance to touch a hair on Cassie's beautiful head, because Luke was going to be sticking to her like white on rice, until they caught him...or Luke killed him.

Maybe some target practice would help him relieve some of his anger, Luke thought, as he carried in the guns into the house and loaded them, before strategically placing them around the house. Putting on his shoulder holster over his t-shirt, he checked and loaded his Sig P228 9mm and slid it in the holster. It had been a while since he'd practiced, so shooting some things up would not only relieve his tension, it would also assure him he was on top of his game.

He was going to take Cassie with him, and give her the snub-nose .38 Special that he pulled out of the cache and loaded. He knew she knew how to shoot a rifle, and shotgun, but she needed a handgun. Having it with her would probably make her feel better too. Shooting it now, might remove some of the fear that he'd seen in her eyes earlier.

Luke ran up the stairs two at a time and burst through the bedroom door. Cassie sat straight up in the bed and her hand flew to her chest, fear sparkling in her eyes.

"Oh, god, Luke...you scared me," she said breathlessly. Her eyes moved to the gun strapped under his arm and the one he held in his hand and they widened. "What's that for?"

"This is for you, sugar and I'm going to show you how to use it," he said with determination.

"I know how to shoot, Luke," she assured him.

"You know how to shoot a handgun?" He knew she knew how to use a shotgun, usually she took one with her when she rode around the ranch. Using a handgun was totally different, and she needed to know that.

"No...but I'm pretty good with a rifle," she said with a smile.

"You need to learn how to use a handgun, darlin'. It's faster and easier to use. Not to mention it'll fit in your purse better than a rifle," he tried to infuse humor into his tone.

Cassie snorted, then pushed up on the bed to sit on the side. "I know why you're doing this, Luke and it's not going to help."

"I think it will...and it'll make me feel better for sure."

Cassie shrugged and stood up. "Okay...", she said then walked over to take the .38 from him, then tested its weight in her hand.

"Careful, darlin', it's loaded."

She almost dropped it and Luke grabbed it from her and put on the safety, then handed it back to her. Cassie chuckled, "I think I'll be more likely to shoot myself in the foot, or you in the ass, than hit a target."

"It's easy as pie, sugar. If I know you, you'll be shooting better than me before we finish this first lesson."

She snorted. "Not likely, but I'm glad you have confidence in me."

He opened the door and spread an arm to invite her to go first then said, "Always, sugar..."

Luke grabbed a stack of aluminum pie tins that Imelda had stored in the pantry, then took Cassie out to the pasture and set the tins up on cross-fence, then handed her the ear protection and goggles he'd grabbed from the truck on the way out.

After counting off seven yards, Luke stopped and drew a line in the hard packed earth with the toe of his boot.

"Isn't that too close?" Cassie asked him.

"No, darlin' this is a close range gun, something you can carry in your purse and can have in your hand in seconds if you're attacked. It's basically point and shoot. I'll show you how to sight it, but you need to practice point shooting."

"So, I have to be about this close to use it?" She asked with a little fear in her tone.

"Yep...but if that scares you I have bigger handguns I could show you how to use. The problem is concealing and carrying them...not to mention they kick like a mule, which affects your accuracy."

"If I aim at someone, I want to hit them...so I'll stick with this one."

Luke got behind her and showed her how to hold the gun and how to balance her weight to help her accuracy. Next, he showed her how to sight it, and then backed away and told her to shoot one of the tins he'd set up.

The shot went wide and she stomped her foot then lined up again and squeezed off another round. That one hit the bottom edge of the pie plate. He walked back over and put his arms around her to line up the shot and give her a few pointers on doing it herself. He used his leg to shift her right leg a little farther back than her left and told her to square up her shoulders.

This time she hit the center of the plate, and she

squealed and pointed the weapon at the ground while she bounced up and down. "That was fun."

Luke smiled at her, she was still the little tomboy he remembered from way back when, the one who did her damndest to outshoot, outride, and out fish every boy in town. She'd done a damned good job of it too.

"Good job, cupcake," he told her then said, "Try to shoot that pie plate with two bullets in a row."

He watched her adjust her stance a little so she was still balanced and was holding the gun properly. She lined up her shot and then squeezed the trigger twice. Those shots hit the pie plate a little below center and she looked over her shoulder and gave him a wide smile.

"Perfect, sugar," he encouraged her then took the revolver and reloaded it before handing it back and telling her to move to her right and take five shots in a row at that pie plate. She took her stance and squeezed off five shots Three hit the lower edge of the plate, and the rest missed.

"There's one more thing you need to know about this kind of gun, sugar. It typically shoots low, so you should aim a little higher than where you want it to hit." He reloaded the gun for her one more time and told her to try again.

This time Cassie put four bullets into the plate just a smidge above center.

"Not bad for your first time," he said and took the gun from her and put on the safety explaining the mechanism to her.

He handed it back to her and then he walked to the fence and lined up cans he'd picked up from the trash for his turn. He walked off a much farther distance for his round then told her to come stand behind him. Once she was safely behind him, he grinned then turned and pulled his Sig and popped off seven shots taking out every can with a single shot to the center in rapid succession.

No, he hadn't lost it, he thought pleased. When he

turned back to her with a smile, he saw her bottom lip was poking out and her arms were folded across her chest.

"Show off," she said then her lips wobbled into a smile and she hooted. "Damn, Luke...that was amazing."

"I went through the police academy sugar, and I've had seven years of practice since then. I thought I'd be rusty though, it's been a while."

"Well if that's rusty, I don't wanna see sharp," she said and then asked him to reset the targets up so she could try again.

Imelda was probably going to be pissed at him for using all of her pie tins, he thought. Regardless of that, he went and put up fresh targets for Cassie, reloaded the .38 and gave it to her.

He'd buy more pie plates for Imelda, Cassie needed the practice. "Try leaning into your target, see if that helps." Luke showed her what he meant then stepped aside. "Start with the gun at your side this time, then take your shots."

She lowered the gun down to side, then lifted it taking five shots at the pie dish, four of them were pretty close to dead center the other was just barely inside the circle. "My arms are tired," she laughed then shrugged. "Guess I'm a wimp."

"No, you're just not used to holding your arms like that for so long, or the weight of the gun while you're doing it, even though it's a light one. That's why we're practicing, so you get used to it. You did good, honey."

Luke told her he was going to take a couple more rounds at the targets and she stood back and watched him intently. He knew she was watching what he was doing and taking pointers from him. Cassie was a smart woman, a quick study, and exceptionally determined when she wanted to master something.

And he was glad she wanted to master shooting the handgun he'd given her. Knowing she wouldn't be defenseless if he wasn't around made him feel better.

***

Tommy Tucker delivered Titan and the mares on Saturday, and Cassie had been babying and loving them since they got there. She'd made him ride Titan for her and then she worked with him on some ground training.

They all tried to bury themselves in getting the new horses settled, and the final wedding preparations made, so they didn't have to think about what was hanging over their heads. James Barton was still on the loose.

As the week progressed though, and the chores with the horses dwindled, and all the wedding plans were in place, everyone at the Double B was edgier than rabbits in a foxhole.

Cole had gotten the restraining order against Barton, not that a piece of paper would stop a bullet, but at least it let the world know that he was a threat to Cassie. And it gave Luke more justification if he had to wind up shooting him.

They'd talked to Sabrina off and on all week and she was frustrated because she didn't have any leads on James yet, and Cole was frustrated because Sabrina wasn't in Bowie yet. Her flight was scheduled to arrive tomorrow at noon in Dallas, and Cole was going to pick her up at the airport.

Luke laughed thinking of how strung out Cole was over Sabrina. It was great to sit back and watch his friend go through the same torture he'd endured with Cassie. Cole had given him hell over Cassie, and payback was a bitch.

"Hey, darlin', hand me another biscuit, please," Luke asked staring over at Cassie who was pushing her eggs around in her plate, but not really eating them. She looked up and handed him the plate of biscuits, a worried frown pinching between her eyes.

Luke grabbed one from the plate and put it on his

plate, then wiped his hands on the napkin in his lap. "What's wrong, sugar?"

"I'm just worried that weasel is gonna ruin our wedding..." she told him and then looked back down at her plate.

"Honey there will be so much firepower at that wedding, I find it unlikely he has the balls to try it."

Luke had arranged for seven armed and uniformed deputies to provide security, as well as a few fed friends he'd made during his term as Sheriff, not to mention he planned to wear his own his own 9mm.

But he wasn't going to tell his lovely bride that.

"I just hate that it has to be that way. We're supposed to be happy and carefree, not on edge and armed to the teeth."

Luke shrugged, "This is Texas, darlin' weddings always call for shotguns," he grinned at her. "I'm sure your daddy will have his handy."

She threw back her head and laughed, and the sound eased some of his tension. God, he loved hearing her laugh. He planned to make sure she had plenty to laugh about for the next fifty or sixty years.

"I'm sure he will...wants to make sure you don't run out on his pregnant daughter," she told him and laughed again.

"Darlin', the only place I'll be running is down that aisle to meet you and our baby."

Cassie smiled and pushed back her chair then came around to sit on his lap and wrap her arms around his neck. She tasted his mouth, licked a crumb from the corner, then traced that talented tongue of hers across the seam before she sealed her mouth to his and kissed the stuffing out of him.

Pulling back from him, she whispered near his lips, "I love you, Luke Matthews. Thank you for making me laugh."

Luke squeezed her to him, thanking God that she was going to be his after all these years. In two days, she'd be his wife, after ten years of waiting. All the wrong women he dated since she left Bowie had just been distractions, a way to bide his time until she came back to Bowie, and back to him. As mad as Luke had been at her, his heart knew what it wanted, and it had wanted only Cassie Bellamy--and always would.

Cassie sat on the porch swing, waiting impatiently for the dust cloud on the driveway to clear so she could see how close Cole's SUV was to the house. Luke sat beside her with his arm slung negligently over the back of the swing behind her.

It irritated Cassie that she was a ball of nerves today, and Cole was cool as a cucumber. He still had his gun strapped to his shoulder, but he acted like it was just another accessory, like the leather belt he wore daily. Her accessory was worry that James would somehow mess up the most important day of her life.

Although the weapon and holster actually looked kind of hot on Luke, Cassie was more concerned with the reason he was wearing it than how it made him look. James Barton still had not been apprehended and her wedding was tomorrow.

Sabrina had handed off the job of apprehending him and had caught the plane from Phoenix to Dallas early this morning, so she could be in the wedding. Cassie was grateful, but secretly wished she'd stayed in Phoenix and kept looking.

Cole pulled up to the house and shut off the car, then Sabrina slid out of SUV and saw Cassie. Cassie stood up then ran down the steps and across the yard with her arms open and Sabrina flew into them and they danced around in circles, finally stopping to look at each other. Luke eventually sauntered up to stand right behind her.

"I'm so glad you finally made it," Cassie grinned widely. "I have so much to tell you."

"I wish I had more to tell you," Sabrina said then

frowned.

"It's not your fault, Bri...you did the best you could. If he shows up here, Luke will take care of him." She tossed a thumb over her shoulder at Luke pointing to his very visible holster and gun.

Sabrina's eyes lit up and she leaned around Cassie to take a better look, "P228--nice!" she said and grinned at him.

"Good eye detective," Luke said and gave her a wink and a big sexy grin.

Cole grumbled under his breath, then walked up beside Sabrina and dropped an arm on her shoulders. "Don't you ladies have somewhere to be?" he asked gruffly and gave Luke a stare.

"Oh yeah, we need to get to the bridal shop for our fitting. Let me go get my hat and boots, I'll be right back," Cassie said then took off running for the house.

She ran up the stairs and grabbed the boxes and her purse, then at the last minute stopped to put the .38 sitting on the dresser in her purse. Luke wasn't going with them to the fitting, so she thought it was a good idea.

She ran back outside and smiled at Luke, "Give me the keys, sugar," she said and held out her hand.

He immediately shook his head, "Nope, I'm driving ya'll there."

Anger surged up inside of Cassie and she stomped her foot. "No, you sure are not! It's bad luck for you to see me in the dress before the wedding."

His face reddened and he moved a little closer to her then said, "It would also be bad luck for the bride to get shot before the wedding. I'm going, end of story."

Cassie looked at Sabrina and Cole for support, but neither of them stepped in. "Cole can drive us. He and Sabrina are armed, and I brought the .38," Cassie told him and gave him an I'm not budging stance.

"I have to get back to the station for a little while," Cole said apologetically.

"My weapon is in my suitcase. I had to check it, so I'll get it out," Sabrina said then walked to the back door of the SUV and opened it to lean inside. When she came back to them, she had a shoulder holster on like Luke's over her tight white scoop neck t-shirt. "We can take the truck, Luke. It'll be okay," she told him and set her suitcase on the ground beside her.

He stared at her for a moment, then stared at Cassie, before he finally reached inside his pocket and tossed Cassie the keys. "You better be careful, cupcake," he told her in a low worried tone.

"God, you'd think I was the only pregnant woman in the entire world," Cassie said and then walked up to him to stand on her tip toes and kiss his unsmiling mouth. "I'll be careful."

"Park next to the store, and go right in, don't loiter outside," he ordered and jerked her roughly against him. "If you see someone following you, come back here or go to the Police station, don't stop. The truck is full of gas, so you don't even have to stop for that. Go there and come right home."

"Jesus, Luke, you need to write all that down," she laughed then tweaked his nose. "We'll be fine, darlin' don't worry."

"You got an extra magazine for your weapon, Bri?" He asked seriously then looked over at her friend.

"In my purse," she laughed then said, "Never leave home without it."

Cole kissed Sabrina's cheek then walked back to the SUV and left. Cassie and Sabrina finally got away from Luke and his instructions and went to the truck. Sabrina had a hard time getting up into the truck, because it was so high from the ground, so Luke came over and gave her a boost. Both of them were laughing when they got inside.

"I need a step stool to get up in here."

"Yeah, Luke has this thing jacked up. He's so tall, it

doesn't bother him, but even I have a little trouble getting up here. Cowboys and their trucks...the taller the better, she winked at Bri then cranked up the monster machine and wrestled the shifter on the steering wheel into reverse.

"I see you got your cast off, you must be relieved."

"You have no idea," Cassie chuckled then told her, "My daddy's in a cast too and he's getting it off today. It was either that or he told his nurse he was gonna saw it off himself."

Sabrina laughed then said, "I can't wait to meet him. He sounds like a character."

"Oh, yeah...definitely," Cassie told her then proceeded to relate the story about him catching Luke climbing in her window when she was a teenager and threatening to fill him full of buck shot. Sabrina was doubled over in gales of mirth by the time Cassie pulled up in front of the bridal shop and turned off the truck.

Her laughter finally reduced to chuckles then just a snicker now and again, and Cassie sat there smiling at her, enjoying seeing her new friend happy. "I'm glad you could come, Bri. Thank you for agreeing to be my maid of honor."

"I can already tell I'm going to have a blast...it's been a long time since I've laughed like this," she admitted then looked down at her hand, her thumb rubbing against a fine white line on her wedding ring finger that Cassie hadn't noticed before.

"What happened?" Cassie didn't want to come out and ask but the sudden switch in Bri's mood told her it must be bad, and she wanted to know.

Silence filled the cab for a few moments then Bri cleared her throat and said, "My husband was a cop too...he got killed in the line of duty almost two years ago."

Cassie gasped in horror then scooted over on the seat to hug Sabrina to her. "I'm so sorry, I brought it up."

"No, it's okay. I need to talk about it...maybe sometime we can get a bottle of wine and I'll tell you all about it."

"Sounds like a plan," Cassie told her and gave her another squeeze before she scooted back over and jumped down from the truck, then leaned back in to get her boxes. Sabrina managed to get down too without breaking a leg, and Cassie clicked the lock button on the key fob then they walked into the boutique.

CHAPTER EIGHTEEN

The kind older woman she'd bought her dress from was happy to see them and led them straight to the dressing rooms, so they could put on their dresses.

Cassie tugged at long-line strapless bra she had to wear under her dress to make it look right. Putting the darned thing on was like shimmying into a corset, and it was a little tighter than it had been last time. If she wasn't mistaken that could be because she had a helluva lot more cleavage bubbling over the top of the cups. It must be the baby making his or her presence known in her body, she thought and smiled.

Once she had the undergarments in place, the woman helped her 'dive' into her dress. It couldn't be called anything else, because she made Cassie put her hands up like she was going to make a swan dive in the lake and point them for a hole she made with the dress, then she eased all the fluffy, frou-frou fabric over her head smoothed it down.

Cassie had to suck in so the woman could zip the zipper. The dress was very snug around the waist now, but she'd only have it on for a few hours, so she could tolerate it that long.

"You look like a dream, Cassie. Your groom is gonna melt when he sees you."

"I feel like a stuffed sausage," Cassie said and chuckled. "Hope I don't pass out before I get to him," she told the woman adjusting her breathing to avoid that right now.

"Oh, is it too tight, sugar?"

"Nah, it'll be fine. We don't have time for more alterations." Cassie looked in the mirror and saw someone she didn't even recognize. Her skin glowed and her eyes sparkled in the white confection of a dress. Her body looked like an hourglass, especially with the extra boobage caused by the baby.

The dress had a sweetheart neckline edged in

rhinestones that led down to a V waist, also edged in rhinestones, and a fluffy tulle princess skirt that stopped at her knees in the front, but cascaded to the floor in the back.

She smiled at the woman then said in a dreamy voice, "It does look good doesn't it?"

"That dress was made for you."

Cassie held her breath then leaned over carefully to pick up her hat and the veil then handed them to the woman. "Can you help me attach this? And do you have a rhinestone hat band I could buy, or even a tiara to put at the crown of my hat?

"Sure, stay here and I'll be right back." Cassie studied herself again in the mirror, her boots went perfectly with the dress just like she thought they would. Spinning around, she looked at the back of the dress in the mirror.

It was perfect...just like the man she was going to marry tomorrow. Emotion clogged Cassie's throat and she fought back the tears burning her eyes.

When the woman came back in Cassie gasped at the beautiful double strand rhinestone hatband she'd attached. She'd also attached Cassie's veil and bunched up a portion of it in a knot at the back. The filmy lacy veil then flowed from the knot and would cascade down her back.

"That's amazing...just right," Cassie said taking the hat from her to put on and survey the final effect. Yep, Luke was going to swallow his tongue when he saw this for sure, she thought and chuckled. "How's Sabrina doing with her dress?"

"Luckily her dress fit just right, she must be a true size 6. I'm working on something for her hair, and shoes to match that won't have to be dyed. Let's go see," the woman invited with a wave of her hand then held the door open for Cassie to go first, then fussed behind her lifting the back of the dress so it didn't drag on the floor, fluffing it as they walked.

When they reached the three-sided mirror at the

pedestal up front, Cassie carefully stepped up and tugged at the neckline of her dress. The woman fluffed her skirt again and Cassie tugged up the neckline of her dress once more. "Do you have straps I can put on this after ceremony, so I don't wind up giving our guests a show? I plan on gettin' down at he reception."

The woman chuckled, "You're a true cowgirl aren't you, sweetie?"

"With all this bling I have on, you have to ask that?" Cassie hooted and then turned her hips left and right to admire the dress again. A gasp behind her had her turning to see Sabrina coming out of the dressing room with her hand over her mouth.

"Oh. My. God. Cassie you look like a country princess."

Just what she'd been going for. Cassie smiled from ear to ear then twirled with her arms out to the side. "Think Luke's gonna like it?"

"If he doesn't he's a blind man," Sabrina hooted.

Cassie ran her eyes over the elegant red dress with the a sweetheart neckline like her own, but unlike Cassie's her dress had straps. The dress hugged the petite brunette's curves to right past her hips then belled out with a kick train in the back. It was perfect.

"That red dress is amazing on you, Bri," she told her maid of honor, "I think we might have to throw Cole in the horse trough to cool him off."

Sabrina chuckled then her eyes turned serious, "You know Cole and I are just friends, right?"

"I think that's what you think, but not what he thinks, that's what I think," Cassie said then shook her head. "Or maybe not what he wants."

"I'm not sure I'm ready for anything else right now. Cole is a nice man and damned good looking, but he's a lawman, and I swore when Kenny got killed I would never date another cop."

"Maybe you should talk to him," Cassie suggested

gently.

"Maybe I will. I'm just enjoying his company so much...it's been a long time, since I've let a man close enough to do that."

"Well, then just be his friend, Bri...and see where things go."

"That's what I'll do, thanks Cassie."

Worry filled Cassie that Cole was already half in love with Sabrina and she was going to break his heart, but she pushed it to the back of her mind to think about later. Today, was her day, and tomorrow would be the big day. That's what she needed to focus on.

"Okay help me get out of this dress so I can take a deep breath," she laughed and stepped down off the pedestal to follow the short round woman back to the dressing room.

Cassie and Sabrina were smiling and laughing when they exited the shop, and walked to the truck with their dresses over their arms, and packages stacked so high in their arms they couldn't even see the truck. Cassie stopped and pushed the unlock button on the key fob for the truck and then shifted her packages to open the door.

Prickles of unease skittered along the back of her neck and caused her hair to stand on end. It felt like someone was watching her. Cassie swallowed thickly then threw her packages in the truck, not caring if they got wrinkled or dirty. She unzipped the purse on her shoulder and stuck her hand inside feeling the comforting steel of the .38 slide into her hand.

She used her thumb to flick off the safety, then moved around the door to look up and down the street. She saw a man's back walking past a shop a couple of doors down and followed him with her eyes until he rounded a corner into an alley. That back looked familiar dressed in a distinctive polo shirt and khaki pants.

Although the man's hair was black, not blonde, she thought he looked an awful lot like James Barton. A shiver passed through her and she thumbed the safety back on the gun then hopped up in the cab and slammed the door, quickly hitting the door lock.

Sabrina's door was still open as she arranged her packages over the seat. "Sabrina get in quick," Cassie said with panic settling in her chest. Her heart was beating ninety-to-nothing inside her chest, and her breathing was fast and shallow.

Her friend looked up at her face, then paled and pulled the gun out of her holster. "What's wrong, Cassie? What did you see?"

"I might be seeing ghosts, but I swear I just saw James. His hair was black, but I'd know that no ass back of his anywhere."

Sabrina took a stance she'd seen Luke using when they were target practicing as she moved her eyes from store to store, then started walking down the street, her gun ready, but pointed downward. "Lock the doors, Cassie and call Cole," she said forcefully.

Cassie leaned over the seat and pulled the door closed then locked it. She cranked the truck in case she had to make a quick getaway, before she pulled out her cell phone and called Cole.

He picked up on the first ring, "Is everything okay?" his asked with anxious concern.

"No--we're in front of the bridal shop in Bowie, and I think I saw James. The hair on my neck stood up like someone was watching me then I saw a man's back turn the corner, and I swear it was him, even though his hair was black."

"Where's Bri?"

"She went after him," she told Cole with dread in her voice. "I'm in the truck with it cranked and the doors locked in case I have to take off."

"If you see him again haul your ass out of there, I'll be there in a second." Cole hung up and a minute or so later she heard sirens wailing in the air a few streets over, then a police cruiser pulled up to the curb by her truck. A policeman got out and came over to stand by her door, with his gun out, while he was talked into a microphone at his shoulder.

Cassie swallowed down the fear that tried to overwhelm her again, then grabbed her purse off the floorboard and unzipped it in case she needed her gun fast. It didn't look like the cop protecting her was going anywhere, but she wasn't taking chances...not with herself, and not with her baby.

A few minutes later she saw Cole come out of an alley down the street with Sabrina, both had their guns in their hands, and Sabrina was gesturing wildly with her other hand. Evidently she was giving him a piece of her mind. He was yelling back at her, and his face was red and his shoulders stiff.

Even though she was scared witless, Cassie wanted to laugh. It looked like they were having their first fight, and Sabrina was giving Cole hell. When Sabrina got back to the truck, Cassie unlocked her doors and she flung the heavy door back like it weighed nothing, then vaulted up inside like an Olympic gymnast.

Obviously in adrenaline overload, Sabrina was breathing heavily, and her cheeks were flushed, as she shoved her weapon back in her shoulder holster roughly, then reached over and slammed the truck door. "That man is a male chauvinist pig," Sabrina grated out between her teeth.

"Welcome to Texas, honey," Cassie told her and chuckled.

"He had the audacity to yell at me for going after James," she huffed out then took the rubber band out of her ponytail to smooth her hair, then refasten it again. "The nerve of the man. James is my fugitive, and I have every right to go after him."

"You sure do...what did he say?"

"He said I should have stayed in the truck and called

him," Sabrina said then got some neck action going when she mimicked him, "I'm the Sheriff in this town and you have no jurisdiction, not to mention he could have shot you," she said in a low comical voice then stuck out her tongue. "He sounded like something out of a bad western movie."

"What did you tell him?" Cassie asked pinching her lips to stop the laughter bubbling inside of her from escaping.

"I told Mr. Big Bad Lawman to go fuck himself," Sabrina hissed through her teeth.

Cassie roared, she couldn't help it, she leaned over the steering wheel, and howled in laughter, picturing this petite woman telling Cole that. She probably put her finger in his chest too. Her laughter was so intense, Cassie had to grip her sides. She heard Sabrina chuckle beside her then guffaw, and before long she was laughing as hard as Cassie was.

The truck door on her side was wrenched open and then Cole was standing there, his face mottled with rage. "Cassie you need to quit all the goofing off and get your ass home, before Luke has a stroke. I called him and he was fit to be tied," he told her then slammed the door.

Cassie's humor fled and she sucked in a shuddery breath then put her seatbelt on, and put the truck in drive. Damn, Cole...he had to go and worry Luke. Now she could only imagine what she'd have to deal with when they got back to the ranch. She groaned then looked over at Sabrina, "Wanna run away together?"

Sabrina chuckled, "I have a feeling where Luke's concerned, you can run, but you can't hide. He'd find you."

"Yeah you're probably right...." She was only kidding about running away, but she had no doubt if she did run away, Luke would track her down to the ends of the earth...she was carrying his baby.

They drove the rest of the way to the ranch in silence, and Cassie had barely stopped the engine when Luke flew across the yard and jerked her door open and pulled her into his arms. "Oh, my god, Cassie...are you alright?"

"Yes, Luke...I just thought I saw James in town. But I'm so edgy, I was probably seeing things."

"And Sabrina, what the fuck, you went after him?"

Cassie whispered by his ear, "Don't go there darlin' or your gonna be in the same fix as Cole."

Luke pinned her an angry glare, but he let it drop and helped her down from the truck, before slamming the door. He took her by the arm to half-walk, half-drag her inside the house. Sabrina followed behind them, and just barely missed having the front door of the house slammed in her face.

"Luke stop being so rude!" Cassie yelled and dug in her heels to stop their forward motion.

"Rude, rude?!" he huffed incredulously his face mottled with rage, "Honey, you ain't seen nothing yet!"

Luke let go of her arm and turned around to face her and then shoved a hand through his hair. "I told you to be careful, and what do you do? You and Sabrina go chasing after someone who looks like James in town. All you had to do was get in the truck, crank it and haul ass home like I told you to do, but you didn't do that did you, Cassie?"

"Luke, you're not my daddy. I don't have to follow your instructions to a T, and you can't tell me what I can and can't do," Cassie told him stiffening her shoulders.

"I'm not your daddy, but I'm gonna be your husband and you need to show a little respect...and think about my baby you're carrying."

Anger coursed up Cassie's body from the soles of her feet. "Respect? Is that what you're showing me? Doesn't sound like that to me, darlin'," She spat then walked closer to him and put her finger in his chest, "And don't be counting your chickens before their hatched. At the rate you're going right now there might not be a wedding tomorrow."

Cassie's breathing had ratcheted up and there was a buzzing in her ears. Spots danced before her eyes as she spun away from him and took off for the stairs. Her knees buckled at the foot of the stairs and the dots closed in to form a black curtain. She could hear Luke and Sabrina calling her name, but couldn't make out anything else.

Suddenly, she felt herself being lifted and heard Luke let out a loud guttural moan near her ear, then her body was jolted as he ran with her in his arms up the stairs.

"Sabrina get me a wet rag...hurry," he said and she felt the soft quilt touch her back, although she still couldn't see anything. Cassie felt hot all over and could actually hear her blood pounding in her ears. She felt Luke place a cold rag on her forehead and wanted to sigh, but couldn't. She fought against the blackness trying open her eyes, but they wouldn't cooperate.

He patted her cheeks and whispered near her ear in a desperate choked voice, "Cassie wake up baby, I'm so sorry...please wake up." A cool rag was placed on her forehead, but she felt water dropping on her cheeks.

She heard Luke tell Sabrina to go call the doctor's number by the phone. More water droplets landed on her face, before another cold rag was put on her throat. She managed to swallow and the blood rushing in her ears slowed down a little, as her breathing settled, then she managed to open her eyes. Luke pulled her up to him and she felt him shiver then felt more droplets of water on her shoulder.

"Just be still, sugar. Sabrina's calling the doctor," he sobbed into her hair and hugged her tighter. What little breath she was able to drag in was trapped in her lungs because he was holding her so tight.

"Luke, let me go, I can't breathe," she whispered then managed to loosen his arms and lay back on the bed and close her eyes for a second, trying to regulate her breathing.

He grabbed her shoulders in a fierce grip and wailed, "Wake up, Cassie--dammit!"

Cassie opened one eye and saw his handsome face was

ragged, his eyes were swollen and red, and tears tracked down his face. She opened both eyes then put her hand to his cheek, "I'm okay, Luke...calm down," she told him weakly then moved her thumb to wipe at the tear tracks on his square jaw.

"I'm so damned sorry, darlin'...I didn't mean to upset you," he told her and placed tiny kisses all over her face then he said, "I was just frantic when Cole called me. Worried that bastard had gotten to you, and I wasn't there."

"Sabrina had it covered, Luke...I'm not even sure it was him. I just got this feeling at the back of neck....and then saw his back."

"I know that feeling...I'm sure Sabrina does too, which is why she ran after him."

"Exactly," Sabrina said as she came back in the room. Relief moved over her friend's face when she saw that Cassie was awake and alert. "The doctor said if you think it's serious, you'd need to bring her to the hospital to be seen...he doesn't make house calls."

Luke immediately slid his arm under and shoulders and then her knees and went to lift her up. "I'm not going to the hospital Luke. I just fainted because I was hot and upset."

"You're going..." he said then lifted her against his chest and stood.

"No, I'm not. There's no need...now put me back down." Luke growled in frustration, but he laid her back on the bed. "Thanks, darlin'," she said then reassured him, "I just need some rest...it's been a long day."

"You're overdoing it, cupcake...you need to slow down."

"I will, after tomorrow," she smiled up at him then patted his cheek, "I promise."

"I'm thinking we should postpone our honeymoon until after the baby is born..."

"No way--we're gonna have a real wedding,

honeymoon included. I'm not waiting eight months to drag the secret out of you."

Luke chuckled and bent down to kiss her lips tenderly, "You are so impatient, Cassie Bee."

"Yep, I imagine by the time I get to two weeks before the baby is born, you might want to move in with Cole for the duration."

"Ain't happening, sugar...after tomorrow you're stuck with me," he told her, his eyes sparkling with love.

Sabrina cleared her throat and said, "I think I'll go get my stuff put away...which room should I take?"

Cassie pushed up to her elbows and was about to get up and show Sabrina her room, but Luke pushed her back down, "You rest, I'll get Sabrina settled."

She huffed out a sigh and laid back against the pillow. "Can you get my stuff out the truck Sabrina? I don't want Luke nosing around."

"Sure..." she said then walked out of the bedroom.

"What happened with her and Cole?" Luke asked sitting back beside her on the bed.

"I'll tell you about it later..." Cassie wasn't sure she wanted to tell Luke about it at all, because he might tell Cole. Especially the part about them just being friends. She wanted Sabrina to have the opportunity to tell him herself. If she gave him that opportunity after the way he'd acted today. Hopefully Luke would just forget about it, and not ask again. "Go help her bring her suitcase up the stairs."

"She carries a gun, and chases bad guys, I think she can handle her suitcase," he told her and then flinched when Cassie punched him in the arm playfully.

"Okay, okay...I'll go help," he said then got up and left her alone.

Cassie didn't tell Luke because she didn't want to scare him, but she was almost positive the man she'd seen had been James. The distinctive striped polo he'd had on was one she'd bought for him last year for his birthday. She'd tell Cole in the morning, and swear him to secrecy. She wasn't letting anything, a fainting spell, or James Barton, ruin her wedding.

Sabrina came back into the room a few minutes later, her arms full of tulle with two boxes propped on top. Cassie smiled then got up to take them from her. She hung them in the closet and smoothed her hand over the dress. "Thanks a lot for bringing this in."

"You're welcome..." Sabrina said thoughtfully distracted before she asked, "Cassie, what made you so sure that man was James today? Other than his flat butt that is," she chuckled.

Cassie poked her head out of the closet and looked around to make sure Luke wasn't there. "Close the door," she said then walked out of the closet to make her way to the bed where she sat down. "The shirt the man had on was the same one I gave James last year for his birthday."

"Well, that could be a coincidence. There are lots of shirts out there like that one, I'd imagine."

Cassie shook her head, then told her, "Not that one. It was pretty distinctive," Cassie ducked her head then admitted, "James always acted like a peacock about his clothes. He thought he was stylish, so when I saw the bright gaudy colors in the stripes, I had to get it for him as an inside joke. Funny thing is he loved it. I laughed every time he wore it."

"We have Diana's place staked out...assumed that's where he'd go, but so far he hasn't been there. I wonder how he got his hands on his clothes?"

"Is she out of jail?" Cassie asked curiously.

"She was never charged, she turned on him...spilled her guts and agreed to testify."

"She's a sneaky one, Bri...had me totally fooled. I'll bet he was staying with her after I kicked him out...and I bet his clothes were at her apartment."

"Well, he hasn't been there."

"She probably met him somewhere, or left them for

him somewhere."

"That's possible, I guess...think we need to tell Luke?"

"No!" Cassie shouted, "We can't tell him! He'll be nervous as a frog in a fruit jar tomorrow anyway and he'll make me that way too. I'm going to talk to Cole in the morning and tell him, so he can let the security guys know."

Sabrina groaned, then came to sit on the bed beside her. "Okay...I just wish it was someone else in charge of protecting you. He just really got under my skin today."

"I'm sure he's feeling like crap about it now..." Cassie ventured then added, "He'll probably apologize tomorrow."

"Doesn't matter...he let me know exactly what he thinks of me--of women--by how he acted today. I can't be friends with him if he feels that way about women. Apologies can't undo some things."

"You're right about the apologies," Cassie agreed, but she wanted to help Cole smooth her feathers too. "But sometimes they do...just see what he says. If his apology doesn't make you feel better, kick his ass to the curb."

"I like your plain talking, Cassie. It's refreshing," she laughed and then leaned over to hug her. "I'm glad we're friends."

"Me too...I don't have many girlfriends left," Cassie told her honestly.

"Me either...I'm kind of a loner these days too, I guess."

"What about your family?"

"My dad died a year ago, actually not long after Kenny, and my mother left when I was really small. I don't even remember her."

Sympathy filled Cassie for all Sabrina had been through in recent years. "No brothers or sisters?"

"One older brother, Gabe...he lives in Mesa. He's a private investigator. I don't see him often."

"Your daddy was a farmer right? How'd you get into law enforcement?"

"My brother...he was military, then he was a Phoenix cop for several years...I was young and idolized him."

"Sounds like you were close...why don't you see him often now?" Cassie knew the value of family, but she also knew how life could intrude on those close relationships. Look at how her previously close relationship with her father had come down to twice yearly visits when she lived in Phoenix.

Sabrina didn't immediately answer her question, instead she twisted her hands in her lap and Cassie saw her lip trembling. She put her hand on Bri's shoulder and told her softly, "I'm sorry...we don't have to talk about it."

Sabrina nodded then said quietly, "Maybe we'll save that one for that bottle of wine too."

"Okay, so how'd you like your dress?" Cassie said brightening her tone and changing the subject to something to lighten the mood.

"Loved it. You did a good job picking it out."

CHAPTER NINETEEN

Luke paced out on the porch, watching the sun set in the distance in a bright orange ball, the same ball of heat he felt curling in his gut. The path he paced was well-worn by now as he tried to rein in the fear and anger that were warring inside of him.

He could have lost Cassie and the baby today, and it made his heart twist around in his chest like someone was wringing it out with the laundry. Swallowing down the knot that formed in his throat, he continued to pace.

Luke need some stress relief...a distraction, that's what he needed. Something to take his mind off of James Barton and his threat to Cassie. Luke was at the point of obsession with it. He wanted to load Cassie up in his truck and drive until the road ended to make sure she was safe and never had to worry about that asshole again.

Walking back inside the house, he grabbed up the phone and dialed Cole. "Hey, buddy..." Cole grunted into the phone letting Luke know he was in the same mood as Luke was. "Wanna go get a beer?" Luke asked hopefully.

Cole's response was another grunt, then he said, "Not in the mood."

"You do know as my best friend and best man you're obligated to get me drunk tonight right?"

Cole snorted and said, "Cassie would kill me...."

Luke chuckled then said, "Nah, in the mood I was in earlier, she'd understand...probably welcome it."

Cole hesitated for a second then he finally said, "Aren't you worried Barton might try to make a move on Cassie?"

"Of course, I am...but if I stay here to protect her, I'm just going to piss her off again..." Luke said then suggested, "I thought maybe you could get a couple of your guys to come sit on the porch with shotguns, while we're gone. The hands are still here setting up chairs for the wedding, and finishing up the gazebo, so I'll get them to stand watch too."

Cole grunted again. "Sounds like you have it all planned out, Slick..."

"I do my best, now get your ass over here, and call your guys," Luke told him authoritatively, but in a playful tone.

"Yes sir, Sheriff," Cole returned snidely.

"Looks like you need an attitude adjustment too, son."

"I need a lot more than that, but I guess I'll have to settle for the beer. I'll be there in a few," Cole told him, his voice lacking enthusiasm.

Luke hung up the phone, and wondered what had gone on between his friend and Sabrina today to put him in such a morose mood. It sounded like it must've been pretty bad, judging from his sour attitude. Luke knew that mood, he was suffering from it himself.

He hung up the phone and then went upstairs to find Cassie. She and Sabrina were sitting on the bed talking like two teenagers having a slumber party. Their eyes sparkled happily as they lounged on the bed telling stories. Seeing Cassie in a better mood did his heart good. At least she wasn't upset anymore. Her fainting spell had been all his fault, and he had been beating the hell out of himself since he'd gone off on her.

How pompous and arrogant he'd sounded, even to himself, when he replayed what exactly he'd said to her. He should have known better than to take that tack with his stubborn cowgirl. But he'd gone and stepped off in it, and almost made her mad enough to cancel the wedding. Luke swallowed hard, and his mouth dried up. He needed that beer, and he needed it soon.

"Hey, darlin'. Cole and I are going grab a beer or two. Guess that's as close to a bachelor party as I'm gonna have."

"Oh? How long are ya'll gonna be out?" she asked with a little fear in her eyes. Luke saw Sabrina's eyes narrow and her lips pinch.

"We're getting a couple of deputies to sit out on the porch until we get back. And the hands are still here working on your gazebo."

"Oh, good," she huffed a relieved sigh then smiled and said, "Ya'll have a good time, sugar...but not *too* good." She raised her eyebrow to give him a warning stare.

"You don't have to worry bout that, cupcake. Wild horses couldn't keep me from marrying you tomorrow."

He walked over to her and tried to give her a quick kiss goodbye, but she wasn't having it and grabbed the side of his face to keep him there then kissed him like she wouldn't see him again for days, weeks.

When she finally released him and he stood up, she said saucily, "Well, if you see Candy, tell her I said howdy," and then she flipped him the bird.

He hooted and slapped his thigh, "I'll be sure to do that, darlin'."

Luke was sitting out on the porch when Cole pulled up in his SUV followed closely by a couple of police cruisers. He smiled and stood to walk down the porch steps, standing at the bottom with his hands on his hips.

Cole got out of the SUV and slammed the door. His face was a thundercloud and Luke smiled trying to get him to lighten up, but his lack of response, told Luke that wasn't going to happen before a couple of beers.

He walked up on the porch then told Luke sullenly, "Let's get this over with."

The deputies walked up behind him and after Luke talked to them, and they assured him they'd keep a good eye on the ladies. Luke put his arm around Cole's shoulder and walked him back to the truck, then slid into the passenger side.

Cole lifted an eyebrow at him then said, "So, looks like you're going to be the only one drinking tonight, huh?"

"Nope, we'll park your vehicle at the station and walk to the bar. If we celebrate too much, we'll call someone to come get us. We're going to throw a good one tonight, friend."

"I need it," Cole told him then slid behind the wheel

and twisted the key forcefully.

Being a Friday night, their old watering hole, the same one they'd been in when Luke met Candy, and basically the only one in town worth anything, was filled with a rowdy crowd whooping and hollering, dancing, drinking and having a high old time. It was a scene that Luke had enjoyed before Cassie had reappeared in his life, but not anymore. The bar was smoky and crowded and Luke just wanted to find a little relief in a few beers then go back home to her.

He smiled at the irony of how much his life had changed in the last month, because of the reappearance of the last woman he'd wanted to see again. With a pat on Cole's back and a firm hand on his shoulder he pushed him toward the bar.

Luke leaned around Cole and told the bartender, "Two tall boys."

"How the hell do you know that's what I want?" Cole grumped and pinned him with angry eyes.

"It's what you're having. No glasses tonight, we're celebrating...no tears in your beer," Luke told him then smiled at a pretty blonde at the end of the bar who was eyeing him and Cole.

"Looks like that cute blonde at the end of the counter, wants a piece of us."

"You've already got all the pieces you can handle, Slick," Cole said gloomily.

"But you on the other hand..." Luke raised his hand and invited her to come down and sit with them.

The green-eyed blonde in the tight white tank top, which showed off her more than ample assets, winked and slid off the stool then grabbed her drink off the bar and pushed her way through the crowd toward them. When she got there, she slid her arm through Luke's and pressed her breasts against his arm. He looked down at her and what would have sent him into overdrive a month ago, did nothing to rev his engine now.

"Hello, darlin'," he drawled and took in the scenery anyway. It was what he was supposed to do, this was his last night as a single man.

Luke took a long slow drink from his beer then sighed and licked his lips. He saw the woman following his movements, then decided he needed to pawn her off on Cole quickly before he got into trouble out of habit. Cole was the one who really needed her attention.

"My friend here had a really bad day, and he could use some cheering up. You think you could do that, sugar?"

The pretty blonde looked up at him, then over at Cole whose stiff back was to them, while he nursed his beer. He hadn't even turned around when the bombshell had walked up to say hello.

"I don't know...he doesn't look like he's in a friendly mood."

Luke elbowed Cole in the back and he grunted. "Turn around here Cole and meet the pretty lady, who's gonna put a smile back on that ugly mug of yours."

Cole took another deep draw on his beer then turned around to face them with a sigh. "Hello pretty lady..." he said in a gruff tone, then he softened it with a twist of his lips. Luke watched as his friend's eyes wandered over her t-shirt that announced to the world that she was a 'country girl' then moved back up to her interested green eyes.

"Why you're right, Luke, she's as pretty as a ray of sunshine..." Cole told him and gave her a smile that should melt her panties. Luke had seen him turn that smile on other women and it hadn't missed in all the years they'd hung out together.

Cole sat his beer on the bar and then stood and grabbed her hand, "Let's dance, sugar," he said then pulled her into the crowd, moving toward the dance floor without waiting for an answer.

Yeah, maybe she could put his normally affable friend back in a better frame of mind, at least Luke hoped so anyway. Luke sat back down at the bar and finished his beer, then ordered another.

Cole didn't come back for a long while, but Luke had seen him on the floor spinning the blonde around the floor, seeming to be having a good time. When they finally walked back to the bar, breathing heavily, Luke smiled and Cole returned it this time. A good sign, he thought. The woman was glued to his side with her arm around his back. Another good sign.

"What'll you have, darlin'?" Cole looked down at her with a smile.

"Bud, please."

"A woman after my own heart," he said then ordered two and leaned on his elbow on the bar, with his arm still around the woman whose name Luke still didn't know.

"You're a miracle worker, sugar. You put a smile on his face," Luke said and tapped his bottle with hers after Cole handed it to her.

She lifted her head and took a long drink of her beer, then said, "Wasn't too hard, he's a great dancer," she told Luke then looked up at Cole and winked at him, "Was pretty hard by the time we finished though."

Luke sputtered and almost spewed his beer across the room, then hooted, "Darlin' not much shocks me, but you just managed to do that."

"Glad to oblige," she told him with a saucy grin. She squeezed Cole's waist and then turned to give him a hug. Cole growled then set his beer down and pulled her to him and bent down to put his lips over hers.

Luke didn't want to see him making out with her, so he turned back around to the bar and motioned the bartender for another longneck. The tension that had him wound tighter than Dick's hatband earlier, had eased a little more with each beer he drank...and he was on number four, so he was pretty near loose now.

In the mirror behind the bar, Luke's eyes snagged on a nice looking brunette who'd just walked in the door. His eyes skimmed over her curvy toned body in the tight jeans she wore with a low cut red western shirt with rhinestones on the chest that spelled out 'cowgirl'.

Luke had seen that shirt before...Cassie had one just like it. And she had a black Stetson with a rhinestone band just like the one the woman wore too. He noticed the woman had her long dark hair curled and tucked behind her ears to show off her dangly feather earrings.

Seeing her wearing what Cassie probably would have worn if she'd come with them, made him miss her, wish that she was here with him. Luke had only been away from her for a couple of hours and all he could think of was getting back home to her.

When the woman lifted her head after showing her ID to the man at the door, Luke's eyes widened and he whispered, "Oh, shit."

Sabrina walked toward the bar with a sashay in her stride, and he saw men all over the bar turn and look, some broke away from their group to trail behind her. Before Luke could warn Cole, her eyes locked with Luke's in the mirror and she headed toward them. She wasn't smiling, and Luke swallowed hard knowing trouble was about to visit them in the form of a 5'3" pissed off woman with a gun.

But she surprised Luke when she walked up to him after a cursory glance at Cole, who was still lip locked with the blonde. "Having fun?" she asked with an edge to her voice hidden beneath the wide smile she gave him.

"Yeah, but missing Cassie..." he told her and drank down half of his fifth beer. "I thought ya'll would be having a girl's night at the house."

"She made me come out...said I needed to come party for her, since she wasn't able to celebrate her last night being a single girl. Guess, I'm a one woman bachelorette party," she chuckled.

Over her shoulder, Luke saw Cole come up for air, dragging his lips from the blonde when he heard Sabrina's voice. Cole's eyes widened when he saw her, right as a medium-built, but stocky cowboy tapped her on her shoulder, and she turned her head and smiled at him.

"Hi, sugar...you wanna dance?" he asked leaning near her ear and sliding his hand to her lower back.

She turned away from Luke and faced the cowboy, putting her hand on his shoulder. "I'd love to, sugar," she purred and he took her hand and led her off through the crowd.

Cole's face turned so red, Luke thought his friend might bust a blood vessel. A vein popped out on his forehead and Luke saw his hands, which were no longer on the blonde, squeeze into tight fists at his side, and he was grinding his teeth into nubs.

The blonde, who was still standing beside him looked up at him curiously. "You, okay, honey?" she asked putting her hand on his arm.

He looked down at her as if he didn't even see her then said, "Fine...get me another goddamned beer Luke," he grated then he loosened his fists and put his arm back around the blonde.

She pressed her body to him and put her hand on his chest, then stood on tiptoe to whisper in his ear. Cole shook his head and then moved away from her, "I'm sorry sugar, but I'm not in the mood. I need to take a break for a few minutes," he told her then sat down on the stool beside Luke again ignoring her to lift the beer to his mouth and almost drink it down in one swallow.

"Well you sure seemed to be in the mood on the dance floor, darlin'," she spat sassily then went to walk away. Cole jumped up off the stool and grabbed her arm, "You know, on second thought, let's go dance again. Maybe I'll work up another head of steam."

Luke saw indecision and desire at war with each other on her pretty face, then she sighed and grabbed Cole's hand to lead him to the floor. Luke watched Cole pull the blonde tightly against him and move her to the edge of the floor, before he spun her into a two-step, but his eyes were searching the floor for Sabrina.

Cole hadn't spotted her yet, but Luke had. She was belly rubbing in the center of the floor with the cowboy who'd asked her to dance. Luke had a bad feeling this wasn't going to turn out well when his friend finally spotted her. Why Cassie had sent her here, and decked her out like she was, he didn't know. She had to know Cole would go crazy.

Maybe she was stirring the pot trying to play matchmaker to get them back on speaking terms. He definitely planned to ask her when he got home, because it was obvious her little scheme was backfiring...big time. All he needed was his best man with a black eye in the wedding pictures. Cassie would kill him, even though this was all her doing.

Luke drank the last of his beer and pushed up from the bar stool, waited a second to get his feet firmly under him, them walked toward the dance floor. It was time for him and Cole to leave.

Luke found him waltzing the pretty blonde around the floor, holding her so tight you couldn't fit a piece of paper between them, then watched Cole stop with her at the corner of the floor where he put his hands on her ass to lift her higher against him, before he made a show of kissing her hungrily. Her body was suctioned to his as her arms went up around his neck and she rubbed her hips against him like a cat on a scratching post.

Hurrying his steps across the dance floor, Luke pushed people aside until he reached them then tapped Cole on the shoulder. He probably should have brought a bucket of cold water with him, he thought as Cole ignored him and continued kissing the woman.

He glanced to the center of the floor and saw that Sabrina had quit dancing too and was staring at Cole and the blonde with tears of anger in her eyes. The cowboy was pulling on her arm trying to get her moving again, but she shrugged him off then turned and stormed off the floor headed straight for the door. The cowboy followed right behind her.

"C'mon let's go Cole. We need to go catch up with Sabrina, she might be able to give us a ride home."

"Nah, I'm staying here, but you go ahead if you want to ride with her," he said then looked down into the blonde's eyes and smiled. "I saw that cowboy follow her out, he'll probably be taking her home," there was pain beneath his nonchalant words, Luke heard it.

"Fine," Luke said then added 'stubborn dumbass fool' under his breath as he headed for the front door to catch up with Sabrina.

The breezy warm night air sobered him up a little when he burst out through the front door of the bar and stepped into the night. Luke stopped and looked up and down the street for his truck. He knew Sabrina had to have driven it to town, because there weren't any other vehicles available to her at the ranch. He finally found it parked across the street down a block, and ran across the road to the sidewalk on the other side.

When he got one foot on the sidewalk, Luke saw her struggling with the cowboy who she'd been dancing with earlier, while he tried to kiss her. The drunk bastard had his hands all over her, and Luke took off at a dead run for them.

He stopped in his tracks through when he saw her knee came up between the guys legs then in quick succession she shoved the heel of her hand into his nose, then gave him a fist on either side of his head near his ears, before stepping on his foot pushing him back on his ass.

The guy laid there rolling around holding his balls curled in the fetal position while he bled from the nose like a stuck pig. Luke wanted to laugh, but he wanted to make sure she was okay first.

Luke walked up to her with a smile on his face, "Good job, darlin'. You okay?" Sabrina might be a small woman, but she evidently packed a wallop, he thought as he looked down at the guy on the ground who was very near tears and chuckled. "Stay here, I need a ride home. Let me go get Cole to clean up the trash...I'll be right back."

"I don't want to see him," she said angrily her eyes sparkling a dangerous sapphire blue.

"You don't have to, sugar...we'll leave as soon as I tell him," Luke told her with understanding then headed back to the bar.

When he got inside, he found Cole sitting at the bar now drinking another beer. The blonde wasn't anywhere around, and his friend looked like hell. His face was strained his shoulders slumped, and his chin about touched his chest. Luke walked over and slapped him on the back,

"You need to call a unit to come pick up the guy out on the sidewalk about a block down."

Cole perked up a little and looked at him, but his voice lacked luster when he asked Luke, "You kick someone's ass again? Do I need to arrest you?"

Luke threw up his hands and laughed. "Not me this time...Sabrina."

Cole vaulted up from the stool and got in Luke's face, "What the fuck do you mean?"

"The cowboy got grabby, and she put him in his place...and then some."

"Holy, shit!" he shouted then pushed Luke to the side and ran for the door. He was across the street and down to the truck, before Luke could catch him.

Luke saw him reach down and jerk the cowboy up by the shirt front, before he pulled back his arm, about to plant his fist in the guy's face. Luke got there just in time to grab his elbow. Sabrina leaned against the truck with her legs crossed and her arms folded over her chest.

"Get a grip on yourself man, or you'll be the one in jail tonight," Luke hissed near his ear. Cole let go of the man's shirt then pushed his shoulder, causing him to stumble then drop to his knees. "Just call someone to come pick him up."

"I wanna beat the fuck out of him," Cole said in a slurred voice, before he walked over and roughly turned the man on his stomach and pulled his arm up behind him then put his knee in the center of the guy's back.

"Don't do it man, you've got to be in my wedding tomorrow. Cassie would shoot you," Luke reminded him. "Besides, I think Sabrina has pretty much already done that for you," Luke told him then gave in to the laughter he'd been holding back.

He wound up leaning against the truck, snorting and gasping for breath, until he saw Sabrina push away from the truck and sashay around to the driver's side with a purposeful angry stride. She pushed the unlock button, then opened the door and launched herself up into the seat and cranked the truck.

Luke grabbed the passenger door and flung it open, just managing to get himself seated before she hit the accelerator. "Whoa, sugar...you're gonna throw me out," he said unsteadily, as he reached to shut the door right before the big truck launched down the street.

She had the seat shoved so far up to reach the pedals, his knees were almost right under the dashboard, he turned them sideways and sat against the door. Her breasts were pressed against the wheel, and her chin was tilted up so she could see over the steering wheel. Luke chuckled at the sight she made. "Cassie should have given you a phone book to sit on."

She glanced at him then back to the road, her hands tight on the wheel at ten and two. "I could probably use two--this big truck compensating for something, honey?" she asked sassily with a grin.

Luke sat up straighter, insulted.   "You sure have a smart mouth on you, honey, for someone driving *my* truck."

She snorted, then said, "I'm driving your drunk ass home in this truck, honey. Be thankful that Cassie won't have to kill you."

He folded his arms over his chest, and shut up. He wasn't going to win a verbal war with this sharp witted woman while his wits were steeped in alcohol.

"Nothing more to say?" she asked with a chuckle. When he didn't say anything, she threw her head back and laughed. "Didn't think so."

"Just drive," Luke told her sullenly. "And don't wreck my truck."

A few minutes later, she pulled the truck to a stop in the yard, then cut the engine and tossed him his keys. "Here you go, stud. Now go answer to your wife."

With that, she opened her door and slid down from the truck, leaving him behind her smiling. Yeah, she was more than a match for Cole. Smart, sassy and more than capable...not to mention beautiful. He hoped his friend could work it out with her. Luke opened his door and got out, stumbling a bit in his alcohol fog, then went inside to face the music.

***

Saturday, the day of her wedding, dawned hot, humid and sticky with gray puffy clouds that threatened rain. They desperately needed the rain, but she desperately didn't want to see it on her wedding day, even if the old wives tale said it meant their love would withstand all weather.

That was fine, but Cassie just prayed it would hold off until after the ceremony, at least. They had tents set up for the reception, so if it rained then, it wouldn't really matter.

Cassie and Sabrina were busy attaching bows to the innermost chairs skirting the aisle. They'd decorate the gazebo next with the flowers the florist had delivered earlier.

"Okay, what's your something blue for today?" Sabrina asked her fluffing out the loops on the bow she'd just placed.

"My engagement ring...it has sapphires."

"Is it also your something new?" Sabrina suggested.

Cassie shook her head and smiled. "That's my dress, hat and boots."

"What about something old?"

"I'm wearing my mama's brooch. It looks great with my dress," Cassie told her shoving baby's breath in her bow's center then hesitating before she said with sentimental tears choking her, "I wish my mama was here for today..."

She heard Sabrina suck in a breath, then felt her kneel beside her, before she put her arms around Cassie's shoulders. "I know how you feel Cassie...but I bet your mama is looking down from heaven today with a smile. I didn't know her, but I believe she'd be proud of all you've accomplished and gone through to get here."

"I'm leaving an empty chair beside my daddy for her today."

"I bet she'd love that." Sabrina squeezed her shoulders.

"Have I told you how much I appreciate you being here today?"

"A thousand times...now stop. You're gonna make me tear up."

Cassie forced a bright smile, and looked at her, "How did last night go?"

Sabrina dropped her hands from Cassie's shoulders and then stood up. "Not good," she said then grabbed a bow out of the box and walked to the next chair.

Remorse filled Cassie, because she'd forced Sabrina to go last night. She'd kept after her until she agreed to go to the bar to check up on Cole and Luke...make sure they weren't overdoing it. And she'd hoped that Cole would take the opportunity to apologize to her. Obviously, that didn't happen. Anger rushed through her and she wanted to strangle Luke's best friend for being so stubborn.

"Cole didn't apologize?" she asked to make sure.

Sabrina snorted then said, "If sticking his tongue down a hot blonde's throat all night is an apology, then yes he did."

Cassie's anger turned to molten lava in her veins and she threw the bow she'd just picked up back in the box and put her hands on her hips. "He did *what?*"

Sabrina shrugged and said, "He hooked up with a blonde and danced her feet off when he wasn't trying to screw her on the dance floor."

"Luke didn't say anything to him?" Cassie would be just as mad at Luke if he hadn't at least tried to talk some sense into the big lug.

"It wasn't Luke's place to do that, Cassie. Cole did what he wanted to do, and so did I."

Cassie grinned at the mischievous note in her friend's tone. "Oh, yeah? What did you do?"

"Danced my feet off with a nice looking cowboy."

"Good for you, Bri," she hooted then said, "I bet Cole was fit to be tied."

"Nah, he just played tonsil hockey with the blonde, and I wound up having to break the cowboy's nose outside the bar."

Cassie's eyebrows flew up to her hairline and she gasped, "Really?"

"Really..." Sabrina laughed then said, "I think he gets the meaning of 'no' now."

"Wow girl, you're my hero."

"I'm no hero...that guy was drunk and all over me..." she waved her hand dismissively then finished."

"Well, it makes me happy to see a woman take care of herself. You'll have to show me some of those moves after the wedding," Cassie told her with a chuckle.

"You got it...now let's get these bows done."

Cassie hurried to pick up another bow and tie it on the next chair. They needed to quit dawdling, but she was having fun working with Sabrina. By the time they finished with the gazebo, she could smell the pork and beef simmering on the spit. The catering crew had arrived at the break of dawn to start cooking. It smelled delicious and her stomach rumbled.

"Let's go grab some lunch, then we can take turns in the shower and start getting dressed. I have Betty Lou from the Cut Up Corral in town coming out to do our hair and makeup. She's old school and will have us looking like Texas belles in no time.

Sabrina groaned then said, "Oh god, Cassie...don't tell me I have to have big hair."

"You got it, sugar. No Texas bride, or bridesmaid would be without it...you'll look great," she assured her friend and looped her arm through Sabrina's and led her toward the house.

CHAPTER TWENTY

Four hours later, Cassie and Sabrina sat in Cassie's bedroom letting Betty Lou put the final coat of shellac, also know as hairspray to non-southerners, on Cassie and Sabrina's hair, and then one more coat of mascara to make sure their lashes were long and lush.

"One more coat of that stuff and I think my smile will be frozen on my face for life like the Joker in Batman."

"My eyelashes are about stuck to my eyebrows," Cassie hooted then said, "But damn, we sure do look good." She turned her head left and right admiring the beautiful style Betty Lou had teased and worked her hair into. She'd drawn up the curls in a loose ponytail at her nape and pulled loose tendrils to frame her face.

Although her eyes were smoky and dramatic, the rest of her makeup was muted, except for her deep rose colored lips. They were the perfect shade, and Betty had glossed them up so they looked plump and full.

"Where's your veil, baby girl? I want to put it on you so you don't mess up your hair trying to do it yourself."

Cassie got up and went to the closet and pulled down the box with her hat and veil, then walked over and handed it to Betty Lou. When she pulled it out, Betty Lou's hand flew to her considerable bosom and she gasped. "Why that is the most beautiful headpiece I've ever seen."

"Thanks," Cassie grinned at the woman's dramatics. It was pretty, but it was just a white Stetson with a veil attached.

"We probably should put your dress on before we put this hat on you," she said gnawing her red lips.

"It's a little early yet..." Cassie told her. They still had an hour before the ceremony.

"I'd wait, but I have another bride to do after I leave here..." Betty Lou told her fingering the large beads at her throat.

"Okay, let me get it..." Cassie wasn't looking forward to being in the dress longer than she had to, but she didn't want to walk down the aisle with messed up hair either. She grabbed the garment bag off the rod and walked back into the bedroom then laid it on the bed and unzipped it. Pulling it out she smoothed layers of tulle then took it off the hanger and handed it to Betty Lou.

"Okay, sugar, I'm gonna get this thing draped on my arms and you just dive right in," she told her. Cassie knew this drill from the times she'd had to do this for the lady at the dress shop. She put her palms together above her head and bent forward and aimed for the open hole in the center of the dress.

The hairdresser helped her shimmy it down over her hips then tugged it down a few times so it sat where it should. Sabrina came over and helped her fluffing the layers of tulle into place and then smiled up at her.

"Don't worry about zipping it yet, I'll do that right before I walk." At least she could halfway breathe until then. She tugged up the top of the gown then dug inside the bodice and tugged up the long line bra again.

"That dress is gorgeous, Cassie. You're gonna be the prettiest bride in Texas, darlin'," Betty Lou told her with tears welling up in her eyes. Cassie hoped she held onto those tears, because with all that blue eye shadow and liner, they'd have a mess if she let them go.

Cassie smiled at her then bent over to give her a hug. "Thanks for helping me today, Betty Lou."

"I wouldn't have missed it, sugar. Your mama would be so proud." She knew Betty Lou had known her mama and had been friends with her, so her words meant a lot.

Cassie felt her lower lip tremble and she sniffed a few times waving at her eyes to try and dry up the moisture she felt there. "Stop or your gonna make me mess up your beautiful makeup job." Cassie glanced over at Sabrina and saw her eyes had teared up too.

Betty patted Cassie's hand and said fussily, "Sit, sit--I need to get your hat on." After a few minutes and a lot of bobby pins, Betty stood back to admire her work. "There you go, darlin'. I don't think a tornado could take that hat off."

Cassie laughed then stared at herself in the tri-fold mirror on the vanity and sighed. All her life she'd had a picture in her mind of what she'd look like on her wedding day, and this was it. And she was marrying the man of her dreams in less than an hour. Betty Lou patted her shoulder and told her to get her lots of 'pictures', then gathered up all her tools and put them back in the big flowered bag she'd brought them in, then kissed her cheek and left.

Cassie had just sat back on the vanity stool when she heard thunder rumble outside. She got up and quickly walked to the window to look out at the darkening clouds. Sabrina was right behind her looking out too.

"Hey is that smoke over behind the barn?" Sabrina asked reaching around Cassie to point at what she saw.

Cassie whirled around and screamed, "FIRE!" at the top of her lungs, then picked up her skirt and ran out the door and down the stairs. She stopped at the phone and dialed 911 and hollered into the phone, "Fire at the Double B..." then dropped the phone and ran out the door heading toward the barn at a full out sprint.

She was halfway across the yard yelling "FIRE!" every few steps when she heard Luke behind her yelling at her to stop. She didn't break stride as she ran toward the orange glow behind the barn, then straight into the thickening smoke at the front.

Luke's heart stopped when he saw Cassie go barreling into the burning barn in her wedding dress. He ran faster than he even knew he could after her, then stopped at the door for a second to search inside for her. He saw her at the far end of the row of stalls to the left, opening stall doors and swatting horse's rears to get them moving toward the front.

The horses blocked his view of her, and he heard galloping hooves coming toward him and dove out of the way at the last minute to keep from getting trampled. Honey was first out, followed by the roan mare that Bud usually rode, then his big black gelding and a couple of others.

He went to go inside, but stopped when he heard more frantic hoof beats then saw two more horses run out then head around the side of the barn. He stepped inside yelling Cassie's name and with his arm bent over his nose to try and keep the smoke from overwhelming him.

Through the thickening smoke he saw her running to the right side of the barn where she'd put Titan and the new mares. He ran that way to intercept her, but saw someone else instead. James Barton stood by Titan's stall with a gas can in one hand and a gun in the other. He had the gun pointed directly at Cassie.

"Barton!" Luke yelled and pulled the gun he wasn't supposed to be wearing out of the holster under his tux. The man spun around with the gun aimed at him and pulled off a shot. Luke dodged to the right and flattened himself against a stall, then raised his gun and fired a shot at James' head.

Somehow the man managed to avoid being hit, so Luke fired off two more shots. One hit him square in the forehead and the second hit him in the chest. A shocked look came over Barton's face, then he fell face forward into the dirt. Good riddance, Luke thought and yelled for Cassie.

He could barely see her through the smoke now, and he yelled her name again. She didn't respond, but one at a time, the new mares ran past him toward the front of the barn. Luke saw hot flames licking at the rafters now and they would reach the hayloft momentarily. When that happened, he knew the place would go up like matchsticks.

Luke covered his mouth and eyes with his forearm

again, then ran down the aisle toward Titan's stall. He stepped over James Barton's body, then flicked open Titan's stall door and slid it open. The horse ran past him, and he slapped his rump to keep him moving.

Coughing violently, Luke stumbled further down the aisle looking for Cassie. He saw a pile of white material sticking out from under the last mare's stall and a pair of white cowboy boots. Panic surged through him and he ran to her and picked her up in his arms and took off for the front of the barn.

Behind him, Luke heard timbers snapping further back in the barn, before they crashed to the floor with a loud boom. Cinders and ashes floated in the air around him as he ran. Luke was lightheaded from inhaling the smoke, and his lungs burned like they were on fire too, but he kept focused on reaching the door of the barn. It was the only way he was going to save Cassie and his baby.

Orange flames were licking at the left wall now, climbing toward the ceiling, so Luke knew their time for surviving was running out. He ran faster, but his legs were getting weak and didn't seem to want to cooperate. Finally he saw light through the smoke and ran outside then collapsed to his knees with Cassie in his arms. He set her down then fell down himself.

Cassie moaned as she started to come awake, fighting at whatever was covering her nose and mouth. Her throat burned, and her lungs felt like they were roasted, and every muscle in her body ached. Finally able to open her eyes she looked around at all the faces surrounding her, staring at her with worry, and then looked at the blue-uniformed man kneeling beside her.

"Are you hurt anywhere ma'am?" he asked her then pressed his fingers to her throat. She shook her head from side to side, but then thought about the baby, and panicked trying to sit up.

The man pressed her back down and she yelled with tears in her eyes, "I'm pregnant!"

"You'll have to have the baby's health checked out at the hospital. An ambulance is on the way..."

"I'm not going to the hospital, I'll go to my doctor..." she told him raspily, then Luke's absence hit her, "Oh, my god, where's Luke?" Cassie wailed and managed to get up even though the medic was trying to keep her lying down.

Cassie pushed through the crowd surrounding her, yelling his name, then saw another crowd gathered a short distance away and ran toward them. She elbowed through to find Luke laying unconscious on the ground as two men worked on him.

His face was gray and soot covered and it didn't look like he was breathing. Cassie sobbed loudly then ran over and slid on her knees beside him. She ran her hands over his thick black hair and asked them in a frantic whisper, "Is he breathing?"

"Yeah, he's breathing, but not evenly...he's still unconscious. Hopefully the oxygen will bring him around in a second. Doesn't look like he was burned anywhere, but he definitely has some smoke inhalation going on. An ambulance is on the way to take ya'll to the hospital to make sure you're okay."

Cassie glanced over at the barn about a hundred yards from where they were and saw only smoldering ashes. She sobbed, for Luke, and for her horses who were alive, but homeless. This was all James Barton's fault. She'd seen the weasel with a gas can and gun in his hands before the smoke got the best of her and she passed out.

"Did anyone see James run out of the barn?"

Cole pushed through the crowd and knelt down beside her, his eyes flicking over Luke then back to her. "Was James in the barn?"

"Yeah, I saw him standing by Titan's stall when I made it over there to let him and the mare's out. He had a gun and a gas can...I don't know anything else because I passed out from the smoke right after I saw him."

"Luke ran in after you and carried you out," his eyes

traveled to Luke then back to her. "You shouldn't have gone in there Cassie..." he told her fervently.

"I know...but I had to. My horses were going to burn up. At least they had a chance if I could let them out of their stalls. There was no way I could stand there and do nothing to help them..." she told him and felt her lower lip tremble as tears started down her cheeks at the same time the rain that had been threatening all day started to fall from the sky in big warm drops.

The crowd around them scattered moving swiftly toward the tent that had been put up for their reception. Her horses were safe, but Luke wasn't. Again this whole mess was her fault.

Cole's eyes glittered with understanding then he hugged her to him and kissed the top of her head. "I know why you did it, and don't blame you, sugar. I'm just worried about Luke, just like you are...but you need to stay calm for the baby."

Cole might not blame her, but she sure as hell blamed herself. If she hadn't been so stupid as to get hooked up with James back in Phoenix, and even invite him here to her home, Luke wouldn't be hurt...her daddy's barn wouldn't be burned to the ground.

Cassie didn't know what James had hoped to accomplish by burning down the barn, but he'd accomplished something, hurting her and Luke, even if he'd died in the process.

He'd also accomplished making her doubt her decision to marry Luke. She'd caused Luke nothing but trouble since she'd been back in Bowie. It was the indisputable truth, he'd even admitted it. Luke probably wouldn't even want to marry her after she'd been the cause of him almost getting killed trying to save her. That thought made her cry even harder.

Cassie swiped at her tears and the raindrops with the back of her hand and came away with black smudges, which made her cry even harder. Her beautiful dress was ruined...as surely as her future with Luke. She got on her hands and knees and leaned to Luke's face to kiss his cheek.

"I'm so sorry, darlin'," she told him in a shaky whisper near his ear then told him repeated she loved him, and begged him to wake up and kiss her.

Just as she heard sirens wailing in the distance, he opened his red rimmed whiskey-brown eyes and looked into hers, then smiled under the mask over his mouth and pulled it off then croaked, "You're alive, cupcake..."

There was relief and disbelief in his raspy voice then he lifted a hand to cup her cheek as tears filled his eyes. "James Barton won't ever hurt you again, sugar. He's dead."

Cassie sobbed as relief washed through her that James was no longer a threat, and Luke was alive, "That's good news, darlin', but don't talk..." She put her finger to his lips then leaned down and placed an emotional kiss there.

Luke sat up and handed the mask to the medic, telling him to cancel the ambulance because he wasn't going anywhere. Then he stood up and pulled Cassie into his arms and hugged her tightly against his chest, softly weeping into her hair. She was crying just as hard now, and both of their bodies were quaking with the emotion raging through them.

Carl Bellamy, Bud, Cole, Sabrina, and Imelda all came over and circled around Cassie and Luke joining in on the hugging and crying. They stayed like that a long while, until the clouds parted overhead and the sun came peeping through.

They all looked skyward and then Carl said, "Looks like a good day for a wedding," then gave a watery chuckle pulling out a white handkerchief to wipe his eyes and blow his nose loudly. Cassie was the first to start chuckling at the ridiculous statement made by her daddy, then Luke joined in, and before long they were all laughing loudly.

Her daddy was the only one not laughing, she noticed

and raised an eyebrow at him when they finally settled down.

"I'm serious, darlin'. You're not going to let James Barton win are you?"

Cassie considered his challenge for a minute, then stiffened her backbone and looked up at Luke who was staring down at her intently. He shrugged then smiled at her his teeth glowing whitely in his handsome soot-stained face.

"Crowd's still here," he rasped.

She laughed at that. Yeah, they were still here because of the fire and excitement, not because they thought there'd still be a wedding today. "Is the preacher still here?"

"Yep, he's making sure the food is well protected," Cole said with a twist of his lips.

The portly preacher who was the pastor of the church where Cassie was baptized, and where her mama and daddy had been married was well known for his love of free food. He was in heaven at the Sunday Socials after church.

Cassie leaned her head back against Luke's chest and looked up into his eyes. "You really still want to do this, Luke?" She looked down at her singed, dirty dress and wanted to weep wildly. "I'm a mess...and all the trouble..."

Luke turned her around in his arms to face him then leaned down close to her face and whispered. "I would marry you if you were wearing a burlap sack, cupcake," he growled and then pulled her to him for a kiss that told her how much he loved her, soft, gentle, sweet and so hot her toes curled inside her boots.

He pulled back just millimeters from her mouth and said, "I love you, Cassie...always and forever...no matter what. You're my kind of trouble, sweetheart, and I want a lifetime of it."

All of her fears and doubts fled and she was filled up by the love shining in his eyes. She put her hand on his cheek and whispered, "I love you too, Luke...always and forever...let's go get married."

He held her away from him a moment and told her with serious eyes. "Only if you promise to go to the emergency room with me after we're done here. I want to make sure you and the baby are okay."

"I promise," she told him then leaned up on her toes and put a kiss on his lips, "On the way to our honeymoon destination, which I still am in the blind about by the way, we will stop at the first emergency room to get all of us checked out."

She heard her daddy let out a whoop behind her and then it was followed by one from Cole and Sabrina, with a final "Yee-Haw" from Imelda. As a group, they walked over to the reception tent and told their guests that there would be a wedding after all, and asked them to take their seats.

Cassie and Sabrina ran back in the house and hurriedly washed their faces and reapplied a minimal amount of makeup, then combed out their hair and put it up in a ponytail, then finally changed into jeans and dressy western shirts Cassie had in her closet.

Cassie cleaned up her white boots with a wet rag and then put them back on, and then cleaned and dusted off her white wedding hat, the one Cole had rescued from the yard, before putting it back on her head. She had another white straw Stetson in her closet and took it down for Sabrina to wear.

They hugged each other then ran back downstairs, grabbed their bouquets from the kitchen table, and ran out the back door where her daddy was waiting to walk her down the aisle. She put her fingers between her teeth and whistled loudly to signal the fiddle players by the gazebo to start the music.

Her daddy laughed then mumbled under his breath, "You can take the girl out of the country...."

"Amen to that daddy," she smiled at him then put her

arm through his.

Cole took Sabrina's arm and they started down the white carpeted aisle that led to the gazebo, where Cassie saw Luke waiting for her looking disheveled, but more handsome than any man had a right to be. After Cole and Sabrina reached the front, and split to stand on separate sides of the gazebo, she and her daddy started walking and her eyes met Luke's. Her heart twisted inside her chest and she felt like she was floating toward him.

As they moved past each aisle of guests, applause sounded behind them, until the whole crowd was standing and clapping by the time she reached the gazebo. Her daddy took her hand, then kissed her cheek, before he placed her hand in Luke's with tears in his eyes.

"Have a good life, darlin'," he said in a choked whisper then walked over to stand in front of his chair, beside the empty chair with a bouquet of white roses, her mother's place.

Cassie swallowed down the emotion churning inside of her and turned to face Luke and look up into his eyes. He gave her a sexy relieved grin, then leaned down next to her ear and whispered fiercely, "You look beautiful, cupcake."

The pastor stepped forward to the top step of the gazebo and raised his hand to quiet the crowd, then he proceeded to say the age old words that would make Cassie and Luke one forever. When he was done, and they'd made their vows, the pastor told Luke to kiss his bride.

Luke grinned at her and then gave the crowd a show they'd be talking about for a long time, as he bent her back over his arm and kissed her like there was no tomorrow. When he finally swung her back up the crowd erupted in laughter and applause.

EPILOGUE

Cassie moaned loudly then hissed out between her teeth, "Luke Matthews, you---are a dead man," she said bearing down and gritting her teeth. "You did this to me."

"Calm down, cupcake...." Luke told her then picked up a few chips of ice from the cup in his hand and put them to her lips, "Here have some ice chips."

"I'm going to shove those ice chips up your a--," she grated and sat up, then moaned, and fell back against the bed clutching the sheets with beads of sweat dripping into her eyes. Her hair was wet and stuck to her face, and she was panting.

Luke took the chance of moving closer to her and then rubbed her belly, "Just breathe darlin', that'll make it better."

He thought her head was going to spin around on her shoulders when she leaned her face up to his and said in a low fierce whisper, "How the hell would you know?" Her eyes were wild and glazed.

"It's what the book said, sugar." Luke was doing everything he could to keep her calm and focused, but he was way out of his element here. He'd read the books, but none of them said he'd be dealing with a possessed madwoman who wanted to kill him...or cut his nuts off as she'd said earlier. He squeezed his legs together and swallowed hard.

"I want you to go find every one those damned books, and burn them. *Now*," she said on an inhale as she pressed down again, then huffed out a breath and then panted.

He'd read about six books on pregnancy and childbirth, so he could help Cassie, but they didn't anyhow prepare him for what he was seeing her go through. Luke almost felt every contraction that racked her body. "What can I do to help you then, darlin'?"

"Get me drugs...lots and lots of drugs."

"The book says those aren't good for the ba--"

She leaned up to him again and pinched his cheeks with one hand. "Say it and you really are going to die," she hissed and Luke believed her...she was that convincing. She gasped then let go of his face and clutched her belly, moaning through another contraction.

"Go get the nurse, I think it's time," she said in a breathless whisper, her face was a mask of pain.

Luke stood and almost ran from the room to go find the nurse. She was behind the round station right outside the door.

"She's ready, come quick," he said desperately.

The fiftyish nurse glanced up at him then back at the chart she was working on and said, "I'll be there in a second."

Luke walked up to the counter and slammed his hands down. This time the woman looked up at him startled.

"You don't understand--I need you to go check on her now. She's in pain."

The nurse's lips twitched, "This your first baby?"

The woman had evidently just come on duty, she wasn't here when he was at the desk last...or she would fucking know this was his first baby. Luke clutched his gut as a pain racked him that made him want to drop to his knees.

"Oh, god..." he moaned and felt beads of sweat breaking out on his forehead.

"You okay?" the nurse asked tilting her head to the side to study him.

"I feel like my gut is about to split open. No, I'm not okay..." he said in a pained whisper. "I need you to go see about my wife...NOW!" he yelled the last word as another excruciating pain ripped through him, and this time he did sink to his knees to ride it out.

Once it passed, Luke sucked in a deep breath then used one hand to push back up to his feet and glared at the nurse.

"Oh, gosh...you're one of those. This is going to be a

fun delivery."

"What the he--" Luke roared as another pain hit him and he staggered back to the door of Cassie's room, then stumbled over to sit in the chair beside the bed. The nurse came in behind him with a syringe. Instead of giving it to Cassie however, she walked toward him.

He leaned away from her and she just smiled. "I'm going to give you something to help you calm down Mr. Matthews.

He felt the blood drain from his face as he stared at the large needle, then back up at the nurse. "Is this because I complained?"

"No, it's because you're having sympathetic labor pains. This will help," she assured him then said, "Roll up your sleeve."

"I'm the one in pain over here and you're giving him the drugs?" Cassie shouted incredulously, then moaned as another contraction squeezed her and she inhaled deeply, then pushed and huffed out breaths and panted.

Luke moaned at the same time and clutched his stomach squirming in the chair. "What the fuck?"

The nurse smiled smugly at him then asked in a sing song voice, "Want the shot now Mr. Matthews?"

He quickly jerked up his sleeve and the nurse stuck him and pressed the plunger to send the medicine into his muscle. It hurt like hell, but nothing like the stomach pains he was having. Sympathetic labor pains? What the hell was that?

He felt the drug move into his system and his brain got a little fuzzy, and he thought the tenseness in his belly had eased some. Breathing a sigh of relief, Luke went to get up to go and help Cassie, when another pain hit him full force, one that almost sent him in a facer to the floor. He grabbed behind him and sat back down huffing through the pain. Just like he heard Cassie doing in the bed.

Jesus, this was just too fucking weird. He had to call Cole to come in here and help him...he was in the waiting room. But the pains were less than a minute apart, and he was falling apart...not even able to get up and help Cassie.

He saw the nurse put on rubber gloves, then go give Cassie a dilation exam. "Yep, she's crowning. I'll go get the doctor."

The woman left the room and Luke and Cassie had two more contractions before the doctor came into the room and grinned at Luke. "How're your labor pains, Mr. Matthews? Did the shot kick in yet?"

Cassie bore down on another contraction and Luke spat out through the pain, "No!"

"Well hopefully it will before you deliver," the doctor told him with a chuckle then went over to check on Cassie.

Luke sure didn't see what was so fucking funny. He was a man--and he was having a baby--literally!

This had to be some kind of strange cosmic joke.

God, if this was what women went through, he was surprised the world's population wasn't dwindling. Surely women talked! He knew he sure as hell would!

When another contraction hit her, he noticed that his was a little less intense, but it still made him want to howl. He heard the doctor announce that the head was out, and Luke was thankful, because both he and Cassie would be out of pain soon. Or so he thought until they had another contraction, this one longer and more pronounced.

"That's it Cassie, bear down...hold it...hold it...and let it go." The doctor coached her and Luke was right along with him. "This looks like a big baby...I thought it was from the ultrasound, but wow."

Cassie had decided she didn't want to know the sex of the baby was before it was born, and Luke had reluctantly agreed. He was surprised, because his wife wasn't long on patience. She hated a secret being kept from her.

How he'd managed to hold out against her less than fair interrogation procedures about the honeymoon, he'd never know. He should have gotten some prize for managing to surprise her with a visit to several Kentucky horse farms, and their nights at the races at Churchill Downs. They'd had so much fun...their whole honeymoon had been amazing.

Cassie had even managed to buy two great broodmares to add to their stock. It was a good thing they'd doubled the size of the barn they'd rebuilt to replace the one that burned down. The way Cassie collected horses, they'd need every stall soon.

Luke tensed up when he heard Cassie have another contraction, then he relaxed and sent up a silent prayer of thanks when he didn't have one. The medicine must have kicked in. He was exhausted from the ones he did have...he could only imagine how Cassie was feeling.

Weakly, he got up from the chair and went to her side and picked up her hand to hold it, then bent down and kissed her cheek. "You're doing good, baby..."

Amazingly, she grinned at him then said, "So are you..." before she gave a belly laugh.

He wondered why she wasn't having contractions anymore then looked down at the doctor who held his daughter up by her feet and spanked her ass. It made him want to go punch the doctor in the nose. Luke could see it was a girl from her lack of male equipment.

Then he heard his baby girl wail, and tears rushed up to his eyes, and a lump formed in his throat. The doctor cradled her then handed her off to the nurse, who suctioned out her nose and mouth, then took her over to weigh her and clean her up.

Luke held Cassie's hand and watched the doctor finish the delivery and then the nurse brought them their baby girl wrapped in a pink and green striped blanket. Her head was covered with a pink knit cap, but Luke could see her dark hair curling around the edge of the cap by her tiny pink ears.

Gently, the nurse put the baby in Cassie's arms and the baby found her thumb and began sucking. Luke sat on the bed then leaned down and kissed Cassie gently on the lips, then pressed a kiss to his daughter's head.

"So what are we going to name her?" Luke asked, since they hadn't really decided yet on a boy and a girl name yet.

She looked up at him with love shining in her sky-blue eyes and said, "What do you think about Annabelle after my mother? Daddy always called her Bella...that means beautiful in Spanish."

"I think it's perfect, darlin'," Luke's eyes filled up and he swiped at them with his arm then drew in a shuddering breath.

"You pick a middle name..." Cassie told him.

"Hmm..." Luke said trying to come up with something. He hadn't known his mother...he knew from his birth certificate that her name was Jewel though. "How about Jewel?

"Beautiful Jewel. That's perfect, Luke...why did you pick that?"

"It was my mother's name," he told her and felt blood rush to his face.

Cassie's eyes filled with tears this time, "I think that's wonderful, darlin'."

Luke leaned down to hug her and Annabelle at the same time, and he thought his life couldn't be anymore complete. He had the family that he'd always yearned for, and so much more. He had a lifetime of triumphs and trouble to look forward to with them and he couldn't be happier.

ABOUT THE AUTHOR

Becky McGraw is a married mother of three adult children, and a Southern girl by birth and the grace of God, ya'll. One of several career changes transplanted Becky and her family to Indiana, where she now lives with her husband and dog Abby.

A jack of many trades in her life, Becky has been an optician, a beautician, a legal secretary, a senior project manager for an aviation management consulting firm, which took her all over the United States, a real estate broker, and now a graphic artist, web designer and writer. She knows just enough about a variety of topics to make her dangerous, and her romance novels interesting and varied.

Being a graphic artist is a good thing for her too, because she creates her own cover art, along with writing the novels.

Becky has been an avid reader of romance novels since she was a teenager, and has been known to read up to four novels of that genre a week, much to the dismay of her husband, and the delight of e-book sellers.

She has been writing fictional short stories and novels for fun, as well as technical copy for her jobs for many years. She was a member of the Writer's Guild on AOL during her last venture into writing romance, as well as a founding member and treasurer of the first online chapter of the Romance Writers of America, From the Heart Romance Writers.

My Kind of Trouble is the first in a series of contemporary cowboy romance novels called Texas Trouble. Please be on the look out for new releases in the series.

Made in the USA
San Bernardino, CA
30 June 2013